Praise for the novels of Maureen McKade

"A story that will tear at your heart . . . terrific."

—*Rendezvous*

"Watch out when sparks start to fly!"

—*Affaire de Coeur*

"A Maureen McKade novel is going to provide plenty of excitement and enjoyment . . . Another triumph."

—*Midwest Book Review*

"Well-done, uplifting, and enjoyable."

—*Rocky Mountain News*

"With a clever story line and sparkling dialogue, she's created a town that will live in her readers' minds and keeper shelves forever. A keeper! *Untamed Heart* is one of the must-read romances of the year!"

—*Literary Times*

"One of the most original romances I've read in a long time. I look forward to reading more from this talented author."

—*All About Romance*

Berkley Sensation books by Maureen McKade

TO FIND YOU AGAIN
AROUSE SUSPICION

AROUSE SUSPICION

MAUREEN MCKADE

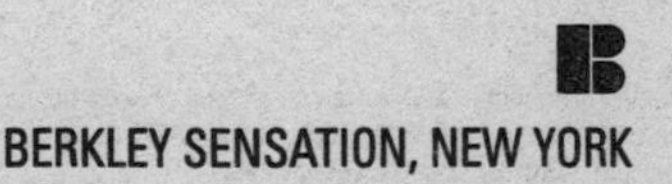
BERKLEY SENSATION, NEW YORK

THE BERKLEY PUBLISHING GROUP
Published by the Penguin Group
Penguin Group (USA) Inc.
375 Hudson Street, New York, New York 10014, USA
Penguin Group (Canada), 10 Alcorn Avenue, Toronto, Ontario M4V 3B2, Canada
(a division of Pearson Penguin Canada Inc.)
Penguin Books Ltd., 80 Strand, London WC2R 0RL, England
Penguin Group Ireland, 25 St. Stephen's Green, Dublin 2, Ireland (a division of Penguin Books Ltd.)
Penguin Group (Australia), 250 Camberwell Road, Camberwell, Victoria 3124, Australia
(a division of Pearson Australia Group Pty. Ltd.)
Penguin Books India Pvt. Ltd., 11 Community Centre, Panchsheel Park, New Delhi—110 017, India
Penguin Group (NZ), Cnr. Airborne and Rosedale Roads, Albany, Auckland 1310, New Zealand
(a division of Pearson New Zealand Ltd.)
Penguin Books (South Africa) (Pty.) Ltd., 24 Sturdee Avenue, Rosebank, Johannesburg 2196,
South Africa

Penguin Books Ltd., Registered Offices: 80 Strand, London WC2R 0RL, England

AROUSE SUSPICION

A Berkley Sensation Book / published by arrangement with the author

PRINTING HISTORY
Berkley Sensation edition / November 2004

Cover design by Brad Springer.
Interior text design by Kristin del Rosario.

For information address: The Berkley Publishing Group,
a division of Penguin Group (USA) Inc.,
375 Hudson Street, New York, New York 10014.

ISBN: 0-425-19919-3

BERKLEY® SENSATION
Berkley Sensation Books are published by The Berkley Publishing Group,
a division of Penguin Group (USA) Inc.,
375 Hudson Street, New York, New York 10014.
BERKLEY SENSATION and the "B" design
are trademarks belonging to Penguin Group (USA) Inc.

PRINTED IN THE UNITED STATES OF AMERICA

10 9 8 7 6 5 4 3 2 1

To RB for Gus.

To Natasha Kern for the awesome title.

To Cindy Hwang for going above and beyond.
To Karen Fox, Paula Gill, Laura Hayden,
Yvonne Jocks, Pam McCutcheon,
Angel Smits, and Deb Stover for your
encouragement to try something different, and
for your laughter and critiques.

And always, to Alan for your love
and support.

My heartfelt thanks.

AROUSE SUSPICION

Chapter One

"He stared at the man who had once been his friend but who now was a heartless mercenary on the wrong side. Longstreet couldn't afford to let their past friendship cloud his judgment or sway his resolve. He had a job to do, and he had never failed yet. He blanked his mind and snapped another magazine into his Glock, then took aim. The pistol barked—"

Nick Sirocco swore and held down the backspace button until the words vanished from the monitor, leaving behind nothing but a pristine white screen and an insolent flashing cursor. He rubbed his eyes and glanced at the digital clock radio precariously perched on a stack of papers and books. 3:20 P.M. Less than twenty-four hours to finish the damned manuscript, which was only half completed.

The phone rang, startling him. Nick poked under a pile of papers where the handset was supposed to be but wasn't. He growled a few choice words and tried to remember where he'd left it. He rolled back his chair from his cluttered desk and rose. His right knee cracked audibly. The joint proceeded to make a muted pop with each step.

Nothing like a couple of hundred parachute jumps to waste a guy's knees.

Fortunately, he didn't have to search long for the missing phone. Gus, his part golden Lab, part Irish setter mutt, came trotting down the hallway, the handset in her mouth. It rang a third time.

"Hand," Nick commanded, and Gus dropped it into his palm. "Good girl." As Nick wiped the doggy-drooled phone across his sweatpants, it shrilled impatiently again. He pushed a button. "Yeah."

"Hey, Nick, how's it going?"

The disgustingly cheerful voice of Steve Hardick, his agent, elicited a groan. "Why're you calling so late?"

"It's not even three-thirty."

"In New York it's after six," Nick reminded dryly as he walked back to his desk. "What's going on?"

In the pause that followed, Nick could almost hear the agent's smile fade. "Is the Longstreet book done?"

Nick squeezed the bridge of his nose and sighed. "Not yet."

"It's due the day after tomorrow, Nick. You've already had two extensions."

"It'll get there on time," Nick assured him. "I'll finish tonight and overnight express it tomorrow."

"It should've been done four weeks ago. You've been dicking around for two months. What's going on with you, anyhow?"

Nick bristled at Steve's nagging tone. He counted to ten to defuse his irritation. It didn't work. "I'm sick and tired of writing the same old thing: beer, bombs, and babes. Hell, Gus has more personality than Longstreet does."

Lying on the floor, the dog looked up at him and wagged her tail.

"Geezus, Nick, you knew this wasn't classic literature when you agreed to write for the line."

"Yeah, well, I needed the job back then, but after three years, it's gotten old. I feel like I'm writing the same frigging book over and over."

"Do you know how many men would give their left nut to write Travis Longstreet books?"

"I could've lived without that visual," Nick said dryly. He sank into his desk chair, the wheels squeaking as if punctuating his comment. "I want out, Steve."

"You're under contract for one more book."

"Get me out of it."

Steve's disbelieving snort came through loud and clear. "This is business, Nick, not some kid's game."

"Writing Longstreet books *is* a kid's game." Nick gripped the phone tighter. "Look, I've been working on something. A cop thriller."

Long silence met Nick's announcement.

"What do you know about cops?" Steve finally asked.

Nick leaned forward, his elbows braced on his thighs, and didn't bother to curb his enthusiasm. "I've been working with an old friend who's been a cop for nearly thirty-five years. He's been helping me out. It's good, Steve, really good."

Nick heard the tapping of a pen against the phone—a sure sign that Steve was thinking. However, the rat-a-tat-tat was annoying as hell.

"There haven't been many police thrillers to hit the lists since Wambaugh," Steve mused aloud. "So you think this book's good?"

"Yeah. And so does my friend." Nick held his breath, knowing he needed Steve's full support.

"What do you have done?"

Nick leaned back in his chair. "Just one chapter. I've been plotting and researching."

"Synopsis?"

"Half there."

"Get the proposal to me by the end of the month. I'll take a look at it. Maybe your editor will make a trade."

"What d'you mean?"

"If Manny likes the idea, maybe I can get him to take this one instead of another Longstreet book. They have two other series writers who should be able to pick up the slack."

Nick sat up straight, excitement sending his pulse into overdrive. "You think?"

"If the story grabs him, Manny'll jump at the chance." Steve paused. "But you have to show him you aren't just another hack."

Nick bristled. "I'm a damned good writer."

"Hell, I know that, but you have to prove it to him. I want that proposal on my desk by the end of the month. And don't piss Manny off by being any later on this book. Day after tomorrow. His desk. No excuses." The line went dead.

Nick punched the Off button and stared at the phone. After writing seven action adventure books starring Travis Longstreet, Nick wanted to tackle something different, something more challenging than a character who shot epithets as accurately as he shot bullets. Two months ago Nick had asked Paddy Hawkins if he'd be willing to act as a consultant for the new book. Faced with a compulsory retirement, Paddy had welcomed the challenge and was just as excited as Nick about the project.

Who would've thought a smart-mouthed punk kid who Officer Hawkins had straightened out over fifteen years ago would be writing a cop book?

And now Nick's agent was willing to give him a shot at playing with the big boys. He grinned and considered calling Paddy with the news but decided to wait until tomorrow. Knowing Paddy, he'd want to go out and celebrate, and Nick had a book to finish.

He rose and settled the phone on its base, then turned off the ringer and muted the answering machine. He didn't need any distractions.

Eleven hours later, with the Longstreet manuscript completed, Nick shuffled off to bed, unaware of the blinking red light on the answering machine.

Five days later

Danni Hawkins juggled a Chinese take-out bag, her backpack, a jumbo iced tea, and two cans of soda as she tried to open the door to the office. Just when she succeeded in turning the knob, the tea tipped, splashing across her tan trousers and onto the cracked sidewalk in front of the door.

"Son of a—" Biting back the rest of her frustration, she righted the cup, stepped over the tea puddle, and entered the office of B. Marshal, Attorney at Law, and D. Hawkins, Private Investigator.

She scurried past Cathy Miller, who sat behind the reception desk, and down the hall to a small break room that doubled as a storage area. She slid her backpack onto a chair and deposited the white bag and the two colas on the Formica-topped chrome table, then stepped into the bathroom. As she tried to remove the brown stain from her pants, Cathy appeared in the doorway.

"Having some trouble?" the petite paralegal asked, her arms crossed.

"No," Danni shot back with as much sarcasm as she could inject into one word. She glanced at the spot and found it had only spread across the material. "Damn!" With more force than necessary, she flung the damp cloth into the chipped porcelain sink. "Is the one o'clock still on?"

"As far as I know. He hasn't called to cancel." Cathy's expression softened. "Are you sure you're up to this? You should've taken the whole week off."

"I'm fine." Danni regretted her sharp tone the moment she spoke. "I'm sorry. I have a lot on my mind." Afraid to meet Cathy's eyes, Danni slipped past her to return to the break room. "Hungry?" she asked with forced brightness. "I brought sesame chicken and General Tso's from Lucky Ling's."

"Does a pig like mud?"

Danni laughed, a rusty but welcome sound after the

somberness of the past few days. "I brought enough for Beth, too."

"She had an appointment at twelve-thirty—the kid your father referred to her." Since Cathy worked for Beth and Danni, she knew both their schedules.

"The juvie who tried to fence a laptop?"

Cathy nodded. "He has two priors. Nothing serious, but the kid's almost eighteen, and the DA wants to try him as an adult."

Having been a cop for two years, Danni could easily imagine the type. Danni's father had spent much of his off-duty time combating the gangs' influences by working with streetwise teenage boys. His colleagues had respected him for his dedication and sacrifice.

It was too bad his daughter had fallen into the "sacrifice" category.

Danni and Cathy emptied the white take-out boxes onto two mismatched plates and nuked the first one in the microwave, which was perched on a stack of Xerox boxes.

Cathy stashed one of the colas in the fridge, then popped open the other over the sink. She held it away from her as it exploded and overflowed into the drain. "Did you shake this or what?"

"Not on purpose. Sorry," Danni answered absently as she watched the plate go round and round in the microwave.

A touch on her shoulder startled her back to the present.

"Why don't you take more time off?" Cathy asked gently. "After all, he was your *father.*"

Danni's throat tightened, and she shook her head. As long as she stayed busy, she could pretend her father was still alive and that she might someday make him proud of her. "I have work to do. I'm already too far behind as it is."

Heavy silence compressed the room. Danni wished she could simply ignore the fact that her father had been buried yesterday with full police honors. Ignore the fact that he'd committed suicide. Ignore the fact that they'd been taking the first tentative steps toward rebuilding their father-daughter relationship.

Danni's stomach twisted, and suddenly the food didn't look nearly as appetizing as it had when she'd picked it up on her way to the office. "Maybe you were right," she murmured. "There's a lot to do."

"Have you gone to the house yet?" Cathy asked.

"The funeral director needed a suit to bury him in. Being a cop was his life, so I figured I'd just have him buried in his service uniform." Her eyes felt hot and scratchy, but there were no tears. There hadn't been, not when the bugler had played taps, and not when she'd walked away from the cemetery with a folded flag in her arms and her father's bronze casket sitting above the ground like some lonely sentry.

Cathy put her arm around Danni's shoulders and gave her a half hug. "Go home. I'll call your one o'clock and reschedule."

Danni was tempted, but she'd already been out of the office for four days. "I can't. I have to start tagging Warner this afternoon."

"Do it tomorrow."

"The sooner I can prove he's screwing around, the sooner we get paid."

Danni had opened her private investigator's business almost two years ago. Even though she split overhead costs with Beth, it was only in the past few months that Danni could afford to eat somewhere that didn't have plastic sporks or offer ketchup in pump dispensers.

The second plate of food finished reheating, and the two women sat down to eat. But the quiet gave Danni too much time to think. "How's Ashley doing?"

Cathy shrugged. "Fine, for an alien."

Danni tipped her head to the side in a mute question.

"Once she hit puberty, it's like she was taken over by a hostile alien," Cathy explained.

"You've been watching too many *X-Files* reruns."

Danni waved her fork and sent a lone grain of fried rice skittering across the tabletop. "You need to get out more."

"Look who's talking." Cathy grinned conspiratorially. "Hey, why don't we go clubbing this weekend? Ashley will be at her father's." Her smile faded. "That is, if you're up to it."

"Sure, why not?" But Danni couldn't meet Cathy's eyes. "I mean it's not like it's that much different now. I actually didn't see Dad that much before he—" Much to her embarrassment, her voice broke, and she cleared her throat. "Before he died."

"He was still your father."

An ember of anger sparked Danni's tongue. "Sometimes I wondered if *he* knew that. He was never around when—" Her rage vanished as swiftly as it had appeared. "It's not fair."

Cathy gave her forearm a gentle squeeze but wisely didn't offer any empty platitudes.

The phone rang, and Cathy hurried out to answer it. Danni tried to listen to the one-sided conversation but only heard snatches. She forced another forkful of General Tso's into her mouth, but even the spicy chicken—her favorite—didn't bring much enthusiasm to her taste buds.

Cathy's heels on the tiled floor alerted Danni to her return.

"Damn reporters," she muttered as she plopped down without her usual panache. "Bob Carlyle from KMCX wanted to interview you for the evening news." Her eyes flashed. "I told him where to go."

Cathy's protective zeal brought Danni a small measure of comfort. Cathy might be petite, but she was as fierce as a mama bear when it came to protecting her family and friends.

"Let me guess. He wanted to unravel the mystery of why a man with a distinguished record who came from a long line of cops would commit suicide," Danni guessed bitterly. "I've been getting calls from reporters at home. I'm actually surprised it took them this long to call here."

Shoving aside her melancholy thoughts, she glanced at her watch. She had five minutes before her appointment arrived. Cathy helped her clean the break room in record time and placed the leftovers in the antiquated refrigerator.

"Don't you have a change of clothes here?" Cathy asked, eyeing the prominent tea stain on Danni's trousers.

"I forgot to bring in another set after the SUV repo."

"Ahh," Cathy said knowingly. "He was the one who thought you were a carjacker."

Danni scowled. "Yeah, like he didn't hear me explain the three missed payments or how the bank sent me to repossess it." The bastard had played dirty, but Danni had some tricks up her sleeve, too. He had ended up in the hospital with a broken collarbone.

"Did the one o'clock say what he wanted?" Danni asked, pausing in her office doorway.

Cathy shook her head. "He said he'll tell you in person."

Danni shrugged, closed the door, and crossed to her desk. Pulling open the lower drawer, she placed her backpack inside. She felt the hard line of her Smith & Wesson in the pack and debated placing the revolver in a more accessible location in case her next appointment was some psycho. Hell, it'd happened before. A delinquent father she'd tracked down had stalked in, waving a knife and threatening to kill her for forcing him to meet his financial responsibilities to his children. She'd disarmed him using defensive moves her father had taught her when she was fourteen years old in case some boyfriend got a little too friendly.

Danni slumped back in her chair and closed her eyes. Not all her memories of her father were unpleasant. She remembered the first time she'd ridden her bicycle without the training wheels. Her dad had hauled her into his big arms and swung her around until she was laughing so hard she almost lost her earlier snack of chocolate cookies and grape Kool-Aid. Years later, when she'd graduated from the Police Academy, her father's proud smile and tentative hug had made her feel the same way.

But it was the memory of his disappointment when she'd turned in her badge that had made her sick to her stomach.

The intercom buzzed, startling Danni out of the eclipsing memories. She leaned forward and stabbed a button. "Yes?"

"Nick Sirocco is here to see you."

"Send him in."

Cathy opened the door, and Danni stood, catching the wink and smirk the paralegal sent her. Then Nick Sirocco strode forward, and Danni understood Cathy's signals.

Danni had been expecting a middle-aged man trying to get the goods on a cheating wife, not someone who looked like he'd just stepped out of a Chippendales gig. Nick Sirocco was a good two or three inches over six feet with broad shoulders that tapered to a narrow waist and hips. Faded blue jeans that hugged muscular thighs and a taut gray T-shirt beneath a weathered brown bomber jacket brought Danni's hormones scampering out of hibernation.

"Danielle Hawkins?"

The deep-timbred voice sent her gaze to his face, only to have her attention captured by startlingly clear blue eyes beneath a high forehead and closely trimmed honey-brown hair. A sense of familiarity washed through her, but she dismissed it. She wouldn't have forgotten meeting someone like Nick Sirocco.

"Yes, I'm Danni Hawkins." She mentally chided herself for reacting like a sex-obsessed teenager. "Nice to meet you, Mr. Sirocco." She extended her hand over her desk, and he crossed the short distance to shake it. His strong, warm grip sent pleasurable currents rushing through her and jump-started parts of her body that had been out of commission for too long.

"Call me Nick." His smile brought creases to the corners of his eyes and mouth.

He glanced down, and she followed his gaze to the tea

stain on her trousers. Her face burned, and she quickly lowered herself back to her chair, grateful for the desk's cover.

So much for first impressions.

"Would you like something to drink?" Danni asked. "Coffee? Soda?"

"A glass of water would be good."

"I'll get it," Cathy offered and closed the door behind her.

Sirocco had obviously made an impact on the paralegal. Cathy was usually adamant about not playing gofer.

He lowered himself to his chair with an animal-like grace.

Danni wasn't used to dealing with drop-dead gorgeous men in her office. The majority of her clients were women, and the few men who sought her help looked like over-the-hill jocks with more gut than hair.

She lifted her gaze to his summer-sky-colored eyes. "What can I help you with, Mr. Sirocco?"

"Nick," he insisted.

Danni usually remained professional with her clients, but if Sirocco preferred less formality, who was she to argue?

"What can I do for you, Nick?" she reiterated.

A crease appeared between his eyebrows, and the discomfort that crossed his features made Danni tense.

"I knew your father," he said.

Danni narrowed her eyes as adrenaline leapt into her veins. "A lot of people knew my father."

"I saw you at the funeral."

She studied him more closely, trying to remember if she'd seen him at the service or the graveside. But she'd kept her gaze downcast throughout most of the funeral and could recall few of those who'd attended.

"You were the only family Paddy had," Sirocco added.

Paddy. Was Sirocco just another bloodsucking reporter who'd dug a little deeper than his colleagues?

A soft knock on the door gave Danni a momentary reprieve. "Come in."

Cathy entered with two glasses of ice water, handing one to Sirocco and placing the other on the desk in front of Danni.

"Thank you," Sirocco said.

Danni murmured the same, and Cathy left them alone. Although Danni hadn't asked for the water, she was grateful. Sirocco's little announcement had given her a case of dry mouth.

"So, how did you know him?" Danni asked after taking a sip.

"He helped me when I needed it." Sirocco shrugged, but his eyes were crystalline. "I owe him."

"It'll be hard to pay him back now." She kept her tone intentionally blunt.

Startled, Sirocco stared at her like he was trying to discover something within her. His lips turned downward as if he didn't find it. "You don't sound like you're real broken up about his death."

Rage tightened its icy claws around Danni's chest, making it hard to breathe. "You don't know anything about me, Mr. Sirocco, so don't you dare presume to know how I feel about my father."

Sirocco's eyes widened minutely, but enough to tell Danni he got her message, loud and clear. "You're right. I don't know you." His voice was cool and flat.

"Why are you here?"

He took a long moment to answer her question. "I need your help."

"Why?"

"Because you have access to people and places I don't." Sirocco set his glass on a stone coaster on the corner of the desk. "I want to find the man who murdered your father."

Three years ago, Danni had been kicked in the belly by a suspect accused of stealing from his employer. He'd been wearing steel-toed boots at the time, and she recalled her desperation when she couldn't catch her breath and how her heart raced as she'd lain on the grimy gray-and-tan linoleum floor, her arms clutched around her middle. She felt much the same way now.

"I don't know what kind of sick game you're playing. My father was upset about being forced to retire in a few months. His gun was found in his hand, and there were burns around the entry wound on his forehead. Powder residue was found on his hand," Danni said, keeping her hands clasped lest he see her trembling. "If he couldn't be a cop, he had nothing left to live for."

"Bullshit." Sirocco's quiet expletive held more intensity than a loud bellow. "If you knew your father at all, you'd know he would never take the easy way out."

If you knew your father at all . . . That was what this all came down to, wasn't it? Had Danni known her father?

Her heart clamored in her chest, and she forced herself to breathe deeply to allay her sudden dizziness. At the time she'd been informed of his death, she'd questioned the suicide ruling. But all the evidence pointed to that determination.

"Why would someone kill him?" Danni managed to ask in a calm voice.

Sirocco glanced away, then brought his sharp gaze back to her. "I don't know. That's why I need your help."

Danni's throbbing head joined in her heart's pounding tempo. "My father is dead. Why can't you let him rest in peace?"

"Because his murderer is walking around out there scot-free." Sirocco dragged a hand over his short hair. For the first time, she noticed dark smudges beneath his eyes. "Paddy left a message on my answering machine the night he was killed. He said he had to talk to me about something important, and that he'd try me in the morning if I didn't get back to him. By the time I got his message, he was already dead."

Danni looked away to regain control of her jagged emotions. Her father had called Sirocco instead of his own daughter the night he committed suicide. But if it was murder . . .

"If he was planning on killing himself, why did he say he'd call me back in the morning?" Sirocco pressed, leaning forward in his chair.

She shoved the old hurts back down into their tattered box. The man had a point. "What's your connection to my father?"

"I've known him for a long time, ever since I was seventeen. He—" The man took a shaky breath. "I was headed down the road to prison when he turned me around."

Danni's eyes widened as a lightbulb flared and realization dawned. "You were one of them. One of the boys he tried to help."

"*Did* help. Like I said, he straightened me out, helped me get into the army. He changed my life."

Danni's life had been changed, too, by her father's involvement with troubled street teens. But it hadn't been for the better. She'd gone with him to the gym until her body began to fill out and "his boys" had started noticing her. At that age, she'd been foolish enough to encourage the attention. After two of the boys had started a fight over her, Danni's father had ordered her to stay home, but he never stayed home with her. He'd always chosen *them* over her.

That decision had been the start of the disintegration of their relationship.

"How nice for you." Danni's rapier sarcasm sliced the air between them.

Sirocco frowned. "I didn't see him for about twelve years. When I got out of the army, I moved back here and started writing books."

Danni noticed a slight hesitation in his speech, as if he were glossing over something or leaving something out of his explanation. She listened more closely.

"We went out to eat a few times. He talked me into helping out with the youth group, giving a hand where I could. You know, coaching some baseball, refereeing some b-ball games, just being there if someone wanted to talk,"

Sirocco explained with a shrug. "I found I liked it, and it made me feel pretty good to be able to give something back."

Danni swallowed a block of bitterness. Her father had never asked her to help. Not even after she'd donned the brothers-in-blue uniform.

"Two months ago, I asked Paddy if he'd help me with a novel I was working on," Sirocco continued. "I needed technical assistance with proper police procedure, and I wanted to use some cop slang to give the book a more realistic feel. He was excited about it and agreed to be my official consultant." A smile played on his lips. "We met once a week to discuss details."

Danni willed herself to remain calm on the outside, despite the emotional hurricane raging within her. "What evidence do you have, Mr. Sirocco?"

His eyes blazed with impatience, and he braced his forearms on his thighs. "He wouldn't kill himself. And if you would take a few minutes to think about it, you'd know that, too."

He truly believed in her father. For a second, she hated Nick Sirocco. She hated that he had more faith in her father than she did.

She hated him because he'd had what she'd been denied.

"Who had a motive?" Danni asked, trying to remain objective, even as adolescent memories rose, ugly and spiteful, inside her.

"I don't know." Sirocco's words came out clipped and harsh. "You're the private investigator; you know the ins and outs of this stuff."

Unable to sit any longer, Danni rose and paced the small space between Sirocco's chair and the door. Her insides felt like fire ants had taken up permanent residence.

Sirocco shifted in his chair so he could watch her. "He was your father," he said softly.

Danni paused, took a deep, shaky breath, and shoved her fingers through her hair, snagging the curls and tugging them back, away from her face. "I didn't know him very well, Mr. Sirocco. He had his life, and I had mine. His ex-partner, Sam Richmond, was more like a father to me than he was."

Sirocco looked like he wanted to ask a question, but instead, he pressed his lips together. "Your dad told me all about you."

Danni's vision blurred with unwelcome moisture. Why couldn't he have talked *to* her instead of *about* her?

"Help me find the person who murdered him." Sirocco's piercing blue eyes demanded her agreement.

Murder. It was such an ugly word, and even uglier when applied to someone she'd known. Her own father.

If there was even a possibility of foul play, Danni had the responsibility to find his killer. Maybe she didn't owe him like Sirocco did, but despite everything, she'd loved him.

And maybe somehow her father could see her and be proud of her.

Chapter Two

Nick watched the indecision play across Danni Hawkins's smooth face. He narrowed his eyes, remembering back fifteen years to the young teenage girl who'd accompanied Paddy to the gym. He recalled her as a tomboy, defeating more than one older boy at a game of horse. She'd been able to sink her shot more often than not when the basketball left her talented hands. She'd only accompanied Paddy three or four times, then he'd shown up alone. She must've decided hanging out with her friends was cooler than shooting hoops with her dad and a bunch of boys.

He studied Danni a little closer, recognizing much of that cocky tomboy in the woman who stood before him now. She had her father's midnight blue eyes—sharp and intelligent—but they possessed a brooding cynicism Paddy's hadn't. She'd also inherited his dark curly hair, but Nick assumed the chestnut glints were from her mother. Who would've figured the gangly kid would turn into a beautiful woman? A woman with one hell of a chip on her shoulder.

She stopped pacing and faced him. "I want to do some checking around first, before I agree to do this."

"So you believe me?"

"To be honest, I don't know what to believe, Mr. Sirocco."

Nick stood and stared down at her, trying not to notice the light smudge of freckles across her nose and cheeks. Or the way they made her seem more vulnerable, and him feel more protective.

As if Danni Hawkins needed to be protected. *Riiight.*

"He said he couldn't wait to get the first copy of the book he was helping me with." Nick smiled without humor. "I planned on dedicating it to him."

Her gaze wavered and dropped. She stepped around him and crossed to the door but didn't open it. Finally meeting his eyes, she said, "I want to hear the phone message from my father."

"You'll have to come over to my place or I'll have to bring the answering machine here."

"You can drop it by tomorrow."

"Then we'll start?"

"We?"

"Someone killed your father. If you investigate on your own and get too close, you could wind up dead, too." Nick took a deep breath, surprised he'd given voice to the bizarre compulsion to protect her. But then, she was Paddy's daughter, and Nick owed the man plenty. The least he could do was try to keep his daughter safe. "Look, Ms. Hawkins, I may not have been a cop or know how to conduct an investigation, but I can handle myself."

"So can I." She raised her chin. "I do this kind of thing all the time."

"So you investigate your father's murder all the time?"

She flinched visibly, and the color leached from her cheeks. It was a cheap shot, but at least Nick had gotten an honest reaction.

She crossed her arms, and Nick recognized the gesture—a defense to keep everyone out and her own emotions locked in. He knew because he'd used it often enough himself.

"If I'm right, the killer was probably someone Paddy knew," Nick said. "In fact, it's pretty likely it was someone in the department."

Her expression flared with disbelief and fear—fear that he might be right. "Christ, Sirocco, you're accusing a fellow cop of killing my father?"

He nodded slowly. "It's the only thing that makes sense." Indecision wavered in her eyes, and Nick pressed his advantage. "You're going to need me to watch your back."

"I don't *need* anybody."

"This is important to me," he added, his voice nearly breaking with intensity. "As important as it should be to you."

Her gaze slid away, and she blinked rapidly. He was afraid she would start crying, and he shifted uncomfortably. Women's tears were one thing he had no defense against.

Finally, she raised her head and peered at him with dry eyes. "I'll think about it."

He could tell even that small concession was difficult. Danni Hawkins was what his drill sergeant would've called a lone wolf.

"I'll bring the answering machine over tomorrow," Nick said.

She nodded and opened the door for him.

He walked past her, his arm brushing hers and bringing a rush of awareness through his blood.

"Mr. Sirocco," she called.

He paused in the reception area and glanced back at her.

"Thank you."

He could tell she meant it by the huskiness in her voice and the haunted look in her eyes.

"You're welcome," he replied quietly.

Outside on the sidewalk, Nick breathed deeply of the rain-tinged air, which hid a multitude of less savory odors.

Danni Hawkins puzzled him. One moment, tough as nails; the next, uncertain and vulnerable.

And what did you expect, Sirocco? She buried her father yesterday, and today you're telling her he was murdered. Nick had poured salt into her wound before it even had time to start healing.

If only he'd checked his phone messages that night. If only he hadn't turned off his ringer.

Thunder rumbled in the distance, reminding Nick he was making like a statue on the sunken, cracked sidewalk. The headache that had dogged him off and on since hearing about Paddy's death throbbed in his temples. Between his guilt and asking questions concerning Paddy at the police department, Nick had slept little the past five days. Despite his attempts to learn anything, he'd been stonewalled by the police rank and file.

Nick knew what it was like. The military was the same way. If someone from outside the closed society started asking questions, that person would be seen as an annoyance at best or a threat at worst. Because of Nick's tenacity, he'd wound up in the latter category. He hadn't planned to go to Danni Hawkins with his suspicions until he had some proof. However, unable to break through the blue wall of silence, he hoped Danni, with her past ties to the department, could slip in and get the information he couldn't.

He unlocked his Jeep Liberty as the first raindrop struck his face. As he drove away, he couldn't help but wonder what could have made a daughter so bitter toward her father, especially when it was Paddy Hawkins.

A man Nick used to wish was his father.

NICK called Danni's office the next day to ensure she'd be there when he arrived. It was later than he'd planned when he rolled into a parking place three car lengths from the office door. Gus had turned her big, doggie-brown eyes on him and suckered Nick into bringing her along. He'd always been a sap where animals and women were concerned.

"Stay," he said to Gus, giving her head a final pat. After making sure the windows were cracked open, he stepped out of the SUV with the phone message machine clutched in one hand. He had no intention of letting it go until Danni agreed to let him accompany her on the investigation.

The receptionist—the nameplate on her desk read Cathy Miller—greeted him with something more than the usual practiced smile. There was no doubt she was interested, but Nick had other things on his mind. Besides, cute Barbie dolls had never been his type.

"Hello, Mr. Sirocco," she said politely.

"Ms. Miller."

"Call me Cathy."

He smiled obligingly. "Cathy. Is Ms. Hawkins in?"

Her gaze flicked away from him. "She's busy. She asked that you leave the answering machine with me."

So that's how Danni was going to play it. Time to let her know he could be just as stubborn. "I'll hang around until she's free and give it to her myself."

Cathy studied him, a speculative gleam entering her eyes. "Wait here, Mr. Sirocco."

The petite woman smiled, but it was the kind of smile that made Nick uncomfortable. The kind that made Nick want to check to see if his fly was open.

She walked to Hawkins's door, knocked lightly, then slipped into the room and closed the door behind her. Nick took a step closer and tilted his head, hoping to hear their conversation, but all he could make out was some mumbling.

He only had a second's warning before Cathy breezed back out. The look on her face told him he hadn't been fast enough in his retreat.

"She'll be out in a minute," Cathy said to him, her eyes laughing.

"Thanks," Nick growled.

Only three years out of covert ops, and already he'd lost

all of his stealth skills. Jimmy and Marquez would rag him mercilessly if they found out.

Only they wouldn't find out, because they were gone, just like the other two men who'd been part of his close-knit Ranger team.

Danni came out of her office, a welcome diversion from Nick's downward-spiraling thoughts.

"Mr. Sirocco," she said coolly.

"Ms. Hawkins," Nick responded deliberately. In contrast to the stained trousers and businesslike jacket she sported yesterday, today she wore chunky black boots, black jeans, and a black, red, and white plaid blouse with a white knit shirt beneath it. Also, yesterday she hadn't been wearing a brown leather shoulder holster with a Smith & Wesson .38 nestled within it.

"I appreciate you bringing me the answering machine." She held out her hand for it.

He shook his head. "We listen to it together."

Danni's lips lost their lushness as she pressed them together. She crossed her arms and rested them below a nice set of breasts. He lifted his gaze to meet hers and wasn't surprised to see stubbornness in her eyes. If he hadn't been at the receiving end of her obstinacy, he would've admired her backbone.

Danni and Nick's staring contest continued until the woman conceded and stepped back. "Come in."

With neither of them speaking, Nick set the answering machine on her desk, and Danni plugged it into an outlet.

"Are you ready?" Nick asked hesitantly. Although he'd listened to the message numerous times, it would be the first time for Danni.

She gave a terse nod.

Nick pressed the Play button.

"You have one old message," the flat monotone stated before Paddy's voice came on. "Message one."

"Rocky, it's Paddy. I need to talk to you. Something's going on at the youth center." He cleared his throat. "I have a feeling I know what it is, but I need your help to prove it.

Call me as soon as you get this message. If I don't hear from you tonight, I'll call you in the morning." A weak chuckle. "Sometimes truth is stranger than fiction."

Nick hit the Stop button as the now-familiar pang of guilt settled in his gut. He lifted his gaze to Danni, who was staring down at her lap. Her long curly hair obscured her face, and he had a hunch the veil was intentional.

He wouldn't push her, not yet. Hearing her father's voice had probably been pretty traumatic.

"So you're Rocky," Danni commented, startling Nick.

Of all her possible reactions, that wasn't even on the list. "Paddy called me that when I was a kid," he admitted. He hadn't liked it in the beginning, but Paddy hadn't cared what Nick thought, and he had come to appreciate the nickname. "He said I was always looking for a fight."

She raised her head, and though her eyes were dry, red lines shot through the whites. "I did a lot of thinking last night."

Although Nick's mind raced, he remained still, waiting for her to continue.

"Did you know Dad was Catholic?" she asked.

"No."

She focused inward. "The Church used to say that if a person killed himself, he'd go directly to hell. They changed their tune on that a few years ago, but Dad grew up believing it. As far as I know, he attended Mass and took Communion every Sunday, and went to confession once every two months like a good Catholic."

"How about you?" Nick asked quietly.

"He made me go with him until he couldn't put me over his knee anymore. But he never stopped going. Never stopped believing. His funeral Mass was the first time I'd stepped inside a church in nearly ten years." She took a deep breath. "Do you have any idea what he might've been talking about?"

Nick's mind took a second to catch up to her question. "Not really. It sounds like he stumbled onto something at center, but . . ." He shrugged. "I don't know what it might've been."

"But he specifically said he needed you to help prove whatever it was. Why?"

Nick had racked his memory for something, anything that might answer that question. *Why*? All he'd done was worsen his headache. "I don't know. It could be anything, from drugs to gang activity to whatever." He threw his hands in the air. "The center is supposed to be a place to get them away from that kind of stuff, but sometimes it doesn't work that way. Some of the kids there have juvie records. Most of the others have had a close brush with the law. Sometimes the center is the last chance they have before juvenile detention."

"You would know. You were one of them," Danni said.

Nick stiffened defensively, then forced himself to ease his tense muscles. "I was one of the lucky ones, thanks to your father."

Danni's jaw muscle knotted, but she didn't look away. After a long bout of silence, she said, "Maybe some of the kids are dealing there. Maybe Dad found out about it."

Nick thought for a moment. "I don't think so. Not that kids don't murder people, but I can't see a kid being that inventive—making it look like suicide."

Danni drummed her fingers on her desk. "You're probably right. But from Dad's message, it seems that his murder was related to the center."

It was the first time she'd actually stated that Paddy had been murdered. Something had convinced her Nick was right. "So what did you find out?" he asked.

She smiled slightly, as if her opinion of him might have risen a notch or two. "I obtained a copy of the coroner's report. Just as I was told, there were burn marks around the entrance wound. There was also gunpowder residue on his fingers, another indicator that he'd fired a weapon."

This wasn't what Nick was hoping to learn. "That's why it was ruled a suicide."

"That's right. Except Dad was at the shooting range that

day, putting in his monthly firearms practice. That could account for the residue on his fingers."

"But wouldn't it have worn off?"

"It can take up to twenty-four hours for the residue to disappear completely from the skin."

Nick sat stiff-backed in his chair, his mind racing. "Did the killer know that he'd been to the range?"

Danni shrugged. "If it was someone in the department, like you suspect, then yes, he could've. The schedules are posted where everyone can see them. But there's something else that's bothering me."

Nick wondered why *all* of it didn't bother her. Hell, it bothered him. Just hearing the cold, analytical words of the autopsy made his skin grow clammy. "What's that?"

"Who did he trust enough to get that close to him?"

Her question solidified a hard fact. "He knew his murderer."

She picked up a green paper clip and bent it open, making it look like a fishhook. "Proving it will be hell."

"I know. I tried."

"I heard." Danni straightened another curve in the paper clip. "It seems you've made quite a name for yourself."

"What're you talking about?"

Danni tossed the now-straight paper clip onto her desk and leaned forward. "Why didn't you tell me you'd pissed off everyone?"

Busted. "All I did was ask some questions."

"You pretty much accused everyone of being involved in a conspiracy." Danni shook her head. "If the killer is hiding within the force, you've built a wall we'll have to take apart one brick at a time in order to find him."

Nick rubbed his throbbing brow. "Nobody believed me. Hell, you didn't even believe me, and you should've been the first one to stick up for Paddy."

Danni's face reddened, and she picked up another paper clip, this one blue, and began unbending it. "You're right. Even though Dad and I weren't on good terms for over ten

., we were slowly starting to mend our fences. I ...uld've known he wouldn't kill himself."

Nick had the insane urge to comfort her in his arms, but he suspected she wouldn't appreciate his sympathy. "You were in shock," he said lamely.

Danni's head came up, her eyes snapping and glittering. "Don't make excuses for me, Sirocco. I screwed up."

Although surprised, Nick understood her lashing out at him. She was in pain, and he kept prodding at the festering wound.

Her phone buzzed.

Frowning, Danni hit a button. "Yes?"

"It's two o'clock," her receptionist said.

Her scowl grew. "Thanks, Cathy." She faced Nick. "I've got a surveillance job."

"Can't it wait? We should go over to the center."

"No. I've already put it off a week, with Dad's funeral and all, and I can't afford to lose a client." She stood and grabbed what looked like a man's old suit coat from the back of her chair. She donned it and tugged her hair out from under the collar. Her curls spilled across her shoulders, catching the light and reflecting reddish tints.

She paused and caught his gaze. "If you're right about the killer being a cop, you're in more danger than I am."

"What're you talking about?"

"You didn't exactly use tact and discretion at the station when you were asking questions about my father. That, and the fact Dad thought you could've helped him tells me you're the one with a bull's-eye painted on your chest."

Nick hadn't even considered his own safety, but that wasn't his foremost concern. Still, if he could use her logic for his objective . . . "You could be right. We should stick together until we figure out who killed him."

A little furrow wrinkled the skin between her eyebrows, like she suspected she'd been played. Then the now-familiar stubborn glint entered her eyes, and Nick held up a hand. "No, Danni." Her name slipped out unintentionally. "One person's already been murdered. If we're going to find the truth, we need to work together. I was in the army, so I know how to take orders." He smiled in what he hoped was a disarming way. "Besides, if you don't let me tag along, I'll just follow you, and that'd be a waste of our natural resources."

Startled amusement tilted her lips upward. "Are you always so full of shit, Sirocco?"

"Only when I'm trying to win friends and influence enemies."

"You've certainly influenced me," Danni said. But Nick could tell most of her hostility toward him had faded. Maybe they could actually work together without maiming one another.

She picked up a backpack from behind her desk and slung a strap over her shoulder. Nick followed her out of the office and stood by the door as she spoke to Cathy.

"I won't be in the office the rest of the day unless Willy has some afternoon delight and I can get the evidence I need right away." Danni picked up the camera with a mega-telephoto lens sitting on the desk corner. "Mr. Sirocco's going with me. We're going to be working together on a temporary basis."

Cathy's gaze slid over to Nick and back to her boss, but not before he noticed the mischievous twinkle in her eyes. "A temporary . . . partner?"

"Something like that."

"Oh, I almost forgot. Sam called to see how you were doing."

"If he calls back, tell him I'll try to touch base this evening."

"Be careful."

Danni gingerly tucked the camera into her backpack. "This job is a piece of cake."

Cathy nodded, but her worry didn't fade. "I know, but humor me."

"I thought Beth was the mother hen in the office." Danni touched Cathy's shoulder. "Don't worry. I'll be fine."

Nick opened the door and allowed Danni to precede him. "Do you want to take my car?" he asked.

Danni shook her head. "I'll drive. My pickup's right here." She pointed to a battered twenty-five-year-old Ford truck with more than a few dents and scratches. It looked like something the Clampetts would drive.

"Got anything newer, like an Edsel?" he asked dryly.

She sent him a glare that might have brought down a lesser man, but Nick Sirocco had been an Army Ranger, trained to endure enemy interrogation techniques.

"It has two very appealing features," she began. "It's paid for, and it runs. Get in, unless you plan to waste natural resources." She walked around to the driver's side.

Knowing he was beat, he said, "I just have to get Gus."

She froze and peered at him over the truck's hood. "Who's Gus?"

"My dog. Gus, short for Augusta," he replied, then added with a shrug, "She likes going for rides."

Sighing, Danni glanced at her watch. "Whatever. Just make it fast. We're already late."

Nick strode to his Jeep to retrieve Gus and the notebook he'd brought as an afterthought. The mutt danced about his legs, her tail wagging with excitement as they rejoined Danni.

Gus trotted over to Danni, who held out her hand with the back faced outward. Gus sniffed her knuckles and gave her approval with a swipe of her tongue. Only then did Danni pet her.

Put two females together, and they start bonding, Nick thought in amusement. *Next thing you know, they'll be exchanging shampoo brands.*

"Gus, come." The dog returned to his side after one more lick to Danni's hand. "Up," Nick said, motioning into the truck's cab. Gus jumped up and settled in the center of the bench seat, tongue lolling.

Nick and Danni climbed in, and she headed south, merging with the early afternoon traffic.

"So where are we going?" he asked.

"A car dealership on the east side. My client thinks her husband's having an affair."

"I thought this was a surveillance job."

"It is. We'll be tailing him to try to get some compromising pictures."

"You quit the force to do *this?* Why?"

Danni's jaw clenched, and the softness she'd revealed earlier disappeared. "My reasons are none of your concern, Mr. Sirocco."

"Touchy, aren't we?"

She glowered but didn't say anything. Paddy had never told him why his daughter left the police force, and Nick hadn't been curious enough to press him. Now he wished he had.

"So the philandering husband's a used car salesman?" Nick commented.

"He actually owns the lot." Her bristles retracted. "But Willy *is* pretty much the stereotypical sleazeball."

He huffed a startled laugh.

They arrived at their destination, which had a sign that read: Willy's Used Cars, No Lemons, Only Lemonade. The place didn't look like much; the dirt lot covered only half a block and the vehicles were either mundane sedans or soccer-mom vans. He couldn't think of a more depressing way to make a living.

Danni drove around to the back of the dealership and parked across and up the street.

"Why here?" Nick asked.

"See that black Mercedes?"

He nodded.

"That's Willy's."

"Our Lothario?"

"Our sleaze."

"Maybe he's only lonely."

"Maybe if he spent more time with his wife, he wouldn't be." Danni angled him a glare, though her sunglasses lessened the impact considerably. "Just like a man to defend another man's right to screw around if he gets the itch."

"I didn't say that." *How the hell had she come up with that?*

"Whatever." She turned her attention to the used car lot and the tiny gray building dropped into the center of it. "Hand me my backpack, please."

He retrieved it from behind the seat and passed it to her.

"Thanks," she said absently.

She withdrew the camera, and Nick returned the backpack to its former place.

Danni pushed her sunglasses up on her head and aimed the camera at the car dealer's office, extending the telephoto lens as far as it would go.

"See anything?" Nick asked.

"No. It's early yet. His wife said when she's called the dealership around three-thirty, Willy's usually gone. Only he doesn't get home until late in the evening."

Nick shot his wrist out from his sleeve. "It's only two-fifty now." He shifted in his seat, moving Gus slightly so he could see Danni's profile. "Was your secretary talking about Sam Richmond?"

"First off, Cathy's a paralegal. If she hears you call her a secretary, you'll be singing soprano for a week."

Nick flinched reflexively. "Point taken."

"And yes, it was Sam Richmond who called. Do you know him?"

"He was Paddy's partner. Used to help out at the center, too. He was a three-point man."

She smiled "I know. Sam taught me how to shoot hoops."

"What about your da—"

"He was always too busy," Danni replied curtly.

Frowning slightly, Nick filed away the information.

Danni kept her gaze aimed at the car lot, her camera lens balanced on the steering wheel. "Do you know of anything that was bothering my father? Maybe a case?"

"He didn't mention anything in particular. His partner,

Karen Crandle, said he'd been upset about something lately, but she didn't know what."

"When did you speak with Karen?"

"She called me after his body was found. She was pretty shook up. I tried contacting her again, but she didn't return my calls."

Danni sent him a sidelong glance. "Did you find out why?"

"At the funeral she apologized. She said it'd been pretty hectic at the station. She looked worn out."

"Did she believe it was suicide?"

"She told me he wasn't looking forward to retiring, but she didn't think he was depressed enough to take his own life. But she believed the evidence."

The air in the truck's cab felt close and sticky, and Nick rolled down his window. The damp breeze carried the scent of more rain. What else was new in the Pacific Northwest?

Gus put her two front paws on Nick's left thigh and stretched her nose toward the window. She wagged her tail across Danni's face.

Danni sneezed and pushed aside Gus's tail. "Next time Gus sits in the back end."

"But she likes riding in the front."

Danni rolled her eyes, but she was smiling. The expression gentled her features, and Nick found himself grinning with her over Gus's antics.

After maneuvering Gus's backside away from her face, Danni became pensive. "Why?" she murmured. "What did Dad stumble across that was big enough to warrant murder? And why didn't he bring it to the attention of someone in the department?"

"Maybe he was trying to learn more before making any accusations."

"Why did he call you that night and not *me?*" Frustration bled into her tone.

"Maybe he didn't want to worry you."

"Or maybe he didn't trust me to help him," she said bitterly.

Stunned, Nick could only stare. Paddy had always spoken about her with pride.

"There's a set of binoculars under your seat if you're interested," Danni said, her intent to change the subject clear.

"Voyeurs R Us," Nick said wryly as he reached for the binoculars. He raised the glasses, but all he could see were dirty blinds covering dirtier windows, so he rested them in his lap. "Do you miss being a cop?"

She continued to peer at Willy's lot. "Sometimes."

"Can you be a more specific? What do you miss?"

Something flickered across her face that Nick couldn't quite identify. Regret? "Why do you care?"

"I'm a writer. I'm curious about everything." *Especially you.*

After a few beats of silence, Danni replied, "I can tell you what I *don't* miss: night shifts, office politics, and shitty coffee."

Nick chuckled.

She placed the camera beside her and lowered her sunglasses back in place. Nick had an idea she was shielding her thoughts more than the sun's rays, especially since the sun was being overtaken by dark clouds.

"I miss some of the people I worked with. I miss the feeling that I was doing something useful," she said quietly.

"And the donuts?" Nick teased.

She chuckled and looked at him. "Only the custard-filled ones."

His gaze lingered on her mischievous smile, and he felt an odd little hitch in his breathing. It wasn't a reaction he expected. But then, Danni was turning out not to be what he expected either.

"So what's the biggest difference between being a cop and a PI?" he asked, surprised his voice was so steady.

"More writerly questions?" Her eyebrows canted upward.

He grinned. "Humor me."

"Don't tempt me, Sirocco." Her teasing tone softened the words. She glanced at the car dealership, then answered him. "Accountability. As a private investigator, I'm accountable only to my client and myself. When I was a cop, I spent half my time filling out forms. That's another thing I don't miss. There was a friggin' form for everything."

"The military was the same way. It's the bureaucratic bullshit used to try to keep everyone honest."

Gus whined and did a familiar dance on the seat. Nick sighed and opened his door.

"Where are you going?" Danni asked.

"Gus has to use the facilities."

"Stay close."

"Yes, ma'am," Nick said with a lazy salute.

He closed the truck door behind him. There was nothing but concrete on this side of the street, so he and Gus crossed to a vacant lot with an equal amount of weeds and rocks.

An old Chevy sped past with a flashy redhead behind the wheel. As Gus took care of business, Nick watched the car turn into Willy's lot. A man carrying a bag came out of the building and jumped into the front seat with her.

"That's him. Get in," Danni called out to Nick.

Caught off guard, Nick called to Gus, who'd found a fascinating scent to follow.

"Hurry!" she yelled. "They're leaving."

"Get over here, Gus," he hollered, but the dog was caught up in whatever she'd discovered. Nick strode toward the disobedient animal.

An engine roared, and Nick spun around to see Danni taking off after the Chevy.

Leaving him and Gus in a cloud of exhaust.

Chapter Three

If Danni had still been a cop, she would've nailed Willy's piece of fluff for speeding, reckless driving, failure to yield, and a host of other moving violations. Danni alternated between cursing the occupants of the car she followed and herself for abandoning Nick. After her talk about him possibly being in danger, she shouldn't have left him behind.

She clamped her lips together and concentrated on keeping the blue Chevy in sight. She'd never slacked on a job, and she didn't plan to start now. Sirocco was a big boy; he could take care of himself for a few minutes.

For ten more minutes she sped through yellow lights and jockeyed around slowpoke drivers, all the while trying not to draw Willy's or a bored traffic cop's attention. She was rewarded when Willy and his paramour turned into a motel parking lot. Sleepy Bye Motel, Hourly and Daily Rates. Danni wrinkled her nose as she parked on the street and watched the redhead sashay into the lobby. With a thigh-length skirt, skintight halter top, and three-inch heels, there'd be no question why the woman was there.

When she came out of the office five minutes later, she

waved a key at Willy. The two-timing worm got out of the Chevy carrying a small nylon duffel bag with his car dealership logo on the side.

A two-timer and an idiot.

Danni stayed long enough to snap some pictures of Willy and the woman entering their room. She hated leaving a job half done even for a short time, but she headed back to find Nick. Although she didn't drive back as recklessly, Danni broke a few speed limits, especially when raindrops began to tap-dance across the windshield.

Arriving back where she'd left Nick, she could find no sign of him or his dog. *Damn! Where had they gone?* She drove slowly, peering through the rain and down each side street. The longer she searched, the more worried she became. If someone was after Nick . . .

Finally, she spotted a familiar denim-clad backside with a dog walking beside it and was surprised by the extent of her relief. Nick had his hands in his pockets and his shoulders hunched against the rain. Both he and Gus looked like drowned rats, which made Danni feel like crap.

She pulled up alongside them and leaned over to shove open the passenger door. "Get in."

Nick halted and glared at her. Gus, however, didn't seem to hold a grudge and hopped in, wet fur and all.

"C'mon, Sirocco. Even your dog has more brains than to stand out in the rain," Danni said, guilt making her tone sharp.

Without a word or a lessening of his rigid features, he slid into the passenger seat and slammed the door. He sat with stiff shoulders and a rigid backbone, his hands jammed in his leather jacket pockets.

Danni's guilt turned to irritation. Fine, if he wanted to act like a five-year-old, so be it. She didn't have anything to apologize for. She was only doing her job. She should be taking incriminating pictures for her client right now instead of putting up with his temper tantrum.

Gus shook, spraying water droplets everywhere, including Danni's eyes. She used her sleeve to wipe her face and grimaced at the wet dog smell, which now permeated the cab.

After a long sigh, she drove back to the motel, trying to keep her mind off her pissed-off passenger. His silent treatment, however, grated on her nerves even as she swore she wouldn't be the one to break the strained impasse.

Nick sneezed.

"Bless you," she said automatically.

He glared.

She glared back.

"I'm surprised you came back for me," he finally spoke.

Danni squirmed in her seat. "Jobs like this are my bread and butter. I can't afford to blow it." She glanced at him. "Know why I drive this pickup? Because it's all I can afford."

Nick scrubbed his rain-dampened face with his palms, then lowered his hands to gaze at her somberly. "I was worried about you."

Warmth fluttered in Danni's chest, startling her. But she was unable to say she was concerned about him, too, even though she had been. Self-preservation was job one in her book. "I came back as soon as I could. There's a blanket behind the seat," she said awkwardly.

"Thanks." He reached back and nabbed the soft thermal blanket Danni used for cold stakeouts. He wiped his hands and face, then the dog's wet fur.

Danni parked across the street from the motel but didn't turn off the truck. The warm air coming out of the vents would ease the damp chill for Nick and Gus.

"Is this where they came?" he asked, looking through the misty rain.

"Room one-thirteen. I'll have to see if they were considerate enough to leave a curtain open." Danni peered at the smoky gray sky and placed the camera in her backpack to keep it dry while it wasn't in use. "I'll leave the truck running."

"I'll go with you." His crooked smile caught her off guard. "It's not like I could get any wetter."

Danni paused, her hand on the door handle. "You don't have to."

He shrugged. "I've never seen a PI in action before."

"You're going to see a whole lot of action you probably don't want to see," Danni warned.

"TMI stuff?"

"Oh, yeah. Definitely too much information." She switched off the truck. "Gus will have to stay here."

Nick nodded and climbed out. Danni joined him.

"Keep down and keep quiet," she said.

"Don't worry. I used to be a Ranger."

"Lone or Power?" Danni smirked.

Before he could retort, she jogged to the end of the motel. She pressed her back against the peeling paint and motioned for Nick to join her. Mumbling about smart-ass women, he scrambled up beside her.

"At least if I was the Lone Ranger, I'd have a faithful companion," he muttered.

"You've got Gus." Danni turned away before he could catch her amused smile. "There should be a window to their room around the corner."

"What if they closed their curtains?"

"Then I keep following Willy until they forget to close the curtains and I can get some dirty pictures."

Nick stared at her. "You enjoy this way too much."

Although Danni could think of a hundred things she'd rather be doing than snapping some raunchy pictures—like cleaning hair out of a drainpipe or unplugging a stopped-up toilet—she waggled her eyebrows. "You ought to see my videotape collection."

"You have videotapes?"

Danni rolled her gaze heavenward, amazed that a former Army Ranger would be so gullible. She blinked fat raindrops out of her eyes. "Come on, let's see if we can finish up here."

Keeping her back close to the wall, she followed the ell of the building. As she did, she was too aware of Nick beside her, his arm occasionally brushing hers. She didn't need this distraction, even though it was one of the more pleasant distractions she'd had in a long time.

"Won't the manager call the cops if he sees us skulking around?" Nick asked. His warm breath caressed her cheek, reminding her how long it'd been since she'd been with a man.

"Puh-leeze. I doubt the scumbag would even call the cops if he found a body in one of his rooms. A *dead* body."

Stopping at the corner, Danni leaned close to Nick, her nose almost touching his short, soft-looking hair. "Their window should be the second one. Try not to trip."

"Yes, ma'am." He gave her a sharp salute, which wasn't too surprising since he'd been in the army. She doubted, though, that he'd used the same husky voice with his commanding officers as he did with her.

Danni crept around the corner and sank into a crouch. She ducked even lower as she passed under the first window, then dropped into a squat, hugging the wall. They were on the back side of the motel, away from the parking lot but facing a gas station less than a hundred feet away.

Nick joined her, his soggy arm pressing against her drier one. If possible, he looked even more waterlogged than when she'd picked him up.

Figuring she was alongside the right room, she set her backpack against the wall, raised up to find a six-inch gap between the curtains, and peeked in. She blinked once . . . twice . . . and hurled herself back against Nick's shoulder, which was only negligibly softer than the wall. Propping her elbows on her drawn-up knees, she buried her face in her hands as she tried to gather her composure. Her shoulders shook with the effort, but it was a losing battle.

Strong hands gripped her upper arms. "What is it? C'mon, tell me. What's wrong?"

Nick's concerned tone shimmied through her bones. It was even better than his husky "Yes, ma'am."

She lifted her head from her hands. "It's Willy. King of the jungle," she managed to say past her muffled laughter.

He jerked his hands away from her like she had a social

disease and plopped down on his backside. He stared at her as if questioning her sanity . . . or lack thereof. "You're laughing."

Danni struggled to get her mirth under control. "Good one, Sherlock." She panted as she wiped at her tearing eyes. "Willy's standing on top of the dresser."

Nick appeared even more bewildered.

"He's wearing a loincloth," she barely managed to say. The memory of his skinny limbs and concave chest nearly sent her into another spasm of laughter. Now she knew what had been in the duffel bag. "And, uh, Ms. Big Boob Redhead is tied spread-eagle on the bed."

"And what's *she* wearing?"

"Nothing."

He tipped his head back and thumped it against the wall. "Shit."

Danni nudged him with her elbow. "Looks like I could've used the camcorder for this one, huh?"

Nick rolled his head toward her. "You're sick, Hawkins. You know that?"

"Prerequisite for the job. Wait here. I'm going to take some pictures."

She retrieved her camera and removed the lens cap. Rising to her knees at the window, she focused the camera on Willy, who beat his hollow chest with his fists, and she clicked four pictures in rapid succession. She shifted and took more shots of the bound woman on the bed, with the loinclothed Willy on the dresser in the background. Pleased with her results, she settled back against the wall and grinned cheekily. "That's a wrap, folks."

A sudden shout and thump, followed by a spine-tingling scream, startled her. She frowned as she met Nick's gaze.

"What the hell?" he asked and rose up to peer into the window. "Goddamn."

Danni crowded up next to him to see what Willy the jungle king and his redheaded temptress had done to produce such a reaction. Willy was lying motionless on the bed between the woman's naked thighs, and she was screaming like a banshee, but the screams weren't ones of ecstasy. "Oh, shit."

Danni tossed her camera back in the pack, snagged a strap, and raced around the motel, peripherally aware of Nick close on her heels. She splashed through puddles formed from the still-falling rain. At room 113, she tried the doorknob, but it was locked. She pounded on the door.

"Help! He's dead! Ohmygod, he's dead!" The hysterical voice came from within.

The locks were the old key type, not the fancy kind with the slide card. Danni dug out her wallet, looking for her one and only credit card to slip between the door and the frame. As she searched, Nick took hold of her arms and moved her away from the door.

A loud crash made her snap her head up. Nick had kicked in the door.

"Way to keep a low profile," Danni muttered, glancing around anxiously to see if anyone had witnessed his testosterone display.

"Hey, it worked, didn't it?"

Danni couldn't argue that, and she rushed into the room, which held a double bed, a dresser, one chair, and a TV. And a scene that could have been from an X-rated movie, except the stud wasn't moving.

Danni grabbed an extra blanket from the shelf above the clothes rack and tossed it over the woman's naked torso. Although Danni was pretty certain Willy's playmate didn't care if another man ogled her attributes, especially one like Nick Sirocco, Danni felt, somehow, less exposed.

As Nick untied the woman, Danni knelt at the end of the mattress and examined Willy, who appeared to have hit his head on the foot of the bed. She rolled him onto his back.

He groaned, and his eyelids flickered open. "What the fu—"

"Lie still," she ordered in her no-nonsense cop voice.

Although confused, Willy did as she commanded. Danni probed the rapidly forming lump on the man's forehead. Fortunately, the skin hadn't split open, and the skull didn't appear to be damaged.

"You should go to the hospital. You probably have a concussion," Danni said.

"What the hell happened?" Willy demanded in a reedy voice that matched his reedy body.

"Don'tcha remember, sweetie? You and me was playing. I was the helpless captive, and you was the jungle hero who was comin' to rescue me." The redheaded bimbo's gaze slanted toward Nick, who held the pieces of rope from her "captivity" in his hands. She winked at him.

Nick winked back.

Danni stifled a colorful comeback. She gave her attention back to the injured Tarzan.

Willy's flush matched the floozy's hair color. "Shut up, Bambi! Just shut up."

Danni glanced at Nick, who mouthed *Bambi?* and she had to look away before she lost it.

"Who are you?" Bambi asked Sirocco.

"Ni—"

"We were just walking by when we heard you scream," Danni interrupted. She wasn't in the habit of kicking a man when he was down, and with the pictures she'd taken, she suspected Willy would find out soon enough why they'd been there.

"We appreciate your help, but you can leave now," Willy said, trying ineffectually to cover the front of his loincloth with his hands. He had obviously lost his excitement for the game.

"You should have your head examined," Danni said, stifling her grin at the unintentional pun.

Willy sent her a sharp look, or as sharp as he could under the circumstances.

She didn't think he appreciated her humor.

"I'll think about it," he said.

Nick gazed down at Bambi and winked. Again. "You and your hero have fun," he said.

The flicker of disappointment on Bambi's overly made-up face told Danni she would gladly trade her ape man hero for the ape who'd kicked in her door. Stifling the urge to roll her eyes, Danni left the motel room, only to find rain pouring down in black sheets.

Just great.

Nick joined her after leaning the door, which he'd kicked off the hinges, against the frame. She checked to ensure her camera was safely stowed in her backpack. They scurried across the motel lot toward the truck and paused to look for traffic before starting across the street.

A squeal of tires was Danni's only warning. She jerked around to see a car barreling through the storm directly toward them. She felt a tug on her arm and fell to the street. Then she was rolling across the wet pavement, another body glued to hers—a bigger and harder body that protected her on the concrete. They stopped abruptly, and Nick groaned, his breath hot against her ear.

Danni scrambled up to try to see the car that had almost run them down, but it had disappeared into the inky rain. She spotted her backpack lying in the middle of the street and grabbed it before it was run over by a vehicle. Hurrying back to Nick, she squatted beside him and laid a hand on his chest. His heart thundered as fast as hers.

"You okay?" she asked anxiously.

He nodded and, with her help, sat up. He rubbed his right arm, grimacing as the rain streamed down his face. "Nothing's broken."

Danni realized he must've hit the curb with his arm. She flinched, imagining the bruise he'd have. "Should I take you to the hospital?"

"No. It'll be okay."

They rose and stepped onto the sidewalk. Nobody was around, or at least nobody they could spot. The rain was easing up, but water saturated Danni's curls and worked its way across her scalp to her nape and rolled down her back. A shiver followed the cold rain's path on her skin.

"Let's get in the truck," Danni said.

Once inside the cab with the happily wiggling Gus,

Nick tugged the blanket out from under his dog and wiped his hands and face. He handed it to Danni, and she found a dry corner without too much dog hair to mop the rain from her face.

"Did you see anything?" Danni asked, her voice low against the backdrop of rain pelting the truck's roof.

"No. It came too fast."

The aftermath of the adrenaline overdose coursed through her blood, and the shakes hit her. She clutched the steering wheel to hide her body's reaction. "Do you think it was a drunk driver?"

Nick shifted his shoulder and grimaced. "Do you?"

"If I thought so, I'd call nine-one-one and report it." Still trembling, she tossed the wet blanket behind the seat. She didn't reach for her cell phone.

Belatedly remembering her camera, she unzipped her backpack and lifted it out. Handling it carefully, she examined it.

"Did it survive?" Nick asked.

Relieved, she nodded and slipped it back inside the pack. "It's in better shape than you are." She eyed him closely, noting the scrape on his left temple where blood oozed. He held his right arm stiffly, telling her the bruise was worse than your standard owie.

With her tremors easing, Danni started the truck and turned the vent fan to defrost. She pulled onto the street, shiny with the watery reflection of the city lights. Her place was on the other side of town, but her father's house was only ten minutes away. It might do them both good to take a hot shower, dry their clothes, and have some coffee before driving another half hour to her office, where Nick's vehicle was parked.

They rode in silence as Danni tried to remember anything about the car or driver who had nearly turned them into roadkill. She didn't want to believe it was anything other than a reckless or drunk driver, but her gut wouldn't let her off the hook.

When Danni turned into her father's driveway, Nick shot her a look. "What're we doing at Paddy's place?"

"You've been here?"

"A few times."

That's right. Nick was the infamous Rocky, her dad's favorite juvenile delinquent. And the object of her first adolescent crush. She squeezed her eyes shut, willing away the bitterness.

"What're we doing here?" Nick repeated, this time with a shade of impatience.

Danni opened her eyes. "I thought we could dry our clothes and have something warm to drink before I take you back to your car."

"Are you trying to get me out of my pants, Ms. Hawkins?" Sultry heat wrapped his low voice in velvet, caressing her as if he'd touched her with his strong, square hands.

She kept her attention trained on the dim porch, trying not to imagine Nick Sirocco sliding out of those snug blue jeans. . . .

Danni cleared her throat, and her mind with it. "In your dreams."

"Or yours."

Damn, the man was too good at this game. Or she was too long out of it.

"Do you mind if I bring Gus in?"

A streetlight illuminated Nick's eyes, as vivid and blue as a mountain lake. She almost forgot the question. But then her gaze shifted to the swollen and bloody bump on his forehead, reminding her why they were here. "No, that's fine."

The rain had diminished to a light mist, but Danni still hurried to the covered porch. Nick and Gus joined her as she unlocked the door. Danni flicked the switch, and light flooded the interior, bringing an avalanche of memories.

Nick closed the door behind them, and Gus trotted into the living room, where she plopped down on the carpet.

Danni set her backpack on the floor, then removed her

jacket, revealing her shoulder holster and damp T-shirt. Glancing up, she noticed Nick eyeing her chest. He was probably comparing her attributes to Bambi's. Danni didn't have a prayer with her 34Bs pitted against a pair of 38Ds.

She resisted the urge to cross her arms, to cover her puckered nipples clearly visible through the damp cloth. A wet T-shirt contest queen she wasn't. She told herself it was merely her body's reaction to the cold. "There's a bathroom at the top of the stairs with towels in the linen closet. Go ahead and take a shower," she said. "If you toss your clothes outside the door, I'll put them in the dryer."

"Thanks," Nick replied.

Danni watched him trudge up the stairs, taking guilty pleasure in eyeing his tight, denim-encased backside. She was surprised he wasn't moving more stiffly, since he'd taken the brunt of the pavement's punishment. *Her* muscles were beginning to feel like she'd hiked up Mount Rainier.

Ignoring her body's demands for a few more minutes, she removed her revolver from the shoulder holster and efficiently wiped it down. It didn't matter if she was a cop or a PI, she had to be able to count on her weapon.

When she was done, she removed the shoulder holster and placed it and her gun on the kitchen table. She put on a pot of coffee, then leaned against the counter. Her gaze settled on the teapot-shaped clock that had hung above the stove ever since she could remember. The pale yellow walls used to make the room cheery even during overcast days, but now they made the kitchen seem old and outdated. The forest green carpet and the heavy furniture throughout the house also spoke of an era when *All in the Family* and polyester leisure suits were in vogue. It seemed her father had stopped time in his own world when Danni's mom left them.

Danni shoved away from the counter and trotted upstairs, passing Nick's pile of wet clothes in the hallway. The shower was running, and Danni could imagine Nick, his head tipped back, as the water sluiced over his hair, down his broad shoulders, and across his muscled back and buttocks. She blinked aside the tempting picture and went into her old room. After removing her T-shirt and black jeans, she tugged on an oversized Oregon State sweatshirt and faded blue jeans with holes in the knees that she found in a dresser drawer.

Nick would need some dry clothes, or he would have to sit in the bathroom for forty-five minutes. Her clothes obviously wouldn't fit him, which left her father's.

She paused in front of his bedroom, her feet suddenly anchored to the floor. She'd only been in there once since her father's death—when she'd gotten his dress uniform for the burial. With her hands clenched tightly and her heart thundering, she pushed open the door and paused.

Her gaze settled on the bare bed frame. The mattress and box spring had been removed, but Danni could almost smell the thick scent of blood. Against her will, her attention shifted to the scrubbed walls, where the blood spatter could still be seen as faint pink stains on the light blue wallpaper. Her stomach rolled, and bile rose in her throat. She forced back the sickness and breathed through her mouth in slow, calming breaths.

Danni found her father's old bathrobe hanging on its usual hook in the closet. She clutched it to her chest and buried her face in the terry cloth. The faded scent of his aftershave surrounded her. She tried not to breathe, to ignore the bombarding memories invoked by the scent, but the sensations were too strong.

When she was four years old, her father used to sit her on the vanity so she could watch him shave. The whole process had fascinated her, from applying the white foam, which he allowed her to help with, to watching him drag the razor across his face, leaving smooth bare skin behind. Then he would tap three drops of aftershave in his palm, rub his hands together, and slap his face. The final act would be the test; her father would rub a freshly shaven cheek against hers. Then she'd giggle and proclaim him ready for work.

A tear rolled down Danni's cheek, and she swiped it away impatiently. That was almost twenty-five years ago, when she'd been Daddy's little girl.

"Do you have anything I can wear?" Nick's shout startled her, and she suddenly realized the shower was off.

"I'm coming." She walked down the hallway and knocked on the bathroom door. "Here." Her throat felt raw.

The door cracked open, and a hand thrust out to accept the robe. "Thanks."

Danni picked up his soaked clothes, gathered her own from her old bedroom, and carried them downstairs to the utility room. She tossed them into the dryer and set the timer.

She heard Nick's padding footsteps on the stairs and returned to the front room. The robe was wrapped almost double around him, but it ended just below his knees. She tried not to stare at the flexing muscles in his calves or his nicely formed feet as he descended, but her gaze kept traveling back to them.

She aimed her eyes above his neck and saw the angry-looking scrape on his temple. "I'll get some antiseptic cream for that."

Nick touched the injury and flinched. "No wonder my head's pounding."

"How's your arm?"

"Sore, but not as bad as my shoulders. They're stiffening up good."

Danni went back into the utility room, found the first aid supplies she knew were kept there, and returned to the living room. "Sit down," she ordered.

"What're you going to do?" Nick asked, making no move to do as she said.

"Nothing that'll ruin your reputation." Danni ushered him into a chair.

She moved to his front, her legs brushing his bare knees. The front of his robe gaped, and Danni was treated to a view of a thoroughly masculine chest with only a light smattering of coarse, golden brown hair. Closing her suddenly dry mouth and dropping her gaze, she opened the smaller of the two tubes. She pinched a dollop on two fingers and carefully rubbed it into the raw scrape on his forehead.

"Ow!"

"C'mon, a big Army Ranger like yourself shouldn't even notice a little owie like this," Danni said.

"It's not the damned owie. Where'd you learn first aid, Atilla the Hun Medical School?"

Danni rolled her eyes heavenward. "Don't be such a wuss." She scrutinized the swollen gash, bringing her face to within an inch of Nick's. "It's still oozing some clear stuff, but that should stop soon." She moved around to stand behind him. "Now loosen your robe so I can check that bruise."

"It's okay." He attempted to stand, but Danni put her hand on his right shoulder, and he flinched visibly. "Damn it, that hurt."

"Lose the robe, or I'll take it off for you."

Grumbling, Nick untied the belt and eased the robe off his shoulders, and partway down his right arm. Danni stared at the smooth skin of his upper back and the delineation of muscle beneath it. Nick Sirocco was a visual banquet.

"Are you going to do something or just stare?" Nick asked.

Flustered, Danni muttered, "Don't flatter yourself."

She examined the ugly bruise on his upper arm. It would be sore, but didn't look serious. She opened the tube of muscle cream and squeezed a long line of it on her palm. After rubbing her hands together to warm it, she massaged the cream gently into his shoulders. As she kneaded the warm flesh with increasingly firm motions, Nick's head drooped forward, his chin touching his chest with only an occasional hitch in his breath.

Danni withdrew her hands, which tingled from both the

muscle cream she'd used and the feel of Nick's sleek skin. She eased the robe back onto his shoulders.

"Does this mean you're done?" Nick asked, sounding like an overtired child.

Danni came around to stand in front of him. "And here I thought you didn't appreciate my nursing technique."

"I appreciate your technique just fine."

Surprised by his voice's huskiness, she dropped her gaze to his, only to be snared by the smoldering heat in the depths of his eyes. Her cheeks felt flushed, and arousal swamped her belly.

He raised his hand, brushed a curl back, and tucked it behind her ear. "Thank you."

"You're welcome," she whispered, wanting to lose herself in almost-forgotten sensual delight.

And knowing she didn't dare.

Chapter Four

THIS was *not* part of the plan. Furthermore, Danni had no intention of getting involved with one of her father's past "projects." Especially this one. She forced herself to straighten, and Nick's hand fell away. Unwelcome coolness invaded the lingering warmth of his touch.

She changed the subject abruptly. "Are you hungry?"

Nick stood, and her gaze dropped to the floor, right where his sexy feet were planted. Was there anything about this man that *wasn't* sexy?

"Is that an invitation?" he asked.

Unnerved by his proximity, Danni brushed past him. "To eat." She flinched. Why did every other sentence out of her mouth sound like some erotic play on words? Not that she was a prude—far from it—but she didn't want Sirocco to get the wrong idea. "I can scramble some eggs."

"Sounds good."

Danni searched her father's fridge and found eggs, portabello mushrooms, gingerroot, and several items she didn't recognize. For as long as Danni could remember, her father had enjoyed cooking—had even fancied himself a gourmet chef. He used to watch Julia Child, then try to reproduce her meals, using Danni as his guinea pig. Usually, the food was delicious. However, there had been a few occasions where it hadn't even come close to edible. Those were the times when her father had pizza delivered, much to young Danni's delight.

She shook aside the bittersweet memories.

Much of the exotic food had spoiled, and the rest was on the verge. She'd have to clean out the refrigerator in the next day or two. Fortunately, there were enough ingredients to spice up some scrambled eggs—Danni's one and only specialty, as she hadn't inherited her father's joy of cooking.

"What can I do?" Nick asked.

She jumped, having forgotten he was there. "Make sure Gus doesn't chew on the furniture."

"She won't."

"Then watch ESPN or something," she muttered.

She was acutely aware of Nick's scrutiny as she chopped an onion, but she ignored him. What had possessed her to offer him dinner? His clothes wouldn't take that long to dry, then they could leave and go their separate ways.

But was that such a good idea after the near hit-and-run?

"It might've been just a case of drunk driving," Nick suddenly said in a quiet voice.

How had he known what she was thinking?

"Maybe we should call the police and let them check it out," he continued with obvious reluctance. "Is there anybody you trust on the force?"

Danni tried to concentrate on preparing their dinner and not the trembling of her hands. During her last month on the force, it had never been a matter of her trusting her colleagues; it had been a matter of them trusting her.

Or maybe her trusting herself.

She scraped chopped onions, mushrooms, and peppers into the pan. They sizzled in the melted butter, and she stirred the mixture, glad to have something to do with her hands. "Before I talked to you, I would've trusted most everybody. Now, I just don't know."

Nick leaned back in his chair and drummed his fingers on the tabletop. "So what do you think? Should we report it?"

"I thought we already had this discussion," Danni said in exasperation. "It wouldn't do any good. There was no one but us around, and even if there had been, they couldn't have seen much in the storm. It was probably a reckless driver."

"Do you really believe that?"

Danni cracked four eggs in a bowl and whisked them with milk as she replayed their brush with the car. Her grip on the whisk tightened, and the mixture splashed onto the counter. She stopped her frantic mixing and stared down into the bowl, her thoughts and instincts taking her where she didn't want to go. "If it had happened a week ago, I would. But now . . . It's too coincidental. My gut's telling me somebody followed us and used the rain's cover to try to take one or both of us out. I think the appropriate question here is, *why?*"

Nick pulled a hand across his face. "Because I stirred up things at the department, and the killer isn't taking any chances."

"He or she obviously thinks you know something." With a none-too-steady hand, Danni added the whipped eggs to the pan. She turned and met Nick's gaze squarely. "Do you?"

He bristled. "What the hell does that mean?"

"Is there something you haven't told me?"

"I wouldn't have asked for your help if I could've figured it out on my own."

Uneasy, Danni added some kind of cheese with a name she couldn't pronounce to the eggs. "Then we need to figure out what they *think* you know. Could you get a couple of plates from the cupboard behind you?"

Nick rose, and his sharp intake of breath revealed his

discomfort. He retrieved two plates and placed them on the table. "Silverware?"

She pointed to a drawer, and he finished setting the table. She spooned out half of the scrambled eggs on each plate. They sat down and ate in a silence that was surprisingly more comfortable than awkward.

"This is good," Nick commented.

"It's the only thing I can cook," Danni admitted with a shrug.

Nick rested his elbows on the table. "So what's the story with you and your father?"

Danni shot him an irritated glance. "No story. We just didn't have anything in common."

"You were both cops."

"I was a cop for two years. Dad spent over thirty years on the force." Her appetite fled, and she rose to scrape the remains of her meal into the garbage. She knew Nick had more questions about her bouncing around in his head, but she didn't like talking about ancient history. What's done was done, and regurgitating old news wasn't going to change anything.

She leaned against the counter and crossed her arms. "How old were you when Dad 'adopted' you?"

"Seventeen, and he never adopted me." His irritation was clear. He stood and set his empty plate in the sink. "Paddy kicked me in the ass when I needed it. He forced me to take a good look at myself, and what I saw, I didn't much like."

"So you joined the army."

"That wasn't the only reason."

Nick walked into the living room and Danni, curious, followed him. He settled gingerly on the sofa, and Danni dropped into the overstuffed chair, her legs folded beneath her.

"What other reason was there?" Danni asked.

"Let's just say there wasn't a whole lot at home for me, besides an old man who was a drunk. And a mother who did anything or anybody he told her." Nick picked up the TV remote and began channel surfing.

Danni knew all about those kinds of kids—kids from broken families, usually with one, sometimes two parents, and a string of "uncles" or "aunts." Those kids were the ones who ended up populating the jails and prisons once they became adults. Nick Sirocco had escaped that fate. Thanks to her father.

Gus snuffled, rose from her sprawl on the carpet, and went to Nick, laying her chin on his thigh. Nick gave her head a pat, and she dropped back down to lie by his feet.

Danni eyed the animal with something akin to amazement. She would've never expected a dog to be so attuned to a person's emotions. Obviously Gus knew her master pretty well.

The phone rang, startling Danni. She hesitated, and it rang again. She hurried into the kitchen to pick up the handset from the gold wall phone. "Hello."

"Danni?"

"Sam. How'd you find me?"

"I called your place first and didn't get an answer, so I thought I'd take a chance on you being at Paddy's." He paused, and when he spoke again, his tone had roughened with concern. "I wanted to see how you were doing, Danni girl."

She shrugged and gazed down at the blue and yellow tiled floor. "I'm all right."

"You don't sound all right. Why don't I take you out to eat, and we can talk?"

She glanced into the living room and met Nick's inscrutable expression. "I've already eaten. But I'd like to talk. How about breakfast tomorrow morning?"

"Our favorite pancake place?"

Danni smiled. "Perfect. Eight o'clock?"

"I'll see you then. Bye."

"Bye, Sam."

She turned away from Nick's too-perceptive eyes and

stared out the window above the sink into the dark evening.

A few seconds later, strong, capable hands settled on her shoulders and kneaded them gently. Danni tensed, then relaxed, as she inhaled Nick's clean scent. Heat flowed from his hands to her shoulders and inward, to encompass her entire body. She wanted to lean back into the solid chest that she knew lay beneath the robe, which was crazy, because she'd known Nick for all of thirty-six hours. And what would he think of her if she suddenly went all soft and maudlin on him? Or if she turned around and kissed him—a wet, take-no-prisoners kind of kiss—that would help her forget for just a little while?

Her face hot from the spicy fantasy, Danni shrugged away from him and crossed her arms over her sweatshirt. "That was Sam Richmond."

"What did he want?" Nick asked, mirroring her pose as he leaned against a counter.

"To take me out to dinner. We're meeting for breakfast, instead."

"I'll tag along."

"The invitation didn't include you."

"I'm not letting you out of my sight until we find out who tried to kill us today."

"Not us. You."

He shook his head. "We don't know that. What if he was after *you?*"

"Why?"

"Same reason he'd try to kill me—he thinks you know something."

Danni restrained a huff of denial. Her father had never confided in her about anything. "I hate this shit," she muttered to herself. She turned to Nick. "So, what do we do?"

"We can either go to your place or mine, but we stay together." His tone brooked no arguments.

Danni wasn't too keen on being apart either, not if someone was out to get Nick. The thought of him laid out on a stainless steel table in the morgue made her stomach churn. "Why not stay here?"

"I didn't think you'd want to after . . ."

Nick trailed off, but Danni could fill in the blanks.

After your dad died in this house.

Danni suppressed a shiver and snapped, "I can handle it, Sirocco. Besides—" she calmed herself. "This place has more room."

"It's too big to defend effectively."

"Spoken like a true soldier," she remarked, half serious. "We'll both be upstairs, and the guest room is across from my old bedroom."

"It would be better if we slept in the same room."

Danni glared at him. "You're not that irresistible."

Nick grinned. "So you won't have a problem sleeping in the same bed and keeping your hands to yourself?"

"Don't even think about it, Romeo."

His innocent look was ruined by the dangerous glint in his eyes. Danni decided on a preemptive strike. "You want to wash or dry?"

"Wash or dry what?"

Her reply was to fling a dish towel at him. She filled one side of the sink with hot water and soap.

"I want to pick up my Jeep tonight," Nick said after taking a rinsed dish from her soapy hand.

"It'll be fine until tomorrow."

"Not in that neighborhood."

"We'll get it tomorrow." She stacked the rest of the dishes in the drainer.

"Are you always so damned stubborn?"

"Only when I'm right."

"And you're always right."

"Not always. Only ninety-nine percent of the time."

"Cocky, too."

"Part of my charm," she said with a shrug. She finished washing the dishes and watched the soapy water swirl down the drain. It was safer than looking at Nick Sirocco.

With a wry smile, he dried the rest of the dishes and

placed them in the cupboard. Danni took the towel and hung it over a chair. "Your clothes are probably dry by now," she said.

"If we aren't going to get my Jeep, I don't need them." His eyes glittered. "I sleep in the nude."

If he intended to get her all hot and bothered with his little announcement, he succeeded. The thought of his lean body spread out between two cool, crisp sheets was a hell of a lot more enticing than sleeping alone in her pink-trimmed room surrounded by frilly curtains.

"TMI, Sirocco," she muttered.

He grinned unrepentantly.

Damn! She was an independent woman, not some blushing virgin. *Definitely* not a virgin.

So why did Nick Sirocco make her feel like a high school nerd with a crush on the star football player?

NICK shifted, barely containing a moan of discomfort when his shoulder protested the movement. His head, too, was pounding despite the three aspirins he'd taken before going to bed.

He punched his pillow, willing himself to ignore his body's buzzing and throbbing. If Danni Hawkins was sharing his bed, he had a feeling he wouldn't have any problem getting his mind off his aches and pains. But Danni was sleeping across the hallway with her door closed. She probably had a chair jammed under the doorknob, too, to keep the sex-starved Sirocco out of her bedroom.

So maybe that wasn't so far from the truth. Nick had little opportunity to meet women, much less date, in his solitary writer's life. In fact, Gus was the only female who'd been in his bed in months. He reached out and encountered Gus's soft fur. The dog was stretched out along his left leg, where she normally slept at home.

Nick touched the bump on his temple gingerly, wondering for the hundredth time who'd tried to run them down. He'd been going over each and every encounter he'd had at the police department but was unable to come up with a viable suspect.

Why would someone go to the trouble of making Paddy's death look like a suicide? What had he known that had gotten him killed?

God, he missed Paddy. He missed the man's common sense and straightforward advice. Paddy was never one to pull a punch if a punch needed to be thrown. He was a firm believer in taking responsibility for your own actions. He would've been the first to tell Nick that the rift between himself and his daughter wasn't the fault of one of them alone, but a combination of their stubborn natures. And Nick could see Paddy in his daughter so easily—the same blunt honesty and wicked sense of humor.

But Danni was a whole lot easier on the eyes than her father.

He recalled her wet T-shirt and the pebbled nipples beneath it. That sight had been a helluva lot sexier than Miss Bambi lying in her full nude glory on the bed. The jungle temptress hadn't tempted him in the least, but Danni and her drenched shirt . . .

Nick felt his erection pressing against his boxers. Despite what he'd told Danni, he always slept in underwear. Maybe he'd just been trying to get a rise out of her—she was so easy to tease. Instead, *he'd* gotten the rise.

He stifled a groan.

If he and Danni were going to remain in each other's space until Paddy's murderer was found, then Nick had better prepare himself for an extended case of blue balls. Then again, he'd been physically attracted to women before, and he'd survived. He suspected he'd survive this frustration, too.

He thought of ice-cold igloos and hairy-footed hobbits, willing his lust—and a certain body part—to deflate. As his testosterone-charged blood cooled, he wondered how big a mistake he'd made by involving Danni. If she was hurt because he'd asked for her help . . .

He wasn't certain his conscience could take any more

blows. He'd already failed four men—fellow soldiers and friends. What would happen if he failed Danni, too?

A low moan sounded, and Gus lifted her head from Nick's leg. The sound had come from Danni's room. Nick listened intently and heard her again, but this time she was speaking. Only he couldn't understand her mumbled words behind the closed door. He debated going in there to see if she was okay.

"No!"

Nick shot up out of bed. Ignoring his body's complaints, he raced across the hall. Gus followed him, whining softly as she pressed against Nick's bare legs. The doorknob turned beneath Nick's hand.

Relief flooded through him when he found her alone and not being attacked.

"Stay," he told Gus.

The dog wagged her tail once and plopped down on the hall carpet.

Nick stepped into Danni's room. In the dim moonlight, he could see her thrashing about on her bed. Her mouth was open in a soundless scream, and Nick reached out toward her, but stopped before his fingers made contact. Bringing someone out of a nightmare was tricky. He knew from experience.

"Danni, wake up," he urged. "Danni, it's Nick. C'mon, it's just a nightmare. It's not real."

She continued to murmur, "I'm sorry. I should've—I couldn't—" Danni opened her eyes, panting as if she'd just run a four-minute mile.

Nick rested his hand on her shoulder, which was damp with fear sweat. "Shhhh, it's okay, Danni. You're safe."

"Nick?" The timid voice didn't sound anything like the self-assured woman he knew.

"That's right," he replied softly. "I heard you yelling in your sleep."

Danni pushed herself upright, and the moonlight reflected in her hair and skin with pale silver brushstrokes. She shoved her sleep-mussed hair back, away from her face. "I'm sorry I woke you. I-I don't usually have nightmares."

Nick perched on the edge of the mattress. "Mind if I turn on a light?"

"Go ahead."

He flicked on the small lamp by her bed and immediately noticed her pallor. Something leapt in the vicinity of his heart. "It's not surprising, considering everything that's happened in the past week."

A wild curl spilled across her creased brow, and he caught the silkiness between his thumb and forefinger. After rolling the strand between his fingers, he reluctantly released it, ignoring the warm arousal meandering through his veins at the intimacy.

"I hate it when I lose control," she said, her fists pressed into her thighs.

"There are some things you can't control, Danni," he said quietly. "Dreams are one of them. Death is another." He glanced out the window as his chest tightened with the memory of those same words being spoken to him. He doubted Danni would heed them any more than he had.

A satiny palm against his cheek guided his gaze back to her face. "And there are some things we *do* have control over." She leaned forward, then stopped an inch from his lips, relinquishing control to him.

Nick's heart hammered in his chest, and he traveled the rest of the distance to her lips, pressing his gently against her sweet, pliant ones. She opened her mouth, granting him access, and he tasted her. Nick moaned deep in his throat. Desire stampeded through his blood. He plunged his hands into her thick hair, the wild tendrils twining around his fingers.

Danni wrapped her arms around Nick's waist and urged him downward. For a moment, he was afraid he'd combust where her hard nipples dug into his chest . . . then he hoped he would. He wanted her with almost frightening intensity.

Her hands crept under his T-shirt, hot and skilled in her

exploration of his bare skin. She pinched his nipples, making him gasp with pleasure. He longed to see her eyes, to see the hunger he knew would match his own, but she kept her gaze aimed at his chest.

"I want you, Sirocco."

Nick hardly recognized her husky voice, but he did recognize the desperate passion in it. She'd just lost her father, and the nightmare had left her even more emotionally vulnerable.

He took hold of her wrists to halt her inflaming touches. "No," he said, his voice rough with suppressed desire. "I won't take advantage of you."

She lifted her head and met his gaze, her face flushed with passion. He'd never seen anything so damned hot.

"You won't be. I just want to forget. Please help me forget," she whispered.

Nick's pulse roared in his ears, his too long ignored libido more than willing to accept her invitation. But he had no right to use her vulnerability to appease his physical needs.

Yet, he understood too well the frantic desire to forget. After he'd been rescued, he'd found too much time to remember. To stop the agonizing memories, he'd spent every spare moment losing himself in alcohol and faceless women. If anybody could understand Danni's need to lose herself in sex, it was him.

He frowned, remembering his empty wallet. "I don't have any protection."

"I do. My backpack. Side pocket."

Nick spotted her bag beside the bed and, cursing his weakness, he leaned over and snagged it. After laying the small foil pack on the extra pillow, he eagerly tugged her baggy shirt off, his hands sliding over the contours of her breasts. Returning to the soft flesh, he captured their fullness in his palms.

He kissed her lips, then moved to her satiny cheek and down to her smooth jaw. He traced her ear with his tongue and dipped inside to tease and tickle.

Danni clawed at his shoulders, and he felt the twinge of his pulled muscles, but it was insignificant compared to the other things going on in and around him. Danni caressed his short hair and nibbled his exposed throat.

It had been a long time since he'd been with a woman, and fiery lust nearly incinerated all other thoughts. His boxers rubbed his too-sensitive erection, sending both painful and pleasurable messages to his brain.

Danni pushed the covers away, revealing smooth, golden skin and baby-blue bikini underwear. Nick took a moment to merely drink in her feminine curves, the gentle indent of her waist, the tempting flare of her hips, and her long, slender legs. His lungs reminded him to breathe, and he drew in gulps of air. Then he skimmed off his T-shirt and underwear and tossed them away.

Danni's hot gaze settled on Nick's groin, then moved back to his face. She reached for him, her expression filled with a need as great as his. He straddled her, a knee on either side of her hips, and leaned down. His hard penis brushed against her soft belly. He froze, afraid he'd embarrass himself. God, it had been too damned long since he'd made love to a woman. And even longer since he'd been this excited, this anxious to slide into a woman's wet heat.

To delay the inevitable, he dropped light kisses on her half-masted eyelids, her cute pug nose, her dainty but oh-so-stubborn chin. He continued the line of kisses down her chest, to each breast, to her belly button, and to the elastic waistband of her bikinis. He raised his head as her warm, musky scent tempted and bedeviled him.

"Yes," she whispered hoarsely.

Nick kissed her navel once more, then divested her of the last cloth barrier between them. He nuzzled the juncture of her thighs, where the scent of her was the keenest. He tasted her, and she arched upward, a cry breaking from her parted lips.

"Now," Danni said, her tone breathy.

Unable to resist any longer, he quickly tore open the flat pack, and his fingers fumbled with the latex.

Nick wanted—no, needed—to go slow. But Danni clearly was ready. She wrapped her willowy legs around his waist and crossed her ankles at his back.

With a groan of surrender, Nick eased into her. Danni's wet, tight heat encircled him, squeezed him. He couldn't *not* move, especially when Danni rocked her hips upward, taking him even deeper.

"Please, Nick, please," she pleaded, the pupils of her eyes nearly obliterating the blue. She raked her nails up and down his back, increasing his need to find release.

Unable to resist both her words and his body's demands, Nick drew back, then plunged into her. She met him stroke for stroke until she climaxed with a strangled cry. The ripples through her body induced Nick's orgasm, bringing waves of ecstasy crashing through him.

Nick collapsed but remembered to roll to the side so he wouldn't crush her. He took care of the condom, turned off the lamp, and reached for Danni, who was well on the path back to slumber.

"Thanks, Nick," she said, her voice husky. She curled against his side, her head resting below his chin and her breath creating moist trails across his chest.

Sated and feeling strangely protective of the warm bundle in his arms, Nick kissed her crown. "You're welcome, Danni," he whispered tenderly.

Chapter Five

UTTER silence and a full bladder awakened Nick. It took him a few moments to realign his brain cells and remember where he was. And why.

A part of him regretted what he'd done, but she'd been so hungry, so passionate. Only a saint could've refused her, and he was no saint.

The empty side of the bed was cool, telling him Danni had risen some time ago. He glanced at the digital clock radio on the nightstand: 8:03 A.M.

Damn the woman! Danni had gone alone to meet Sam Richmond for breakfast. After their conversation about sticking together, she'd still gone without him.

He threw off his covers and found his muscles were even sorer than they'd been last night. Of course, the sexual aerobics probably hadn't helped. Well, maybe it hadn't helped his muscle aches, but it had helped him overcome his insomnia.

He stood carefully, tugged on his boxers, and hobbled down the hall to the bathroom he'd used last night. Once that mission was completed, he slowly swung one arm, then the other, in a wide arc to loosen them. A few minutes later, the tight muscles eased enough that he could actually lift his arms without grimacing.

Grabbing the borrowed bathrobe, Nick went downstairs, the creaking steps a harsh contrast to the empty silence. Gus was sprawled on her side on the carpet in the living room, in much the same position she'd been last night before she'd followed Nick to bed. Rather, his first bed.

His irritation with Danni grew. Why didn't she understand that she could be in danger—deadly danger? Why did she have to be so damned stubborn about this?

He smelled coffee and ducked into the kitchen to find a nearly full pot. There was also a bowl of water on the floor for Gus. Nick's irritation with Danni eased slightly.

He found a cup and filled it with the rich, dark brew. Gus padded into the kitchen, her toenails clicking on the tile. She paused beside Nick and waited until he petted her before lapping some water and returning to the living room.

As Nick drank his coffee, he spotted a white piece of paper with his name on it on the refrigerator, held by a Golden Gate Bridge magnet. He unfolded the note.

"Nick. Don't leave the house. Unless someone followed us last night, you should be safe. Danni. P.S. I let Gus out to take care of business this morning and gave her some hamburger from the freezer."

No apology or mention of where she'd gone. All she'd told him last night was that she was meeting Sam Richmond for breakfast. He crushed the note in his fist and tossed it onto the counter, then found the phone book and punched in a number.

"D. Hawkins, Private Investigations. How may I help you?" the voice at the other end answered.

What was her name. Karen? Carol? No, Cathy.

"Cathy, it's Nick Sirocco. Did Danni tell you where she was going to be this morning?"

"Mr. Sirocco," Cathy purred. "I haven't heard from

Danni since you left *together* yesterday." After a slight pause, she asked, "Did you have a good time?"

Momentary panic shot through him, then he realized she couldn't know what transpired between him and Danni during the night. "We got the pictures for your client." Although he knew that wasn't what she was fishing for, he wasn't about to bite. "Danni said she was going to meet Sam Richmond for breakfast this morning. Do you know where they might've met?"

"Their usual breakfast spot is the Pancake Parlor."

"Thanks." He ended the call before Cathy could ask him any more questions. He riffled through the phone book and got the address for the restaurant, then called a cab.

Nick took a quick shower and brushed his teeth with his finger and toothpaste. It felt strange to use Paddy's toiletries, but Nick figured he wouldn't have minded. However, Nick suspected he wouldn't feel so generous about him sleeping with his daughter.

After nabbing a door key from the key rack in the kitchen, Nick left Gus asleep on the carpet and locked the house. Impatient, he went onto the porch to watch for his taxi. A gray-haired woman wearing a dress four decades out of fashion emerged from the house next door. She did a double take, which might've been funny, except that Nick was too busy composing his tirade against Danni.

"What're you doing over there, young man?" the old lady demanded in a surprisingly strong voice.

"Waiting for a cab," he replied.

Her eyes narrowed behind round, wire-rimmed glasses. "Did you know Patrick Hawkins?"

Nick sighed at the unavoidable cross-examination. "He was a good friend." He suddenly realized he had an opportunity to ask some questions about the night Paddy died, and he may as well take advantage of it. He stepped over to the edge of the porch. "My name's Nick Sirocco."

"Mrs. Sarah Countryman. Was that Danielle with you last night?"

Nick wasn't surprised she'd noticed their arrival; every neighborhood had a Mrs. Sarah Countryman. "That's right."

Mrs. Countryman crossed her arms and fixed him a glare behind her round lenses. "When I was your age, men and women didn't spend the night together under one roof unless they were married or related. Which are you?"

Damned if Sarah Countryman didn't make him feel like a schoolboy. "Neither." He couldn't even reassure her nothing had happened under that roof, unless he wanted to lie, and he had a feeling Mrs. Countryman was a human lie detector. "I suppose it was pretty quiet with just Paddy living here, huh?"

Mrs. Countryman's expression lost some of its harshness. "He was a gentleman. He did as good a job as a man can do raising a girl alone. But Danielle was quite the handful—rebellious and stubborn in high school. Poor Patrick had no idea how to handle her. I tried to help, but I was busy teaching up until ten years ago, about the same time Danielle graduated."

Although Nick was there to learn more about the night Paddy died, he couldn't help being curious about Danni. "With all the kids Paddy worked with in the youth center, you'd think he'd be the last person to have trouble with his own."

Mrs. Countryman straightened her thin shoulders. "Maybe that's the reason he *did* have trouble with his own daughter. He was too busy with those others."

Shit. It'd been staring him in the face all along. He'd sensed Danni's initial animosity toward him, but he'd put it off as her abrasive personality. But if she had been jealous of her father's attentions to him and other kids like him, it was no wonder she was bitter. It would also explain the rift between father and daughter.

It didn't, however, explain why someone would murder Paddy.

"Did you see or hear anything the night Paddy died?" Nick asked.

She tilted her head to the side, eyeing him shrewdly. "The officer I spoke to that night told me he committed suicide."

"Did you believe him?"

"Why would he lie?"

Nick gave her what he hoped was a reassuring smile. "No reason." He spotted a blue-and-white cab coming down the street. "It was nice meeting you, Mrs. Countryman."

"Good-bye, Mr. Sirocco." Her expression was thoughtful as she returned to her house.

Nick wondered if she knew anything useful. Maybe he could speak with her later, after he talked some sense into Danni, if that were possible. He slid into the taxi's backseat and gave the driver the restaurant's address.

"I don't know, Danni," Sam Richmond said. "The rain was pretty heavy. It would've been easy for a driver to miss seeing you."

Danni counted to ten as she took a sip of her coffee liberally laced with cream and artificial sweetener. "I heard a squeal of tires, then it was almost on top of us."

"Us?" Sam squinted at her, his craggy face drawn in a scowl. "Who was with you?"

Hearing the bell above the door, Danni glanced at the entrance and spotted a familiar face, but his angry expression wasn't even in the same universe as the look he'd given her last night when they'd— She cut the memory off before it could take substance. That had been a mistake—both hers and his.

"Hello, Hawkins," Nick said to Danni, his voice so cold the words froze in the air.

Sam stood. "Rocky, what're you doing here?"

"Sam." Nick shook his hand. "Danni promised me breakfast, then skipped out."

Danni's cheeks flushed hotly. "I did no such thing,

Sirocco. I left you a note and told you to stay put until I got back."

"Maybe I should leave," Sam said, nabbing his ball cap from the tabletop.

"Stay." Nick and Danni spoke at the same time.

Sighing, Sam lowered himself back into his chair. Nick sat in the seat next to Danni. She tried to inch away from him, but he grabbed her chair and held it in place.

"You're not getting away from me again, Hawkins," Nick warned.

"Cut the macho crap, Sirocco," she growled back.

Sam's eyes twinkled. "You two obviously know each other well."

"Apparently not well enough," Nick said.

Danni picked up her coffee cup and was tempted to dump the contents in Nick's lap. One glance at him told her he knew what she was thinking, and she damned well better not follow through.

"So you were the one who almost got run down with Danni girl, huh?" Sam asked, breaking the tension.

Nick shot Danni a look she couldn't translate but answered the question. "Yes. Hard to say if it was accidental or intentional, though."

"Danni thinks it was intentional."

"She also has an overactive imagination," Nick said in a patronizing tone.

To hell with just a cup of coffee; Danni was going to dump the whole carafe in his lap. "*She* is sitting right beside you, and *she* thought you were certain it was intentional, too."

Nick shrugged. "I tend to see things clearer the morning after."

Danni tensed, reading his layered meaning. She didn't need this complication, but it was her own fault. When Nick had awakened her last night, all she wanted to do was forget, to let the heat of passion burn away the nightmare's icy grip. That she was incredibly attracted to Nick Sirocco only made it that much more pleasurable. It wasn't the first time she'd used sex to forget, but she'd never enjoyed it quite so much.

"I told him about your suspicions," Danni said. "But he already knew."

Sam nodded and pinned Nick with a sharp gaze. "Sergeant Rodgers told me you were at the station asking a lot of questions. He said you think Paddy was murdered." His expression hardened. "Can't you let him rest in peace, Rocky? We all knew how hard it was on him being forced to retire. The force was his life. He told me six months ago that if he retired, he'd go crazy."

Nick's lean jaw tightened. "He had resigned himself to retiring and was even talking about trips he was planning. He started helping me with a project and was excited about that, too. And he was going to continue his volunteer work at the youth center." Nick fixed his gaze on Danni. "He also told me he was looking forward to spending time with his daughter, if she'd let him."

Danni's breath caught in her throat, and her heart tripletimed in her chest. Had her father actually confided in him? If so, why hadn't he mentioned it before now?

Sam's bushy eyebrows furrowed across his brow. "He told you a helluva lot, Rocky."

"We were friends."

The waitress stopped by and dropped off another cup for Nick. Instead of letting him fill it himself, the woman picked up the carafe and did it.

"Thank you," Nick murmured.

"You're welcome. Is there anything else I can get you?" she asked, her hip pressed against Nick's arm.

He looked past her breasts, which were level with his face, and smiled. "No, thank you."

Danni watched the disappointed waitress walk away and wasn't surprised when the woman turned to take another look before disappearing into the kitchen. But the twitch of jealousy in Danni's stomach was a surprise.

"Look, I know you thought of Paddy as a father, Rocky, but I think you're wrong here. He was found in his own bed with his own service revolver in his hand. There was no sign of a struggle," Sam argued. His expression turned melancholy as he looked at Danni. "I don't understand why you're helping him, Danni. You've seen the evidence. You were a cop. It's a tragic but straightforward suicide. There's no reason to search for a killer who doesn't exist."

Torn between her surrogate parent and the man who'd stolen her father's affections, Danni shouldn't have had any problem making her decision. But she'd heard her father's message on Nick's answering machine. And the more Sam tried to talk her out of continuing the investigation, the more determined she became to unravel the mystery.

"Too many things don't add up," Danni said. "If everything Nick said about Dad is true, then there was no reason for him to kill himself."

"You're missing motivation, Danni," Sam said. "Even the greenest rookie knows there has to be a motive if there was a murder."

"I know, I know," she said impatiently. "Finding a motive will give us the killer."

Sam laid his giant hand atop her fist. "I wish I could help you, Danni girl, but your dad and I didn't see each other that much since I retired." He smiled self-consciously. "Nancy's kept me busy doing things around the house that I hadn't gotten around to for twenty-five years. And since we bought the boat, we've started fishing every weekend."

Danni grasped his hand, pleased to hear he'd finally started doing the things he used to talk about. "I'm really glad to hear that, Sam. How's Nancy doing?"

Sadness entered the older man's face. "Better. But the doctors say there's really nothing to stop the degeneration of nerves. She'll end up in a wheelchair." He forced a smile. "That's why we have to make the best of what time we have."

"Dad told me one time that he wished he'd found a woman like Nancy." Danni glanced down to hide the unwelcome sting of moisture. "I think he was too afraid to try again after my mom left us."

"He used to tell me the same thing, even after Nancy was diagnosed last year." He released Danni and stood. "I better get going. I told her I'd clean the windows today. She likes the sun shining in the house."

Danni stood and hugged Sam, and his strong arms gathered her close. He'd been the one she'd gone to when she'd been picked up joyriding in high school, and he'd been the one who talked her father out of sending her off to a private girls' school.

"If you just need to talk, give me a call, Danni. You know my number," Sam said.

She nodded and stepped back.

Sam insisted on picking up the tab and left Danni with stone-faced Sirocco.

"Let's go." Danni started to follow in Sam's wake.

Nick grasped her wrist and tugged her back to the table. "Sit down, Hawkins. You and I are overdue for a little chat."

Danni balked, but the determined glint in Nick's eyes didn't bode well for a successful escape. She perched on the edge of her chair. "So talk."

He crossed his arms and leaned back. Slanting her a steely look, he asked, "Why?"

Danni's mind came up with a few different versions of that question, like, *Why did you meet Sam without me?* and *Why did you tell him about the car incident?* and *Why did you want to make love last night?*

She chose the least difficult one. "You were sound asleep when I got up." She refused to dwell on how long she'd lain there, tracing the ruggedly handsome lines of his face with her gaze and soaking in the warmth of his body as she lay within his arms. "I figured I could meet Sam and be back before you woke up."

"Then why leave a note?"

She should've known he wouldn't let her off the hook that easily. "Just in case."

"A note that didn't even tell me where you were going."

Danni plopped an elbow on the table and ran her hand through her unruly curls. "Lighten up. It's broad daylight."

Nick continued to peer at her coolly. "Do you want to know what I think?"

"Not really." She knew she was acting like a petulant child but couldn't stop herself. She was too accustomed to looking out for herself, and that meant hiding her feelings and thoughts behind a well-used mask.

Nick's gaze slid away, then back to her. It was the first sign of discomfort since he launched his inquisition. "You were afraid to face me after what you did last night."

"What *I* did?" She poked him in the chest. "I wasn't the only one in that bed."

"I wouldn't have been if you hadn't pulled me down."

She sneered. "Yeah, like you were so unwilling."

Nick's nostrils flared, but his voice didn't change its volume. "I admit it. When a beautiful woman invites me, I rarely say no."

It took a moment for Danni to process his words, and the one that resonated was "beautiful." "I had a nightmare. I wasn't thinking straight." She paused, her cheeks heating. "But that doesn't mean I didn't enjoy it. Because I did. Enjoy it, I mean."

Nick's lips quirked upward, and the corner of his eyes crinkled. "I know."

She renewed her glare.

"I did, too," he added softly.

Danni's heart missed a beat, then made up for it by doubling her pulse. The sultry glow in Nick's eyes vividly reminded her of their lovemaking, and Danni had little defense against so potent a memory. Except she had to ignore it. "It's not something we'll repeat," she stated, proud that her voice remained steady. "We're temporary *professional* partners."

The blatant desire in his eyes faded. Relief with a niggling of something she didn't want to consider allowed her to breathe easier.

"Until we find your father's killer."

"And we go our separate ways," Danni felt compelled to add.

"Until we go our separate ways," Nick reiterated.

Danni's cell phone rang, and she unzipped the small pocket on her backpack to nab it. "Hawkins."

"Danni, it's Cathy. Beth needs to talk to you."

"About what?"

"Hold on. I'll get her on the line."

Danni had rarely heard Cathy so rattled.

"Danni?" Beth said.

"What's wrong, Beth?"

"Remember the boy your dad asked me to defend?"

"Yeah."

"He was found dead at home this morning." Beth's voice trembled. "They said he slit his wrists."

Danni closed her eyes. "I'm sorry, Beth."

"Look, I know this is probably a bad time to ask, but I want you to check into it. I can't believe he would do such a thing. He was going to make a deal."

Light-headedness assailed Danni. "You think it was murder made to look like suicide?"

Nick sat up straight, his expression full of questions.

"Yes," Beth replied. "Cathy told me about your suspicions about your dad's death. I know this won't be easy for you, but I need your help."

Danni wasn't surprised Cathy had told her. The three women had become good friends in the past two years. "It's okay. I'll look into it. Who were the reporting officers?"

There was a shuffle of papers. "Joe Tygard and Alex Levin."

"I know them." Danni rubbed her throbbing brow. "Nick and I'll run down to the station this morning and see what we can find out."

"Thanks, Danni. Bye."

"Bye."

Danni punched the Off button.

"Well?" Nick demanded.

Danni slumped in her chair. "Two days before Dad died, one of his boys was arrested for trying to unload some stolen merchandise. Dad asked Beth, the lawyer I share office space with, to defend him. Last night the kid slit his wrists. He's dead."

"What was his name?"

"Matt Arbor."

Nick dropped his head back and rubbed his eyes. "Goddammit."

"You knew him?"

"Yeah. At the center. He didn't strike me as the type who'd take suicide as a way out."

"Beth doesn't think he did either. She said he was going to make a deal."

"What kind of deal?"

"She didn't say. Maybe he was going to give up his accomplice. I don't know." She stood, feeling three times her age. "I'm going to the rest room. I'll meet you at the truck." She tossed him the keys and picked up her backpack.

In the ladies' room, she splashed cold water on her pale face. Blindly, she reached for some paper towels and dabbed her cheeks. Good thing she hadn't put on her usual makeup this morning, even if she did look like death warmed over.

She tossed the towels into the refuse container and gripped the edge of the sink. Leaning into it, she stared at her reflection, at the haunted eyes.

Were the two murders related? *Were* they murders? Or was she simply caught up in Nick Sirocco's theory? Although all the evidence was circumstantial and the product of gut feelings, Danni couldn't help but believe her father hadn't committed suicide. Was it because Nick believed it so strongly? That could be part of it. But now, with the suspicions regarding Matt Arbor's death, another finger pointed at criminal conspiracy.

They needed the common denominator and the motive.

The common denominator was simple: the youth center, which her father had mentioned in the message he'd left on Nick's answering machine. And Nick had been involved with the kids, too.

So had Nick been the target of the driver last night?

Or had it merely been an accident?

With her mind going in circles, Danni exited the rest room and joined Nick in the truck. He sat in the driver's seat, but she didn't feel like arguing.

"I thought we could stop at my place first so I can pack a bag and get some dog food for Gus," Nick said.

"All right. Then we'll go to the station." She wrapped her arms around her backpack and held it close to her chest like a shield.

Nick didn't start the truck, and she looked up, only to find him studying her.

"Are you okay with all of this?" he asked.

The compassion in his face made her eyes burn, but she didn't want his sympathy. She wanted to learn the truth.

"No, I am *not* okay." Anger was much easier to deal with than the grief that kept trying to escape. "I'm not okay with some bastard murdering people and making it look like suicide. I'm not okay with almost being turned into hamburger on the street. And I'm definitely not okay about having to look at people I've known for years as murder suspects."

"I know." He squeezed her shoulder lightly before starting the truck.

She stared out the window as Nick drove. She rarely sat in the passenger seat of her truck, and it unsettled her, just like everything else that had happened since her father's death.

Nick pulled into an average-looking apartment complex and found a parking place close to the entrance. She opened her door and almost struck Nick as he came around the truck. He appeared exasperated but didn't say anything.

Danni realized he'd come around to open her door. For

as long as she could remember, she'd fought to be equal with her peers, and that included opening her own doors. But she supposed it was kind of nice of him in a quaint, old-fashioned way.

He unlocked the front door, and they entered the foyer where Nick checked his mailbox. Danni didn't see anything but junk mail: a credit card offer, an ad addressed to Occupant from a local office supply store, a Cabela's hunting catalog, and a fishing magazine.

Frowning, she followed him up one flight and down the hallway to number 207. She surveyed the typical dingy-colored carpeting in the hall—it was easier to hide the dirt. The walls were a neutral tan, just like her own apartment complex.

"Son of a bitch!"

Nick's bellow startled her out of her musings, and she peeked around his broad shoulders to look into his apartment. Either he was a slob, or someone had broken in while he was gone and trashed the place.

His reaction told her it was the latter.

Chapter Six

Danni reacted instinctively, using her body to shove Nick to the side, away from the open doorway. She grabbed her revolver from her shoulder holster and held it two-handed, the four-inch barrel aimed at the ceiling.

"They could still be in there," she hissed at Nick. Pressed against his side, she felt his muscles bunch.

"It's empty," he argued.

"You don't *know* that."

"If the burglar was in there when we got here, he's gone now." He started to move away.

Danni gripped his sleeve and jerked him back. Her lips nearly touching his ear, she said, "Dammit, Sirocco, stay put. We need backup. Call nine-one-one."

Nick glared at her. "You call. I'm going to see what they took." His glare shifted to her hand still on his arm, his message clear.

Apprehension filled Danni, and she shook her head. "We don't go in until the police get here."

Nick's lips pulled down in a scowl, and he slumped against the wall. Relieved that he saw things her way, albeit reluctantly, Danni released him. With her left hand, she fumbled in her jacket pocket for her cell phone and thrust it at Nick when she found it. "Here."

He took it, although Danni could tell he didn't want to. She divided her attention between listening to Nick call it in, and his apartment, straining to determine if there was anyone inside. Only the sound of the traffic on the street and Bob Barker's "Come on down!" on a neighbor's television down the hall intruded on the quiet.

"Somebody's broken into my apartment at 4398 Wintergreen Place, apartment 207," Nick said into the phone.

Danni couldn't make out words, only the unruffled tone of the operator. She listened to Nick as he gave his name and answered the standard questions: Did anyone require medical assistance? Was he in any danger? Were the perpetrators still in the vicinity?

Damned good question.

Nick pushed the End button on her cell phone. "He said the police should be here in about ten minutes."

Nick held the phone out to her, and Danni dumped it back in her pocket. He suddenly shoved away from the wall. She made a grab for him, but the fool disappeared into his apartment before she could stop him. Grumbling her choicest expletives, she rose to follow him.

She stood at the edge of the doorway, her muscles tense and her stomach reinforcing the warning signals in her head. Readjusting the revolver in her damp palms, she licked her dry lips.

Move it, Officer Hawkins.

The voice was so real, Danni almost glanced around for Scott. But he'd been gone for over two years now.

She gritted her teeth and charged into the apartment. Her finger rested on the trigger guard as she dropped into a firing stance and swept the room with her gun and gaze.

Nick's eyes widened, and he raised his hands. "Easy. It's just me."

Danni examined the room before relaxing her pose, but not her temper. "Have you checked out the rest of the apartment?"

He shook his head.

"Stay here." She moved down the hallway and swept the bathroom, bedroom, and office. Empty.

She deposited the weapon back in her holster as she strode back to the living room where Nick stood.

"What part of 'Stay put' didn't you understand?" she demanded.

"I *knew* the apartment was empty."

"And how the hell did you know that?" Danni was too angry to bridle her sarcasm. "Are you a psychic as well as an idiot?"

"Look, I figured whoever had been here was gone by now, and if by some long shot he was still here, I might be able to catch him," Nick said, his temper obviously rising.

"Catch him? What if the perp had a gun or a knife?"

"I was trained in hand-to-hand combat."

"Hell of a lot of good that would've done if he shot you."

Nick's jaw muscle corded. "What's your problem?"

"Besides you?" Danni held Nick's seething gaze, refusing to give an inch. Or offer any more of an explanation for her blistering reaction. She had no intention of slicing open an artery and letting him watch her bleed. Her past failures weren't any of his business.

Unless they get him killed, too.

Danni swallowed her caustic guilt, wishing she could work the case alone. But even if she was granted her wish, there was no guarantee that Nick would remain safe if someone was after him.

I'm damned either way.

Danni looked away from Nick's exasperated face and released the breath she didn't realize she'd been holding. "So, is anything missing?" she asked with feigned casualness.

"I don't know." His hooded gaze surveyed the surrounding mess.

"Don't touch anything."

"Don't worry. I've watched *CSI* once or twice."

Danni couldn't stop the twitch that caught her lips. She turned her attention to the chaos around them, and her humor faded.

Throw pillows, magazines, and books lay carelessly across the living room floor. The cushions had been tossed off the sofa and recliner. The galley-sized kitchen hadn't been spared, with canisters' contents spilled across the counter and cupboard doors left ajar with dishes, glasses, and mugs—some broken, some not—littering the counters and floor.

She picked her way down a short hallway and inspected the bathroom. Towels were heaped in the tub, and the gaping shower curtain hung by only a hook or two. The medicine cabinet contents had been swept into the sink.

She continued to the next room, which was obviously Nick's office. A fairly new computer sat on the desk, but it was the only thing that seemed to be in its proper place. The monitor was dark, but the orange light beneath it indicated the power was on. Files were strewn about, books were tossed from the bookshelves helter-skelter, and computer CDs were scattered across the carpeted floor and desktop.

Danni frowned at the mess. She'd seen numerous breaking-and-entering cases when she'd been on patrol, but this didn't have the feel of a typical robbery.

Somebody had been looking for something specific.

She turned to go back to the living room and nearly plowed into Nick, who stood directly behind her. He caught her arms and steadied her, then immediately released her. But not before Danni felt his hands trembling in the scant seconds he'd clung to her. Despite his bravado, the violation of his apartment had gotten to him. Her irritation with him faded, replaced by sympathy.

"If this was a typical break-in, your computer would've been stolen," she said.

"Maybe they were in a hurry and didn't want to handle anything that big."

She glanced at Nick. It was obvious he didn't believe

his own words, although he wanted to. "Is anything missing?"

"Hard to tell." Frustration sharpened his words. He moved around her, their arms brushing in the narrow hall.

Danni followed him to his bedroom but stopped in the doorway. She catalogued the Mission-style bedroom set, which included a queen-sized bed that had either been left unmade or had been torn apart by whoever had broken in—Danni supposed it was the latter. There was a matching dresser and a nightstand on either side of the bed.

She noticed Nick kept his hands by his sides as he visually searched his dresser top and open drawers that had clothing hanging out of them. Maybe CSI *had* taught him a thing or two about not botching up a crime scene. Not that Danni believed the perpetrator would be caught.

His brows drew together as he peered into the dresser's top drawer.

"What is it?" she asked.

He straightened and met Danni's gaze. "If you were a thief, wouldn't you steal a diamond ring? Easy to pocket and even easier to fence?"

Danni's breath stalled in her throat. Although she knew he was merely asking a rhetorical question, her mind was stuck on the diamond ring. Was it his own? Or was it an engagement ring—for a woman? If so, *had* he been engaged? Or was he dating someone seriously now?

Ice settled in the pit of her stomach. Even though they'd done the dirty deed last night, she knew very little about Nick Sirocco.

"Police. Freeze!"

Startled back to the present, she turned her head to see two patrol officers she didn't recognize with their revolvers aimed at them. She stifled a sigh, then laced her fingers and rested them on her head. If they'd stayed outside where they were supposed to, the police wouldn't be treating them like suspects.

Nick took a step toward the policemen. "We're the ones—"

"Hold it," the younger cop ordered, his fingers twitching.

Danni grabbed Nick's jacket sleeve and tugged him back to her side, then quickly placed her hands back on her head. Nick already had someone after him. He didn't need a nervous rookie blowing him away by accident. "Do like me, and don't make any threatening moves until they sort this out," she said to Nick in a low voice.

For a moment she thought he would argue, but he only shook his head in frustration and copied her position.

"I have a weapon in a shoulder holster," Danni announced to the policemen. "I'm a private investigator. My ID and my license to carry are in my jacket."

While the older patrol cop kept his weapon trained on them, the rookie relieved Danni of her weapon and found her ID and license. He handed them to his partner, then searched Nick.

Five minutes later, Danni took back her possessions, and she and Nick were ushered into the hall. There they were interviewed by the younger cop while the older one, Porter, checked out the apartment. Danni recognized the drill immediately. Though she tried to get ahead of his questions, Shenders, the rookie who still had acne, plodded along methodically.

"Was anything stolen?" Shenders asked after he'd gotten their names and addresses.

"Not that I could see," Nick replied. "But I haven't done a thorough search."

"Anyone who might have a grudge against you? Maybe someone has a reason to think you have something of theirs?"

Danni crossed her arms and caught Nick's quick glance. She shook her head minutely.

"Nobody I know of," Nick replied, his tone neutral.

The older cop, Porter, joined them. "I couldn't find any sign of a forced entry."

"So you think I just invited someone in to do this?" Nick asked, waving a stiff arm at the apartment.

Porter's narrowed eyes were almost lost in his fleshy face. "I'm not suggesting that, sir. I'm only stating what I found." He hitched his belt up under his belly. "Who else besides you has a key?"

Nick hesitated just long enough for Danni to notice. "Nobody."

She frowned, suspecting he lied. Why wouldn't Nick tell them? Maybe the woman who he intended to give the ring had a key?

She struck the nagging thought down but found she couldn't dismiss that damned ring from her mind.

"Not even your . . . friend?" Porter asked. There was a short but discernible pause before 'friend' as the veteran cop's knowing gaze slid to Danni.

"She's not a friend. She's a business associate," Nick said.

She wondered if he made a habit of sleeping with business associates. Then she couldn't decide if she should feel insulted or not.

"We'll check the door and windows for fingerprints, but that's all we can do." Porter's sour expression told Danni he didn't believe Nick's claim about their relationship.

"Don't you bring in people who collect physical evidence?" Nick asked.

Danni laid her palm on Nick's forearm. "Not in cases like this. It's impossible to send a team out to every B and E. Every cop is trained to gather fingerprints."

"How do you know that, ma'am?" Shenders asked, his young voice surprised.

"I used to be patrol."

Porter stared at her. "Hawkins. I remember you." He nodded slowly. "It was your father who killed himself last week."

Danni gritted her teeth, feeling the tug of her jaw muscle in her cheek. She should've kept her mouth shut. "Yes."

"Poor bastard," Porter muttered, then cleared his throat as his round cheeks reddened. "I'm sorry, Ms. Hawkins. I didn't know him well, but from what I heard, he was a good cop."

Danni's throat tightened, cutting off her ability to speak. She merely nodded.

"I'd like to go inside and start cleaning up. I want to find out if anything was stolen," Nick said.

Danni was grateful for his timely intervention, whether it was deliberate or not. One glance at his blue eyes, and she knew it was intentional. She was surprised by the choked feeling in her throat.

"Give us fifteen minutes," Porter said, then turned to his partner. "Run down and get the fingerprint kit."

After taking the fingerprints on the door and windows, the two cops also fingerprinted Nick and Danni to eliminate theirs from the ones they'd found. They also interviewed the few neighbors who were home, but nobody had seen or heard anything.

The older policeman handed Nick a card. "If you find anything missing, call this number and leave the information."

"Thanks," Nick said, accepting the card with the precinct's phone number.

The two cops didn't offer Nick any false hopes, but wished him luck in taking care of the mess, and left.

Danni leaned against the wall as she used a handwipe to try to remove the ink from her fingertips. She glanced up from her futile task and watched Nick do a slow three sixty in the middle of the living room, which looked like Hurricane Elmo had paid a visit.

"What were they looking for?" Nick asked, abandoning the pretense that it was a simple robbery.

"Good question. We figure that out, and we'll probably figure out what Dad discovered."

"Something that got him killed."

Danni nodded, feeling twitchy and restless. "Yeah."

"There's another thing," Nick said quietly. "Paddy was the only other person who had a key to my place."

The implications were clear. Whoever had killed her father had taken the key.

Suddenly anxious, Danni shot out her wrist and glanced at her watch. "It's almost eleven. Throw what you need into a bag, then we have to get over to the station to talk to the two officers who found Matt Arbor's body."

"I want to straighten up first."

Danni opened her mouth to argue, but the lost look in Nick's expression stopped her. With both of them working, it wouldn't take long, and she knew it would ease Nick's mind. They might also find out if anything had been taken.

"I'll clean the kitchen," she volunteered.

Startled, Nick met her gaze, and his eyes softened. "Thanks. Be careful of the glass."

Danni nodded. She should have resented him for warning her like she was a child, but instead she was flustered by his gratitude and concern.

"After we finish here, we need to go to Paddy's," Nick said.

"Why?"

He picked up a leash from one of the piles on the floor. "Unless you want to clean up more messes . . ."

Damn. She'd forgotten about Gus.

NICK was relieved to find Gus hadn't had any accidents, but her entire body was quivering to get outside. He accompanied Gus into Paddy's backyard. As the dog took care of her business, Nick racked his brain trying to figure out why his apartment had been trashed. What were they looking for? Did they think Paddy had stowed something at his place? Or did they think Nick knew more than he did?

About what?

He hadn't told Danni, but he would've sworn he'd turned off his computer before leaving his place the day before. Yet it had been on when he'd straightened his office. He'd searched his files, but there was nothing there that would even remotely be related to Paddy's death. Maybe the person who'd broken into his place was a Travis Longstreet fan and couldn't wait for the next book. Nick shook his head at the ridiculous notion.

He wasn't going to find any answers standing in the middle of Paddy's yard. He whistled for Gus, who accompanied him back into the house.

He followed Danni's voice to the kitchen, where she was talking on the phone.

"All right. Tell her to come by the office at three o'clock. I'll have the pictures developed by then," she said with a curt tone.

Danni listened silently for a few moments, and her face lost some of its tension. "Yes, Cathy, I took my vitamins this morning." She raked a hand through her curls, and her gaze darted to Nick. She turned away, but he could've sworn he saw a blush in her cheeks. "No, I don't need *that* to relax," she said in a low voice he could barely hear.

Nick's face flared with heat. He suspected Cathy was trying to get the scoop from Danni about their night together. It sounded like Danni wasn't the kiss-and-tell type.

Thank God.

Danni hung up the phone and faced him. "My client wants to see the pictures of her jungle hero and his temptress at three o'clock. That's not going to be a fun appointment. Willy's wife will probably try to hire me to string him up by his balls."

Nick shuddered. "Thanks for *that* image."

One side of Danni's lips curved upward. "Sorry." She glanced at Gus. "Do you want to bring her along?"

"I thought you didn't like extra passengers."

"Four-legged aren't bad. It's the two-legged that I have trouble with."

The twinkle in Danni's eyes startled Nick and reminded him of Paddy. The older man's dry humor had never failed to make Nick either laugh or groan. It was one of the things he'd liked best about his friend.

"Make sure her tail stays on your side of the cab," Danni added with the Hawkins quirked eyebrow.

"Yes, ma'am." Most of Nick's anger and frustration from the morning's festivities bled away under the familiar-yet-not banter.

After gathering some items for Gus, Nick followed Danni out to the truck with the dog.

"What about my Jeep?" Nick asked, suddenly remembering he'd left it parked by Danni's office yesterday.

Danni waited until they were in the truck to answer. "Cathy said it was still there." She paused. "It even had all its tires."

"It's a miracle," Nick muttered.

Danni rolled her eyes. "It's not that bad a neighborhood. You can pick up your car after the appointment with Wilhelmina Warner, Willy's wife." She darted him a glance. "And yes, that's her real name."

Nick chuckled. "I'd never use a name like that in one of my books—too unbelievable." He shifted as Gus sat down, pressing her eighty-plus pounds against his side. "I've got the notes for that book I was working on with your dad in the Jeep. I'd hate to lose them."

Danni backed out of the driveway and joined the sparse traffic on the residential street. "Dad never told me about it."

Nick decided to ignore her bitter twang. He shrugged and glanced out his side window. "I asked him to keep it between us until I sold it."

"Were you afraid somebody would steal your idea?"

"No. Superstition."

Danni braked for a stop sign and sent Nick a sidelong glance. "You're the last person I'd guess was superstitious."

Nick grinned. "Writers are notoriously superstitious. Just among the ones I know, one has to wear red socks whenever he writes, another won't sit down at his desk until he's finished the *New York Times* crossword puzzle, and there's one woman who has a half-hour conversation with her characters every day before starting to write."

Danni continued driving. "So what's your fetish?"

Nick arched his brow and leered.

"I'm not talking about leather, whips, or chains here, Sirocco."

"I was thinking feathers myself."

She laughed. "There may be hope for you yet."

"Are you saying you like feathers?"

"I'm saying my fetishes are none of your business."

"Just when I thought we were becoming friends." Nick sighed dramatically.

Danni grinned but didn't comment.

She stopped at the one-hour photo shop she always used to have the film of Willy's extracurricular activity processed, then drove to the police precinct headquarters. She pulled into a parking garage next to the station and found a slot where Gus could watch the comings and goings, but where the truck was out of direct sunlight.

Danni switched off the vehicle, then turned to Nick. "When we go in, I want you to be seen and not heard."

"Why?" Nick asked.

"I think they'll be more open to answering questions from someone who used to be one of them."

"Are you referring to the thin blue line?"

She pressed her lips together. He'd irritated her.

"All I'm saying is you're an outsider, and in a cop's world, that makes you one of 'them' instead of one of 'us.'"

Although Nick didn't like the idea of having to play the silent sidekick, he understood her reasoning. Besides, he'd tried breaking through that wall and had failed miserably.

"All right." Nick ensured the windows were cracked open, then stepped out of the truck. "Stay," he commanded Gus, who stared at him with betrayal in her eyes. "We won't be gone long."

He joined Danni, who was waiting behind the truck.

"She'll be all right," Danni said, motioning to Gus. "We

shouldn't be here long. If Alex and Joe are on duty, they'll be out on patrol. We need to find out where."

They walked side by side across the concrete parking lot. Once inside the precinct, Danni spoke with the officer working behind the desk. She surrendered her gun, which would be held in a lockup area while she was in the building. She and Nick were then given visitor badges and allowed to go to the briefing room.

Danni led him through the dull corridors and into a large room littered with battered tables, plastic chairs, and a desk at the front where a beefy man with a crew cut sat. He glanced up as they entered and stood, holding out his hand. "Hawkins."

She shook the ham-sized hand and smiled. "Hey, Sarge. How's the wife and kids?"

Rodgers grimaced, or maybe it was a smile. Nick couldn't be certain.

"Good. Susan, my youngest, just started college. Wants to be a teacher."

"She can't be that old yet."

Rodgers guffawed. "Look who's talking. I remember when your dad used to bring you down here riding on his shoulders."

Danni's smile faltered, and she waved a dismissive hand. "That was a long time ago."

"Yeah, it was. Better times." He glanced at Nick. "I recognize you."

"I—" Nick began.

"He's a writer doing some background for his next book," Danni interrupted.

Rodgers narrowed his eyes. "He was asking a lot of questions about Paddy."

"Part of my research," Nick put in smoothly.

Rodgers grunted and gave his attention back to Danni. "So what brings you to my little island paradise?" He motioned to their less-than-lavish surroundings.

"I've been hired to look into the death of a juvie named

Matt Arbor. He was arrested for trying to sell stolen merchandise about two weeks ago," she replied.

Rodgers ran a hand over his spiky gray hair. "I don't remember him, but then we arrest a lot of kids. You know how it is."

"This one supposedly committed suicide last night."

"Maybe he recognized the wickedness of his ways."

Nick stiffened, not liking the man's callousness. Danni, however, didn't show any reaction one way or another.

"Or maybe somebody else recognized the wickedness for him," she said.

Rodgers frowned. "Are you saying it wasn't suicide?"

"That's what I'm trying to find out. Since Levin and Tygard were the first officers on the scene, I wanted to ask them a few questions."

"They're on the swing shift. Won't be in until eight tonight."

"I suppose we'll have to come back then. Do you think I could see the kid's file?"

"You know the rules."

"What's it going to hurt? He's dead."

"You're not a cop anymore."

She flinched but managed a weak smile. "Couldn't hurt to try."

Nick stepped forward. "Can't you at least check his file and tell us if it's been officially ruled as a suicide?"

"How'd he off himself?" Rodgers asked.

"Slit his wrists," Danni replied.

"Then it's suicide."

"What if it's not? What if it was made to look like a suicide?" Nick asked.

Rodgers glared at him but spoke to Danni. "He was asking the same type of questions about Paddy. Folks liked Paddy, and didn't like this guy stirring things up."

Danni lifted her chin. "Maybe things need stirring up. I'm beginning to wonder about Dad's death myself."

Sergeant Rodgers's eyes narrowed. "What's he been filling your head with?"

"Facts," Nick said. *To hell with staying quiet.* "Fact one: Paddy Hawkins supposedly commits suicide. Fact two: less than a week later a boy he helped seems to have done the same."

"Coincidence," Rodgers said.

"I don't believe in coincidences."

Rodgers held Nick's gaze for a minute, then turned back to Danni. "Look, I know you're upset about your father's death, but going around accusing people of covering up, or worse, committing a murder, is foolish. It's not going to bring him back. Paddy's dead. Let him rest in peace."

"What if he isn't resting in peace?" Danni asked softly.

The beefy sergeant flinched.

"Thanks for the information, Sarge. We'll be back this evening."

Nick opened his mouth to continue the argument, but Danni latched onto his jacket and tugged him out of the briefing room.

"He's a jerk," Nick said in a low voice.

"He's only doing his job."

Danni's calm answer seemed a strange contrast to her typically spitfire attitude.

"How well do you know him?" Nick asked her.

"He was my shift supervisor. We were both at the low end of the totem pole, so we usually ended up with the swing or night shifts."

"Did he know Paddy pretty well?"

"They weren't real close, but they'd shared a drink after work a few times." She eyed him warily. "What did he tell you about Dad?"

"Not a damn thing. Nobody did."

They stopped at the entrance desk to leave their visitor badges and retrieve Danni's revolver.

"What next?" Nick asked as they walked back to the truck.

"Lunch."

Nick's stomach rumbled on cue. All he'd had for breakfast was coffee, and it was already after one. "Where?"

"Why don't you pick the place?"

"Why don't you?"

"Because you're buying." Danni grinned, and her eyes twinkled with deviltry.

Nick grumbled, but Danni's smile was worth the price of a meal.

Chapter Seven

Castle Burgers wasn't what Danni had in mind when she'd suggested Nick choose where they eat lunch. But then, he did pay, so she couldn't complain too much. And Gus had approved of the grease-bomb burger Nick brought back to the truck for her.

After lunch, they drove to Danni's office via the photo shop. She found herself often checking the rearview mirror. Although she couldn't see a tail, her neck was stiff with tension. She didn't like that Nick had blurted out their theory of her father and Matt Arbor's deaths being related. Granted, she didn't *think* Sarge could be involved in anything illegal, especially not murder, but she hadn't seen him in a long time. People changed.

She had changed.

She rubbed the back of her neck. Was she growing paranoid? No, not paranoid, but wary, which was certainly justified by the near hit-and-run yesterday and Nick's apartment getting trashed. In fact, she had a right—even a responsibility—to be suspicious of every vehicle that followed them for more than three blocks.

What information did they think Nick possessed?

Or were the mysterious *they* after them both?

And if it was both of them, what about her place? Had her apartment been ransacked, too? She hadn't been there since yesterday morning. . . .

Damn it!

She made a tire-squealing U-turn, throwing Gus against Nick.

"What the hell?" Nick asked, one arm braced on the door and the other wrapped around his dog.

"We're making a detour."

"Where to?"

She glanced back to see if anyone had copied her abrupt one eighty, but she didn't see any familiar vehicles. "My apartment."

Nick stared at her a moment, then comprehension filled his features. "If they didn't find what they were looking for at my place, they might search yours."

"Give the man a prize."

Why hadn't she thought of that possibility earlier? She'd been so distracted by the damned diamond ring, she wasn't thinking straight. Never before had she let her personal feelings intrude on a case. What was wrong with her? What did it matter if Nick was seeing a woman? It only meant he was a normal, red-blooded male. It also meant he was screwing around behind his girlfriend's back . . . with Danni.

"They can't do much worse than what they did to my place," Nick said.

"Gee, that's reassuring." Although Nick had picked up on her tension, he was mistaken about the reason. Instead of correcting his assumption and asking him point-blank if he had a girlfriend, she'd resorted to her usual defense—sarcasm.

Real mature there, Danni.

She turned into her apartment complex and parked in her slot. Focusing her attention on her third-floor balcony, Danni eased out of the truck.

"Stay," Nick said to Gus. He closed his door and joined Danni on the asphalt. "Should we call nine-one-one?"

Danni cast him a sidelong glance. "*Now* you're worried about calling for backup?"

Nick flushed with a mixture of embarrassment and irritation. "You were right back at my place. I should've waited."

Danni nearly stumbled in her shock. He didn't strike her as the type to admit he was wrong without some incentive. "I'd like a copy of that, signed and notarized."

"Real funny, Hawkins."

Danni bit her tongue to keep from bursting out with laughter. God, if she thought that was hysterical, she must be stressing big time. *Focus,* she told herself and cast her gaze back to her apartment.

"Let's first find out if my place has been broken into. If we call without checking and there's no sign of a B and E, the cops aren't going to be real happy with us," she said.

Nick hesitated, then nodded reluctantly.

"Stay behind me," she told him.

Annoyance flashed in his eyes, but he did as told.

They crept up the stairs cautiously. Danni held her gun close to her hip as they climbed, not wanting to scare any innocent tenants who might happen by. Her pulse thrummed in her ears, creating a percussive accompaniment to her cadenced breathing. Magnified sounds from the street and other apartments filtered up the stairwell, bouncing off the walls before being absorbed by the carpeted steps.

An explosive *thwump* brought her to an abrupt stop, and she swiveled around, aiming her revolver at the stairs below them. Nick's solid body pressed against her.

"It was a door slamming," he whispered and settled his big hand on her wrists, pressing the barrel of the gun downward.

Feeling foolish, Danni didn't meet his gaze but continued her ascent, her heart beating twice as fast as a minute earlier. God, she was strung tighter than a drug addict.

They stopped on the landing of the third floor, and Danni cracked open the door to the hall. She peered through the thin gap but could see nothing but the familiar brown carpet and tan walls with flea market pictures hung throughout the hallway. After opening the door wider, Danni slipped through, and Nick followed on her heels. Although she'd never admit it, Nick's presence bolstered her and reminded her of what it used to be like having a partner to watch her back.

Shaking her mind free of the ambushing melancholy, Danni kept close to the inner wall as she sidled down the hall to her apartment. Once there, she pressed her ear against the door but heard nothing. She slipped her key ring from her pocket and slid the key in the doorknob. It turned with a tiny click.

"It's still locked," Danni said quietly.

"That's good, I guess." Nick's lips pressed into a thin line. "Be careful."

Danni rolled her eyes in a *Look who's talking* fashion. But she kept her motions deliberate and slow as she turned the knob and swung the door open. Her heart shot into her throat, and Danni half-expected the perpetrator to be staring back at her from the living room. Instead, she found the apartment in exactly the same condition as she'd left it. Although she was certain she hadn't had any unwanted visitors, she followed ingrained police procedure and checked each room. Nothing. She slid her weapon back into her shoulder holster.

"I wonder what they were looking for," Nick said, standing in the middle of the living room.

Confused, Danni glanced at him. "What?"

Nick motioned to the newspapers, magazines, and pieces of mail scattered across the sofa, dishes lying on the kitchen counters, and the piles of clothes on the living room floor. "Look at the mess. Whoever trashed my place obviously did the same to yours."

Danni's face burned. "Not exactly."

Nick's quizzical expression would've made her chuckle if she weren't so embarrassed.

"This is what it looked like when I left yesterday morning," she muttered, looking everywhere but at him.

So she wasn't the poster child for Neat Freaks Anonymous. Why did she care what he thought about her housecleaning abilities anyhow?

Nick stared at her like she'd just announced she was a mass murderer. "You actually live in this?"

Danni surreptitiously nudged a pair of black lacy underwear lying on the floor beneath a blue T-shirt. "It's not usually this bad. I was in the middle of sorting my clothes so I could do the laundry when—" She broke off, irritated with herself. "Look, I don't have to explain anything to you. I can do whatever I please in the privacy of my own home."

Nick only grunted, which might have meant he agreed. Or it might have meant he thought she was Oscar Madison's female counterpart. Either way, she didn't care . . . much. A woman's home was her castle.

"You know what this means?" Danni asked.

"You don't have any clean clothes?" Nick's expression oozed innocence, but his eyes twinkled.

Danni glared at him; then she remembered what she was about to say. Her exasperation fled, replaced by apprehension. "It means you're the one they're after, not me."

Nick turned away. "I know."

Troubled more than she cared to admit, Danni wandered into her kitchen and began to move the dirty dishes from the countertop to the dishwasher. She always thought better when she had something to occupy her hands, and she had plenty to think about. The most important was Nick's welfare. He'd stirred up a hornet's nest, and these hornets didn't just sting—their venom was deadly.

Since she liked Nick more than she should, it made the situation even more difficult. It wasn't every day a woman got up close and personal with a boy she'd had a crush on fifteen years ago. Little Danni Hawkins had both despised and envied seventeen-year-old Rocky. Adolescent hormones and father issues had confused the hell out of her then. But it seemed grown-up hormones were still doing a number on her.

"Do you want me to do anything?" Nick asked from directly behind her.

Startled, Danni swung around. She wasn't a small girl—not with sturdy Irish bones and muscles honed from hours at the gym and self-defense techniques—but Nick's solid physique and broad shoulders made her feel like a sapling in the shade of a towering oak tree. It was both comforting and disconcerting.

She raised her head to meet his eyes. "Like what?"

Nick shrugged. "Do your laundry?"

Danni crossed her arms and leaned against the counter. "What would you do if I said yes?"

"I'd ask where you kept your laundry soap."

He *sounded* serious, which only confused Danni more. She was accustomed to figuring people out within five minutes of meeting them, but Nick defied her intuition. Or maybe old feelings were mixing with new, clouding her judgment.

She suddenly realized Nick was waiting for an answer. "Uh, no, that's okay. I'll take care of it later."

"Suit yourself."

He took a deep breath and shoved his hands into his pockets, drawing Danni's attention to his hips. The man definitely filled a pair of jeans nicely. Irritated by her wayward thoughts, she jerked her attention back to his face, but not soon enough.

Nick grinned knowingly, and Danni held her breath, expecting some lascivious comment. Instead, he picked up a dirty plate and glass from the counter and piled them in the dishwasher.

"If you want, we can stay here instead of your dad's place," Nick suggested, continuing to clear the countertops.

The offer was tempting. There were emotional land mines in the house where she'd been raised, not to mention it was the place her father had died. She glanced at Nick, suddenly noticing how small the kitchen—hell, her whole apartment—was. Being in such close proximity to Nick Sirocco when night fell was *not* a good idea.

"We've got more room at my Dad's," she said. "And a yard for Gus."

Nick shrugged. "Suit yourself. If we're going to be there, why don't you put your dirty clothes in a basket and wash them at your dad's? We might be there awhile, and you'll need some clothes."

Startled, Danni pushed away from the counter and headed toward the living room. "Good idea."

"And don't forget those little black panties," Nick called.

Danni spun around and found him grinning like a cat that found the entire pitcher of cream. For the second time in less than ten minutes, her face flamed with embarrassment. Unable to come up with a snappy retort, she harrumphed and hurried to carry out her task . . . before he spotted her white lace thong, too.

WILHELMINA Warner fanned the stack of explicit photos across Danni's desk. "Willy told me a customer hit his head with a car door." The woman glared at the pictures as if everything was their fault. "I'm going to string him up by his balls."

Danni glanced at Nick, who sat in the back of her office. He caught her gaze and crossed his legs, then shuddered melodramatically. She coughed to stifle a rising chuckle.

"Better yet, I'll hire one of them Sopranos to take him out," Mrs. Warner continued ranting. "Maybe leave a horse head in his bed like they did in that movie—what was it?"

"*The Godfather,*" Danni supplied. She kept her clasped hands resting on her desk, keeping her amusement hidden behind a calm, professional mask. "Mrs. Warner, it is against the law to hire someone to commit murder, and if you continue to talk of doing so, I'll be obligated by law to report you to the police."

Wilhelmina snapped her mouth shut and looked like a thirteen-year-old who had been told she couldn't hang out with her friends at the mall. Her chin quivered.

Stifling a sigh, Danni reached for the tissue box behind her and passed it across the desk to the woman. She'd had more than her share of tawdry cases, and each one followed the same pattern when the truth was revealed: anger, tears, then depression. It didn't matter if the client was male or female, each reacted the same. Just like grief, except for the denial stage. Danni provided the undeniable proof. She only wished she could offer some morsel of comfort.

By habit, she picked up a paper clip and proceeded to unbend it. She unbent another while Wilhelmina dabbed at her mascara-streaming eyes and cringed when the woman blew her nose. It sounded like a party noisemaker reject.

"Why? After giving that worm thirty-two years, why would he do this to me?" Mrs. Warner gazed at her with wounded eyes, obviously wanting Danni to give her an answer she could accept.

Danni fumbled around for some well-meaning platitude but came up empty. "I'm sorry, Mrs. Warner, but I don't know." She shrugged. "Why do men do anything?"

She tossed another straight paper clip with more force than necessary onto her desk and glanced at Nick, who sat quietly in a corner. She'd told her client that he was a writer researching his next book, and the fifty-something woman had reluctantly agreed to let him observe.

"Maybe he was bored," Nick suddenly said.

Danni tensed and aimed a glare at him. The deal was that he could stay for the meeting but was to remain silent. She should've known that was beyond his abilities.

"Now—" Danni began.

Mrs. Warner turned in her chair to peer at Nick. "What do you mean?"

Nick came to perch on a corner of Danni's desk. Danni felt the urge to give his nice-looking backside a poke with her letter opener.

"Your husband sells used cars day in and day out. Maybe he just wanted some excitement in his life," Nick said.

Mrs. Warner's double chin quivered again. "I-I've never refused him."

Danni wanted to bury her face in her hands. She could live without knowing any more sexual exploits of Willy and his wonder wurst.

"When was the last time you tried something different? Have you ever told him *your* fantasies?" Nick asked.

Feathers and handcuffs flitted through Danni's mind, jolting her libido. She tried to concentrate on her exasperation at Nick for playing sex counselor, but the pictures his question conjured—especially when he was starring in her fantasy—made it nearly impossible to focus.

Mrs. Warner's gaze turned inward even as her plump cheeks reddened. "But I thought Willy loved me."

"I'm certain he does." Nick spoke with so much certainty that Danni almost believed him. "Do you still love your husband?"

Mrs. Warner glanced at the pictures in her hands, and a tear rolled down her face. "After seeing these, I shouldn't, but I just can't help myself. Yes, I love him, but how can I compete with *that?*" She pointed at a picture of the spread-eagled Bambi.

"You don't have to compete. You're married to him. Your husband has clearly made a serious error in judgment, but that doesn't have to mean your marriage is over."

Mrs. Warner raised moisture-filled eyes. "What can I do?"

Danni cleared her throat.

He ignored her.

What else is new?

"Buy something sexy," Nick replied. "When your husband comes home from work, pretend it's your first time together, and give him an evening he won't forget."

His voice had dropped to a low, seductive tone that sent a shiver down Danni's spine, but this wasn't about him or her. And he had no right sticking up for some two-timing twit.

"He *cheated* on you, Mrs. Warner," she reminded her client. "He's the one who should be making it up to *you.* Five minutes ago, you were ready to string him up by a sensitive part of his anatomy."

"We've been together for over half my life. I have to try," Mrs. Warner said.

Danni wanted to scream in frustration. Nobody should have to put up with being treated like pond scum. She sighed. "It's up to you, Mrs. Warner. I did what you hired me to do."

Mrs. Warner stuffed the incriminating pictures back in the brown envelope and stood. She lifted her chin. "Thank you, Ms. Hawkins. At least I know what I'm up against now." She turned to Nick, and her stern expression softened. "And thank you for your advice, Mr. Sirocco."

"My pleasure, Mrs. Warner." Nick shook her plump hand. "I hope you're able to work things out."

"Me, too," she said wistfully.

Danni escorted her client out, then returned and closed the door behind her. She propped her hands on her hips and narrowed her eyes. "What the hell was that about?"

Nick frowned. "What?"

"Do you see a sign anywhere—*anywhere*—in this office that says Marriage Counselor?"

He crossed his arms. "She doesn't want a divorce."

Danni gave herself a shake, wondering if she'd heard him correctly. "And you know this how? Did she tell you?" She feigned surprise. "But how could she have? I was with you the entire time."

"She's been married to the guy for over thirty years. She doesn't want to throw that away without a fight, and I don't blame her."

"Dammit, Nick, when people break their marriage vows, they don't deserve forgiveness. They'll never change."

Nick studied her, and Danni had the insane urge to escape his keen gaze. What was he seeing?

"Is that what happened with your mother?" he asked, his tone and expression surprisingly gentle.

The air gushed from Danni's lungs, and her heart raced. The room dipped in and out of focus, until all she could see was the past.

"Go to your room, Danielle," Daddy ordered.

Six-year-old Danni pouted, but when Mommy glared at her, she skipped out of the living room and up the stairs. Only she didn't go to her room. She sat at the top of the stairs, where her mommy and daddy couldn't see her. But Danni could hear them.

"So who were you sleeping with this time, Glenda?"

Daddy's voice boomed, and Danni shrank back but couldn't stop listening.

"As if you care. You'd rather work eighteen hours a day than come home and take responsibility for your own family." Mommy sounded mad.

"If I didn't have that job you hate so much, you wouldn't be able to afford your fancy clothes and fancy fingernails."

Danni stuck her thumb in her mouth, not caring that she was a big girl now and wasn't supposed to do that anymore. She had never heard Daddy and Mommy yell at each other before, and Danni was scared.

"If you weren't so tired every night, I wouldn't have to go out and find someone who treats me like a woman."

"How many men have you been with?"

"Ten or twelve. Who keeps count?"

Danni heard a funny sound, like when Mommy would slap her face, but a lot louder.

"I bet you feel like a real man now, don't you?" Mommy said, her voice shaking.

"Goddammit! I've put up with more than any other man would have. Get out!"

A tiny sob made it up Danni's throat, but the thumb in her mouth prevented it from escaping. There was the sound of the door opening and slamming, then silence.

Scary silence.

Danni rolled onto her side and curled into a tight ball.

"Danni, did you hear me?"

She shook herself free of the vivid flashback and found Nick's hands on her arms, his worried face close to hers.

"Wh-what?"

"Are you all right? You're white as a sheet," Nick said.

Danni's mouth felt like ashes, and her head pounded. "I'm fine. I'm just getting a headache." It wasn't exactly a lie. It just wasn't the entire truth.

It was clear by the clenching of his jaw that Nick didn't believe her, but he didn't press.

Danni moved around him to her desk and sat down, grateful that her trembling legs didn't have to support her any longer. She'd carried only vague memories of the night her mother had left.

What had triggered that repressed memory?

It must've been a combination of the adultery case and Nick's quiet question. At some level, Danni had known her mother had been unfaithful, which probably accounted for her wariness of commitments. But she never knew her father had kicked her mother out of the house. She'd always believed her mother had simply abandoned them.

"Is there anything else you need to do here?" Nick asked.

She'd almost forgotten he was in the room. "I-I don't think so. I'll check with Cathy to be sure, though." Instead of walking out to the receptionist's desk, she picked up her phone and punched the intercom. "When is my next appointment, Cathy?"

"Nothing until Monday at ten A.M.," the receptionist replied. "Is Mrs. Warner's case closed?"

"Yes. Go ahead and send her the final bill." She placed the phone back in its cradle, feeling somewhat calmer. She glanced at Nick, who'd sat down in the chair Mrs. Warner had occupied. "Nothing until Monday."

"That gives us five days to concentrate on Paddy's and Matt Arbor's deaths."

Danni swallowed the acid in her throat and focused on Nick's words. "We should talk to Matt's parents."

"His mother. From what he told me, his mom never married his father. In fact, I don't think he even knew who he was."

Danni wasn't surprised. She pushed herself upright and was relieved when her knees didn't buckle, although her head was throbbing. "Let's go talk to her now. Maybe she can tell us who he hung out with."

"Maybe we should go back to the house so you can lie down." He paused. "You've had a rough week."

She glared at him, irrational anger catching her off guard. "I've survived over twenty years without a mother. I don't need one now."

Nick held up his hands, palms out. "I was only trying to help."

"Don't."

She scowled at the straightened paper clips on her desk and swept them into the wastebasket impatiently. After ensuring her desk drawers were locked, she led the way out of her office. She stopped by Cathy's desk. "Do you have Matt Arbor's address?"

"I can get it." The administrative assistant typed in some commands on her computer. She scribbled an address on a Post-It note and handed it to Danni. "What're you going to do?"

"Talk to his mother."

Cathy's pixie face was somber. "He had an appointment with Beth the day before he died."

"What was it about?" Nick asked.

With unusual seriousness, Cathy answered, "He wanted to cut a deal."

"Beth told me," Danni said. "Do you know if he went into any details?"

"I don't think so, but you should probably talk to Beth."

Danni pointed at her closed door. "Does she have a client?"

Cathy nodded apologetically. "It's going to be at least an hour, but you can wait if you want."

Danni caught Nick's eye, but he was strangely non-committal. She shrugged and said to Cathy, "We'll talk to her tomorrow. When is she free?"

"In the morning. Her first appointment is at eleven."

"Pencil me in for ten." Danni rubbed her brow, hoping that she wasn't getting one of her rare migraines. "We're going to talk to Matt's mother."

She was aware of a pair of identical worried glances but didn't acknowledge them. Although she was accustomed to Cathy's mother-henning, she wasn't used to having anyone else—especially this man—care about her well-being.

"It can wait until tomorrow," Nick said.

She shook her head, then realized what a dumb move that was as the ache behind her eyes increased. With any luck, the migraine would hold off a few hours, until she'd interviewed Ms. Arbor, as well as Levin and Tygard at the station.

After that, she could collapse for the night and her usual nightmare would give her a respite.

Chapter Eight

NICK followed Danni into an apartment building that had graffiti liberally splashed across its tired brick facade. The grease-stained walls and crumbling plaster in the entrance, as well as the smell of stale cigarettes, dirty diapers, and rotting garbage, reminded him too much of the place where he'd grown up. He'd worked hard to shed his past, but it still lurked within him, eager to emerge when way-laid by such powerful sensory triggers.

"Cher Arbor, 1C," Danni said, her finger on the decrepit line of mailboxes. "I wonder if her parents had a Sonny and Cher fixation."

Nick, too caught up in his past miseries to appreciate Danni's dry humor, shrugged impatiently. He just wanted to get this over with.

Danni led the way down the reeking hall, and Nick was careful not to brush against the yellowing walls. At 1C, Danni stopped and knocked. A baby's wailing and a man's guttural expletive drifted from another apartment, and Nick gnashed his teeth as déjà vu swept through him.

"Knock again," Nick said between thinned lips.

Danni pounded harder. "Ms. Arbor, are you in there?"

After another minute, there was a scuffing on the other side. Two locks clicked, and the door cracked open with a chain still offering a semblance of security.

A pale blue eye surrounded by bloodshot white peered at them through the slit. "What d'ya want?"

"I'm Danni Hawkins, a private investigator." She held up her ID. "I'd like to ask you some questions about your son Matt."

"He's dead." Her tone was as lifeless as her eye.

"Yes, we know, that's why we're here. His lawyer, Beth Marshal, asked me to look into his death."

The eye blinked, then shifted to Nick. "Who's he?"

"Nick Sirocco," he answered.

She closed the door and unlatched the chain, then allowed Danni and Nick to enter. Cher Arbor tightened the sash around her faded pink robe, then pushed her flyaway hair out of her face.

"Mattie mentioned you," she said to Nick. "Said you used to be just like him but got out of the neighborhood and done good."

Her admiration made him self-conscious, but he managed a smile. "That's right. I grew up about five blocks from here. The building's condemned now."

"Just like this place'll be in a few years," Ms. Arbor said grimly.

He glanced around the tiny apartment that had a water-stained ceiling and cracked paint on the walls. The furniture was at least thirty years old, but it appeared Ms. Arbor tried to clean it once in a while. Unlike his mother, who never did anything more strenuous than lie on her back. He brought his attention back to the pitifully thin woman.

"How'd you get out?" Ms. Arbor asked curiously.

"The army."

Ms. Arbor stared at something over Nick's shoulder. "That's what Mattie was planning on doing—joining the army. See the world. It had to be better than this." She motioned to her surroundings, her loathing evident.

"I'm sorry about your son, Ms. Arbor," Danni said softly. "My father thought a lot of him."

"Officer Hawkins—he was your father?"

"That's right."

Ms. Arbor clasped Danni's hand. "He was a good man, tried to help kids like my Mattie make a better life for themselves. You must've been proud."

Danni shifted from one foot to the other, her body language screaming her discomfort. Nick opened his mouth to relieve her of answering, but she beat him to it.

"I'm finding out how good a man he was," she confessed quietly.

Ms. Arbor stared at her a moment, then seemed to shake herself. "Sit down. Would you like some coffee? I think I have some soda, too. Mattie used to drink it."

"No, that's all right. We're fine," Danni assured as she perched on the sagging sofa. "We don't want to take a lot of your time, but we have some questions we'd like to ask."

Only when Ms. Arbor lowered herself to a mustard-yellow vinyl chair across from the couch did Nick sit down at the opposite end of the sofa from Danni. A spring pressed into his left buttock, and he repositioned slowly, not wanting to embarrass their hostess.

Ms. Arbor reached for a pack of generic cigarettes, tugged one out, and lit it. She blew the smoke away from Nick and Danni. "I don't know what I can tell you. I didn't see him that much. I work the night shift at Landy's Truck Stop. As soon as Mattie got home, I usually had to leave for work. And when he left in the morning, I was asleep." Her voice was raspy, either from grief or her cigarette habit.

"What time did he usually get home?" Danni asked.

"Around eleven."

"Did he ever tell you where he was? Who he was with?"

Ms. Arbor grasped the lapels of her robe with her left hand, tugging it closed at her neck. Nick couldn't help but notice her fingernails were stained brown with nicotine, just like his parents'.

"I asked him, but mostly it was 'nowhere.'" She attempted a laugh and failed. "You know how kids are nowadays."

"Did he go to the youth center very often?" Danni asked.

A spark of life lit her sallow face. "When he did tell me anything, it was about that place. He liked it, I think. I mean, it's hard to say with a seventeen-year-old. Seventeen. Already a man." She shook her head. "His father was only sixteen."

"Matt told me he didn't know who his father was," Nick interjected.

Ms. Arbor leaned over to tap her cigarette ashes into an empty can with a tomato soup label. "He didn't. I didn't either. I was fifteen and boy crazy. One of three boys—all of them sixteen—was his father. I never knew which." She said it matter-of-factly, like she was describing a stranger.

Nick felt a wave of empathy for Matt.

"Did you know any of Matt's friends? Who he hung out with?" Danni continued her questioning.

"There were two boys he used to talk about. He brought them home one time. Gary and Marsel. I don't know their last names."

"Can you describe them?" Nick asked.

"Marsel's black, tall, skinny, usually wears those baggy pants that look like they're going to slide right off him. Gary's shorter. Long brown hair. Has eyebrows that go all the way across his forehead, like there's only one."

"I know them," said Nick. "I've seen them hanging out at the center."

"Is there anybody else you can think of? A girlfriend maybe?" Danni scribbled in a notebook she'd taken from her jacket pocket.

"If he had one, he didn't tell me about her," the woman said with a snort of derision. "Guess he didn't want to scare her off."

"Did you know he was involved in theft?"

Nick scowled at Danni for being so blunt. The woman had lost her son less than a day ago.

"No." Ms. Arbor punched out the butt of her cigarette against the inside of the can. "I tried to teach him right from wrong." Her thin face crumpled. "But I couldn't even do that right."

Nick leaned forward and laid a hand on hers. It was cold and bony. "You can't blame yourself, Ms. Arbor."

"He's right," Danni said gently. "At a certain point, children have to become responsible for their own actions, regardless of how they were raised."

Although Ms. Arbor probably only saw empathy in Danni's sad smile, Nick could read the self-reproach and wistfulness in her dark blue eyes. He curled his hands into fists to keep from touching Danni, from offering—what? Sympathy? She'd prefer indifference.

"A friend of mine used to say raising a kid was like a crapshoot; sometimes you roll a seven and sometimes you hit snake eyes," Danni said. "Just remember you did the best you could. That's all anyone can do."

A tear slid down the older woman's cheek, and she brushed it away with the back of her hand. "Thank you."

Nick noticed that Danni gave Ms. Arbor time to regain control of herself instead of continuing immediately with her questions. He suspected Danni had been a good cop, compassionate and caring, much like her father, yet she probably didn't even recognize the similarities.

"Was Matt depressed or upset about anything?" Danni asked, keeping her voice low and solicitous.

Ms. Arbor shook her head, then reached for another cigarette. She tried to light it, but her hands shook too much. Nick took the cheap lighter from her and flicked it. The woman leaned close to the flame and took a few puffs to get the tobacco burning.

"No," Ms. Arbor finally replied. "If anything, he was excited about graduating from high school and getting away from here."

"Do you think Matt killed himself?" Danni asked.

"No," Ms. Arbor replied firmly without hesitation.

"Do you have any idea who might've wanted him dead?"

Ms. Arbor lowered her graying head, shaking it slowly.

Danni leaned forward to meet Ms. Arbor's downcast gaze. "Did he mention anyone he had a fight with recently? Maybe had a grudge? Did he cross anyone?"

"No. No, I-I don't know." The woman's voice was thick with tears. "I just don't know."

Danni opened her mouth, and Nick touched her arm. When she glanced at him, he shook his head. He was certain Matt's mother didn't know anything more.

He could see the reluctance in Danni's features, but she nodded once, accepting his unspoken request.

"Thank you, Ms. Arbor," Danni said. "I'm sorry if I upset you, but I just want to find the truth."

Ms. Arbor lifted tear-filled eyes. "I do, too. I-I'm sorry I wasn't much help."

Danni mumbled a few words of sympathy, then stood. "We'll let you know if we learn anything."

The woman tugged her robe snugly about her emaciated body. "Thank you."

She escorted Nick and Danni out with a shuffling gait and closed the door behind them. They walked down to the truck in silence that lasted until Danni pulled away from the curb.

"Do you believe her?" Danni asked.

Nick scratched behind Gus's ears. "Yes. Boys Matt's age don't tell their mothers anything important."

"Are you speaking from experience?"

Nick glanced sharply at Danni, expecting to find mockery. Instead, she appeared genuinely curious. He shifted his gaze to the passing street. "My mother didn't care what I did, as long as I stayed out of the way." The words came out with far more resentment than he intended.

Danni's hands clenched and unclenched the steering wheel. "Maybe I was lucky my mom left when she did."

Nick's mouth gaped, surprised by her admission.

"So, you know those two boys, Marsel and Gary?" Danni asked, abruptly changing the subject.

Still caught up in Danni's confession, Nick took a moment to switch gears. "They hang out at the center quite a bit." He glanced at his watch. "It's a little early for them to be there now, but we could stop there in a few hours."

"Sounds like a plan," Danni said. "Let's swing back by the office so you can get your car, then drop it at the house."

TWO hours later, after eating Chinese takeout and leaving Gus at the house, Nick and Danni headed over to the youth center.

As Nick drove, he divided his attention between the road and Danni. She had her right ankle resting on her left knee. Her right foot jiggled constantly, and her fingers tapped a counterrhythm on her thighs. However, she'd been uncharacteristically subdued, not even arguing when he suggested they take his vehicle this time. The only time she'd shown some fire was when he'd asked what was wrong. He'd gotten a resounding, "Nothing."

"Would you quit watching me like I'm a ticking bomb?" Danni asked in irritation.

"You aren't, are you?" Nick half-teased.

Danni turned her head and leveled him with a look. "Only if you keep staring at me."

Nick braked for a red light, easing to a stop. "They might clam up around you."

"Huh?"

"Matt's friends. Maybe you should let me talk to them."

"You tried that already. All it got you was a group of pissed-off cops."

The light turned green, and Nick stepped on the accelerator. He couldn't deny her criticism, but he had a definite advantage with these kids; he'd been one of them. "This is different." He tossed her a smile. "No thin blue line."

Danni grunted and crossed her arms, which Nick assumed was her version of giving in gracefully. From his side vision, he watched the streetlights play across her strong yet feminine face, striping it with ever-changing darkness and light—one moment cold and forbidding, the next open and guileless.

Like two people resided within her.

Which one was the true Danni Hawkins?

Nick turned in to the youth center's parking lot. The center was located where gang boundaries converged, in a decrepit neighborhood that had been abandoned by everyone but those who couldn't afford to leave. No colors were allowed at the center, creating a level playing ground for those who came to play some ball or just shoot the breeze with friends. The neutral territory had survived for over twenty years because of people like Paddy Hawkins who didn't put up with any bullshit.

Nick parked in the well-lit parking area close to the building that had once been an abandoned warehouse. He recognized most of the other cars as belonging to volunteers.

Nick opened his door and started to get out, but he noticed Danni remained motionless. "Aren't you coming in?"

She blinked, and her curved eyelashes swept cheeks that appeared ghostly white in the streetlights. "It's been a long time."

Nick quelled the urge to ask her how long. He didn't know why it was so important, but he wanted her to confide in him on her own. Seconds ticked by as he waited.

She buried her hands in her blue and brown plaid jacket pockets and stared at the youth center. "I was fourteen when Dad banished me from here."

"What about when you were a cop? Didn't you come by then?"

She turned toward him, and her eyes appeared impossibly huge in her pale face. "No. This was Dad's place. I never tried to be included in that part of his life again."

Nick digested the information, and for the first time, felt

a spark of anger at Paddy. The man could alleviate pain and hurting in strangers' kids but hadn't recognized it in his own child.

Danni opened her door and slid out of the SUV. Troubled, Nick joined her and walked by her side.

As they neared the center's entrance, the door flew open, and Paul Gilsen, a dark-haired man Nick's age, exited. He stopped and smiled in recognition.

"Nick. I was wondering where you've been," Paul exclaimed, holding out his hand.

Nick grinned as he shook his friend's offered hand. "It's been awhile."

"A couple of weeks, since before . . ." Paul trailed off, his lips turning downward.

Nick's smile faded. "Yeah, I know." A cleared throat reminded him of Danni's presence. "Paul Gilsen, this is Danni Hawkins."

Paul switched his full attention to Danni, and his brow crinkled. "Paddy's daughter?"

Nick could almost see the effort it took Danni to nod calmly.

"That's right," she replied stiffly.

"Paul and I hung out together when we were kids," Nick said. "We both made it out of the neighborhood."

Danni eyed Paul. "Did you join the army, too?"

The two men laughed and exchanged a look.

"He was a jarhead," Nick said. "Joined the marines."

"Got out after four years," Paul said. The rivalry between their two military alma maters had become a running joke. "But I didn't come back to the city until last year. When I stopped by here for a visit, I ended up volunteering, just like Nick."

"What do you do here?" Danni asked.

"I help with the computers, teach the kids how to use them." Paul shook his head. "The young people today need to know at least the basics, or they're going to be left even farther behind." He glanced at his watch. "I have to get going unless I want to stand up my date." He turned to

Danni and smiled amiably. "It was nice seeing you again, Danni."

She nodded but didn't say anything.

Nick waved good-bye to his friend, then turned back to Danni. "Again? You knew him before?" he asked curiously.

"Yes."

"And?"

She focused on him. "And nothing." She opened the door. "Come on."

Shaking his head at her obstinacy, he joined her. They walked down a hallway, which had the administrative office on one side and a large room with a dozen computers in it on the other. There was a light on in the office, but the computer room was locked, since Paul had left and there was no one to supervise the young people. Metal doors at the end of the hall led into the gym, and Nick continued through them. Danni followed, and they paused just inside the basketball court.

Sweat permeated the air. The sounds of boys' grunts, bouncing basketballs, and tennis shoes squeaking on the floor filled their ears. Nick watched the pickup game, allowing memories to wash through him. In contrast to the bleak memories Matt Arbor's apartment building brought back, these memories were filled with fondness and warmth. He'd spent countless hours in this same gym, forgetting about what awaited him at home and dreaming of the day he could finally escape.

"Do you see either of them here?" Danni asked.

Startled out of his recollections, Nick blinked and searched the gym. A handful of spectators sat along the sidelines, cheering the players. Tony Mullen, a cop and center volunteer, was acting as referee for the game. Finally, Nick spotted Marsel playing basketball, but Gary was nowhere in sight.

"Marsel. He's going in for a layup," Nick said.

He watched the tall teenager sail through the air and sink the ball with deceptive ease.

Danni whistled low. "He's talented."

Nick led the way down the sidelines, where they stood behind a dozen girls. When the boys on the court took a break, some of them joined Nick, slapping his palm in greeting. After some good-natured teasing, he introduced Danni to them, intentionally not giving her last name. He wasn't sure if she wanted the kids to know she was Paddy's daughter.

She took the boys' adolescent leers in stride—no doubt another skill learned as a cop. When they realized they weren't going to fluster her, they started drifting back onto the floor.

"Hey, Marsel, can I talk to you a minute?" Nick asked the tall, skinny teenager.

Swaggering back to them, Marsel shrugged. "What about, man?"

"Matt."

Marsel pressed his lips together and shuffled his feet. "Never figgered him to off himself."

"Me neither." Nick paused, ensuring he had Marsel's attention. "We think he was murdered."

Marsel's dark eyes widened. "I heard he slit his wrists."

"Somebody could've done it to him, made it look like suicide."

"Who?"

"That's what we want to find out," Danni spoke up.

Nick sent her a glare, which she ignored.

"Tell me what he was into," she said to Marsel.

The kid stared at her and shook his head. "Don't know."

Nick scowled at Danni. Like it or not, she was an outsider, and these boys, either a short step away from delinquency or already there, weren't going to give her squat.

"C'mon, Marsel, you were his friend," Nick said. "We're not talking about lifting some televisions or computers. We're talking murder."

Marsel glanced around, his agitation clear. "I don't know nothin' 'bout murder. Matt and me hung out together, but we weren't joined at the hip or nothin'. He did his thing. I did mine." He turned back to the game. "I gotta go. We're leadin'."

Marsel jogged back onto the court, his long, baggy shorts barely held in place by his slim hips.

"He knows something," Danni said.

"Probably, but how do we get him to trust us?"

"I thought you said they'd talk to you."

Nick leveled a glare at her. "He might've told me more if you hadn't jumped in. Didn't I ask you to let me handle it?"

Danni folded her arms across her chest, and her eyes flashed. "Just like you let me handle Mrs. Warner and Sergeant Rodgers."

"That's different."

"How?"

Nick fumbled around for a reason but could only come up with, "Because." He laid his hands on Danni's taut shoulders. "I think Marsel will tell me more, but it'll have to be in his own time."

"We don't have time, Nick. We have two deaths ruled as suicides. If we don't come up with something soon—"

The distinctive sound of gunfire outside startled them. The rapid staccato told Nick whoever it was had an automatic weapon.

"Get down," he yelled, then grabbed Danni and yanked her down onto the floor, covering her body with his as more shots rang out.

Chapter Nine

DANNI lay still beneath Nick's protective cover as her mind raced, already sorting out what was happening. Windows shattered under the rapid-fire barrage, and bullets pinged against the metal bleachers. She tried to draw out her revolver, but Nick's pressing weight gave her little freedom to move.

"Stay down," he said, sounding impatient and pissed off.

She wanted to argue, but she could barely breathe, much less mount a verbal dispute.

Abruptly, the firing from outside ceased, and tires squealed on asphalt. Eerie silence followed. Danni became aware of the grit beneath her cheek and Nick's hot breath against the back of her neck. She smelled sweat but wasn't certain if it was hers or his.

Nick eased off her, and Danni rolled onto her side, sucking in a big gulp of air. Her gaze met Nick's dark, anxious eyes.

"You all right?" he whispered hoarsely.

She nodded, surprised at the concern in his voice and

features. Shoving her hair out of her face, she scrutinized him. "You?"

"Fine." He sat up, and his gaze surveyed the huddled bodies. "The kids."

Assured that Nick was unhurt, Danni quickly switched her attention to the teenagers who were milling around cautiously. Unsure if the shooting was actually over or if this was only a lull, Danni didn't rise but rolled onto her hands and knees. With Nick beside her, she hurried over to the group of girls who'd been watching the game. They were shifting slowly, and Danni could hear some panicked whimpers.

"Was anybody hit?" she asked the shell-shocked young women.

They shook their heads. Danni exchanged a relieved look with Nick, then turned back to the girls. "Move over there and keep down until we know for certain that the shooters are gone." She pointed to a corner of the gym shielded by bleachers folded against the wall.

The girls obeyed, helping one another crawl to the somewhat protected spot.

The man who'd been refereeing the game scuttled over to the basketball players to check on them. Danni and Nick joined him. They all remained doubled over, hoping they'd be less of a target.

"Everyone all right?" Nick asked, his hand moving across the boys' shoulders and arms to reassure them.

The teenagers nodded, their expressions filled with a mixture of fear, anger, and shock.

"I called it in as soon as the shooting started," the referee said to Nick.

"Fast thinking, Tony," Nick said. "Let's get over by the girls."

The boys bellied across the floor to join the cluster in the corner. Keeping low, Danni and Nick brought up the rear.

"Who the hell would open fire on the center?" Nick muttered as they followed the kids.

Danni didn't even try to formulate an answer. She wondered the same thing herself. There had been too damned many coincidences in the past week: her father and Matt's mysterious deaths, the attempted hit-and-run, the ransack of Nick's place, and now this drive-by shooting at the youth center. If she hadn't been convinced her father's death was murder before, she was certain now.

Danni glanced at Nick, who was speaking to the referee. Nick was the common denominator. But of *what?* Had he and her father seen or heard something they shouldn't have? And if so, why didn't Nick remember it? Or maybe they hadn't realized the significance at the time, and then Dad had figured it out the night he'd called Nick.

Her head pounded with even more intensity than earlier at the office. It hadn't graduated into a migraine then as she'd feared, but she suspected she wouldn't be so fortunate this time. She took a deep breath and let it out slowly, hoping she could hang on long enough to get through the question-and-answer session with the police.

Diverting her thoughts, she turned to Marsel, who was at the edge of the group. His complexion was ashen, and his gaze darted about, as if he expected a gunman to jump out of the walls. He wiped his brow with his hand, and sweat dripped onto the wooden floor.

Danni's instincts tingled, and she crawled over to the kid. "Are you all right?" she asked Marsel. "You look like you've seen a ghost."

Marsel snorted and avoided her eyes. "I ain't been shot at before."

Something more than flying bullets was bothering him. In this neighborhood, gunfire wasn't all that uncommon, and Marsel didn't strike her as a blushing virgin in the juvie game. She shifted a little closer to him and confided, "I'll tell you a secret. The first time somebody shot at me, I damn near peed my pants. And I was a trained cop."

Marsel lifted his startled gaze to her, his brown eyes wide.

Danni followed up, now that she had an opening. "Do

you have any idea who might want to shoot up this place? From what I understand, it's neutral territory."

A droplet of sweat rolled down the side of Marsel's dark face and dripped onto his Chicago Bulls jersey. "How should I know? The only thing I shoot is hoops."

Danni stifled her impatience and managed a cajoling tone. "Come on, Marsel. Are you telling me that you don't know who the badasses are in the neighborhood?"

Marsel laughed, but it lacked strength or amusement. "You been watchin' too many hood movies. Round here, everybody minds their own business or—" He broke off and glanced around anxiously. He obviously knew more than he was saying.

"Or what, Marsel?"

The teenager shot her a glare, but a tic twitched in his jaw. "Or nothin'."

Danni grasped his sweaty arm. "If you know something about Matt's death, you could be in danger."

Marsel's lips twisted into a scowl. "Look, I don't know nothin'. Find yourself someone else to harass."

Before Danni could continue, the metal doors burst open, and four cops charged in, their guns drawn.

The volunteer raised his hands and called out, "Officer Tony Mullen here. We were all inside when the shooting started."

Danni turned back to Marsel, but the teenager had joined the other basketball players. She curled her hands into fists. Marsel knew something, and it could be vital to uncovering the truth, but she didn't have any leverage to use against him. She hoped Nick's confidence in the kid wasn't misplaced.

One of the patrol cops stepped toward them, and Danni recognized Sergeant Rodgers. The department must've sent out all but the administrative types to the center, since the supervisor rarely answered calls.

"Is anyone hurt?" he asked.

"No," Mullen replied. He wiped his brow and stood. "Did you find anyone?"

Rodgers holstered his service revolver and shook his head in disgust. "Whoever it was is long gone."

The teenagers pushed themselves to their feet. Danni began to rise and found Nick's extended hand in front of her. She grasped it and he pulled her up effortlessly. Their gazes locked, and Danni felt the subtle awareness between them shift up a notch. She recalled with sudden lucidity how Nick's body had covered hers and how safe she'd felt. She'd always insisted she could take care of herself—and she could—but she had to admit she was coming to like Nick's protective streak.

Realizing they still held hands, she released him and stepped back. "Thanks," she murmured.

"Nick, Danni, what are you two doing here?" a woman asked.

Danni turned to see Karen Crandle. Dressed in her patrol uniform, her father's former partner still managed to look fashionable with her shoulder-length, stylish blond hair and just enough makeup to enhance her attractive features. Now, however, her expression was filled with concern.

"We just came to talk to the kids," Nick replied.

"About what?" Karen asked.

"A boy who killed himself last night," Danni answered.

Karen nodded somberly. "Matt Arbor. He wasn't a bad kid." She shook her head. "Hard to believe he committed suicide."

"We're not sure he did," Nick said. "Do you know if Matt was into anything more than lifting computers?"

Karen's brow furrowed in concentration. "No. Paddy might've known something, but I think he was as surprised as me when Matt got picked up on the stolen goods charge."

"That happened only a couple of days before Dad died," Danni said.

"That's right." Karen frowned, and her gaze traveled from Danni to Nick and back. "Am I missing something here?"

Danni grimaced, partly from her headache and partly from the mystery. "I wish I knew."

Sergeant Rodgers joined them. "Have you gotten their statements, Crandle?"

Karen reached into her breast pocket and pulled out a small notebook and pencil. "I was just working up to that, Sarge."

Rodgers cast her a disgruntled look, then glanced at Danni. "You and Sirocco keep turning up like a couple of bad pennies."

"You can't blame a drive-by shooting on us," Nick fired back, his antagonism obvious. "We were in here."

Her head throbbing, Danni didn't have the time or the patience for any male posturing. "Let's just answer their questions and get out of here."

"Levin and Tygard are outside," Sarge added. "After Crandle gets your statements, you can grab a couple of minutes with them."

With all the excitement, Danni had forgotten she'd planned to talk to them this evening. Although she preferred to go home and collapse in her bed, she might as well take advantage of Sarge's olive branch. "Thanks."

The sergeant moved on, leaving Karen to take Danni's and Nick's statements. Once they were done with the routine interview, Karen laid a hand on Danni's forearm. "I'm sorry about your father. I'm really going to miss him." Her eyes glimmered with moisture, then she hurried away to question the remaining witnesses.

Danni sighed and rubbed her pounding temples. "What a mess."

Nick rested a hand on her shoulder. "Did the headache come back?"

Danni's belly fluttered under his scrutiny, and déjà vu washed through her. She'd experienced the same feeling in this gym fifteen years ago after she'd been knocked down during a basketball game, and Nick had helped her up. Although her father liked the youthful Rocky, he hadn't approved of his daughter's crush on him. She'd met her dad's order to stay away with rebellious anger, but now Danni could recall her underlying hurt with painful clarity.

"I'm fine," she lied, keeping her gaze averted. "Let's go find Alex."

Once outside, Danni found the area lit up like a carnival midway with almost as many bystanders milling around. Half a dozen patrol cars surrounded the center with their strobes revolving. She squinted against the rotating red and blue that turned the night into a nauseating miasma of purple. Her throbbing head broadcast queasiness to her stomach, and she swallowed to allay the sickness. This was definitely turning into a migraine, but she had to hold on just a little longer.

She spotted Alex Levin finishing up with a witness and made a beeline toward him. The policeman glanced up. Recognition brought surprise, then a fond smile to his face.

"Danni," he said in greeting.

Despite her headache, she grinned. "Hi, Alex. Been a long time."

"And whose fault is that?"

Danni's grin faded. As much as she wished she could deny his good-natured accusation, she recognized the truth behind it. Once she left the department, it had been too awkward to stay in touch. "I'm sorry. It was just . . ."

Alex hugged her and said close to her ear, "Hey, it's okay. I understand how tough it was losing Scott."

The lump in Danni's throat threatened to choke her as she clung to him. Scott, Alex, Joe, and she had gone through the Police Academy together and became close friends. After their break-in time with seasoned veterans, Scott and Danni had been paired together, and later Alex and Joe. The four had maintained their friendship until Scott had been killed.

"I'm sorry about your dad," Alex said.

Danni gathered her composure and released him, stepping away to give herself some space. "Me, too."

Alex's cool, assessing gaze flicked to Nick. "You used to come by the station with Paddy. Sirocco, right?"

Nick nodded, but there was wariness in the gesture. "That's right."

Danni shifted to draw Alex's attention. "Did anybody see the shooters?"

"Nothing we can use." The patrolman flipped open his notebook. "Dark sedan, ranging from an eighty-one Ford to a ninety-eight Chevy."

"More than likely gang related," Danni said in frustration.

"Probably. We'll have to see what the physical evidence folks come up with." He studied her. "What're you doing here?"

Danni gave him the abbreviated version about Matt Arbor, then asked, "Were you and Joe first on the scene of his alleged suicide?"

Alex crossed his arms, and in the succession of red, blue, and white lights, his expression appeared almost sinister. "Yes. We looked for signs of foul play but didn't find any. Nothing on the door or windows suggested a forced entry." He shrugged. "There was nothing but the body and a razor blade in the tub."

Although Danni had seen her share of suicides, the picture Alex painted made her head pound even harder, and she almost succumbed to the nausea.

"Was he dressed?" Nick asked.

Any other time Danni would've been upset by his butting in, but now she was grateful. Besides, more often than not, his questions were relevant.

Alex nodded.

"Were the slashes consistent with someone who slit his own wrists?"

"As far as I could tell."

"What about the angle of the slashes? Did they look like Matt made them?"

Alex scowled and looked at Danni. "What's this about?"

"We don't think Matt killed himself," Nick answered, drawing another glare from Alex.

"We think Dad's and Matt's so-called suicides are related," Danni said. If there was anybody she trusted in the department, it was Alex.

The patrolman deliberately looked at Nick. "I heard you were asking a lot of questions about Paddy a few days ago."

"You heard right," Nick said, his mouth set in a stubborn line.

"Did you find anything?"

A tic appeared in Nick's jaw. "No."

Alex's expression relaxed. "Everybody liked Paddy."

"Not everybody," Danni said, siding with Nick against her old friend. "He didn't kill himself, Alex."

Her friend appeared troubled. "You didn't know him that well, Danni. You said yourself that Paddy had better things to do than be your father."

Moisture burned in Danni's eyes. She blinked it back and crossed her arms, hoping no one noticed her weakness. "Maybe, but he was still my father, and I have to learn the truth."

Alex grasped her upper arms and gazed at her intently. "He's gone, Danni. Doing this won't change anything. You still won't get his approval."

She jerked away from him, letting anger cover the slicing grief. "I want the person who murdered him. I don't care about anything else." She took a deep breath to dispel the betrayal she felt. "Will you call me if you hear something about Matt Arbor's death?"

Alex stared at her a long moment before nodding. "You know I will. Hey, Helen and I'll have you over for dinner soon."

The invitation was thrown out almost as an afterthought, but Danni managed a smile. "I'd like that. Say hi to her for me."

Alex nodded, and Danni turned away, not even stopping to say hello to Joe, who was taking statements. Nick matched her pace as they walked back into the center, where there were no strobes to aggravate Danni's headache.

Nick stopped Danni just inside the gym. "Wait here, and I'll ask Karen if we need to stick around."

Danni, unable to generate any irritation, nodded slightly. It hurt too much to do anything more.

She leaned against the wall and watched Nick approach the female cop. Karen smiled, and Nick returned it. He stepped close to her—so close their bodies almost touched—and spoke to her. Karen nodded and leaned nearer, her breasts brushing his chest. Then he hugged her. Tightly.

Jealousy caught Danni unaware, and she gasped at its sharp edge. Were Karen and Nick dating? She recalled the damned diamond ring. Was it for—She cut off the thought, telling herself it wasn't any of her business. Still, if Nick was seeing Karen, why had he slept with her?

Danni's head felt like it was being used as a drum, and she closed her eyes to the people in the gym. The voices, distorted by the gym's size, made her stomach dip and glide. She needed to get home, to someplace dark and quiet.

A touch startled her, and her eyes flew open, only to have the movement and lights overcome her tentative control. She stumbled away from Nick and down the hallway into the nearest bathroom. The vomit rose caustic and bitter in her throat. She flushed once, then again. Finally, she sank back on her heels in the bathroom stall and ran a shaking hand across her clammy face.

She hated this loss of control, ever since her first migraine at fifteen. At least their frequency was rare, maybe one every year or two. It shouldn't have surprised her to get one now, after her father's death and everything else that had happened in the past week.

"Danni, are you all right?" came Nick's low, gentle voice.

She took another swipe at her damp forehead, then pushed herself upright. She leaned against the stall's door until her legs stopped their impersonation of Jell-O and eased the door open. Nick stood in front of her, looking worried.

"It's a migraine, isn't it?" he asked softly.

She gave him one tiny nod and shuffled to the sink to splash cold water on her face. She groped for the paper towels, and Nick passed her a handful. Grateful, she dabbed at her forehead and cheeks. After tossing the towels into the wastebasket, she gripped the edge of the sink and hung her head.

"I'm sorry," she said. "If I'd known it would get this bad, I would've taken one of my pills before we left the house."

Nick made light, soothing circles across her hunched back. "Think you can make it out to my Jeep?"

"I hope so," she said with a weak smile.

Nick placed an arm around her shoulders, and she leaned into his side. He led her out of the rest room—the men's, she noticed with a grimace—and down the hallway. She was grateful that they didn't run into anyone. As soon as they stepped outside into the artificially lit night, the rotating red and blue lights sent a blinding jolt of pain through her head. She closed her eyes and buried her face against Nick's shoulder, knowing he would guide her safely to his car.

Once in the vehicle, Danni leaned her head back against the headrest and closed her eyes. She was grateful Nick remained silent as he maneuvered the SUV out of the labyrinth of prowl cars and forensic vans.

It'd been a long time since she'd had such a bad migraine.

And even longer since she trusted anyone as much as she trusted Nick.

Chapter Ten

MUTED sounds of a dog barking and the occasional car engine eased Danni's journey back to the living. She kept her eyes closed, caught in the never-never land between asleep and awake.

How did she get here—wherever *here* was? What time was it?

Something damp brushed against her cheek, forcing her to abandon her floating haven and seek answers. She flinched when a blurred furry face with an open mouth and lolling tongue filled her vision.

"Gus, down," came a quiet command.

The dog obediently dropped to the floor beside the couch, laying her head on her crossed front legs. Her brown gaze, however, remained on Danni.

A weight settled beside Danni's legs on the sofa.

"Welcome back," Nick said in a low voice. "How're you feeling?"

Everything returned in a rush: the shooting at the center, the ensuing onslaught of her migraine, Nick guiding her to his vehicle, and the long, painful ride to her father's house. After that, things got hazy. Her jacket and shoulder holster were missing, and she had a vague recollection of Nick removing them. Her shoes, too, were gone.

The living room was dim, but the slanted sunlight coming through the sheer curtains allowed her to make out Nick sitting by her feet at the end of the sofa. He sat at an angle, leaning toward her, his elbows braced on his knees and his hands clasped.

"Better," she answered, pushing her hair off her forehead. "How long?"

Nick glanced at his watch. "It's nearly eight. You've been out all night."

Danni wasn't surprised. Migraines did that to her. It was just that she usually woke up without a nurse on duty. She glanced down and found herself covered by a soft blanket, then looked at Nick again. He wore the same clothes he'd had on last night, although his hair was tousled and his whiskers needed their morning shave. She noticed a rumpled blanket on the big recliner and realized he must've stayed down here all night to keep an eye on her. That revelation made her glance away uncomfortably.

"How's your headache?" he asked.

"Pretty much gone." Her fingers curled into the worn blanket. "If I take my medication and lie down as soon as it comes on, it usually goes away within a few hours."

"But because you were too stubborn to say anything, you didn't take your medication or lie down, so it was an especially bad one." Nick's smile tempered his blunt words.

Her face heated because she knew he was right. Damn him for reading her so well.

"I had a friend who had migraines," he added. "He was almost as stubborn as you."

His teasing tone made her roll her eyes and smile, even as his comment made her wonder about his past. She'd known Nick for over fifteen years, had sex with him two nights ago, yet she didn't *know* him. He'd told her he'd been an Army Ranger, which she knew was an elite group. Special training, special missions. Special men.

"Are you hungry?" Nick asked, interrupting her thoughts. "I had the corner grocery deliver some food an hour ago."

Danni focused on her stomach and realized how empty it was. No wonder—she'd lost everything when she'd gotten sick last night at the Center. "I could eat."

"I'll put something together." Nick stood but remained beside the couch, looking down at her. "I'm sorry I stirred up bad memories."

"What?"

"That's when your headache started, after Mrs. Warner left your office." His lips pulled downward in a rueful frown. "When I asked about your mother."

Danni's lungs felt tight, and her eyes suddenly burned. She leaned over to pet Gus to hide her reaction. "I hadn't remembered that he kicked my mother out of the house. I always thought she left on her own. Dad never told me."

"Maybe he was trying to protect you."

Danni swallowed hard, trying to ignore the festering anger that rolled through her, but she couldn't. "Maybe he was just protecting himself."

Although she kept her gaze aimed at Gus, Danni could feel Nick's scrutiny. She was afraid to look up and see what was in his eyes. Afraid there would be disappointment and reproach. Finally, he moved away, and Danni let out a shaky breath.

She threw off her blanket and stood. Her bladder sent out a warning signal, and she hurried upstairs to the bathroom.

When she returned to the main floor, she found two steaming cups of coffee and two bowls of grayish matter on the table.

"I hope you like oatmeal," Nick said, sitting down. "It's the only thing I can make without burning it."

Although she wasn't a big fan of oatmeal, Danni sat down to eat it with an abundance of milk and sugar. Realizing she was famished, she ate quickly and scraped the bowl clean, then sat back to drink her coffee at a more leisurely pace. She was grateful Nick didn't feel the need to talk. It was nice, though, to share breakfast with a warm body. God knew it was rare nowadays she awoke in the company of a man.

The fact that it was Nick only made it better.

They rinsed their bowls and placed them in the dishwasher. Nick leaned against a counter and crossed his arms.

"They shot at the center because I was there," he said, his low voice filled with vehemence.

"We don't know that," Danni said, startled by his muted anger.

"Don't we?" His eyes flashed. "They could've killed or hurt some of those kids, and it would've been my fault."

Danni didn't find this martyr side of him very attractive. "No. The blame lies squarely on whoever did the shooting."

"I was the one who stirred things up by asking about Paddy and getting you involved, then with Matt getting killed . . ." Nick took a deep breath, visibly trying to compose himself. "I have to figure out what's going on before anyone else gets hurt."

Danni could feel waves of anguish rolling off him. "If you're to blame, then I am, too," she said firmly. "We're in this together."

Nick tilted his head and studied her. "I don't want anything to happen to you, Danni."

The intensity of his voice made her look away. "I can take care of myself. If nothing else, Dad taught me that."

Nick took her chin between his forefinger and thumb and tilted her face upward. "I heard what Levin said last night." His eyes darkened. "You always had Paddy's approval. You don't have to prove anything to anybody."

He was wrong. Danni had never lived up to her father's expectations, even after she became a police officer. Oh, he'd been proud when she'd graduated from the Academy and when his precinct had hired her. But she'd seen the look in his eyes—the longing for the son he never had. The son Nick had become.

She turned her head, forcing Nick to release her. "The only thing I want to prove is that Dad didn't commit suicide."

Nick scrubbed his face, his grizzled whiskers rasping against his palms. When he looked at Danni, she couldn't tell if he was infuriated or worried. "I shouldn't have gotten you involved in this."

Danni glared at him. "The hell you shouldn't have. He was *my* father."

"And if something happens to you, he's going to come back here and kick my ass."

Danni stifled the spiteful words that sprang to her tongue. "I'm going to shower. We have a meeting with Beth this morning."

She spun around and ran upstairs, startling Gus. Keeping her mind blank, Danni grabbed some clothes from the bag she'd dropped in her room yesterday afternoon. She carried them into the bathroom, turned on the tap, and stripped as the water heated. Once she stepped under the spray, she gave in to her seething frustration.

Wasn't it enough that Nick stole her father's affections years ago? Wasn't it enough that he'd come back home and once again insinuated himself in her father's life?

Why, after her dad's death, did Nick still deny her the right to be her father's daughter?

Where did he get off telling her she shouldn't be involved? If anybody had the right to learn the truth, it was her. Paddy had been *her* father, and she'd loved him. Her only sin had been in not telling him, and her penance would be finding his murderer.

Resolve strengthened within her. It was her right and her responsibility to find the killer, no matter what Nick wanted.

She showered quickly and dressed. As she was tucking her knit shirt into her jeans, she heard the telephone ring.

Dashing out of the bathroom, she shouted downstairs, "I got it."

Danni nabbed the phone in her father's bedroom, keeping her gaze averted from the pale spatters on the wall. "Hello."

"Danni, it's Sam."

She smiled, and some of her tension leached away. "Hi, Sam. What's up?"

"I think I should be asking you that question. I had coffee with Harry Rodgers after he came off duty this morning. He told me about what happened at the center."

Danni walked to a window and pushed the curtain back so she could see the street below. Sarah Countryman, wearing a wide-brimmed straw hat, was working in her flower garden, and a man was standing impatiently on the boulevard, waiting for his poodle to finish watering a signpost. The ordinary sights made last night's events more surreal.

"Nobody was hurt," she finally said.

"That was pure luck," Sam said. "Harry said, judging from the shell casings, seventy-five to a hundred rounds were fired at the building."

Although she'd been there, she hadn't realized the number had been that high. "Do they have any suspects?"

"No, but the gang unit has gotten involved. They're going to poke around, see if anything's been brewing."

Even though she wasn't convinced it was a simple gang shooting, Danni said, "Good idea."

There was a long pause at the other end of the line. "What's going on, Danni girl?"

Ignorance seemed the easiest route. "What do you mean?"

"What're you and Rocky up to?"

"I told you. We don't think Dad killed himself."

"Dammit, Danni, why can't you just let it go?"

Danni leaned her forehead against the cool glass. "I have to do this, Sam."

He muttered something Danni couldn't understand,

then asked, "Did the shooting have anything to do with your investigation?"

"I don't know. Maybe." She sighed, and her warm breath fogged the window. It didn't feel right holding out on the one man she'd always trusted without reservation, so she explained about Matt Arbor and the connection with her father. "If somebody's getting nervous, they might have followed us to the center."

"Then staged the shooting as a warning?"

"It's possible."

"But why kill Paddy? And this boy? What's going on?"

"If I knew that, I'd have the answers, Sam."

"You're thinking corruption, aren't you?"

Danni shifted her weight from one stocking foot to the other. "We both know it happens."

"And Paddy wouldn't stand by and let it continue if he found out." Sam sounded resigned.

"I may not have known him that well, but I do know Dad would've never accepted a bribe or covered for someone who did. That could be the reason he was killed."

"All right," Sam finally said. "I'll do a little digging with my sources in the department. If I learn anything, I'll let you know."

"Thank you," Danni said with heartfelt gratitude.

After a moment's silence, Sam asked, "So, are you and Rocky getting along any better?"

Danni smiled despite herself. "Like cats and dogs."

Sam chuckled. "Paddy had a lot of respect for Rocky. I know he trusted him."

Danni's amusement faded. "Yeah, I know."

"Do *you* trust him?"

Nick had come to her with his suspicions, then proceeded to irritate the hell out of her. He also punched too many of her buttons, which was why they'd ended up doing the horizontal tango their first night together. And if she hadn't come down with a migraine, there could easily have been a repeat performance last night.

But did she trust him?

"I trust him more than I trust anybody on the force right now," she finally replied.

"Then stay close. If you're right, you're both targets."

A shiver shimmied down Danni's spine. "We will."

"Be careful, Danni girl."

"I will," she promised. "Bye."

She hung up the phone and put it back in its cradle. The sound of the shower roused her out of her somber thoughts. She went into her bedroom and shoved her feet into a pair of black Skechers. Feeling half dressed without her shoulder holster, she walked to the bathroom door. The shower had been turned off.

"Where's my gun?" she asked, raising her voice.

The door suddenly opened, and a cloud of steam emerged. Danni blinked and found Nick, wearing only a towel around his trim waist, standing in the doorway. His damp hair was mussed, spiked in every direction like he'd just toweled it. Water droplets remained on his chest, and her gaze followed one as it rolled down between his pecs, leaving a damp trail through the light smattering of hairs. For one insane moment, she wanted to lean forward and lick away the droplet and taste Nick's skin.

"Top dresser drawer in your room," he said.

Her heart pounding and her body tingling, Danni forcibly lifted her gaze to his face. "What?"

He smiled crookedly, but his eyes smoldered, turning blue to stormy gray. "Your shoulder holster. It's in your dresser. Do you want me to take you into your bedroom and show you?" His silky tone resonated with double meaning.

Danni snapped out of her sensual review of Nick's near-naked body and felt her face flush with embarrassment. She took a step back, putting more space between them. The sizzling tension eased to a low undercurrent of awareness. "Uh, no, thanks, I can find it."

Danni escaped to her room, shutting the door behind her. She dropped onto her bed and closed her eyes, but she could still see Nick's broad shoulders, the breadth of his chest, and the delineation of muscle in his arms and torso. Her hormones were charging to Nick's reveille. She tried to order them to retreat, but her mind taunted her with memories of their lovemaking: the feel of his lips on hers, the smooth-coarse texture of his chest, the sleek skin on his back and buttocks.

She lightly touched her sensitive nipples through the layers of shirt and bra. She imagined it was Nick's hands, and heat shot through her, hardening the nipples and increasing the tight coil in her belly.

Suddenly she jerked her hands to her sides and flopped back onto the bed to stare at the ceiling. Was she so deprived that just the sight of Nick's body turned her into a sex addict?

To distract herself, she studied the faded paint on the ceiling and counted the number of ridges. Gradually, arousal's heat cooled, and she stood.

Trying to forget her humiliating reaction, she focused on donning her shoulder holster and checking her revolver. She was grateful Nick had enough experience with guns to empty the cylinder before placing the weapon in the drawer.

Digging into her closet, she pulled out an old black leather jacket that reached midthigh. With nothing left to do, Danni took a deep breath and left her room.

She heard Nick downstairs talking to Gus and couldn't help but smile. Even though he irritated the hell out of her sometimes, Nick had qualities she admired and respected. His meddling with Mrs. Warner had annoyed her, but she'd also understood he was trying to help the woman. And as much as she hated to admit it, she could see why he didn't want her working on her father's case. She didn't agree with his reasoning, but she could respect it.

Realizing she was wasting time, she descended the stairs. Nick, now dressed in brown jeans and a snug black T-shirt, was in the kitchen filling Gus's food and water bowls. He straightened when she entered the room.

"Gus should be okay in the house this morning," Nick

said. "As long as we stop by early this afternoon to let her out."

"No problem," Danni said, keeping her gaze averted from the cotton stretched taut over his pectorals. She checked the side pocket of her backpack and pulled out her truck keys. "Beth's expecting us at ten, so we should get going."

Nick nodded, grabbed his weathered brown leather jacket, and followed Danni out of the house.

Sarah Countryman was kneeling in her flower garden, just as she'd been when Danni had seen her through her father's bedroom window. She wore her usual housedress with an apron over it.

"Good morning, Mrs. Countryman," Danni said.

The seventy-something woman looked up, and a smile lit her face, which was shaded by her straw hat with a faded yellow ribbon around it. "Hello, Danielle." She began to push herself to her feet, and Nick took hold of her arm and helped her. "Thank you, young man." She eyed him closer. "You're the one I spoke to yesterday morning."

Nick's smile could've charmed a band of femi-nazis. "That's right. Nick Sirocco."

Danni frowned. He must've talked to the older woman after she went to meet Sam for breakfast.

"Yes, you were interested in the night Patrick died," Mrs. Countryman said.

Danni's glower intensified. "You didn't mention any of this to me," she said to Nick.

He shrugged. "It didn't seem important." He turned back to the older woman. "Your flowers are beautiful. You must give them a lot of loving care."

Two pink spots blossomed on Mrs. Countryman's wrinkled cheeks. "Since I don't teach any longer, my flowers have become my students. They must be tended with patience and attention."

"Your students must've liked you."

She chuckled. "Not all of them."

Danni smiled, remembering the times she thought Mrs.

Countryman was a nosy old lady. Later, she'd realized the ex-teacher had only been concerned about her.

"Did you remember anything else about the night he died?" Nick asked.

Mrs. Countryman brushed her face with her gloved hand and left a smudge of dirt on her pink-rouged cheek. "When the police officer told me Patrick had killed himself, I didn't question him. However, after I spoke with you, I thought about that evening. He had a visitor about nine o'clock. I know it was nine because *Will and Grace* had just come on." She hid a naughty smile behind her hand. "If my students knew I watched such a show, they would—what's the word?—freak." She cleared her throat. "I glanced out my window, but all I could see was a tan or gray sedan."

"Did you see the driver?" Danni interrupted.

"Not then. However, I heard the car start later, after *ER* was done, and I was getting ready to retire for the night. I merely caught a glimpse of the back of his head, but I could tell he had long, light-colored hair."

"How long?"

"To his shoulders."

Danni exchanged a glance with Nick. She hadn't heard about an evening visitor the night her dad died. It appeared it was news to Nick, too.

"Did you hear anything while he was there?" Nick asked.

Mrs. Countryman shook her head. "But then, I was watching my programs."

"Thank you for the information," Danni said.

The woman's eyes narrowed behind her round spectacles. "I have this feeling you're involved in something dangerous, Danielle Hawkins."

"We're only interested in learning the truth."

Mrs. Countryman eyed her a moment longer, then turned her schoolteacher glare on Nick. "I see you spent the night with Danielle again, young man. I do hope your intentions are honorable."

"I had a migraine last night," Danni interjected. "Nick was kind enough to stay with me."

Mrs. Countryman merely arched a pencil-thin eyebrow.

"Good-bye, Mrs. Countryman," Danni said, anxious to escape her reproving gaze.

Nick leaned forward and thumbed away the dirt smudge on the older woman's cheek. "Good-bye."

Mrs. Countryman blushed. "Good-bye."

Bemused, Danni walked to her truck and unlocked it. Nick hopped into the passenger seat. Without looking at him, Danni turned the key in the ignition and pulled out onto the street.

"I've never seen Mrs. Countryman blush before," Danni commented.

"She reminds me of my grandmother," Nick admitted. "On my mother's side. You never would have believed she and my mom were related."

"Why didn't you live with her instead of your parents?" Danni asked, intrigued by this slice of Nick's past.

Nick turned to gaze out the window, giving Danni a view of the back of his head. "Her favorite saying was, 'You make your bed, you have to lie in it.' I guess she figured I was my mother's problem, not hers."

Without thought, Danni reached across the seat and gave Nick's knee a gentle squeeze. "You didn't get a break, did you?"

Nick turned, glanced down at her hand, then met her eyes. "Your father was my break." He covered her hand with his. "I don't know what would've happened to me if he hadn't been there."

Danni's throat grew tight, but the usual bitterness didn't materialize. She gave her attention to driving but kept her hand on his knee, where it was comfortably enveloped in his warm grasp.

Chapter Eleven

When they arrived at the office, Nick reluctantly released Danni's hand so she could turn off the ignition and withdraw the key. She'd surprised him when she'd rested her palm on his knee as they'd left Paddy's house. However, the biggest shock was that she'd kept her hand there the entire drive.

He waited on the uneven sidewalk for her to join him, kicking at the weeds coming up through the cracks. He didn't approve of the neighborhood where Danni's office was located, but then it wasn't his place to judge. However, now he understood the occasional remark Paddy had thrown out about his daughter's pride and refusal to accept any help. Nick had always liked women with a mind of their own, but Danni took the concept light-years beyond any other person—male or female—he'd met.

Danni joined him, and he allowed her to precede him into the building.

"Good morning," Cathy said, her voice far too chipper. Nearly half of her face was hidden by a blond curtain, and the one eye he could see possessed a lecherous twinkle. "What's wrong? Didn't get much sleep last night?"

Nick rolled his eyes heavenward. The woman had a one-track mind.

"Migraine," Danni simply said.

Cathy's impish expression disappeared, replaced by genuine concern. She tucked the obscuring hair behind her ear. "Oh, honey, you should be at home resting."

"It was gone this morning, thanks to Nick." Her gaze slid across him, as if embarrassed to admit she'd relied on someone other than herself. She glanced around. "Where's the newspaper?"

"In the break room. I read about the shooting at the youth center." Cathy's eyes widened. "Don't tell me—"

"We were there," Nick confirmed, glancing at Danni's somber expression. "Fortunately, no one was hurt."

Danni corroborated his words with a nod. "We don't know if it's related to Dad or Matt Arbor's deaths, though." She headed down the short hallway that Nick assumed led to the break room.

Nick started to follow, but Cathy stood and latched onto his arm.

"You aren't taking advantage of her, are you?" she asked, her voice pitched low.

The question was preposterous; he couldn't even fathom Danni allowing anybody to use her. But then he noticed Cathy's thinned lips and narrowed eyes. The woman was serious—so serious that Nick wouldn't put it past her to use a dull knife on his sensitive parts if he gave her the wrong answer, even in jest. "No."

Cathy kept her laser gaze locked on him, and Nick didn't dare look away. He'd known army interrogators with less brass than this tiny receptionist. He'd underestimated her, at least when it came to protecting her friends.

The smile she suddenly leveled at him would've done a barracuda proud. "Good. I'd hate to have to kick such a fine-looking butt." She waggled her eyebrows. "Unless you're into that sort of thing."

One moment she acted like a guardian angel, and the next, a nymphomaniac.

Women! He'd never understand them. Even Danni, who was more straightforward than her flaky friend, had her Sybil moments.

Danni came out of the break room, reading the paper as she navigated down the hall. She was so intent on the article, she almost walked into Cathy's desk. Nick shot out his arm to stop her before she collided with the corner.

Danni glanced up, acknowledged his assistance with an absent head bob, then returned her attention to the paper. "It says here that the authorities believe it was gang-related, and they have little hope of determining who the actual shooter was."

Nick snatched the paper from Danni to scan the story himself. He swore under his breath. "If this had happened at some country club, the cops wouldn't be so fast to call it a lost cause."

"Welcome to the real world," Danni said, her lips curled in cynicism.

He shoved the paper under her nose. "You think this is right?"

Danni's temper flared. "No, but acting like it's a big surprise is naive. Don't tell me your Rangers never carried out a mission that was politically motivated rather than an actual threat against our national security."

Nick blanched at the memory of his last mission, when he'd lost his team members in the cause of "national security."

"Nick?"

Danni's voice startled him back from the oppressive humidity of the Central American jungle and the stench of death. It had been a long time since the suppressed memories had been disturbed. "What?"

"Are you ready to talk to Beth?"

He nodded quickly. Anything was better than dwelling on that chapter in his life.

"Just knock on her door and go in. She's expecting you," Cathy said.

Danni led Nick to a door opposite hers. He heard music

from the lawyer's office. By the sounds of it, the attorney was a Pavarotti fan. Danni knocked and opened the door, sticking her head in. "Do you have a few minutes?" She'd raised her voice to be heard above the operatic solo.

Pavarotti was cut off in mid-aria.

"Come in," a woman said.

Nick followed Danni into the office, which was almost twice as large as Danni's. It was also more elaborately decorated, with a mahogany desk and matching barrister bookcases. The woman sitting behind the elegant desk peered at him with dark eyes above a pair of narrow reading glasses, which were perched on her slightly flared nose. Her curly black hair was cut close to her scalp, giving her a no-nonsense appearance. This was a person who didn't tolerate bullshit from anyone. However, her smile that greeted them was warm and friendly.

The lawyer rose and extended her hand across her desk. "Beth Marshal. So I finally meet the mysterious Nick Sirocco."

Nick grinned as he shook her hand, not surprised by her firm grip. "Not so mysterious, I'm afraid."

Beth laughed. "Sit down."

By habit, Nick waited until the two women were seated before he lowered himself to the chair beside Danni's.

Beth leaned back in her leather chair and removed her reading glasses, allowing them to hang from a silver chain around her neck. "Have you learned anything new about Matt's death?"

Danni shook her head. "We talked to the two officers who were first on the scene. They said there was nothing to suggest anything but suicide."

Beth's lips thinned. "He didn't kill himself."

"How can you be so certain?"

"He wanted to make a deal. He would give up the names of those in charge in exchange for no hard time."

Leaning forward, Nick planted his elbows on his thighs and hung his clasped hands between his knees. "Those in charge?"

Beth nodded. "Yes. Those were his exact words. I asked him what he was involved in, but he clammed up. He said he wouldn't tell me anything more until I could guarantee him no prison time."

"Prison would have been hell for a kid like him," Nick said. "He wouldn't have lasted more than a month or two, unless he got himself a protector." Paddy had told him the prison facts of life years ago, when Nick had been poised on the edge. His graphic descriptions of what cons did to fresh meat had fueled young Rocky's nightmares for weeks. It'd also helped him decide which side of the law he wanted to be on.

"Did you know him?" Beth asked.

"From the youth center. I was doing some volunteer work there with Danni's father."

Beth laced her fingers together and rested her hands on the desk blotter. "Then you probably know more about him than I did. Who did he hang around with? Maybe some of those kids are also involved."

"In what?" Danni asked. "Some kind of theft ring?"

Beth threw up her hands. "I don't know. I'm just throwing out possibilities here."

Nick slumped back in his chair and rubbed his jaw thoughtfully. An organized crime ring operating out of the center sounded a lot like a plot idea he'd had for the book proposal he was putting together. Except Paddy had scoffed at its plausibility. With all of the off-duty cops who volunteered there, it would be impossible to hide something of that magnitude.

Unless an officer—or more than one—was involved.

"Did Matt talk about anyone in particular when he spoke with you?" Nick asked.

"Just Danni's father. He respected him." Beth's brow furrowed. "At first, Matt was adamant about not making a deal. It was only after Paddy Hawkins died that Matt changed his tune."

Nick's heartbeat kicked up a notch. "Why?"

The attorney lifted a shoulder and shook her head. "Your guess is as good as mine."

"He knew Dad was murdered," Danni said.

Nick turned to see dark savagery in her eyes. "You don't know that."

"Why else would Matt suddenly want to deal? And why else would someone then kill him before he could cut that deal?"

"All right. Let's operate under the assumption that both your father and Matt were murdered," Beth began in a logical, lawyerly voice. "Let's also assume Matt was working within an organized crime ring. Why would anyone murder two people over a stolen laptop?"

When Beth put everything together into such concise terms, Nick couldn't help but wonder if he was out in left field with his suspicions. Why *would* a small-time theft trigger a cavalcade of deadly events?

"Because it's not just small-time," Danni said with an air of certainty. "There's obviously more going on here than we're seeing." She stood, and Nick turned in his chair to watch her pace. "How was Matt caught?"

Beth pawed at some files on her desk and pulled one out. She lifted her reading glasses into place and scanned the file. "When he tried to pawn the laptop, the shop owner spotted the registration number on the hot sheet." She paused, meeting Danni's and Nick's gazes. "The computer was taken from the backseat of a stolen Jaguar."

"What?" Danni asked.

"The laptop computer Matt was caught fencing was from a stolen Jaguar," Beth reiterated.

Nick's spine tightened. "Did Matt steal the Jag?"

"He said he didn't."

"Was the car recovered?" Danni asked.

"As of the day before Matt died, no," Beth replied. "I don't know if it's been found since then."

"Why wasn't he charged with the theft of that, too?" Nick asked.

"No hard evidence."

"Matt being in possession of a laptop from a stolen car would be circumstantial, at best," Danni said, nodding somberly.

"Right," Beth said.

"For argument's sake, let's say Matt didn't commit grand theft auto. Did he lift the computer before or after the car was stolen?"

"That is your bailiwick, not mine," Beth said dryly.

"So Matt didn't tell you?"

"No. He admitted to trying to fence the stolen item, but that was all." Beth rested her elbows on the chair arms and steepled her fingers. "One thing I did notice. When he first came to see me, Matt was pretty cocky and certain he was only going to get his hand slapped by the courts. When I saw him after your father died, he was completely the opposite: anxious, frightened, almost to the point of paranoia. I tried to get him to tell me what was wrong, and that's when he offered to deal."

"He knew who killed Paddy," Nick said quietly.

"And that's why he was murdered, too," Danni added, equally as softly.

"It's all speculation," Beth argued. Then her expression fell. "And it's all we have."

Nick wanted to argue, but the lawyer was right. They needed something—something concrete—to support their claims.

"Marsel," Danni suddenly said.

Nick frowned. "What about him?"

"Who is he?" Beth asked, her question overlapping Nick's.

Danni blinked, as if surfacing from a trance. "He was one of Matt's friends. I think he knows what's going on, or at least he has a piece to the puzzle." Her features became more animated. "Last night, when we were all gathered in the corner of the gym, I talked to him."

Nick remembered seeing them together, and he'd wondered what she and Marsel were discussing.

"I asked him what Matt was into. He wouldn't answer,

and he wouldn't look me in the eye. I'll bet he knows where Matt found that laptop. He might even know who stole the Jag."

"Why didn't you tell me this last night?" Nick asked, irritation coloring his tone.

"We were a little busy," Danni snapped. Then she relented a bit. "Besides, migraines make it a bitch to think."

Nick couldn't argue. He'd seen how devastating the headache had been for her. "All right," he said grudgingly. "Maybe I can get him to open up."

"What about the other boy Matt's mother mentioned?"

"Gary. I'm surprised he wasn't at the center last night. He's usually hanging around in the evenings."

Danni met Nick's gaze. "Maybe he knew what was going down."

"Or he was a part of it," Nick said reluctantly. He didn't want to believe Gary was capable of that level of violence, but how well did he know the kid? He'd shot a few hoops with him, but he had no idea what Gary did when he wasn't at the center.

"Do you know where he lives?" Danni asked Nick.

"No, but he does have a girlfriend." He furrowed his brow as he tried to remember her name. "Annie, Angie. No." The name struck him then. "Angela, that's it. And she was there last night."

"Which means if he was involved in the shooting, he didn't give a damn that his girlfriend was inside the gym." Danni's lips drew into a thin line, and her eyes flashed.

Nick held up his hand. "Slow down, Danni. We don't know for sure Gary was involved. Or that he knew his girlfriend would be there."

She struggled with her temper and finally sent Nick a brief nod. "You're right. I shouldn't jump to conclusions."

Beth chuckled without humor. "Seems to me we've done a lot of that."

"Jumping to conclusions and hypothesizing aren't the same," Nick said with an edge of annoyance. "Danni and I should go back to the center and see if anyone knows where Gary or his girlfriend live."

He stood, and Danni followed suit.

"If you think of anything else, Beth, let us know," Danni said.

"I will. You two be careful," Beth cautioned. "If our theory is right, they've already killed two people. Two more won't matter."

Nick caught Danni's eye and knew what she was thinking. The killer or killers had already tried once—twice if the shooting was related—and failed. Which meant their theory had some credibility. It also meant they'd probably be trying again, and maybe next time Danni and Nick's luck would fail.

He followed Danni to the reception area and gave Cathy a nod as Danni said good-bye to her. Once outside, Nick climbed into the passenger seat of Danni's truck.

He couldn't banish his fear for Danni's safety. His conscience reminded him of those he'd been unable to protect. Fractured memories flared in his mind's eye, like a camera flashing pictures. He remembered the bloody bodies of his fellow Rangers sprawled around the helicopter's wreckage. It'd been a miracle he hadn't been killed.

He could almost smell the past—the sharp tang of rage and anguish—as he'd realized he was alone on foreign soil and his duty was to carry out his mission. It was part of The Ranger Creed: *"Readily will I display the intestinal fortitude required to fight on to the Ranger objective and complete the mission though I be the lone survivor."*

He'd lived by the creed for eight years. It had given him something to believe in, and he had done so, body and soul. Even now, he could recite the entire Ranger Creed. Even now, a part of him continued to believe in it. Even now, he believed he had dishonored it four years ago.

"Never shall I fail my comrades."

"Nick."

The silky voice and light touch on his arm snapped him out of his grim musings. He focused on Danni's oval face only inches from his. Her eyebrows were drawn in concern. "What?"

"What's wrong?" she asked, not shifting back to sit on her side of the bench seat.

He looked away to escape the worry in her deep blue eyes, so different from the detachment usually found there. He hadn't confided in anyone about those days spent alone in the jungle after his fellow Rangers' deaths—not the shrink he'd been ordered to visit after he was rescued and not Paddy. He wasn't about to spill his guts to Danni, yet it was her death he feared, the possibility he'd fail her, too.

He cupped Danni's cheek in his palm and brushed his thumb across her peach-velvet skin. Her eyes widened at the contact.

"I don't want to lose you, too, Danni," he said, his throat tight.

"Nothing's going to happen to me." She clasped his hand resting against her cheek and smiled. "Because if it does, it's *your* ass Dad's going to come back to kick."

Nick laughed, startling himself. He turned his head and kissed the center of her palm. "Let's go to the center."

Danni studied him a moment longer, and her gaze felt like a lover's caress. Nick's breath caught, and his gut clenched with something akin to lust but tempered with affection and respect. Before his control gave in to the impulse to kiss her breathless, Nick looked away, and Danni scooted over to her side of the bench seat.

As she drove to the center, Nick concentrated on the drab city scenery of concrete and gray buildings to forget the sucker punch to his heart. Even if he wanted to pursue a relationship with Danni, his timing sucked. He needed a clear mind to unravel the mystery surrounding Paddy's and Matt Arbor's deaths. And keep Danni alive.

"None of the kids will be around the center this early," she said.

"It's not them I want to talk to. It's the volunteers who might know where Gary or Angela live."

"It's a long shot." Danni sighed. "But I don't have a better idea."

She parked in the center's lot beside a silver Audi. "What kind of cop can afford an Audi?" she asked.

"It's Paul Gilsen's," Nick replied.

Danni wrinkled her nose. "Oh."

They walked across the asphalt to the door.

"You don't like him," Nick said.

She shrugged. "I thought he was a show-off when we were kids."

Nick laughed. "People change, Danni. Look at me."

Danni took him literally and surveyed him from head to toe. "Yes, they do."

Her enigmatic comment baffled him, but before he could ask what she meant, they entered the center. Nick led her to the office where a gray-haired woman sat at a dented and scratched metal desk.

She glanced up, and her wrinkled face lit with a smile. "Nicky."

"Hello, Marge," Nick said. "How's my favorite secretary?"

She shook a finger at him with mock severity. "It's administrative assistant nowadays, not secretary."

Danni smirked, and Nick spied the amusement in her eyes. Less than three days ago, Nick had received the same admonishment from her about Cathy's job designation.

Nick cleared his throat self-consciously. "Marge Hilyer, I'd like you to meet Danni." He intentionally omitted Danni's last name, uncertain if she wanted the center volunteers to know she was Paddy's daughter. "Danni, this is Marge, the center's administrative assistant." He enunciated her title carefully.

"It's nice to meet you," Danni said, shaking the older woman's hand. "Have you been working here long?"

"I used to be an executive secretary before I retired six years ago. A week after retiring, I was bored out of my skull." Marge's hazel eyes twinkled. "I found this place and volunteered my time and expertise and haven't regretted it for a moment."

"The place would fall apart without her," Nick said.

Pink blossomed on Marge's cheeks. "Nicky exaggerates terribly, but that's one of his finer qualities." She eyed Danni like she was examining a melon at the market. "Are you married?"

"No," Danni replied warily.

The older woman beamed. "Isn't that a coincidence? Neither is Nick."

He rolled his eyes. "Marge, I don't think—"

She ignored him and leaned conspiratorially toward Danni. "Did you know he's a famous writer? And he used to be an Army Ranger? I don't know about you, but I've always been turned on by a man in uniform."

Nick couldn't believe he was listening to a seventy-something woman talking about her sexual turn-ons.

Danni leaned close to Marge and peered at Nick with a devilish spark in her eyes. "Maybe if we ask him nice, he'll model it for us."

Nick raised his hands in a warding-off gesture. "Enough already."

Marge and Danni shared laughter, and Nick couldn't help but grin in spite of his embarrassment.

"Maybe we can talk about why we're here sometime this century," Nick said with a lift of his eyebrows.

"No need to be so grouchy," Marge said. She winked at Danni, then gave Nick her attention. "What is it you wanted, Nicky?"

"We're trying to track down a couple of kids named Gary and Angela." Nick described them.

Marge thought for a moment, then shook her head. "Sorry, they don't ring a bell. But then, I'm usually gone by the time most of them show up in the evenings." She pursed her lips. "Maybe Paul knows them. If they've used the computers, he'll have their names and addresses."

"Thanks, Marge. I saw his car in the parking lot."

"He's in the computer room. He dropped off donuts

when he came in an hour ago." She motioned to a box of Krispy Kremes behind her. "Help yourself."

After only oatmeal for breakfast, Nick didn't waste time opening the box and plucking out an original glazed donut. Danni opted for a cherry-filled one.

They left Marge's office and went down two doors to the computer lab. Paul was at a station, and he glanced up, startled to see them, then smiled a greeting. Dressed in khaki Dockers and a blue button-down shirt, Paul stood and joined them.

"Nick," Paul said, extending his hand. "What's going on?" Nick motioned to his sticky hand, and Paul laughed, dropping his arm to his side. "You must've stopped at the office first."

"We did. Thanks." Nick popped the last piece of the donut in his mouth.

Paul's curious gaze moved to Danni. "It's nice to see you again, Danni."

"Mr. Gilsen," Danni said with a tiny incline of her head.

"You used to call me Paul."

"We were kids then."

Nick frowned at Danni's hostility. Even if she thought Paul was a jerk as a kid, it was strange that she harbored such a strong dislike for him over the years.

"Yes, we were. Stupid kids who didn't know any better." Paul stared at Danni, as if his words imparted a deeper meaning—one Nick wasn't privy to.

Danni hugged her torso in an uncharacteristic self-protective gesture. "Maybe."

Nick didn't understand the undercurrents running between them, although he guessed it involved something that happened years ago. Despite his curiosity, he didn't press for an explanation. He would ask Danni later.

"We're trying to locate a boy and girl who hang out at the center," Nick said to Paul. "We were hoping they used the computers here." He described Gary and Angela. "Do you know them?"

"I have a couple of Garys that use the computers, but

neither matches your description," Paul answered. "And no Angela. Sorry."

Nick shrugged, hiding his disappointment. "It was a long shot. We'll just have to come by this evening and see if they're here."

"Why are you looking for them?"

"We just want to talk to them about Matt Arbor."

"The boy who killed himself?"

"That's right. Gary used to be a friend of his."

Paul shook his head. "Sad thing. I knew Matt. He was a good kid. He used to do reports for school on the computers here."

"Do you think he killed himself?" Nick asked bluntly.

"He didn't strike me as the type, but then it's hard to say. Remember Davey?"

The name brought a remembered image of a round-faced boy with acne and glasses into focus. He'd been the same age as him and Paul. "Yeah."

"Nobody thought he'd kill himself either," Paul said, shaking his head sympathetically. "Who knows what demons Matt was fighting?"

Nick slid his hands into his jacket pockets. "I suppose."

Paul glanced at his Rolex. "I have to get back. Good luck with your investigation."

"Thanks."

Paul ushered them out of the room and made sure the door was locked, then walked with them out to their respective vehicles. He lifted his hand in farewell as he sped out of the parking lot.

"He still drives like a kid," Danni muttered.

"What is it with you and him?" Nick demanded. "Every time you two are in the same room, the temperature falls about twenty degrees."

"He's an asshole."

Danni stuck the key in the ignition, and Nick grabbed her hand before she could turn it. "He's a successful businessman."

"A leopard can't change its spots."

"Cut with the clichés and tell me what's going on."

Danni let out a huff of air and sank back into her seat, crossing her arms. She stared out the windshield, but her eyes were unfocused. "One night after Dad had ordered me to stay away from the center, I snuck over here. Paul was in the gym playing basketball." Her lips twisted into a self-mocking scowl. "I was young and an idiot, and Paul was older and I thought smarter. He was also cute."

Nick blinked at the obviously juvenile description, surprised Danni had used it.

"He had a car, and I was stupid enough to go with him. Alone."

Nick's heart skipped a beat. Had Paul . . .

"He drove over to the park, and we started necking. Before I knew it, he wanted more." She scrubbed the back of her hand across her mouth, as if trying to remove a bad taste. "He didn't get it, but I ended up with some bruises and a lesson learned the hard way. I called Sam, and he came and got me." She paused and swept a hand across her eyes. "I never told Dad."

"Why?"

Impatience flared in her face as she locked gazes with him. "Because *I* would've been the one in trouble, not Paul. Dad had ordered me to stay away from the center, and I disobeyed him."

"You were almost raped," Nick nearly shouted in his frustration.

Danni cringed, then glared at him. "Why don't you yell a little louder? I don't think the people three blocks over heard you."

Nick snapped his mouth shut. When he spoke again, he kept his tone lower but no less intense. "Dammit, Danni. Paul Gilsen was the one at fault, not you. Paddy wouldn't have blamed you."

Danni clenched her jaw. "You only saw my father through rose-colored glasses, Nick. He wasn't perfect." Bitterness bled into her voice. "Believe me, I know."

Nick opened his mouth to argue but abruptly closed it.

He chose to stare out the side window as Danni started the truck. Was Danni right? Had he put Paddy on so high a pedestal that he could do no wrong?

Sometimes he wondered if he and Danni had known two separate people named Paddy Hawkins. It seemed the only thing those two Paddys had in common was that neither one would've killed himself.

Chapter Twelve

WITH no leads they could follow, Danni decided to take a drive around the run-down neighborhood surrounding the center. At one time, she'd known the area intimately: corners where drugs traded hands like hamburgers in a fast-food restaurant, alleys where hustlers—male and female—plied their damaged goods, and buildings where gangs dealt both tributes and retributions. Then there were the decent folks who couldn't afford to move but refused to give in to the hopelessness surrounding their homes.

"Where are we going?" Nick asked.

Accustomed to working alone, she replied curtly, "I used to patrol this area. Maybe I'll recognize someone."

Nick nodded. He seemed to sense her brooding mood and didn't press for details. Or try to draw her into a conversation.

Besides, they had nothing to talk about. They'd tacitly agreed to disagree about her father. They wouldn't be able to question Gary until the evening, and that was providing he was at the center. So for now, the case was at a standstill.

She cruised up and down garbage-strewn streets bordered by crumbling buildings and broken sidewalks overgrown with weeds. Knots of belligerent kids, dressed in gang colors, glared at them as they drove past. The teenagers should've been in school, but the dropout rate in this area was the highest in the city. A truant officer would be taking his life in his hands by coming into this neighborhood to enforce public school policy.

"I could've been one of those kids."

Nick's voice was so low Danni wondered if he knew he'd spoken aloud.

"Don't you have a college degree?" Danni asked, her gaze darting between Nick's profile and the street.

"I went to college under the ROTC program." He shrugged. "After graduation, I owed the army four years. I stayed in eight."

"When did you start writing?"

"I've kept a journal for years."

His sheepish smile seemed incongruous with his tough-guy background, both as a teenager on the streets and as a Ranger in the army. It gave him a boyish vulnerability that made Danni uncomfortable because it reminded her too much of her adolescent crush on him.

"When I got out of the army, I couldn't get anything besides night security. While I was on the job, I started reading the Longstreet books. One night I decided to try to write one. Two months later, I sent it in, and they bought it." He shrugged, almost apologetically. "That was the start of my illustrious writing career."

There was a self-deprecating note in his voice, like he was embarrassed, and Danni shot him a questioning look. "Do you enjoy writing them?"

"I used to." He bounced his fisted hand on his knee. "The novel Paddy was helping me with was my chance at writing something more."

Although Danni didn't know a thing about writing and publishing, she did understand the difference between a novel and an action-adventure series book. "What do you mean *was* your chance?"

"I don't think I can do it without your dad's insights. What he didn't know about being a cop wasn't worth knowing."

For a split second, Danni considered offering her expertise. But then Nick could have asked for her help, and hadn't. Obviously he didn't think her insights were anywhere near as valuable as her father's. "Why don't you ask some other officer? How about Sam Richmond?" she suggested, ignoring the dull ache of disappointment, of not being good enough again. "He's retired and would probably get a kick out of helping you."

"It wouldn't hurt to ask." Nick suddenly turned toward her. "What about you? You used to be a cop."

Startled, she wondered if she was that transparent. But even if she'd like to help, she couldn't live up to her father in Nick's eyes. "That's right. I *used to be* a cop."

"What happened?"

Danni put on her blinker and made a right at a corner surrounded by condemned buildings with boarded-up windows and deteriorating bricks. "My partner was killed. It was my fault." She managed to say it without her throat closing or her eyes tearing.

"I don't believe it."

Irritation rose hot and acrid. "You can find his grave at the Hillside Cemetery."

"That wasn't what I meant." Nick's voice was soft and far more understanding than she deserved. "If you really believed it was your fault, you wouldn't be carrying a gun and a PI card."

Everyone, including the review board, had told her the same thing. So maybe she wasn't at fault, but she *had* lost her nerve—the assurance needed to act when someone's life was on the line. Therefore, she'd resigned so there'd be no more Scotts dying because of her.

But here she was again, facing the same dilemma, with Nick's life on the line.

Her chest constricted, and for a moment she couldn't breathe. She didn't want this—the responsibility of another person's life. She'd already proven she couldn't handle it. What other proof did anyone need other than her partner's grave?

"Are you trying to strangle the steering wheel?" Nick asked gently.

Startled, Danni suddenly noticed the painful cramping in her fingers and her white knuckles. She consciously loosened her grip, flinching slightly when nerves tingled back to life. "Just being a careful driver."

She read the skepticism in his arched brow but ignored it.

She spotted a black man wearing layers of ragged clothing and pushing a cart filled with aluminum cans across a deserted lot. Stinging memories invoked by Southpaw's appearance caught her off guard. She swung over to the curb and parked with a short squeal of brakes.

Nick, his hands pressed against the dashboard, asked, "What're you doing?"

"Visiting an old friend."

He followed her line of sight to the raggedly dressed man who halted his cart on the sidewalk ten feet away. "Do you know him?"

"Yeah." She hopped out of the truck and closed the door behind her.

Curious, Nick cracked his window to eavesdrop.

"How's it going, Southpaw?" Danni asked the homeless man.

"Ain't goin' nowhere," Southpaw replied. "Ain't been the same without you or your daddy round to roust me."

"Yeah, I know." Danni stared over the man's shoulder. "Nothing's the same anymore."

The melancholy in her voice sent a wave of sympathy through Nick. Why couldn't she talk to him like she spoke to this near stranger? But maybe it would've been better if Nick were a stranger instead of a constant reminder of where she'd ranked in her father's life.

Southpaw picked up a Coke can, examined it, and

placed it back in his cart before capturing another one. "The Babe wouldn't quit the team."

Danni's shoulders stiffened, and she stepped closer to him, although Nick figured he had to be pretty rank wearing all those layers of clothing in the warm weather. Why would some crazy guy's ramblings interest her?

"What do you mean?" she asked.

"Your daddy weren't no quitter. Bottom of the ninth, no outs, bases loaded. Ain't no way he'd sacrifice."

"Then what happened?"

"New team come in." He picked up another can, hefted it in his left hand like it was a baseball. "Wild pitch." Southpaw wound up his arm and let the can fly. It clattered onto the sidewalk some twenty feet away.

Puzzled, Nick wondered what in the hell they were talking about. In a way, it reminded him of the coded messages he'd used on covert assignments, but this wasn't Bosnia or Iraq or one of a dozen other political hotbeds. And the old man sure as hell wasn't an operative.

"What new team?" Danni's words were mild, but from the expression on her face, she was struggling to contain her impatience.

"Other team been around longer. Ain't gonna let go of the pennant." Abruptly, Southpaw wrapped his gnarled hands around the cart's handle. "Gotta go. I'm late for batting practice."

Danni grabbed the cart. "Wait." She dug into her pocket and pulled out some dollar bills, then thrust them at the man. "Here. Buy yourself a Coke and a hot dog at the concession stand."

Southpaw grinned, revealing stained teeth and a gap in the bottom row where he'd lost two. "Maybe I'll get me some peanuts instead."

She patted his shoulder. "You get whatever you want, Southpaw."

"You always was a good girl, Danni." For a moment, the homeless man seemed lucid. Then, mumbling to himself, Southpaw lumbered down the street, stopping to pick up the can he'd thrown and continuing toward some place known only in his mind.

Danni shoved her hands in her jeans pockets and stood gazing after the man for a minute or two before returning to the truck cab. She settled in her seat without glancing at Nick.

"Who is he?" he asked quietly.

She kept her attention focused down the block, on the solitary figure. "Everyone calls him Southpaw. I saw him just about every time we patrolled this area. I used to give him some money now and again. Felt sorry for him."

"What was with the can throwing?"

Danni's attention turned inward, toward some memory Nick wasn't allowed access. "He used to be a pitcher for a minor league baseball team. Never made the big time, except in his mind."

"Drugs?"

She shook her head. "A bat alongside the head."

Nick inhaled sharply, and his gaze followed the pathetic man pushing his cart filled with imagined baseballs. "Where does he live?"

"Corner of Fifth and Dupont, in a cardboard box. He thinks he's at training camp." Danni took a deep breath. "We should get back to the house and let Gus out."

Nick sat back as Danni pulled into traffic, his mind on the strange conversation. "What were you talking about?"

Danni shoved her hair back from her brow. "He sees and hears everything on the street, but his mind processes it in baseball terminology. I think he knows something about Dad, but I couldn't figure out what he was trying to tell me."

"He seemed almost normal at the end."

"It comes and goes, but usually he lives in this ballpark in his head." Danni sighed. "The sad thing is, he had enough talent to make it to the big leagues. Dad took me to a game once. Southpaw was the starting pitcher. I was about seven or eight years old." She smiled self-consciously. "I wore my baseball glove, hoping I'd catch a ball."

Nick grinned, picturing young Danni in curly pigtails, a baseball cap, and her glove, waiting impatiently for a ball to come her way. "Did you catch one?"

"No. Dad bought me ice cream after the game to make up for it."

"So you do have some good memories of your father."

"I guess." She flexed her shoulders. "I wish I knew what Southpaw was trying to tell me."

"Maybe we should look him up tomorrow and see if you can get anything else from him," Nick suggested.

"We can try." Danni didn't sound very confident.

A black-and-white patrol car rounded a corner ahead of them. It slowed as Danni approached it, and Nick recognized Karen Crandle, Paddy's former partner, in the driver's seat. The two vehicles stopped, and Danni rolled down her window.

"What're you two doing here?" Karen asked, her bent arm resting on the open window. Her new partner, a man nearing fifty, leaned over to look at them.

"I used to patrol around here. I thought I might see someone I recognized," Danni replied.

Karen made a head motion behind her. "Someone like Southpaw?"

"Yeah."

"What did he have to say?"

"Something about wild pitches and a new team," Danni replied vaguely. "You know how he is."

"Scrambled eggs for brains," Karen's partner commented with a disgusted scowl on his fleshy face.

Danni tensed, and Nick, too, felt a measure of annoyance toward the cop. He laid his hand on Danni's arm, hoping she'd let the insensitive comment go. Her muscles relaxed, and Nick gave her forearm a squeeze.

"Has there been any word on the street about the shooting last night?" Danni asked.

"Lots of it, but nothing that'll help track down the shooter," Karen said. "You'd think everyone was deaf and blind in this neighborhood."

"That's the way it is here," Nick said.

"That's right. You're from the neighborhood. Do you still know people here?"

"No. Most of them are either dead, in prison, or got the hell out like I did."

Karen shaded her eyes against the midday sun. "I'll let you know if we hear something."

"Thanks. We appreciate it."

Karen lifted a hand in farewell and drove on.

Danni continued down the street, a faint scowl marring her face.

"Something wrong?" Nick asked.

"No," came the succinct reply.

Knowing Danni was again hiding something from him, he said casually, "Nice of Karen to keep us in the loop."

"Yeah. Nice."

"You don't like her?"

"Obviously not as well as you."

Nick recoiled at her caustic tone. "Are you jealous that I know your father's partner better than you do?"

Her glance slanted across him. "Should I be?"

Aggravation took the place of bewilderment. "Spit it out, Danni. I can't read your mind."

Fury flared in Danni's eyes. "Are you sleeping with her?"

Danni's question caught him unaware. His mouth opened, but he wasn't sure how to respond to the unexpected accusation.

"Look, I don't care, and it wouldn't be any of my business, except that if you are, you sure as hell had no right crawling into my bed the other night," Danni said, her voice as tight as her fingers squeezing the steering wheel.

Danni's insinuation that he slipped into her bed and seduced her brought his own temper to its boiling point. "You're right. If I was sleeping with her, it's none of your damned business. Besides, I wasn't the one looking for sex that night. As I recall, you were the one doing the asking."

Danni's jaw muscle jumped. Good! He'd managed to

piss her off as much as she'd pissed him off. What the hell kind of man did she think he was? The kind who couldn't keep it tucked in when he was in the company of a beautiful woman? There was no doubt that both were beautiful. So why had he chosen the infuriating Danni to break his months-long celibacy?

Maybe I'm just a masochist, he thought, because it *was* Danni he wanted, not Karen or any other woman.

Nick sank back in his seat, crossed his arms, and stared out the windshield. He should apologize to Danni, tell her that he and Karen had never dated, much less slept together. But some stubborn—and self-righteous—part of him wouldn't let him speak the words.

Did Danni think that little of him, to believe he screwed women indiscriminately?

He closed his eyes. No other female could provoke him as quickly and as completely as Danni Hawkins. Yet he still felt attraction humming between them, the same fascination he'd felt years ago for the fourteen-year-old daughter of his surrogate father, when she'd been strictly off limits.

The truck slowed and stopped. Nick opened his eyes to find Danni already out of the cab and striding toward Paddy's neat white frame house. He gnashed his teeth and followed in her blustery wake.

She unlocked the door, and Gus charged out, nearly bowling her over as the dog leaped up to greet her. Danni's stormy expression faded under the onslaught of affection, and Nick paused on the sidewalk to simply observe her.

She was a woman of contradictions: tough-skinned but softhearted, standoffish but passionate, brash but guarded. He suspected she rarely let anyone see the entire package—the real Danni Hawkins. However, Nick was becoming obsessed with learning everything about Paddy's daughter, thorns and all.

Gus trotted over to Nick and jumped up to place her front paws on his waist. He petted the golden dog and scratched behind her ears, feeling some of his irritation with Danni bleed away.

Nick gave Gus a few minutes to take care of her business, then called the dog to the porch. Danni had left the front door open, and he entered with Gus crowding against his legs to go through the doorway at the same time.

He locked the door behind him and stood in the entrance, listening for Danni. He followed muffled sounds to the kitchen, where she was pulling out the makings for sandwiches from the refrigerator. Without saying a word, Nick arranged ham and cheese slices on a plate. He set it on the table, along with the loaf of bread and condiments.

"What do you want to drink?" Danni's tone was neutral, and she didn't look at him.

"Water's fine."

She retrieved two bottles of water from the refrigerator and placed one at each of the place settings. They ate their sandwiches in silence, sharing some of the ham with Gus.

"What's the plan for the afternoon?" Nick asked after the table was cleared.

Danni shrugged. "Do whatever you want. I'm going to wash clothes."

"Would you mind washing some of mine with yours?"

Her glare gave him her answer.

Hoping he'd get a rise out of her, Nick smiled at her thorny expression. "I take it that's a no?"

She planted her hands on her hips. "How about *hell* no? Do I look like a cleaning lady?"

"From the shape of your apartment, definitely not." He was playing with fire, and enjoying it too much.

"You're treading on thin ice, Sirocco."

"I always did like a challenge." He winked, which made her cheeks redden.

She stomped out of the kitchen without replying.

Nick would've laughed, but hc preferred his body without any broken bones.

• • •

DANNI dumped her last load of clothes from the dryer into a basket. She glanced at the washer, which held some of Nick's clothing. He'd put them in after asking politely if it was all right to use the machine. Her conscience tugged at her sense of fair play. She could have tossed some of his laundry in with hers, but her injured pride had stopped her. It wouldn't hurt to transfer his clothes to the dryer now that she was done. After doing so, she carried her basket into the living room to fold her clean clothes.

Nick and Gus were sitting on the floor watching some old black-and-white comedy on the TV. Nick glanced up at her. "Are you done with the dryer?"

"I already put your clothes in it," she said defensively. She didn't want him to think she wasn't still angry with him.

"Thank you." His quiet voice and direct gaze were sincere.

"You're welcome," she mumbled, then picked out a pair of trousers to fold from the basket at her feet.

Although she kept her gaze averted, she could feel Nick's scrutiny. Maybe she was being churlish, and maybe his sex life wasn't any of her business, but when he hadn't denied sleeping with Karen Crandle, she'd been hurt. Which was almost laughable, because she never let herself to be hurt by a man. Have some fun, then walk away.

"I should take Gus out. She's been penned in all day," Nick said.

She wanted to tell him to go ahead, leave so she could be alone, without his distracting presence. But there was still someone out there trying to kill him, and she'd be damned if she allowed another partner to be killed. "Give me a few minutes to finish up, and I'll go with you."

Nick shot her a startled glance. "You don't have to."

"There's someone out to get you."

"We don't know that for sure."

"You're not going alone."

"I won't be alone. I'll have Gus."

"Can Gus shoot a gun?"

"I haven't taken her to the range lately. . . ." Nick was obviously struggling to suppress a grin, but his eyes twinkled.

Danni found her own lips curving upward. "Yeah, well, that probably means she isn't weapons qualified, so I'd better go with you."

Nick stared at her a moment, then acceded with a shrug. "Sure, the more the merrier."

Danni quickly finished her task and grabbed her jacket to toss over her shoulder holster, which she hadn't removed since she'd donned it that morning.

Nick snapped a red leash to Gus's collar, and they left the house. Danni tucked her hands in her pockets and tugged the jacket snug against her torso. She walked beside Nick with Gus trotting happily ahead of them.

"How long will we have to do this?" Nick asked.

"Walk Gus?"

He shot her a half-annoyed, half-amused look. "Stick so close together."

Disappointment made her frown before she could control her reaction. "Until we figure this thing out."

"And if we never figure it out?"

"We will," Danni said firmly, hoping to convince herself as well as him.

"But if we don't—"

"We will." She calmed her frazzled nerves. "We have to, for Dad's sake."

"And yours?"

His quiet question gave her pause. "Yes. Mine, too," she replied almost in a whisper.

She expected him to repeat what Alex Levin had told her, that she couldn't gain her dead father's respect, but Nick didn't. Instead, he said with a strained voice, "For my sake, too."

Damn, he was always throwing her off balance, alternately pissing her off and forcing her to empathize with him. She wanted to stay angry with him but felt the emotion drain away. Sometimes he and she were so much alike it frightened her. Other times, it was as if they were from two diverse universes.

She sensed he had something more on his mind but didn't know if she had the right to pursue it. Especially since she'd already treaded on forbidden ground by asking him about Karen Crandle.

"Would he still be dead if I'd gotten his phone call the night he died?" Nick finally voiced in a husky tone. "He never let me down in all the years I'd known him, and the one time he called me for help, I let him down."

Danni didn't know how to respond. She was torn between being hurt that Dad had called him rather than her, and wanting to console Nick, tell him that Dad's death wasn't his fault any more than it was hers.

She ended up moving closer to him, so her elbow brushed his as they walked.

The Smith & Wesson tucked into her shoulder holster was a comforting weight against her side. Although hypersensitive to Nick's closeness, Danni remained alert for slow-moving cars and out-of-place strangers. Maybe there was too much cop in her to let down her defenses, or maybe she simply cared too much for Nick. Either reason was enough to keep her vigilant.

Gus trotted along ahead of them, occasionally stopping to water a yard. The neighborhood had grown quiet as children were called in for dinner. They were a block from her father's house when Gus decided to do her job on a sculpted green lawn.

"I hope you have a bag to pick that up," Danni said.

"I don't. Do you?"

She groaned and tugged at his arm. "Then don't let her do it here."

Nick remained immovable. "When you gotta go, you gotta go."

She leaned close to his ear, so close she felt the tickle of his soft hair against her forehead. "This is Mr. Grewen's place. He always wins awards for his lawn."

He grinned unrepentantly. "Consider Gus's contribution as fertilizer."

"That's not funny." But Danni had a hard time keeping a straight face. "As soon as she's done, we have to make a run for it."

"You're not serious, are you?"

Grewen's front door opened, and a tiny man with white hair and black horn-rimmed glasses stepped onto the porch. "Who's out there? What're you doing to my grass? Is that a dog? You get that dog off my lawn! I'm going to call the police and have you arrested!"

Danni grasped Nick's wrist. "C'mon."

Fortunately, Gus was finished, and Nick fell into a loping run beside Danni. Gus raced ahead of them, her tongue lolling. If Danni didn't know better, she would've sworn Gus was laughing at Mr. Grewen.

Nick turned into her father's driveway, but Danni grabbed his sleeve. "This way. If he sees us go in here, he'll send the cops."

With only a slight veer, Nick kept pace with Danni as they dashed past the house. Danni felt like she was eight years old again, running away from mean Mr. Grewen after she cut through a corner of his yard.

She glanced at her companion, who hollered, "How far do we have to go?"

"Just around the next corner."

Danni plunged ahead and skidded around the next block, but didn't stop until a huge brick house hid them from Grewen's view. She leaned over, placing her palms on her knees, and gasped for air in between laughter. Beside her, Nick panted and Gus pranced around them as if wondering why they'd ended the fun so soon.

"Would he really call the police?" Nick asked after regaining his breath.

"He's done it before." She read the disbelief in his features. "I was eight years old. He wanted me hauled in for trespassing because I cut through his yard. Dad convinced him not to press charges." She remembered her father's exasperation with Grewen and his defense of her. It was a memory she'd forgotten until now.

"A hardened criminal by eight, huh?" Nick teased.

"Didn't know you were spending time with an ex-con, did you?" she bantered back.

"Prettiest ex-con I've ever seen." Nick swept a wayward curl behind Danni's ear, his hand lingering and following the curve of her neck.

Desire jolted through her veins, and she knew she should step back, but his half-lidded, smoldering eyes trapped her. They drew her nearer until she could smell his body's muskiness, made more potent by their unscheduled sprint. His minty breath feathered across her lips, and she knew with absolute certainty he was going to kiss her.

Chapter Thirteen

As Nick drew Danni closer, he decided to hell with the fact that they were standing on a sidewalk in the middle of a family neighborhood. His palms followed the curve of her waist and glided down to her hips, then he leaned in to capture her lips.

Suddenly, Danni jerked out of his embrace and stared up at him, her cheeks flushed and her eyes snapping. "You bastard," she said through clenched teeth.

Reeling from her abrupt withdrawal, he growled, "What the hell?"

She whirled around and stomped away into the growing dusk. Shaking his head in frustration, Nick trailed after her with Gus straining at the leash. He breathed deeply, and as the cool air circulated through his hot blood, his mind cleared.

Why had she run off like some high school virgin?

The answer wasn't long in coming. Earlier, he hadn't denied her claim that he was sleeping with Karen Crandle, so in Danni's eyes he was merely living up—or down—to her opinion of his moral standards.

Shit.

"Danni!"

She didn't slow her pace and was already nearly a block away.

"Dammit." He started jogging, and Gus, on her leash, loped alongside him.

He glanced up as a dark sedan neared, and his muscles tensed. It passed him slowly, and he let out a gust of air he hadn't realized he'd been holding. After last night's shooting at the center, it was difficult to stop looking at every person, every vehicle as potential danger.

An explosive shot suddenly ripped through the quiet evening, and Nick instinctively dived into a thick hedgerow next to the sidewalk. Thorns raked his face and clothing, and he heard Gus's surprised yelp at being hauled into the brambly bushes with him. Once in the middle of the thick brush, he wrapped his arms around the squirming dog and bent over her, hoping to calm and protect her.

But there was no more shooting. Eerie silence blanketed them for an interminable minute.

"Nick! Nick, where are you?"

Danni's frantic voice and the sound of her searching among the thick bushes made him uncurl from his hunched position. He released Gus, who whined and nosed her way out of the shrubbery.

Following his dog, Nick struggled through the heavy growth, biting back his aggravation with the sharp thorns. He lowered his head and was able to protect his exposed skin but couldn't see a damned thing.

Fingers closed around his arm. "Come on," Danni said, her voice close.

He allowed her to assist him out of the underbrush and stood shakily.

"Are you all right?" Danni asked anxiously, peering up into his face.

"Yeah. The shooter missed." He wiped at a tickly feeling along his cheek, and his hand came away smeared with blood. "But the thorns didn't. Did you get the license plate?"

Danni shifted her weight from one foot to the other, clearly uncomfortable. "Nobody was shooting at you."

Nick stared at her. Only a deaf person wouldn't have heard the attack. "You didn't hear it?"

"It was a car backfiring."

He replayed the sound of the "shot" again in his mind. He'd heard enough weapons' fire to realize Danni was right. His face heated with embarrassment. "Christ, I can't believe I thought that was a gunshot." He must be more on edge than he realized.

A light came on, and the owner of the hedgerow stepped onto his porch. "What's going on out there?"

"Just walking our dog," Danni hollered back. She grabbed Nick's arm. "Let's get back to Dad's place."

As soon as they were back in Paddy's house, Danni went upstairs and returned with the first aid kit. The way things were going, they'd need a new one soon.

"You've got quite a collection of scratches," Danni said. "Sit."

Mute, Nick eased onto the kitchen chair she'd pulled away from the table. With firm, steady fingers, she raised his chin to examine his face. She washed the shallow cuts first with water, then peroxide.

Nick caught a glimpse of guilt in her eyes and frowned. He captured her hand and asked gently, "What's going on, Danni? You said yourself it was only a car backfiring."

Her gaze flickered to him, then slid away. "What if it wasn't? What if it *had* been a gunshot?"

"It wasn't."

Her expression flared with impatience. "Dammit, Nick. If that had been a shooter, you'd be dead!"

Nick had no idea why she was dwelling on what-ifs. "A car backfired, and I overreacted. End of story."

She jerked her wrist out of his hold and tossed the gauze she'd used to clean his abrasions in the wastebasket under the sink. Leaning against the counter, she crossed her arms and studied the floor like it hid the mysteries of the universe. Nick, however, noticed her hands trembling.

Concerned, he rose and moved to stand in front of her. She continued to stare downward. He brushed a dark curl behind her ear and allowed his fingers to linger in her silky hair. "What's really bothering you, Danni?" he asked tenderly.

The wall clock ticked off countless seconds as Nick waited for her reply. He sensed she was fighting inner demons, but there was nothing he could do unless she let him in.

Finally, she raised her head, and moisture glimmered in her eyes. However, her voice was filled with self-directed anger. "If that had been a real hit, you'd be dead because I was acting like a jealous teenager instead of doing my job." A tear spilled down one cheek, and she blinked, preventing any more. "I'm sorry." Her voice broke.

Her apology settled someplace in Nick's chest, making it hard to breathe. "I'm sorry, too." He licked his dry lips and fanned his fingers across her damp cheek. "There's no reason for you to be jealous, Danni. I have never slept with, nor do I plan to sleep with Karen Crandle. In fact, you're the first woman I've been with for close to a year."

Danni's eyes widened. "You're kidding."

He smiled self-consciously but didn't regret his confession. He raised his right hand. "Scout's honor. Working at home, I don't get a lot of opportunity to meet women."

"But you volunteer at the center."

He chuckled. "If you haven't noticed, the only women there are either young enough to be my daughter or old enough to be my mother. And neither appeals to me."

"But Karen—"

"Isn't you," Nick finished softly.

A pink flush flooded Danni's cheeks, but she raised her hand and traced the curve of his jaw. "So, there's no significant other in your life right now?"

He shivered at the feather-light caress of her fingertips. "I wouldn't say that."

The dark blue irises were almost eclipsed by her pupils. "I'm not looking for anything serious."

Her breathy tone shot straight to Nick's gut. He shifted closer, so only a hairsbreadth separated them. "Neither am I."

Danni wrapped her arms loosely around his neck. "So what do two unattached people who are attracted to one another do if neither wants a relationship?"

Her warm breath spiked his nerve endings, and her sinfully seductive voice sent pleasurable signals scampering to his groin. He brushed her nose with his. "Play canasta?"

"I prefer gin."

"Strip poker?"

Her smile was anything but angelic. "Why don't we forget the poker part and just strip?"

Nick definitely liked that suggestion as his erection surged against denim. He nudged his hips against her, letting her feel him. "My kind of woman."

She leaned back and kept her hungry gaze locked on his as she unbuttoned his first button, then the second and third. Holding his shirt open, she kissed the center of his chest.

Nick groaned and cupped her soft backside in his palms and tugged her body against him. She raised her head and licked her lips, like a cat that had discovered a whole pint of spilled cream. Slipping her arms around his waist beneath the now fully opened shirt, she continued her exploration of his pectorals using her lips and tongue.

Bolts of pleasure seared him. There was nothing tentative about Danni's actions. Her kisses were like her: brash, bold, and passionate.

As hot as her caresses were, Nick wanted more. He wanted to touch *her*—skin against skin. He leaned close to her ear, yielded to the temptation to give it a tender nip before whispering, "Upstairs."

Danni shivered, and he felt her nod.

They tiptoed past Gus, who was sound asleep on the living room floor, and ascended the stairs. At the top of the staircase Nick paused, uncertain which bedroom to use.

Danni tugged him down the hall to her room, where

they'd made love the first time. She released him and stepped back, removing her shoulder holster and placing it on the nightstand. She pulled her shirttails out of her jeans and reached for the hem.

Nick's hands settled on hers. "Let me."

She gave him a short nod and raised her arms. Prolonging the sensual torment, Nick eased the shirt over Danni's head slowly, revealing a black lace bra with alluring glimpses of skin beneath it. He tossed the shirt aside.

Danni and Nick's gazes locked as he palmed her lace-covered breasts and rolled her nipples between his thumb and forefinger. She reached back and unsnapped her bra. As she slipped the straps down her arms, Nick released her and removed the undergarment, baring her breasts.

His breath caught in his throat, and he leaned forward to capture an already taut nipple in his mouth. Danni moaned, and her head fell back, giving him full access to her breasts. As he worshiped her with his lips, she stroked his bare torso, alternating between a barely there touch and an erotic play of fingernails.

Nick unsnapped and unzipped her jeans, then shoved them down her long legs. Danni kicked them off impatiently. His lusty gaze drank in the sight of her wearing only a pair of lacy underwear; they looked infinitely better on Danni than on her apartment floor.

"Someone still has too many clothes on." Danni's eyes sparkled with a mixture of desire and mischief.

"*Someone* should probably take care of that."

Almost before Nick had gotten the words out, Danni was upon him, and a minute later, he stood naked in the middle of her bedroom.

She eyed him and licked her lips. "Much better."

"Not quite." He hooked his fingers in the waistband of her panties and spent a moment caressing her smooth belly beneath the black lace. Sliding lower, he felt her damp heat, her readiness for him.

Danni's eyes widened, and her breath quickened. "You

damned well better get down to business soon, Sirocco." Her voice was husky with need, and her legs trembled.

He laughed, but he, too, was reaching the end of his patience. He skimmed down her underwear and knelt before her as she lifted one foot, then the other. The underwear joined her other clothing already scattered across the floor.

Her muskiness filled his senses, and he grasped her hips, bringing her forward to taste her.

"Nick!" Danni cried out at the first touch of his tongue.

Smiling, he continued to pleasure her. Her hands kneaded his shoulders, and her little mewls of passion brought Nick dangerously close to the edge. Danni's legs trembled, and he barely managed to rise and guide her to the bed.

He grabbed the foil pack from his wallet. Yesterday he'd felt like a kid hoping to get lucky when he'd bought the condom from a rest room vending machine. Now he wished he'd bought more than one.

He knelt between her long legs and braced his hands on either side of her head. Her dark, curly hair fanned across the pillow, framing her flushed face. Leaning down, he buried his nose between her neck and shoulder. She smelled of shower soap with a faint tinge of sweat—all woman and all Danni.

She ran her hands down his chest and belly, then grasped his hardness. Nick jerked his head up and thrust into her soft yet firm grip. He was close. Too damned close.

He seized her skillful hand, his body poised on the edge and his breathing harsh. "Easy, Hawkins."

She laughed, but the sound was thready. "Too much woman for you, Sirocco?"

He couldn't help but chuckle. Danni was pushy both in bed and out. "Damned straight."

Their heated gazes met, and the air crackled between them.

"I want you now, Nick," she whispered.

She wrapped her shapely legs around his waist and

urged him downward with a strength that didn't surprise him. He forced himself to stay motionless and grinned down at her. "Impatient?"

The impact of her glare was diminished by her kiss-swollen lips. "Horny."

He laughed, but understood too well. Lowering his body, he kissed her and eased into her tightness. Sensations washed over him and threatened to overcome his control before he was completely sheathed.

He tried to remain still, but Danni didn't cooperate. She thrust her hips upward, taking his full length into her. Thought spiraled away, and Nick matched Danni's driving rhythm as she lunged up to meet him. Their bodies glided together, and the wave of pleasure crested higher and higher.

Suddenly Danni screamed, and her body tightened around him, drawing his orgasm from him with powerful pulses.

As the aftershocks faded, Nick eased out of her and disposed of the condom. He lay down beside her, their heads touching on the pillow.

The first time they'd made love, it had been an act of desperation prompted by a nightmare, and immediately afterward they'd fallen asleep. This time, Nick took pleasure in the afterglow of their lovemaking and the intimacy of merely lying close, their bodies cooling.

Danni could be exasperating as hell at times, but in bed she became a fiery lover who gave as well as received with equal amounts of passion. Just thinking about the teasing, sexy twinkle in her eyes sent renewed desire arrowing through him.

He turned his head toward her. "Still horny?"

She snorted. "Fishing for compliments, Sirocco?"

He stifled a grin. "No need to strain yourself, Hawkins."

Danni laughed, which made her breasts jiggle enticingly. "All right. You were good. Very good. Satisfied?"

Nick rolled onto his side and propped his head on his hand to look down at Danni. Her cheeks remained flushed, and she didn't appear embarrassed by her nudity. Even as he slid his gaze across her pale skin, she didn't try to cover herself. "Oh, yeah. Definitely satisfied."

"I'll take that as a compliment." She smiled smugly.

Nick wasn't accustomed to his lovers being so assertive. Or to bantering during lovemaking. Yet it fit Danni, and he was finding it fit him, too.

His stomach growled, eliciting more laughter from Danni.

"Men." She shook her head in mock exasperation. "Sex, then food."

Nick feigned offense. "Hey, us growing boys need to eat."

Devilish mischief danced in Danni's expression, and she reached down to fondle him. "Growing?"

He groaned, but felt lust creep into his blood once more. If only he'd bought another condom . . .

Releasing him with a gentle squeeze, Danni raised her head and gave him a quick kiss. "We should eat something before we go to the center."

Although Nick would've preferred to stay right where he was with Danni right where she was, his sense of responsibility wouldn't allow him the luxury. He nodded but remained lying on the bed to watch Danni's reverse striptease. And found himself growing hard as her delicious curves disappeared under denim and knit.

"Time for a cold shower, Rocky." Danni smirked and tossed his shirt over his face.

By the time Nick lifted it off, Danni was gone. Shaking his head and grinning, he pushed himself upright and tugged on his clothes. With a grimace, he carefully zipped up his pants and joined Danni.

When he entered the kitchen, she was leaning into the refrigerator, giving him an eyeful of her sexy ass. His arousal, which had waned, returned with a vengeance.

"What're you hungry for?" Danni asked, gazing at him over her shoulder.

Unable to resist, Nick stepped close and cupped her tempting anatomy. "What did you have in mind?"

Danni straightened and turned around. She backhanded his chest lightly. "Obviously not what you do."

"Hey, have pity on the celibate man."

"I don't think so, buddy, since your period of celibacy is a thing of the past." She grinned. "Dinner. Food. Get your mind back on track, Sirocco."

Although Nick would've liked to leave his mind—and body—on a more enjoyable track, he couldn't help but chuckle. "All right. How about pasta?"

"You volunteering to cook?"

"You want to risk food poisoning?"

Danni groaned. "Pasta it is, as long as we have a bottle of sauce to heat up."

Working together with surprising ease, Nick and Danni put together a salad, spaghetti, and garlic bread. Nothing boiled over, burned, or spilled, so they deemed it a success.

Nick pushed his empty plate back. "I should've gotten some wine to go with it."

Danni wiped her mouth with a napkin. "Neither one of us goes anywhere alone."

Although Nick grumbled, he knew Danni had a point.

"When's the best time to go to the center?" she asked.

Nick glanced at his watch: 7:40. "The kids start to show up around eight, so we can leave as soon as we're ready."

While Danni took care of the dirty dishes, Nick let Gus outside. Fifteen minutes later, Nick was driving to the center, having left Gus snoozing happily in the living room.

"How do you want to do this?" Danni asked.

"We find Gary. We ask him some questions. Take it from there."

"What about Marsel?"

Nick glanced at her, forcing himself to ignore the lingering trace of their lovemaking in her slightly swollen lips. "You really think he knows more than he told us?"

"My gut says yes."

He grinned. "Who am I to argue with your gut?"

Her face relaxed into a quirked smile that faded as she darted glances in her side mirror. "Take a right here," she suddenly said.

Forty-eight hours ago he would've *not* made the turn, just to piss her off. Now, however, he obeyed her command without question. As he jerked the steering wheel around, the centrifugal force pressed Danni toward him. She pulled herself back into place, and her gaze flew to the mirror.

"Still there," she said tersely. "You know how to lose a tail?"

Nick shot a sharp look at the rearview mirror. All he could see were headlights. "How can you tell it's a tail?"

"It is."

He sucked in a deep breath. "Hang on."

Coming to another intersection, he yanked the wheel into a left turn and stepped on the gas. His Jeep shot forward. He touched his brakes and made a skidding right onto a more heavily trafficked street. Weaving in and out of the vehicles, he spared a glance at Danni, who had one hand locked around the door's handhold and her other braced on the dash. Her attention, however, was focused on the mirror. "Still there?"

She nodded grimly. "Yes."

"Can you see what kind of car it is?"

"All I can make out is a light-colored sedan." Danni paused. "Mrs. Countryman said a gray or tan car was at Dad's the night he died."

Nick swore under his breath and executed another left turn, then a quick right. He accelerated for three blocks, then turned left, with another fast right. "Did we lose them?"

Danni peered in the mirror for a full minute before replying. "I think so."

Nick wheeled his SUV into another right turn. "Just to be on the safe side."

She leaned back in her seat. "Damn it. I wish we

could've turned the tables. We might've been able to see who it was."

Nick divided his attention between the street and Danni. "How many were in the car?"

"Only the driver."

Nick hated the helplessness that chewed at his insides. Why were they being targeted? What did they think he and Danni knew?

"You know what this means?" Danni asked quietly.

"What?"

"I spotted the tail not long after we left Dad's house. Whoever it is, they know where we're staying."

Chapter Fourteen

DANNI could count on one hand the people who knew she and Nick were staying at Dad's place: Sam Richmond, Beth Marshal, Cathy Miller, and Mrs. Countryman. Cathy might be flighty, but she was a loyal friend. Beth had been the one to ask Danni to look into Matt Arbor's death, so it was doubtful she was working against them. And Danni suspected that the retired schoolteacher had never so much as jaywalked in her life, much less attempted murder.

What about Sam? No, he couldn't be involved. He and Dad had been friends for years, and he was like a second father to her. She recalled how rough this past year had been on Sam. Just after he retired from the force, his wife Nancy had been diagnosed with a debilitating disease that would eventually leave her bedridden for the rest of her life. Now, while Nancy was still able to get around, they were doing many of the things they'd put off: road trips with a new motor home and fishing with a fancy boat Sam had recently bought.

All those things took money. A lot of money.

"Danni?" Nick asked, obviously sensing her troubled thoughts.

She took a shaky breath. "I was just thinking about the people who know we're staying at Dad's: Beth, Cathy, Sam Richmond, and Mrs. Countryman."

Nick nodded somberly. "One of them might be involved."

Danni cast a glance at the side mirror and was satisfied that their tail hadn't found them again. "But I can't imagine any of them murdering Dad."

"Can't or won't?"

Part of her hated that he made her doubt her judgment, while her pragmatic side knew those would be the same questions she'd be asking if their positions were reversed. "I've known Cathy for two years, ever since she started working for Beth and me. She had excellent references, and I've never had any reason to mistrust her."

Nick digested her words. "And Sam?"

She gnawed at her thumbnail, wondering if she should confide her suspicions. In a way, it felt like a betrayal, yet she couldn't shake her misgivings surrounding his recent purchases. "I've known him since I was a kid. He was always there for me."

Unlike Dad, who was always there for you.

She tried to stem the rising resentment the thought evoked, but the feeling was so ingrained it was hard to ignore.

Nick swung into the youth center's lot and parked. He turned off the vehicle and shifted in his seat to face Danni. "You're not telling me everything."

She didn't want to confess her worry that Sam wasn't as perfect as she'd always believed. However, she knew he wouldn't let this go, so reluctantly she told him. "You know Sam retired last year?"

Nick nodded. "That's when Karen Crandle was assigned as Paddy's partner."

"That's right. Did you know that Sam's wife has a degenerative disease that will eventually make her an invalid?"

Nick's face softened with sympathy. "No."

"They have maybe a year, eighteen months at the most before that happens." Danni paused and tried to convince herself she wasn't betraying her old friend. "Over the past year, he's bought a new motor home and a fishing boat, plus they've taken quite a few trips."

Danni could tell by Nick's expression that it took only a second or two for the implications to sink in.

"Where did he get the money?" he asked in a tone that didn't expect a reply.

Danni felt compelled to defend her surrogate father. "He was a good cop, Nick. He put in thirty-five years, and there was never a black mark against him."

"Nobody's saying he wasn't a good cop. But maybe circumstances forced him to do something he never would've done otherwise."

Miserable and sick that she was even considering Sam a suspect, Danni tipped her head back and scrubbed her face. "Damn it. He wasn't involved in Dad's death. They were best friends."

Nick rubbed her upper arm soothingly. "There's another possible explanation. Maybe somebody followed us from the center or your office."

Danni blinked and wondered why she hadn't thought of that. "That seems more likely."

"It doesn't rule Sam out."

As much as Danni wanted to disagree, she knew he was right. "No, but it does open more options." She took a deep, shuddering breath. "We should go in."

Nick studied her, his concerned gaze feeling like a warm caress. "Are you all right?"

She managed a crooked smile. "I will be."

He brushed her cheek with his fingertips. "You aren't alone, Danni."

Her throat tightened, and tears burned her eyes. All she could do was nod her gratitude, but it was enough. Nick smiled gently, then moved away and slipped out of the SUV.

Danni opened the passenger door and was flustered

when Nick was there to take her hand and help her out. He locked the doors with the press of a button on his key ring.

They entered the center and heard the murmur of voices in the computer lab, as well as muted shouts and sneaker squeaks coming from the basketball court. Alex Levin came out of the administrative office.

"Alex," she called.

The cop turned and smiled. "Hey, Danni. What're you doing here?" Then he glanced at Nick. "You have a run-in with a cat, Sirocco?"

Danni had forgotten about the angry red scratches on Nick's face.

"A bush," Nick replied blandly.

Before Alex could question him further, Danni said, "Nick and I are looking for a couple of kids."

The policeman narrowed his eyes. "This have anything to do with Matt Arbor's death?"

Danni glanced at Nick, who shrugged. She turned back to her former Academy classmate. "As a matter of fact, it does."

Alex darted a look up and down the hallway, his expression wary. "The autopsy came back on Arbor today," he said in a low voice. "They found a tranquilizer in his blood."

Danni's mind raced. "Forced?"

"It's possible, or he took it to help him carry out his own suicide." Alex shrugged. "We've seen it before."

"What was it?"

"A barbiturate. Just enough to make him sleepy."

"Or pliable enough to kill without a struggle." Danni glanced at Nick, seeing a reflection of her own grim thoughts.

Alex shrugged. "Maybe. Which kids are you looking for?"

"Marsel and Gary," she replied.

"Friends of Arbor's?"

"That's right. We want to ask them some questions."

Alex stabbed a thumb over his shoulder toward the

gym. "I saw Marsel come in about half an hour ago. Gary hasn't been in for a few days."

"You know an awful lot about what goes on around here," Nick said.

"Nick," Danni warned.

Alex held up a hand. "No, it's okay, Danni." He faced Nick and crossed his arms over his broad chest. "I'm here a couple of nights a week. I used to see you hanging out here with Paddy quite a bit, too." There was thinly veiled accusation in his voice.

"I was one of the kids he helped years ago," Nick admitted.

"Paddy helped a lot of kids. Too bad he didn't give Danni half the time he gave them."

Although Danni was grateful for Alex's support, she felt uncomfortable making Nick the bad guy. "It was a small price to pay for what good Dad accomplished."

"That's not what you used to say."

"Yeah, well, maybe I'm finally growing up."

Alex looked from Danni to Nick and back, then nodded slowly. "As much as I disliked Paddy for the way he treated you, I admired him, too," he admitted. "He's practically a legend around here."

Danni's gaze wandered around the center where her father had spent so much time. She could almost imagine his booming voice echoing through the hall and gym. He would've been furious about the shooting last night and taken it as a personal affront. He probably would've shaken down the neighborhood to uncover the shooters.

Alex flicked a glance at his watch. "I've got to get going. Helen's expecting me at nine." Alex kissed Danni's cheek. "I'll let you know if I learn anything more."

"Thanks."

Alex lifted a hand in farewell, then jogged down the hall and out the door.

"Do you trust him?" Nick asked, staring after Alex.

"Yes. He didn't have to tell us Matt's tox results."

After a few moments, Nick nodded. "How come you and he didn't . . . y'know, get together?"

She wrinkled her nose. "It would've been like dating my brother."

Nick laughed. "He does seem a little protective."

"You don't know the half of it." She tipped her head toward the gym. "Shall we?"

Danni pushed the metal door open and slipped into the gym with Nick's reassuring presence at her shoulder. Two groups were playing half-court basketball; on one side were girls, the other boys. Danni leaned against the wall and watched the girls, experiencing a sense of envy. When she was in high school, the center was more of a boys' hangout. It seemed the place had changed with the times.

She spotted a familiar blond woman with the girls and pointed toward her. "Isn't that Karen?"

"Yep. Paddy talked her into volunteering. It's good for the girls to see positive female role models."

"Maybe I'll start coming down here and helping out." At Nick's startled look, Danni added defensively, "If Karen can do it, I can."

"Paddy would like that."

Nick's quiet words sent a shaft of pain and longing through her. If only she and her dad had had more time. Danni suspected old wounds could've been healed, and she might've had the father-daughter relationship she'd always longed for.

"There's Marsel," Nick said.

It wasn't difficult to spot the tall, gangly teenager with his baggy red shorts and overly large jersey among the half-dozen boys.

"There seem to be fewer boys here tonight," Danni commented.

Nick frowned. "Maybe the shooting scared some of them off."

She scanned the gym, noting the boards that had been nailed over the windows broken by last night's shooters. "Maybe that was their intention."

Nick leaned against the wall. "What if we're wrong about this, Danni? What if the drive-by had nothing to do with us?"

"Don't you think the timing was a bit coincidental?"

He raked a hand through his short brown hair. "Or maybe with your dad gone, the gangs don't think they have to toe the line anymore."

"What do you mean?"

"Your dad was one of the founders of the youth center. He was the one who got the gangs to sit down and hammer out a truce to make the center a safe zone." Nick took a deep breath and exhaled slowly. "With Paddy gone, maybe they think they don't have to honor the agreement any longer."

"What would they gain from shooting the place up?"

"Reputation?"

Before Danni could comment, the boys took a water break.

"Marsel," Nick called.

Although Marsel looked like he wanted to ignore them, he shuffled over. "Hey, man, I told the cops all I know 'bout the shooting."

"What makes you think we're here to talk about that?" Nick asked.

Marsel shrugged. "Why else?"

Danni stifled the urge to jump in and ask questions. Nick believed Marsel would be more inclined to open up to him, and she was willing to let him try.

"Matt Arbor," Nick said. "What was he into?"

"Don't know—"

"Cut the crap. You were his friend. Where'd he lift the computer?"

Marsel fiddled with the hem of his jersey. "He never said."

"Bullshit. You two were tight."

Marsel shifted his red-sneakered feet. "So I hung out with him. That don't mean I was his mother."

Nick leaned close, his face a scant inch or two from the

boy's. "You were his friend. Why won't you help us find his killer?"

Danni fisted her hands in her jacket pockets as Nick and Marsel engaged in a staring contest. Beads of sweat rolled down the teen's face, and Danni was certain little of it was from his physical exertions on the court.

Finally, the boy glanced away. "Look, man, if I knew anything, I'd tell you."

"Would you?" Nick asked, his voice low.

Marsel lifted his chin, defiance in his eyes. "When I know somethin' for sure, I'll tell you."

Danni read between the lines; Marsel had his suspicions, but he didn't have any proof. She pulled out her card and handed it to him. "You can get hold of us any time at this number."

Marsel stared at the card for a long moment before he tucked it into his sock.

Nick latched onto his arm, drawing his attention. "If you think something's going down, use that number. We'll come right away. No questions asked. Got it?"

Marsel blinked in surprise and nodded. "Yeah, man, I got it."

"One other thing. Have you seen Gary tonight?"

"About half an hour ago. Geek room." He tipped his head toward the main hallway. "Computers."

"Thanks." Nick released the teenager.

Marsel retrieved his jacket and left amid grumbles from the five remaining basketball players.

Danni watched him go, her muscles tense. "Didn't Gilsen say he didn't know Gary?"

"Maybe it's Gary's first time in there."

"Let's go find out."

Danni and Nick exited the gym and walked down the hallway to the computer room. Was Paul Gilsen involved in this mess somehow? Or was her judgment tainted by something that had happened fifteen years ago?

The door to the lab was open, and she and Nick entered. Only three of the twelve computers were in use. It was obvious something was keeping the kids away from the center tonight.

At a station close to the door, Gilsen was helping a pink-haired girl with a gold stud in the side of her nose. He looked up when Danni and Nick approached him and smiled, but the expression quickly disappeared. "What happened to you?" he asked Nick, motioning to his face.

"You oughta see the other bush," Nick answered with a chuckle.

Gilsen frowned, then turned back to the teen. He gave her a few more instructions before motioning for Nick and Danni to join him in a corner of the room.

"We heard Gary was in here earlier," Danni said without preamble.

Gilsen crossed his arms over a pale blue dress shirt. It looked like he'd come straight from work and just removed his jacket and tie before coming into the center. "Is that the boy you were asking about earlier today?"

Danni nodded.

"I just got here about half an hour ago. If he was using a computer, he left before I came in."

Danni wanted to accuse him of lying but had no reason except for her own prejudice.

"Who was watching the room before you came in?" Nick asked.

"Alex Levin." Gilsen smiled. "He's not a computer geek, but he knows enough about them to help out."

Danni felt like she'd been kicked in the gut. They'd told Alex they were looking for Gary. Why hadn't he mentioned that the kid had been in the computer room?

"Marge told us that anyone who uses a computer has to have their name and address on file. If Gary was in here earlier, Levin should've gotten that information, right?" Nick asked.

Gilsen snapped his fingers. "That's right. Let me check the cards. I'll be right back."

Danni watched him wend his way to a desk at the front of the room. He was stopped by one of the teenagers to answer a question, which he seemed to handle with patience and friendliness.

"He has a car like the one that tailed us, but if he got here half an hour ago, he couldn't have been the one," Nick said quietly.

"Or he's lying."

"Have you considered he might *not* be involved?" Exasperation colored Nick's tone.

"Have you considered he *might* be involved?" Danni fired back.

"Mrs. Countryman said the person at Paddy's that night didn't have dark hair, like Paul's." Nick shifted impatiently. "Damn it. Don't you think we should be questioning Levin? And Sam Richmond?"

"We will," she said reluctantly.

"Fine."

Gilsen plucked an index card out of a box and carried it over to Nick and Danni. "Here."

Danni accepted it with a mumbled thanks. "Gary Otis. 4562 Horner, apartment D," she read aloud. She handed the card to Nick, retrieved a small notebook from her jacket pocket, and jotted down the address.

Nick handed the card back to Gilsen. "Thanks, Paul. We appreciate it."

"No problem."

"Mr. Gilsen," the pink-haired girl called out.

"Be right there." Gilsen gave Danni and Nick a shrug. "Duty calls."

Although she wanted nothing more than to put a few miles between herself and Gilsen, she had another question. "What were you doing here earlier today?"

"Two things. After I read about the shooting in the paper, I wanted to make sure the computers weren't damaged. I also updated the antivirus program. I received a message at work this morning about a new virus and wanted to make sure the computers here were protected against it."

His smarmy smile made Danni's skin crawl, but she managed a civilized nod. "Thanks."

After Nick and Gilsen exchanged handshakes, Danni didn't waste any time making her escape. Outside, Nick unlocked his SUV, and they climbed in.

"Do you know where Horner Street is?" Danni asked.

He nodded as he pulled out of the parking space. "Yes."

His curt reply made Danni wonder if she had tripped a memory land mine. "So, you want to talk about it?"

He shot her a sharp glance. "What?"

"How you know Horner Street."

"I grew up around here. I know all the streets."

"But there's something different about Horner."

He sighed. "That's where Davey lived."

It took Danni a moment to recall where she'd heard the name. "The boy who committed suicide?"

Nick nodded. "He didn't belong here. He was smart and liked to read and learn. He helped me with my homework a few times. If he hadn't killed himself, he could've done something with his life."

"Maybe he couldn't see any other way out of the neighborhood?"

"Maybe. I just wish I'd known."

"If he was determined to do it, you couldn't have stopped him."

Nick gave her a small smile of gratitude.

The address was less than ten minutes from the center, and Nick parked under one of the few unbroken streetlamps. The apartment complex where Gary lived was one signature away from being condemned.

They paused on the sidewalk in front of the crumbling building, and Danni checked her revolver and placed it back in her shoulder holster. "I answered more than a few domestic calls around here when I was on patrol."

"No surprise there," Nick said dryly.

As they approached the entrance, they could hear raised voices and ugly words, then a baby's squall. Despite Danni's less-than-happy memories of dealing with domestic disturbances, she suspected Nick's memories were far more vivid and personal.

The security lock on the entrance was broken, and it appeared to have been that way for years. Nick opened the door, and they entered the fetid-smelling foyer. Not wanting to spend a lot of time there, Danni quickly found apartment D on the second floor. She pounded on the door and heard someone approaching.

"Who's there?" a voice asked.

"That's Gary," Nick whispered to Danni.

"My name's Danni Hawkins. I'm a private—" A loud expletive from inside the apartment interrupted her.

Then came the sound of running feet, more cursing, and odd pounding noises.

Nick shoved a shoulder against the apartment door, and the rotting wood gave way easily. He stumbled inside, and Danni followed, her revolver clutched in her hand.

She rushed toward an open window and stuck her head outside. She spotted someone jumping off the bottom of the fire escape. Her gut told her it was Gary. She tucked her revolver in its holster and used both hands to climb out onto the rusty ladder to give chase.

"Danni!" Nick hollered.

"I'm going after him."

Danni heard Nick shouting at her, but her sole focus was on the boy who might hold the key to her father's death.

She dropped the last four feet to the ground, nearly turning her ankle when she landed on a piece of garbage. She scanned her dim surroundings and heard a clatter of metal to her left. She ran in that direction and spied a shadowy movement in the litter-strewn passageway.

She forced her legs to pump faster. Her vision adjusted to the dimness, and she managed to avoid tripping or stumbling as she chased her quarry. Although she was in good shape, her breathing filled her ears, and her heart thundered against her ribs.

Gary slipped in and out of sight in the darkness, but

Danni was gaining on him. She didn't think he had a weapon, or he would've used it. Or maybe he was just waiting until he had a closer target. . . .

Realizing she hadn't seen Gary's bobbing figure in the last thirty seconds, Danni slowed her pace. She came to the corner of an intersecting alley and flattened against the wall. Her heart pounded in her ears, making it difficult to hear anything beyond that and her rapid breathing. Not knowing who or what lay ahead in the darkness, Danni drew her gun.

She peeked around the corner and gasped. A figure loomed directly in front of her.

Chapter Fifteen

Nick tore down the creaky apartment stairs three at a time. Stumbling out of the dilapidated building, he halted on the sidewalk. Scanning one way then the other, he quickly picked a direction and bolted around the corner into the back alley.

"Stick together, she says," he muttered as his eyes adjusted to the darkness.

Although his tone was furious, Nick's worry outweighed his anger. Gary was obviously guilty of something, or he wouldn't have taken off. If he was involved in murder, he was desperate, and desperate people committed desperate acts. And Danni had gone after him alone.

Fortunately, Nick could take some consolation in the fact she'd been a cop and knew how to defend herself. Still, police procedure was like Ranger regulations in that you always had someone watching your butt, and Danni had broken that number-one rule.

Nick swore as he stumbled and tripped over the debris littering the narrow alley. After a few minutes of following twists and turns, he realized he didn't know where the hell he was, much less where Danni was.

He heard a faint scuffling, and hoped it was Danni and not a stray dog scrounging for dinner. As he moved toward the noise, he searched the shadows for the impulsive woman and the teenager. Nothing.

He tilted his head and recognized the nearly inaudible rustle of cloth. He found himself reverting to his covert training. Controlling his breathing and moving with silent footsteps, he approached the intersecting alley. . . .

And found a gun pointed at his chest.

Before he could react, the weapon's barrel tipped upward.

"Goddammit, Sirocco!" The familiar voice was followed by a resounding palm slap against the brick wall. "I almost blew your head off."

Nick sagged in relief, but then fury coursed through his blood, giving him another dose of adrenaline. "What the hell did you think you were doing, going after him alone? How did you know he wasn't just waiting for you at the bottom of the fire escape with a gun? Or that he wasn't leading you into a trap?" His fists trembled at his sides. "Was all the stuff you spouted about sticking together just a bunch of crap?"

Danni reholstered her revolver and planted her hands on her hips. "I couldn't let him get away. He could be the key."

Nick grabbed her shoulders and barely restrained himself from shaking her. "A lot of good that key would do if he killed you."

"No problem there. He got away." Sarcasm oozed from Danni's voice.

Too frustrated and incensed to be rational, he released her and stamped back along the route he'd come. "Let's get out of here."

"But—"

"Now."

If Danni didn't get her ass in gear and follow him, he was going to throw her over his shoulder and haul her back to Paddy's. Another wave of anger crested through him as he realized she'd managed to turn him into some prehistoric caveman ready to drag her away by her hair.

He was relieved when he heard her footsteps behind him. However, he also heard curses that would've embarrassed seasoned Rangers.

He found where he'd parked his SUV, which fortunately was in one piece, complete with hubcaps. Once he and Danni were in the vehicle, he peeled out onto the street.

Strained silence enveloped them all the way back to Paddy's house. Danni sat with her arms crossed tightly over her chest, glaring out the windshield. If she glanced at him, he didn't notice.

She had no right being ticked off. *She* was the one who'd acted rashly and ignored her ironclad rule about sticking together. Nick had only gone after her to guard her backside, like she'd insisted they do for each other ever since she'd heard the phone message left by her father.

Braking sharply, Nick parked along the curb in front of the house. Danni reached for the door handle, but he grabbed her wrist before she could escape.

"Don't you ever run off by yourself like that again," he said in a low, menacing tone.

"Or what?"

Her contempt provoked Nick further. "Or I'm going to find Paddy's handcuffs and cuff us together."

She pressed her lips together, and her nostrils flared, but she didn't challenge him.

He released her, and she jumped out of the vehicle. By the time Nick made it to the porch, she had the door open. He followed her inside and snapped the two locks into place after shutting the door behind them.

Gus merely glanced up from her prone position on the living room carpet and thumped her tail once, then closed her eyes. Obviously, she didn't need to go outside.

Danni tossed her jacket on the sofa and climbed the stairs.

"Where are you going?" Nick asked.

She paused and glared at him over her shoulder. "To bed. Did you want to come with me?"

Three hours ago the question would've been asked in a playfully seductive voice. Now, however, her tone cut with razor-sharp sarcasm.

He scowled at her. "Damn it, Danni, don't make me the bad guy here. How can we watch out for each other when you go flying off like damned Wonder Woman?"

"He was getting away. I *had* to go after him."

Nick marched to the foot of the stairs and stabbed a forefinger up at her. "And if he'd had a gun or a knife? What then? You'd be hurt or dead."

"Or *he* would've been."

"You don't know that." He struggled to regain his composure. "Losing one Hawkins was hard enough."

Danni's eyes widened, but then stark bitterness filled her features. "Too bad you lost the most important one."

Fury, disbelief, exasperation, and regret swirled through Nick. How could she not realize that her life was just as important to him as her father's had been? In three steps he was beside her on the stairs, and he gripped her shoulders tightly. He wanted to yell at her, but he had no idea what words to use—they all jumbled together with his chaotic feelings.

Instead, he followed his instincts and ground his lips against hers. He tasted a hint of blood—hers or his?—and gentled the bruising kiss. He teased her lips, urging them apart so he could show her how much she meant to him, not because she was Paddy's daughter, but because she was Danni.

Her lips yielded, and a soft moan vibrated in her slender throat as their tongues intertwined. She wrapped her arms around him, pulling him impossibly closer.

Only when Nick felt the need for oxygen and a less precarious position than the stairs did he ease away from her. He rested his chin on her head as his pulse and breathing raced. He was gratified to hear Danni struggle to bring her own body back under control.

"It was a stupid thing to say," she whispered, her gaze downcast.

"Yes, it was." Nick kissed her pert nose. "Too many people I've cared about have died. I don't want to lose you, too."

Surprise flashed through her eyes, followed by uncertainty. She took a deep breath and eased away from him to return to the living room. After dropping to the floor to sit cross-legged with her back against the sofa, she bent down to stroke Gus.

Nick rubbed his brow where a headache throbbed and followed Danni down the stairs. He sat on the couch, his leg brushing her shoulder. "I didn't hurt you, did I?"

She turned her head to cast him a smirk that was marred slightly by her red, swollen lips. "Nah, I'm as tough as I look." She waggled her eyebrows. "It was actually pretty hot."

Nick chuckled. Just when he thought he knew her, she'd throw him a curveball. Did she have any idea how thoroughly exasperating and desirable she was?

He reached out to run his fingers through her thick hair. A silky curl wound around his finger like an affectionate lover. "It *was* pretty hot." He sobered. "But I'm still sorry for losing control like that."

He felt a shudder pass through her. "And I'm sorry for running off like I did. I'm just not used to having a partner."

"And I am?" He kept his voice light as he continued to toy with her soft curls.

"You have Gus."

"Who I keep on a leash."

Danni leaned away from him, and her hair slid through his fingers, leaving them forlorn and empty.

"No way. Cuffs can be kind of sexy, but a leash?" Mischief sparkled in her eyes.

Nick's heart rate quickened. "Do you still have your handcuffs?"

"Wouldn't you like to know?" She laughed and shifted until her back was resting against Nick's legs.

He leaned back against the sofa, content to merely watch Danni pet Gus. The fear he'd carried since Danni had run off to chase Gary loosened its talons. He hadn't lied about caring for her. In fact, if anything, he'd understated his feelings. Not many people could make him lose control, but she did. In record time. One moment he'd been furious with her, and the next, he'd wanted her with fierce intensity.

The seesaw of emotions frightened him. Was he falling in love with Danni?

He dismissed the possibility immediately. It was a moot point. Danni had made it clear that she wasn't looking for a serious relationship, and he'd be damned if he'd lose his heart to someone who was only interested in sex as a form of recreation.

Danni rose gracefully. "I'm going to the kitchen. Would you like something?"

"No, thanks."

She nodded and walked away.

Gus raised her head to gaze longingly after her. Then the dog sighed and lay back down, which elicited a smile from Nick.

You and me both, Gus.

A familiar beep came from the kitchen, but Nick couldn't understand the subsequent tinny voice on the phone's answering machine. Curious, he went into the kitchen to find Danni punching a number in the phone.

"Who was that?" Nick asked.

"Sam," she replied, obviously listening to the ringing at the other end. "He invited us over for dinner tomorrow evening."

"Good. That'll give us a chance to ask him some questions."

Danni didn't appear happy, but she didn't argue either. They both knew there were too many things that didn't add up for the retired police officer.

"Hi, Sam. It's Danni," she said into the receiver. "Sorry it's so late, but I just got your message. Nick and I would love to come over tomorrow evening."

Nick leaned against a counter and listened to the one-sided conversation.

"Six o'clock sounds fine. Is there anything we can bring?" She smiled. "Just ourselves. Right. How's Nancy feeling?" A long pause, then Danni spoke again. "I'm glad to hear it. You tell her to take it easy. She doesn't have to cook anything fancy for us." Another break, and her expression sobered. "I'm looking forward to it. Yep. Good night." She hung up the phone.

"Well?" Nick asked.

"Six o'clock dinner at their place." Danni gazed past him, her eyes unfocused.

"What else?"

She seemed to shake herself. "Sam said he had something for us."

"About Paddy's death? Or Matt's?"

"He didn't say, but I got the impression it might be about both."

"So their deaths are related?"

Danni pressed her lips together and shrugged. "We've been making that assumption. Sam may have evidence either linking them or blowing our theory to hell."

Nick's mind raced, and his mouth followed. "If Sam had something to do with it, he might try to feed us some BS to convince us Paddy and Matt committed suicide so we stop snooping around."

Danni crossed her arms, and a familiar stubborn expression took residence. "No, I don't believe it."

Nick leveled a steady gaze on her, refusing to be drawn into another argument. She was too smart to let her emotions get in the way of the investigation. He just had to let her figure that out for herself.

Finally, Danni closed her eyes and tipped her head back. "God, Nick, I don't *want* to believe it."

He placed his hands on her shoulders and massaged them gently. "I don't either."

"It'll kill Nancy if Sam is involved."

The anguish in her voice made Nick look away in empathy, but one of them had to remain objective. "How about we hope for the best but prepare for the worst?"

Danni cracked open her eyes and a smile played at the corners of her lips. "Spoken like a true Boy Scout."

He snorted. "Hardly. Not where I grew up."

She narrowed her eyes as if examining him under a microscope. "So tell me about yourself, Nick Sirocco."

Her gaze was steady, her expression curious but not morbidly so. Still, it was an ingrained habit to keep his past to himself. Paddy had known the most about his childhood, and much of that he'd surmised from what Nick *didn't* say.

Nick smiled disarmingly. "I grew up in the neighborhood, went to college, spent eight years as an Army Ranger, and the last four as a writer. End of story."

Danni placed her palm over his heart. "*Who* is Nick Sirocco? How did he escape the neighborhood? And don't tell me it was all my father's influence. He saw something in you. What was it?" Her eyes appeared even darker blue, blending seamlessly into her black pupils.

Nick searched for an answer, but only found a memory he'd buried long ago. He stepped away from Danni to cross his arms and stare out the window above the sink. "I wondered that myself. When I was sixteen, before I knew Paddy, he caught me lifting a guy's wallet. He convinced the man not to file charges, but Paddy laid into me about right and wrong. I asked him then why he was wasting his time. You know what he said?"

Danni shook her head.

"He said *I* was the one wasting time, and that if I wanted to end up in prison, I should keep on wasting my time." Nick smiled wryly and slid his hands into his jeans pockets. "But he said if I had higher aspirations than being Bubba's girlfriend, he'd help me. And he did."

"And you climbed out, unlike a lot of kids."

Nick shrugged. "I wasn't the only one. Paul Gilsen got out, and two other guys I knew did, too."

"Did Dad help Paul, too?" Her voice sounded stiff.

Nick recalled those days when all he could think of was escaping his parents, the dealers on the corners, the gangs in the streets, and the pall of hopelessness that hung over the neighborhood. "He spent some time with Paul, but he was more Sam's project than Paddy's."

Blaring silence made him turn toward Danni. She stood rigid, her lips pressed together and her face pale. "What's wrong?"

"Sam never told me," she said, her tone cold. "Not even the night I called him after Gilsen tried to . . ." She wrapped her arms around herself.

Without thought, he gathered Danni close and rocked her trembling body. "Maybe he just didn't want to upset you any more than you already were."

Danni, her face pressed into his chest, didn't speak. Nick would've preferred angry or sarcastic words rather than this uncharacteristic silence.

"All this is wild speculation, Danni," he said gently, her soft tendrils tickling his lips. "Sam may not be involved in any of this, and he may have a good explanation as to why he didn't tell you about Paul back then."

Danni finally raised her head. "But—"

"It's late, and we should go to bed," he interrupted. "You can get your answers tomorrow."

She nodded and stepped back. Cold air replaced warmth, and Nick tried to ignore the sense of loss. Although he admired Danni's self-reliance, he felt an innate need to defend and shelter her. But she would never tolerate that. He could just imagine her response if he confessed his odd protective streak.

He let Gus outside one last time, and when the dog returned, she jumped onto the sofa and curled up in a corner. She stared up at Nick with liquid brown eyes.

"Uh, do you mind?" Nick asked Danni, motioning toward Gus.

"No." Danni patted the dog's head, then said in a stage whisper to her, "Just don't tell anyone. It may ruin my badass image."

Danni's disguise worked well. But hidden beneath the badass image lay a compassionate, fiery woman who believed in right and wrong, and whose passion far outweighed her cynicism.

"Your image is already ruined," he said, his voice husky.

Danni glanced at him and flushed. "I'd better lock up the house," she murmured.

Nick smiled and flicked on the light at the top of the stairs. Once she was done checking the doors and windows, he trailed her up the staircase and down the hall.

She paused in front of her bedroom door and gazed at Nick over her shoulder. "Since the person who followed us knows we're here, it might be safer to sleep in the same room."

Nick's heart skipped a beat, and it had little to do with lust. For the first time—without the aid of a nightmare or a rampant libido—she was reaching out to him. He kept his voice light, fearful that she might rescind the offer. "Same room or same bed?"

She grinned crookedly. "I suppose it wouldn't make sense for one of us to sleep on the floor when there's a perfectly good double bed." She held up a hand. "Sleep only. I'm exhausted."

"Don't worry. I'm beat, too."

She smiled with relief and gratitude.

Nick kept his back turned to Danni as he stripped down to his boxer briefs and slid between the sheets. Danni, wearing an oversized T-shirt, curled up by his side but not close enough that they touched.

Nick would've preferred lying in one another's arms, but he remained motionless. He had to allow her to decide where she was comfortable, both physically and emotionally.

However, after a few minutes, she snuggled closer, resting her head on his shoulder. "Thank you," she whispered.

Relieved and heartened by her trust, Nick wrapped his arm around her and kissed her forehead. "You're welcome."

NICK threw off his covers and stood before he even knew what had awakened him. Darkness surrounded him, and he glanced at the digital clock—1:03 A.M. Then Gus's barking registered, and his sleep-muddy brain cleared.

"Does she have to go out?" Danni's quiet voice reminded him where he was.

"She usually whines instead of barks."

Danni rose and slid her revolver from its holster where it lay on her nightstand. "After everything that's happened, I'm not taking any chances."

Nick blinked at the pale vision of Danni in the oversized shirt—long legs, bare feet, and holding a gun between her hands like Dirty Harry. Only Clint Eastwood never looked that sexy. "You're not dressed," he whispered.

Although he couldn't tell for certain, he thought she gave him a visual once-over.

"And you are?" she asked.

Wearing only his skivvies, he couldn't argue. Gus's barking continued, telling him they didn't have time to dress. "All right, let's go."

He began walking toward the door, but Danni's hand stopped him. "I have the gun. I go first. Behind me. Now."

Although he wanted to argue with the hardheaded woman, it *was* her gun, and she *had* been trained as a police officer. Reluctantly, he did as she ordered.

Danni cracked open the bedroom door and peered into the hallway. "Clear."

She slipped out, and Nick followed on her heels. He wasn't going to let her get away from him again.

At the top of the stairs, Nick gazed down into the living room and spotted Gus by the front door. She jumped up and down, her front paws scraping the door. Her ears were straight up.

"You sure she doesn't just have to pee?" Danni asked Nick in a low voice.

"She would've come up to get me."

They crept downstairs, and Nick moved to Gus's side. "Shhh, easy girl," he crooned. Gus stopped barking, but her body vibrated with tension.

Danni peeked through the living room curtain. "I can't see anything." She opened the curtains wider, and her lips turned downward. "Someone broke into my truck."

Two gunshots and breaking glass sent Nick diving for the carpet with an arm wrapped around Gus. His heart lodged in his throat. "Danni!"

"I'm fine," she said from her position on the floor. "You?"

"Peachy. That isn't a car backfiring this time."

"No kidding."

"I'm going to try to get to the phone and call nine-one-one." He laid a hand on Gus's back and commanded, "Stay."

As Nick inched toward the kitchen, tires screeched, and a car roared away. He looked back at Danni. "Are they gone?"

She nodded, then rose and dashed into the kitchen, mumbling something. Nick stood and fell in behind her.

"Edward, Charles, Union. Edward, Charles, Union," Danni repeated over and over.

In the kitchen, she hit the light switch, and he blinked in the sudden brightness. She fumbled in a drawer, pulled out a pad of paper and a pen. "Edward, Charles, Union." She wrote "E, C, U" as she spoke.

"What's that?" he asked Danni, pointing at the slip of paper.

"The first three letters of the license plate. I caught them as he drove off."

"Did you see his face?"

Danni shook her head. "It was too dark. We were lucky he didn't tape over his license plate." She met Nick's gaze. "I'm pretty sure it was the same car that tailed us."

Nick wasn't surprised. Instead, he was frustrated and angry. "We have to call the police."

"If the neighbors haven't called already."

Nick reached for the phone but drew back his hand when he heard distant sirens growing nearer. "Great Neighborhood Watch program."

Her lips thinned. "Too bad they weren't watching the night Dad died."

Chapter Sixteen

DANNI blinked in the sunlight that slanted across her face and threw an arm over her eyes to block the bright rays. Disoriented and groggy, she tried to remember where she was.

A movement beside her startled her and brought back the memory of the evening's festivities. She barely stifled a groan. She and Nick had finally fallen back into bed at four that morning, after three hours of questioning by the police.

The crime scene unit had shown up, too. The CSIs had found two bullets—nine millimeter—lodged in the living room wall, and one shell casing outside behind the truck. They'd taken pictures of the tire marks on the street, but the photos wouldn't do any good unless the perpetrator's car was found. Not unexpectedly, there were no other fingerprints besides Danni's and Nick's on the truck.

Danni had given the investigating officer—a detective she'd known while on the force—the first three letters of the license plate. She knew it was little to go on, and Detective Rearden didn't offer any gratuitous hope. However, there was one car Danni intended to check out personally.

If the plate started with the same three letters, Danni planned to do some interrogating herself.

She wondered what Nick's reaction would be if Gilsen was involved. In fact, she didn't even know how close the two men were. Before she and Nick became connected at the hip, had he socialized with Gilsen?

Nick shifted beside her, and warm breath cascaded across her neck, followed by a moist tongue. Smiling, she said quietly, "Don't get any ideas. We've got work to do."

A snuffle was her only answer.

"You can't sleep all day either," she teased. Without turning over, she reached behind her to wake her sleeping companion . . . and encountered a furry body.

Danni yelped and rolled away. The bedspread wrapped around her, and she dropped to the floor in an undignified mound.

"Problems?"

The familiar voice and its accompanying dry wit made her sit up so she could see over the bed—and Gus—to where Nick stood framed in the doorway. Dressed in black jeans and a white turtleneck, he held two steaming cups of coffee. He looked like he'd just stepped out of a for-women-only greeting card, except for the smirk that bedeviled his eyes and ruined the fantasy.

"When did you get up?" Danni asked irritably to cover her embarrassment.

He shrugged. "About seven-thirty. Couldn't sleep any more." He strolled to the side of the bed and perched on the mattress, then held out a cup to Danni, who still sat on the floor feeling like a badly wrapped mummy. "Want some?"

She glared at him, then wriggled around until she had both arms free, and accepted the coffee with a mumbled "thanks."

After taking a sip of the rich brew, she looked up at Nick, noting his clean-shaven jaw. His blue eyes were brighter than usual, highlighted by the white turtleneck, and his jeans were just tight enough to snap her hormones to attention.

She met his gaze and found him studying her, his eyes twinkling with amusement. Here she was sitting cross-legged on the floor with bed hair and a defective toga, while Nick could've just stepped out of a *GQ* ad. Life just wasn't fair.

"I must've been tired. I didn't even hear you get out of bed," she said.

His humor faded. "You've been under a lot of stress."

"So have you," she said, annoyed by his patronizing tone.

A corner of his lips hitched upward. "Touché." He took a drink of coffee. "Alex Levin called this morning. He wanted to know how you were doing."

"How'd he know I was here?"

"By now everybody on the police force knows you and I are here."

The police report. Danni had forgotten how well the brotherhood-in-blue gossip mill operated in the department. A call about a late-night shooting at Paddy Hawkins's place involving his daughter and Nick Sirocco would be tempting fodder for even the most tight-lipped.

"Did he have any news?" Danni asked.

"No." He gazed down into his cup. "I wanted to ask him why he lied about not seeing Gary last night, but I figured I should wait and let you handle it."

It took a moment for Danni to switch gears. "Is he on duty today?"

"Until four."

Danni glanced at the digital clock radio on the dresser—9:55. "I didn't realize it was so late."

She handed Nick her coffee cup and pushed off the blanket. Her panties and thighs were exposed, and she quickly tugged the T-shirt down over her underwear. Her face warmed under Nick's appreciative gaze. "If you don't mind . . ."

"Not at all." Nick's eyes gleamed with mischief.

She shook her head in exasperation, then extended her hand. "If you're staying, make yourself useful."

Setting both coffee cups on the nightstand, Nick grasped her hand and pulled her up and toward him so she stood between his knees. He placed his hands on her hips, his fingers splaying across her lace-covered bottom. His face was level with her breasts.

The intimacy made her breath catch and her heart stammer. "I have to shower."

"I like you this way, smelling like you and me."

"And Gus," she couldn't help but add.

Nick chuckled and tilted his head back to gaze at her. He reached up to tuck a strand of hair behind her ear. "You're beautiful when you fall out of bed."

Danni failed to contain the laughter that bubbled up. "You need glasses, Sirocco."

"You need a better mirror." He slid his hands up her back and behind her neck, then gently tugged her head downward.

Tumbling into his eyes, Danni brushed his lips with hers, tasting his faint minty toothpaste and smelling his fresh soap scent.

Nick broke the kiss but didn't draw away. "I wish we had more time," he whispered. "I'd show you how beautiful you are."

"With a better mirror?" Danni asked, her voice husky.

Regret tinged his smile. "You should get dressed. We have a lot to do today."

Danni had slept with her share of men, but none like Nick. Usually, her bed partner wanted a quickie before getting up, whether she was running late or not. She suspected Nick wouldn't have been averse to a morning round of lovemaking, but there was more in his eyes than simple lust. He actually cared about *her.*

At least for now. The attraction was a matter of proximity and inevitability. After they solved her dad's murder, Nick would leave, and the allure would fade.

Hating that her throat felt like she'd swallowed sandpaper, Danni moved out of Nick's arms. On the way out of the bedroom, she patted Gus, who was still sleeping sprawled on the bed.

Twenty minutes later, a fully clothed Danni trotted downstairs with Gus on her heels. The coffee and shower had done miracles in bringing her back to life.

"Nick?" she called out.

"In the kitchen."

Danni pushed through the swinging door, and Gus crowded through with her. The dog trotted to her food bowl and chowed down.

Danni found Nick sitting by the table, which was covered by papers and note cards. "What're you doing?"

Nick propped his elbows on the sea of papers. "Since you were still sleeping when I got up, I figured I'd work on my book proposal."

"Is this the one Dad was helping you with?"

He nodded.

Danni pulled out a chrome and vinyl chair and sat down beside him. "Can I help?"

Nick tilted his head and peered at her. "Maybe."

Frowning, she picked up a sheet of paper and read the scrawling across it. "It's a mystery?"

"Police thriller."

"What's the difference?"

"A thriller is a more intense mystery."

She wrinkled her nose. "More blood and gore? That sort of thing?"

Nick smiled. "Not exactly. Just more edge-of-the-seat type of thing."

"Ahhh." Danni continued scanning Nick's notes. "You're using the youth center?"

"A *fictional* youth center where crooked cops are running a crime ring using the kids they're supposed to be helping."

Startled by the similarities of his book and her suspicions, she asked, "Was Dad the only one who knew about this?"

"He and my agent, but I only gave my agent a general idea."

Danni stared at the page, not reading any more but thinking. She suddenly recalled her dad's phone message to Nick the night he was killed. What had been his exact words?

She jumped up and ran up to her childhood bedroom where her backpack lay in a corner. Unzipping it, she rummaged around for the answering machine. Her fingers scraped plastic, and she tugged it out. She stared at it, wondering if she had the courage to hear his voice again. She'd only listened to the message once, in her office when Nick had brought it in. It seemed like months ago, instead of only days.

She dashed downstairs with the answering machine clutched to her chest.

Nick met her in the living room, his expression quizzical. "What's going on?"

"I want to listen to Dad's message again." She continued into the kitchen and set the machine on the counter, then plugged it in. Her heart slammed against her ribs, and she was glad when Nick joined her. His presence gave her the courage to push the Play button.

Although she was prepared to hear her father's deep voice, it still caused her to flinch. She closed her stinging eyes as she listened to his painfully familiar voice.

"Rocky, it's Paddy. I need to talk to you. Something's going on at the youth center. I have a feeling I know what it is, but I need your help to prove it. Call me as soon as you get this message. If I don't hear from you tonight, I'll call you in the morning. Sometimes truth is stranger than fiction."

Danni stabbed the Stop button. " 'Sometimes truth is stranger than fiction,' " she quoted. "What do you think he meant?"

"I told you I didn't know," he said, confused.

"He's talking about your book, Nick." Danni paced,

punctuating her words with her hands. "Knowing you were a writer, I should've figured it out when I first heard it."

Nick stared at her as realization dawned across his features. "He discovered a crime ring working out of the center."

"And a cop or cops are involved."

"Just like my fucking book." His voice was strained, his eyes dazed.

Danni stopped and nodded. "Now all we need to do is fill in the characters."

Nick sank into a vinyl chair. "Son of a bitch."

Danni dropped into the chair she'd abandoned minutes earlier. "So which cops are involved?"

Nick seemed to struggle to pull himself together. "Levin? Sam? Sergeant Rodgers?"

"Or one of fifty others who volunteer at the center. And which kids?" Although they had more information than they had two days ago, Danni felt like they were back to square one. She took a deep breath. "Tell me about your book. The *Reader's Digest* version."

Nick scrubbed his pale face with his palms, then slouched in his chair. "Two cops, along with an assorted number of crooked players, recruit juvenile delinquents they're supposed to be helping to steal for them. One of the kids goes to the good guy cop—" He smiled. "A gruff old patrolman who reminds me a lot of Paddy. The bad guys kill the kid, and the story follows the good guy cop, who's been targeted, as he tries to break up the auto theft ring."

"Auto theft?" Danni asked pensively.

Nick straightened. "Like the stolen Jaguar where Matt found the laptop he tried to pawn." His excitement disappeared. "So Paddy was killed because someone saw my notes and thought they were real?"

Danni didn't want to believe it, but her gut was telling her the pieces were finally starting to fit together. "Or Dad said something about it," she said softly.

"No. Paddy knew I didn't want anyone to know about it." Nick stood, as if unable to sit in one place. "What about the shooting at the center? If they were trying to scare us off, you'd think they'd do it here or someplace less crowded. Why take a chance with so many people around?"

"Maybe the warning wasn't for us."

"Who then?"

Danni's mind scrambled for a theory. "The police believe it was a gang-related shooting. What are some of the initiation rites for a gang?"

Nick frowned. "Robbing a convenience store? Taking out a rival gang member?" His scowl deepened. "Stealing a car?"

"Maybe the shooting was just to show everybody whose turf this is."

"But why wouldn't these ring leaders recruit gang members?" Nick answered his own question before Danni could speculate. "Because gangs are loyal to each other and nobody else. That leaves using kids who don't belong to a gang."

Danni was impressed by Nick's reasoning. "Kids like Matt, Marsel, and Gary?"

"As far as I know, they weren't in a gang. But we don't know that they're involved in anything either."

"What if Matt ratted out to Dad? Just like in your book?"

Nick rubbed his jaw thoughtfully. "When was Matt arrested for the theft?"

"Two days before Dad was killed."

"Why didn't Paddy tell me then? Why wait until he was in danger?"

"Knowing Dad, he probably wanted to check things out before saying anything to anybody, especially if those involved were cops he knew." Danni's throat tightened. "That's what I would've done."

Nick leaned against a counter and gazed at Danni. "We can't trust anyone."

"Except each other."

Her eyes softened, giving him a glimpse of her faith in

him. It was an unexpected gift that made his heart clench. "Except each other," he repeated in a husky voice. "So how do we do this?"

"We treat everyone like a suspect, including Sam Richmond, Alex Levin, and Paul Gilsen." She raised a hand to halt his objection. "I know he's not a cop, but he could be a crooked player."

"We'll have to check his license plate against the partial you got."

"So why did they break into my truck?"

"To find that." Nick made a sweeping motion toward the table filled with his story notes. "What they think is evidence against them."

"Why didn't they get into your Jeep?"

"Maybe we scared them off before they could."

It sounded reasonable. "Wouldn't they wonder why they haven't been arrested if you have evidence against them?"

Nick shrugged. "Maybe they thought that without Paddy, we couldn't make a case."

Danni stood and raked her fingers through her hair. "And so by killing him, they eliminated their biggest threat. But obviously someone saw your story notes, and they're not certain what you know. However, they are worried enough to ransack your apartment and break into my truck to find them."

"And try to kill us," Nick added.

"So who besides Dad might've seen your notes?"

Nick threw up his arms. "Nobody. I was always careful about that."

Frustration vibrated through his words, and Danni knew he needed something else to focus on. "Let's sort out what we have." She held up one finger. "First, we have Matt Arbor arrested for trying to fence a stolen laptop computer, which just happened to come from a stolen car. Then we have Dad, who asked Beth to represent Matt, who initially didn't seem very worried about the charge. But after Dad died, he told Beth he wanted to deal."

"So, did he know who killed Paddy?" Nick interjected. "Is that why he was killed?"

"If our theory is right, yes on both counts." Danni added a second finger. "Second, we have Dad's message to you the night he was killed. He obviously suspected he was in danger. What had he found out? How did someone get close enough to him to stage his suicide?"

"It had to be someone he knew but didn't suspect was involved."

Danni nodded. "Good point. Mrs. Countryman saw a car at Dad's place the night he died. Probably the same car that followed us and that was here last night."

"The car we're assuming is Paul's," Nick said grimly.

"But here's where the fly in the ointment comes in. The person in that car had lighter-colored hair. Gilsen has dark hair."

"Maybe Mrs. Countryman's eyes weren't working too well."

"Or it could've been an accomplice."

Nick grimaced. "The person who knew Paddy well enough to get close to him." He paused. "Sam Richmond has gray hair. Levin's is light brown. Both would pass for 'lighter-colored' hair."

Although on one level she'd known Sam and Alex were viable suspects, Nick's comment settled like a ball of lead in her stomach. "I know. Do you know where Gilsen works?"

"He told me once, but I can't remember."

"We'll have to stop by the center and see if your friend Marge has that information."

"How about some brunch first?" Nick suggested.

Now that Nick had reminded her, she was hungry. It'd been a long night. "We'll stop someplace on the way."

Danni helped Nick gather up his book notes and put them into a folder, which Danni tucked into the backpack. She also tossed the answering machine in the bag. What they had couldn't be called evidence, but someone apparently thought it was and had killed her dad because of it.

Leaving Danni's truck with its broken window in the driveway, they took Nick's SUV. As Nick pulled onto the main street, Danni's cell phone rang.

"Hawkins," she answered crisply.

"Danni, thank heavens you're all right," Cathy said, relief evident in her voice.

"Why wouldn't I be?"

"Beth heard from a friend of hers on the force that somebody shot at you last night."

Danni rolled her eyes heavenward. Did the whole city know? "Someone broke into my truck. Gus woke us up."

There was a long pause.

"Gus? Isn't that hottie Nick's dog?"

Danni grinned and glanced at Nick, who shot her a quizzical look. "Yes, Gus is hottie Nick's dog."

Nick mouthed, *Cathy?*

Danni nodded and fought the urge to laugh at his exasperated expression.

"So, are you going to tell me what Gus and Nick were doing at your place?" Cathy asked, her innuendo crystal clear.

"It was Dad's place, and we were all sleeping." *At least at the time of the shooting.* "How're things at the office?"

"Quiet, but I have two messages for you. One's from a potential client. He'd like you to track down his fiancée who ran away with his engagement ring. He'll pay you a finder's fee of two thousand dollars in addition to your normal charge."

Two weeks ago Danni would've jumped at the chance to bring in some extra income, but she wasn't about to drop her dad's case, especially when they were getting close. "Call him back and tell him I'm too busy. What's the other message?"

"It's from Sergeant Rodgers. He wants you to call him at 555-7302 as soon as possible."

"Did he say what it was about?"

"No. I tried to find out, but he wouldn't even give me a hint."

"Okay, thanks, Cathy. I'll call him right away." She folded her phone and looked at Nick. "Sergeant Rodgers left a message at the office for me to call him."

"Any idea what it's about?" Nick asked, splitting his attention between the road and Danni.

"None." Curious and worried, Danni punched in the numbers Cathy had given her.

The phone rang once before Sarge's bellow answered. "Sergeant Rodgers."

"Sarge, it's Danni Hawkins. I just got your message."

"It's about damned time," the crusty sergeant swore. "You know a kid named Marsel Malone?"

"Yes. How'd you know?"

"Found your business card on him. He's at Memorial. Hit-and-run. Broken bones and a severe concussion."

Danni sucked in a sharp breath and pressed her free hand to her forehead. "Any witnesses?"

Sarge snorted. "Nobody sees anything in that part of town."

She was aware of Nick casting her concerned glances, but she remained focused on the conversation. "Any description of the car?"

"Dark green Taurus. It was found abandoned five blocks from the scene. Big dent in the hood with Malone's blood. No prints. Owner reported it stolen at six this morning."

"Dammit." Danni squeezed her eyes shut. "Thanks for the information, Sarge."

"Find out what the hell's going on." The sergeant hung up.

"What happened?" Nick demanded as he parked in the center's nearly abandoned lot.

Danni told him about Marsel's "accident."

"They must've figured another suicide would be too much of a coincidence." Nick's eyes flashed with anger.

"I want to swing by Memorial and see him after we talk to Marge." Danni propped her elbows on her knees and buried her face in her hands. "Damn it! How many more people are going to be hurt or killed before we find out what's going on?"

"We're doing the best we can, Danni." Nick said quietly. A hand settled on her shoulder, squeezing it in reassurance. "Come on. Let's see what Marge has for us."

Chapter Seventeen

Nick glanced at the piece of paper in Danni's hands, then through the rain-spattered windshield at the high-rise office building. "Do we have a suite number or company name?"

"This was all Marge had besides Gilsen's work number, and his voice mail picked up when I tried calling." She sighed. "Maybe we should drive around and see if we can spot his car."

As Nick drove, he surveyed the downtown area filled with cars and pedestrians. "He probably parks in a parking garage, and it would take all day to search them. It'd be easier to drop by the center tonight and see if he's there."

"We're supposed to be at Sam's place for dinner this evening." Her voice was laden with impatience. "I suppose we can stop at the center after dinner. But right now, since we're close to the hospital, let's check on Marsel."

Nick's stomach growled, reminding him that their plan to have brunch before going to the center to talk to Marge had fallen by the wayside. "Let's grab something to eat first."

"Sure, why not? We're not accomplishing anything here anyway." Her sour tone vibrated with frustration.

Nick reached over and squeezed her knee. "Hey, we'll figure it out. It's just going to take more time."

"Yeah, well, I never was very good with that patience thing."

He arched an eyebrow in feigned astonishment. "Really?" His attempt to coax a small smile from Danni succeeded.

"I got it from Dad. He was the same way," she admitted.

Nick recalled several times when Paddy's patience seemed in short supply and chuckled. "You're right. But I never saw him lose his temper."

Danni sobered and stared out the windshield. "I did. Once."

He sensed her melancholy and gently prodded her. "When?"

She didn't speak for a minute, and Nick was certain she wouldn't answer him, that the pain was too deep to share. He empathized only too well.

Nick turned into a fast-food drive-in and parked beneath a large metal canopy beside a menu and intercom. After getting Danni's selections, he pressed the call-in button and placed their order. Not long afterward, a teenage girl brought out their drinks and passed them through Danni's open window.

"Your order will be up in a few minutes," the carhop said with an oft-used, too-bright smile.

Nick sipped his slushie drink, while Danni drank her diet soda.

"I was six years old," Danni said quietly as they waited for their food.

It took a moment for Nick to figure out she was referring to his earlier question about her father's temper. "What happened?"

She plucked at her straw. "From what I remember, Mom wasn't a candidate for the Mrs. Brady award. She wanted me to be quiet in the house during the day, and at night she was gone more than she was home, so it was pretty common for Dad to put me to bed. He used to tell me she was at a meeting or playing cards with her friends. I don't know if he was lying to protect me or if he really believed it.

"One evening after dinner, they got in a big fight. Dad ordered me to my room, so I went upstairs but stayed at the top of the steps where I could hear everything. They didn't know I was there." Danni paused to take a sip of her soda.

Nick could imagine little dark-haired Danni, already willful enough to disobey her father.

"They were yelling and saying words that would've gotten me in trouble if I'd have said them," she continued, a wry note in her tone. "After a while there was this other sound—I recognized it because I'd heard it before when Mom punished me for being too loud. Dad hit her." Danni twirled her straw around and around between her fingertips. "That's when Mom left. I never saw her again."

Nick's heart ached, and he reached over to clasp her hand. It was a poor substitute for what he really wanted to do, but bucket seats weren't conducive to embraces. "I'm sorry, Danni."

She shrugged but kept her face cast downward. "It was a long time ago." She sniffed once and raised her head, revealing glistening eyes. "I'm sure it wasn't bad compared to what you had to put up with."

Abruptly, all the memories he'd buried rose from their graves to haunt him.

"My parents didn't fight much," Nick began before he even consciously decided to confide his whole sordid past. "At least not when I was younger. I used to come home from school only to be kicked out because my mother was 'working.' My dad was usually drunk, but not so drunk that he didn't forget to take the money for services rendered." Years-old resentment thickened Nick's voice. "Those were the 'good old days.' Later, when I was a teenager, after Mom lost her looks, and business was harder to come by, they used to fight." He laughed, a sharp, humorless sound. "By that time I was bigger than Dad, or he probably would've had *me* turning tricks."

Danni didn't appear shocked. During her time as a cop, she'd most likely seen worse. "I'm sorry, for all the good that does now," she said softly.

Nick gazed out his side window to lay the memories to rest once more and regain his composure. When he'd gone to Danni to get her help in discovering who killed Paddy, he never expected to spill his guts to her. Of course, he hadn't expected to sleep with her either, and he'd done that and more. If the case were progressing as quickly as their attraction to one another, it would've been solved by now.

The perky carhop brought out their tray and hung it on Nick's window. After he paid for the meal, she retreated, leaving Danni and Nick to eat.

He passed Danni's two plain burgers to her, as well as the small fries she'd ordered. Then he unwrapped his burger with the works and, even though his hunger had fled, he forced himself to eat it all.

Glancing at Danni, he noticed she only nibbled her food. More than likely she, too, hadn't enjoyed the trip down memory lane. That, coupled with the increasingly complex maze surrounding Paddy's and Matt's deaths, had pretty much ruined their appetites.

Fifteen minutes later, the carhop returned for the tray, which held half of one of Danni's burgers and most of her fries. Danni stowed the other untouched burger on the floor between the two front seats.

"Snack for later?" Nick asked, hoping to lighten the mood.

"I'm hoping we run into Southpaw," she replied.

Nick had forgotten about the former baseball player. Although he didn't have Danni's faith in the crazy homeless man, there were few other leads to follow.

Ten minutes later, Nick parked in the Memorial Hospital visitors' lot. He turned up the collar of his brown leather jacket against the drizzle as he waited for Danni to join him at the back of the Jeep. She had slung her backpack over a shoulder, not wanting to risk leaving his story notes and the answering machine in the vehicle.

Warily, he glanced around the dreary surroundings, half-expecting to spot a light-colored sedan, but he didn't see anything suspicious. He didn't chide himself for his paranoia this time.

They entered through a pair of automatic doors and stopped at the information desk. The grandmotherly woman working there gave them Marsel's room number, and Danni and Nick boarded an elevator to ride to the fourth floor.

"Even if he has regained consciousness, they may not let us talk to him," Nick said.

Stubbornness glittered in her eyes. "If he's awake, we'll talk to him."

Nick shrugged, recognizing an immoveable force when he encountered one. Besides, he knew her well enough to know she wouldn't push the injured boy too hard.

The door to Marsel's room was open. The boy was hooked up to a monitor and had an IV in his left hand. His right leg was encased in a cast, and there was a purplish lump on his right temple.

A woman sat in the chair beside his bed, her back to them.

Danni knocked softly on the door as she and Nick entered.

The heavyset woman came to her feet and faced them. Fear filled her dark eyes. "Who're you?"

"I'm Danni Hawkins, and this is Nick Sirocco," Danni said.

The woman's shoulders slumped with relief. "Marsel's talked about you," she said, looking at Nick.

"I volunteer at the center," he said. "Are you Marsel's mother?"

"Olivia Malone," she introduced herself.

Nick shook her hand. "Nice to meet you, Ms. Malone."

"Call me Olivia," she said, shaking Danni's hand.

"How's he doing?" Nick asked.

Olivia looked at her son, and her brow furrowed in worry. "As well as can be expected. Three broken ribs, broken leg, bruises all over his body, and a bad concussion."

"We were sorry to hear about his accident," Danni said. "Do the police have any leads as to who did this?"

Olivia shook her head and said bitterly, "Not a one." She tucked the sheet around Marsel's still body.

Nick glanced at Danni, asking her mutely what she wanted to do now.

"Was Marsel into anything illegal?" Danni asked his mother.

"No way," she replied with conviction.

"How can you be so certain?"

Olivia glared at Danni. "He promised me he'd stay out of trouble and get himself a basketball scholarship. He was going to get out of the neighborhood and do something with his life." She looked at Nick. "That's why he was at the center all the time. He was practicing."

"He was at the center whenever I was there," Nick said to Danni.

"Marsel's a good boy," Olivia said with a mixture of pride and defensiveness. Her expression grew cloudy. "And now, because of some careless driver, he probably won't get that scholarship."

"What did the doctor say about his injuries?" Nick asked.

"He'll heal, but he's going to need some kind of therapy for his leg. By the time he's back to normal, his chance for that scholarship will be gone." Olivia dashed a hand across her eyes.

No one spoke as they gazed at Marsel's ashen complexion.

"Did Marsel ever talk about a boy named Matt?" Danni asked, breaking the silence.

Olivia nodded. "He used to have a friend named Matt, but he killed himself a few nights ago. Marsel was pretty upset about it." She tilted her head, remembering something. "The day after Matt's death, I walked to the corner store to pick up some milk. I heard Marsel arguing with another boy—I think his name was Gary—in the alley. They were talking about Matt."

"What were they arguing about?" Danni asked.

"I only caught a few words here and there, but I got the impression Marsel thought Gary might've been able to help Matt."

"Did you hear any other names?" Danni asked.

Olivia lowered herself to the chair beside the bed and laid her hand on her son's arm. "Yes. A Gilcrest or Gilyard, something like that."

Danni squatted down beside the chair so her gaze was even with Olivia's. "Could it have been Gilsen?"

The woman thought for a moment, then nodded. "It might've been."

A nurse dressed in a colorful uniform entered the room. "Would you all mind stepping out into the hallway? I need to assess the patient."

"When does the doctor expect him to regain consciousness?" Olivia asked the RN.

The nurse, whose name tag read Kera, replied, "The doctor is hoping he'll come out of the coma in the next thirty-six hours. But even if he does wake up in the next day or so, there's a strong possibility he won't remember much leading up to the accident."

Olivia nodded in resignation. "Thank you."

Nick helped the woman from the chair and guided her out of the room, with Danni following. They walked down the hall to the small corner waiting room near the elevators.

"Is there anyone who can sit with you?" Nick asked Olivia.

"My sister's coming after she gets off work."

"Is there anything you need?" Danni asked.

"Just for Marsel to wake up," Olivia replied, a quaver in her voice.

Danni touched her forearm, then dug a business card out of her backpack and handed it to her. "Call us if you need anything, or if Marsel's condition changes."

Olivia tucked the card in her shirt pocket, then clasped Nick's hand in her right hand and Danni's in her left. "Thank you. Both of you."

"You're welcome," Danni said.

"When Marsel wakes up, tell him we'll stop by to see him," Nick said.

"I will," Olivia promised.

Nick and Danni left the woman alone in the waiting area and rode down to the main floor. The elevator doors opened, and they stepped out to see Karen Crandle, in uniform, walking toward them.

"Hello, Karen," Nick said.

The slender, blond cop glanced up, startled. "Hi. What're you doing here?"

"We came to see Marsel."

"That's where I'm headed. Sarge wanted us to stop by to see if he woke up yet. I'm supposed to get his statement."

"He's still unconscious," Nick said.

"Is anybody with him?"

"His mother."

Karen nodded, her expression pinched. "I've seen Marsel at the center. He's a good kid."

"Yeah, he is," Nick said.

The cop glanced at the elevators. "I think I'll go up and introduce myself to his mother. Maybe she knows something."

"Where's your new partner?" Danni asked.

Karen rolled her eyes. "He wanted some coffee. He said I could handle Marsel alone. Knowing him, he bought half a dozen donuts to go with his coffee."

"Kinda takes the stereotype seriously, huh?" Danni said.

"Tell me about it. But at least I don't have to put up with

him too much longer—less than a day." Karen brightened. "Are you coming to Hennessy's tonight?"

With everything that had happened, Nick had totally forgotten about the get-together. "We're going to Sam Richmond's for dinner."

"What's going on at Hennessy's?" Danni asked.

"Farewell party," Karen answered. "Two weeks ago I put in my notice. I got a lateral transfer to Denver. My sister, her husband, and kids live there, so I thought it'd be nice to be close to family." She paused. "The party starts at four-thirty. Why don't you stop by before you go to dinner?"

"We'll try to do that," Nick said. "When do you leave for Denver?"

"Two days." She glanced at the watch on her slim wrist. "I have to get going." An elevator dinged open, and Karen stepped into it. "I expect to see you both at Hennessy's later."

Nick lifted his hand in farewell, and the elevator doors closed. He started walking toward the main door with Danni beside him.

"I didn't know she was leaving," Danni said thoughtfully.

"I remember Paddy saying something about it. She even talked to him before she actually put in her notice, asked him what he thought she should do," Nick said.

"And Dad told her to move closer to her family?"

Nick heard her lingering bitterness. "No matter what you thought, he always believed family was the most important thing in the world." He took a deep breath, hoping he wasn't overstepping his bounds. "Your father used to tuck you in bed. He took you to baseball games. He brought you to the center until your adolescent hormones got you in trouble. He always kept your latest school picture in his patrol car and talked off anyone's ear if they asked about you. Does that sounds like a man who didn't want anything to do with his daughter?"

Danni stared straight ahead as they walked across the

damp asphalt to the Jeep. "No." Her voice was so low Nick had to strain to hear her.

Nick waited until they were in the SUV to speak. He traced her somber profile with his gaze and resisted the impulse to touch her. "I know it's going to take longer than a few days to believe it, but he was damned proud of you, Danni."

She didn't answer, but he thought he noticed a hitch in her breathing when she turned away from him. Stifling a sigh, he started his Jeep. "Where to now?"

She remained silent for so long he began to wonder if she'd heard him. Finally, she faced him again. There was no sign of the earlier anguish in her features, only cool determination. "If Gary ran from us, maybe he had something else going on last night."

Nick didn't need a map to follow her line of thinking. "Maybe steal a car? Who can you trust in the department?"

"Nobody." Her lips curled as she opened her cell phone. "But I happen to have an administrative assistant who can check public records for auto thefts committed last night."

She punched in some numbers, and Nick listened to her ask Cathy for the information.

"She'll have the list printed by the time we get there," Danni said after punching off the phone.

"What're we looking for?"

Danni smiled crookedly. "We'll know it when we see it."

Damned if Nick didn't believe her.

Chapter Eighteen

DANNI was disappointed when she and Nick didn't spot Southpaw on their circular route to her office. He must have been catching a nap in a vacant building or on a park bench. Not that she expected him to tie the case up in a pretty bow, but he often surprised her with his extensive but jumbled knowledge of the goings-on in the neighborhood.

As soon as Danni and Nick walked into the office, Cathy—true to her word—handed Danni a printout of the auto thefts reported that morning. There were only fourteen vehicles on the list, which gave Danni a decent shot of finding that arcane something that might solidify their theories.

Danni carried the list into her office, and she and Nick both sat on the client side of the desk to scan the sheet.

"A 2001 Honda Accord, 1996 Ford Expedition, 1998 Toyota Camry," Nick read aloud.

"Probably all stolen for their parts," Danni mused aloud. "There's an amazingly large market for parts for the most common vehicles."

"Chop shops," Nick said absently as he continued to peruse the listing. "A 1999 Ford Taurus." He glanced up with startled comprehension.

Danni gritted her teeth. "The one that hit Marsel." She took over reading aloud. "A 2003 Dodge Ram, 1999 Jeep Wrangler, 2003 BMW 530i." Her breath caught, and the back of her neck tingled. "Matt stole the laptop from a Jaguar, right?"

"That's right." Nick appeared bewildered. "Why?"

She held up a stalling hand and scanned the remaining stolen automobiles. Nothing else came close to the BMW in terms of price and luxury. Her mind racing, Danni stabbed the intercom button.

"Yes?" came Cathy's tinny voice.

"I want a list of all the stolen vehicles over the last six months."

"It's a good thing we ordered extra reams of paper this week."

Even through the speakerphone, Danni could hear her friend's dry tone. "How long will it take?"

"Give me an hour."

Although Danni wanted the information yesterday, she knew better than to snipe at Cathy. Her friend would only snipe back. "You got it. Thanks." She flicked off the intercom.

"What?" Nick asked, his brows drawn downward. Only he could make quizzical look sexy.

"If you were operating an auto theft ring, what kind of cars would you go for?"

He thought for a moment, then his eyebrows lifted in comprehension. "Expensive ones to make the risks worthwhile."

"Bingo." She pointed to the BMW on the list. "A BMW was stolen last night. Maybe that was why Gary ran from us. The laptop was lifted from a Jaguar, which means Matt could've stolen the Jaguar."

Nick slouched in his chair, obviously pondering her words. "If it's an auto theft ring, where does the computer fit in?"

"The kids are probably paid a certain fee for the cars they lift. When Matt saw the laptop, he figured it'd be a nice bonus."

"In other words, Matt got greedy."

Danni leaned forward and placed her elbows on her thighs. "And when the boss found out what Matt had done and that the boy had gone to my dad to save his own skin—"

"The boss ordered Matt killed," Nick finished, straightening excitedly.

"Or the boss did it himself. We don't know how many people are involved. When we get the new list, I want to record the dates each luxury car was stolen and where it was stolen from. Then we'll have to get into a computer at the department to look up each of the case files."

"And how do we intend to do that?"

"Alex Levin."

Nick's eyes widened. "He could be involved."

Danni nodded reluctantly. "I know, but if he isn't, it'd be a good idea to have him on our side."

"And if he is involved?"

"Then maybe he'll get desperate, and we can take him down."

Nick scowled. "Or he'll take *us* down."

"Either way, I think the risk is worth it." Danni reached for the phone, then drew her hand back as her conscience slapped her. This involved Nick, too, and he deserved to have a say in the matter. "What about you, partner? Do *you* think the risk is worth it?"

Nick wrinkled his brow as if it were a trick question. "What if I said it's not?"

She took a deep breath. "Then we don't ask Alex for help." Although she thought Alex was innocent, it wasn't about only her anymore. Nick's life was on the line, too.

He studied her, his features neutral. Danni tried to match his expression, but it was difficult with his intense blue eyes leveled at her. She managed not to fidget as he considered her question.

"You said you went to the Academy with him?" he finally asked.

"That's right."

"And he's never given you a reason not to trust him?"

"Never," she replied honestly.

"All right. Call him."

Danni's throat tightened, although she would've been hard-pressed to explain why. Or maybe the why was as simple as discovering Nick trusted her judgment.

She gave him a quick nod, then called the department and left a message for Alex to call her.

Danni stood. "Would you like a cup of coffee or a soda?"

"Coffee, please."

"Two coffees coming up."

Danni slipped past Cathy, who was on the phone, and retrieved two steaming cups from the break room. She returned to her office and handed Nick one. Her heart quickened as their fingers brushed.

Danni chastised herself as she moved to her chair on the other side of the desk. Sweating hands and a palpitating heart were for hormone-driven adolescents, not a twenty-eight-year-old woman who'd dated enough boys during high school and college to staff a luxury hotel.

"So now we wait?" Nick asked.

"Now we wait."

For an entire five minutes, Nick remained silent, drinking his coffee and keeping his gaze aimed at the toes of his hiking boots. Danni wasn't certain if she wanted him to talk or not. In fact, when it came to Nick, she wasn't certain about much of anything, which was a condition she rarely found in herself.

"So—"

"What—"

Danni and Nick spoke at the same time.

"You first."

"Go ahead."

Their voices overlapped again.

Danni pressed her lips together and saw that Nick did the same thing. They laughed.

"I was just wondering when you need to have your book written," Danni said.

Nick grinned wryly. "Since I haven't sold it yet, never. However, I told my agent I'd have the first few chapters to him by the end of the month."

"That's only two weeks away."

"Yep." He sighed. "But I've decided not to write it."

"Why? Because Dad isn't here to help you?"

Nick rubbed his eyes. "Partly. But mostly because it's the reason Paddy's dead. If I hadn't—"

Danni leaned across the desk. "Your book isn't the reason Dad is dead. He's dead because some son of a bitch killed him. Period."

"But if I hadn't—"

"You didn't squeeze the trigger. Besides, how could you have known that your idea was more fact than fiction?" Danni gentled her voice. "If Dad were here, you know what he'd say."

Nick quirked a smile. "He'd tell me to quit feeling sorry for myself."

"I was thinking more along the lines of, 'Quit acting like a jackass.' "

Amusement glimmered in his eyes. "That, too."

Their gazes locked, and warmth flowed through Danni. She'd always scoffed at talk show guests who spoke of soul mates, but the connection she felt with Nick made her reexamine her cynicism. They'd spent over seventy-two hours in each other's company and had yet to kill one another. Of course, there had been a few instances . . .

Just for kicks, she imagined spending more time—a few days, weeks, months . . . the next fifty or so years—with him. Amazingly, the thought didn't make her want to check herself into a psych ward.

A knock brought Danni back to the present. "Yes?"

Cathy opened the door and stuck her head in. A lecherous smile lit her face. "I'm not interrupting anything, am I?"

Nick ducked his head and rubbed his brow. "For crying out loud."

Danni hid a smile behind her hand. "What is it, Cathy?"

The assistant turned serious and crossed to the desk. She held out a sheaf of papers to Danni. "Here's the first month of car thefts. The second month is printing now. I'll bring them in as they come off the printer."

Excitement surged through Danni as she took them. "That'd be great. Thanks."

Cathy's gaze deliberately moved from Danni to Nick and back. "Well, I'd hate for you two to get bored in this little tiny office all by yourselves where no one can see what—"

"I hear a printer calling your name," Danni interrupted deliberately.

The petite blond wrinkled her nose. "No rest for the weary."

"Or the wicked," Nick muttered.

"I didn't realize you'd noticed." Cathy winked at him. "Let me know if you need anything else." She exited like a stripper leaving a stage.

Danni held up a hand. "Don't say it. She's a good friend and the most efficient administrative assistant I've ever seen."

Nick sighed but his eyes twinkled. "I have to admit she does kind of grow on a person."

"Like a fungus," they said simultaneously, then laughed.

Danni grew serious and split the papers into two piles. She handed Nick one. "Look for luxury, high-end vehicles. When you find one, jot down the date and address of where it was stolen." She pushed a pad of paper and a pen at him.

Nick nodded and set his empty coffee cup aside.

An hour and a half later, Danni and Nick stacked six months of scrutinized auto theft records in the middle of the desk. Danni had compiled a list of twenty-seven. Glancing at Nick's amazingly neat handwriting, she noticed he had almost as many.

Nick rubbed his eyes with the heels of his hands. "I never realized how many cars were stolen each day."

"It's a national pastime," Danni said absently. "Our next step is to figure out if there's any pattern as to when and where they were stolen."

Nick sighed, but bravely began reading off addresses so Danni could enter them in her computer. Forty-five minutes later, two facts became evident.

"Most of them were stolen from their homes, and they were stolen at night," Danni said.

"Isn't that common?"

Danni picked up a paper clip and straightened it. "It's more common for automobiles to be taken from public places, like mall parking lots or parking garages. It's usually too difficult for a thief to sneak into a neighborhood—especially an upscale one—to steal a car from the owner's garage."

"So this tells us what?"

Danni tossed aside the ruined paper clip and picked up a new one. "One, that the thieves knew the addresses of their targets, which means they were either under surveillance or somebody tipped them off. Two, they knew how to bypass the security systems."

"How do we know the victims had security systems?"

"Because anyone who has money for expensive toys also has a security system these days."

Nick grunted. "I'll buy that. Is there a three?"

Danni dropped yet another straightened paper clip on her blotter. "Not yet. I think this is where we need Alex's help." As if on cue, the intercom buzzed. "Yes?"

"Alex Levin on line two," Cathy announced.

Danni arched an eyebrow in Nick's direction, then punched the blinking light on her phone. "Thanks for calling back, Alex."

She went on to explain the favor she needed. Her friend

was more than willing to help, and since he was at a terminal, she started feeding him the information.

Half an hour later, her hand was cramped from writing, but from the twelve thefts Alex had called up on his computer, one thing became glaringly obvious. She looked at Nick's anxious expression and gave him a thumbs-up. But before she ended the call with Alex, she had one more question for her friend.

"Last night, I got the first three letters of the license of the person who broke into my truck. Detective Rearden is running the list, but there's one person I'd like to check. Could you punch Paul Gilsen's name into Motor Vehicles and take a look at his plate number?"

Alex grumbled, but she could hear his fingers tapping unevenly on a keyboard.

"What're you doing?" Nick asked quietly. "If he and Gilsen are in this together, you've just tipped them off."

Danni covered the phone and opened her mouth, but closed it abruptly when Alex spoke.

"Looks like he has only one car—a 2002 silver Audi." The policeman spoke in a low voice, like he didn't want anyone to overhear him. "Number is Edward, Charles, Union, three, nine, two."

Danni's heart hammered against her ribs, but she kept her voice even. "Thanks, Alex. I really appreciate this."

"Are you going to tell me what's going on?" Alex asked.

"Sorry. Too soon. Once we've got our ducks in a row, I'll explain. Honest."

"Just don't get your ducks shot off."

Danni smiled. "We'll be careful. Thanks again."

After exchanging farewells, Danni ended the call and gave Nick her undivided attention. "There wasn't enough time to check on all the thefts, but out of the dozen he pulled up, eleven of the cars were taken when the owners were on vacation."

Nick tilted his head. "How did the thieves know they were out of town?"

"Exactly," Danni said as excitement thrummed through her. "Someone involved in the ring must have some connection to a security firm—or firms—which would make sense since at least one of the thieves would have to know how to bypass the system." She paused as another possibility struck her, and her enthusiasm wilted. "Or they have someone within the department feeding them the information."

"How—"

"People often inform the police when they'll be out of town. When I was on patrol, we'd make sure to check on those places at least a couple of times each shift." She brightened as she thought of another possibility. "People stop their mail and newspapers when they go on vacation. What about someone from one of those places passing on information?"

"Not very likely. My money's on a dirty cop," Nick said quietly.

Although she was no longer a police officer, she felt a loyalty toward her former brothers in blue. However, her gut was agreeing with Nick. More than likely, some cop was taking bribes for giving the ringleader the dates and addresses of vacationers.

And now she was fairly certain who that ringleader was.

"Care to guess what letters Paul Gilsen's license plate starts with?" she asked, arching an eyebrow.

Nick didn't look pleased; he'd obviously figured that one out. "It'd be easy enough for him to make contact with different cops at the center," he said. "Feel them out. Find out which ones might be open to a little graft."

Danni sighed. As far as she was concerned, her gut instinct about Gilsen had been validated by the matching partial plate. However, she didn't enjoy hurting Nick. "I'm sorry. I know you and Paul were friends."

"A long time ago. I guess he didn't escape the neighborhood after all." He glanced at his watch, his face an expressionless mask. "It's three-thirty. I have to go back to the house to let Gus out."

"We should change for dinner, too." Danni gathered their notes and the printouts and slid them into a large envelope.

Nick picked up Danni's backpack and slung it over a muscled shoulder, while Danni carried the papers.

Cathy was busy on the telephone again and merely waved as they left.

When they arrived at Paddy's twenty minutes later, Danni scanned the neighborhood with a practiced eye but saw nothing that roused her suspicions. Nick let Gus out in the backyard while Danni checked the answering machine for messages and found the light blinking.

"Danni, it's Karen. I heard you and Nick were staying at Paddy's. I just wanted to tell you how much I respected your father. He taught me a lot about being a police officer. He also talked my ear off about you." Quiet laughter. "I really hope you can drop by Hennessy's later. I know your dad will be there in spirit."

"Who was that?" Nick asked as he and Gus came in the back door of the kitchen.

"Karen Crandle, just reminding us to stop by Hennessy's."

Nick leaned against the counter and crossed his arms, while Gus went to sit by Danni's feet. "What do you want to do?"

As she considered his question, Danni unwrapped the second burger she'd gotten for lunch and squatted down by Gus. She tore a chunk off the cold sandwich, and the dog took it from her fingers. "She was Dad's partner."

Nick nodded but didn't speak. It seemed he was conceding this decision to her, just as she'd given him the choice to trust Alex Levin earlier.

Danni gave Gus another piece of the burger. "It wouldn't hurt to drop by on the way to Sam's."

"And maybe Paul Gilsen will be there."

"Do they know each other?"

"They both volunteer at the center."

Duh. If Danni didn't have a mangled burger in her hands, she would've struck her forehead in exasperation. "We might be able to ask him some questions. He'll be less likely to try anything in a bar surrounded by cops."

Nick glanced down at his feet. "You didn't ask Levin why he lied to us last night."

It took Danni a moment to recall what he meant. She fed another piece of hamburger to Gus before speaking. "About seeing Gary in the computer room?"

He met her gaze steadily. "Yes."

Danni forced herself to hold his gaze. "If he's at the party, I'll ask him then."

Nick's attention shifted to Gus, who was staring at the remains of the burger in Danni's hand. "Go easy on that, Gus. We're going to be gone a few hours this evening."

Danni looked at the dog, who stared at them with pleading, liquid brown eyes. "Don't turn those baby browns in my direction—beam them at your master."

Gus let out a short bark, then nosed Danni's hand.

"All right. Just one more," Danni said. She fed her the last chunk of meat, then tossed the wrapper and the remnants of the limp bun in the garbage.

"You may have a mess to clean up when we get back tonight," Nick warned.

"She's your dog."

"You're the one who gave her the burger."

"But she's *your* dog." She glanced at the ugly teapot-shaped clock above the stove. "We'd better get ready if we want to stop at Hennessy's first." Suddenly feeling more lighthearted than she had in some time, Danni charged out of the kitchen, hollering, "First dibs on the shower."

Five minutes later, Danni felt a cool breeze as the shower curtain was pushed aside and Nick joined her beneath the steaming spray. Muscled arms wound around her waist from behind, and she leaned into his welcome warmth.

She tipped her head back against his shoulder and gazed

up at his sinfully sexy smile. "Is that your rifle, soldier, or are you just glad to see me?"

He nuzzled her ear with his nose and whispered, "This rifle's locked and loaded, baby."

Laughing, Danni turned within his embrace and put her arms around his neck. "Fire at will, soldier."

"Yes, ma'am."

Nick then proceeded to earn his sharpshooter's badge.

DANNI shifted on the passenger seat of Nick's Jeep, her body still humming with lingering pleasure. Shower sex wasn't new, but shower lovemaking definitely was a novel—and fulfilling—experience.

Nick glanced at her, a knowing grin on his freshly shaven face. "Something wrong?"

Danni searched for a snappy comeback, but her body and brain were too content to dredge up a sarcastic retort. "Not a thing, unless having this strange urge to shower again is wrong."

He chuckled and reached over to clasp her hand, which rested on her thigh. "It must be contagious; I've got the same urge."

"We're both out of luck. No urges satisfied until we get back to the house."

"Is that a threat?"

"A promise."

Nick's gaze fastened on her lips, and his eyes smoldered.

Danni glanced out the windshield to see the curb growing closer. "The road, Nick."

He jerked his attention back to driving and smiled sheepishly. "Drive. Now. Urges. Later."

Danni's cheeks warmed, and she lowered her window to breathe in the cool, damp air. It took the remainder of the trip to Hennessy's to bring her body temperature down to normal.

After Nick found a parking place a block from the popular police hangout, he and Danni got out of the Jeep. Danni glanced at her backpack on the floor between the two seats.

"We'll only be there a few minutes," Nick said, obviously guessing her thoughts. "And I don't think we had a tail over here."

Danni granted him a quick smile. "How would you know? You barely kept us on the road."

In the late afternoon shadows, Nick's flush was barely perceptible. "I didn't see a light-colored sedan following us."

Danni took pity on him. "I didn't either. And nobody knows where we're parked." She shut the passenger door, leaving the backpack inside the SUV, and joined Nick on the sidewalk.

He took her hand in his, as if it were the most natural thing in the world. Danni curled her fingers around his without a ripple of awkwardness. It felt . . . natural.

Hennessy's was as full as Danni had ever seen it. She paused just inside the door, frozen for a second by the déjà vu of familiar faces and shoptalk. Phrases and tones sparked memories of coming here after work with her former partner Scott.

"Danni?"

Nick's gentle voice enticed her out of the past. She squeezed his hand, silently thanking him. He smiled down at her.

She allowed him to tug her through the crowd as she kept her face down, hoping no one would notice her. She hadn't even considered how difficult it would be, being around her former colleagues again.

"Danni?"

She glanced up at the sound of her name and spotted Joe Tygard directly in front of her. "Joe. How are you?"

He frowned. "Is that all I get after all this time—'How are you?' " The husky redhead picked her up and hugged her tightly. "Damn, it's good to see you again. Alex told me he's talked to you a few times this week."

"He answered some questions for me," Danni said, embarrassed. "I'm really sorry I haven't kept in touch, Joe. It's just . . ."

"I know. You, me, Alex, and Scott—the four musketeers. Nobody could stop us."

"Only a bullet." Danni's throat constricted as she remembered that night when she'd failed her partner. She blinked back moisture and suddenly became aware of Nick's scowl directed at Joe. "Joe Tygard, this is Nick Sirocco. Nick, Joe Tygard. We went to the Academy together."

Nick shook Joe's hand, the grip lasting longer than usual. She shook her head at the sterling example of male posturing.

"Tygard," Nick said.

"Sirocco," Joe said.

They finally ceased the arm wrestling contest.

"I didn't see you at Dad's funeral," Danni said to Joe.

"I was out of town with my fiancée. Visiting the future in-laws," Joe replied.

"I didn't know you were getting married."

Joe ducked his head as his face reddened. "Alex said I should call you."

She punched his arm. "You should've."

Joe surveyed Nick from head to toe. "So, this your latest?"

It was Danni's turn to flush. "Not exactly."

"Yes," Nick said a split second later.

She glared at Nick. "We're investigating Dad's death."

"I thought it was ruled a suicide," Joe said, puzzled.

"That's the official ruling, but we believe he was murdered." Danni paused. "Is Alex here tonight?"

Joe shook his head. "I saw him in the locker room before I came over here. He and Helen are going up to a B and B in Seattle for the weekend. They were leaving as soon as he got home."

Danni hid her trepidation. "Alex didn't mention that when I talked to him earlier."

"I'm not surprised. He told me it was Helen's idea. He wasn't too keen on it, but you know how Helen can get sometimes."

Danni did know how stubborn Helen could be.

"He'll be back Monday?" Nick asked.

"He said he would be. Anything I can help you with?"

Danni shook her head. "No, but thanks." She smiled. "It was good seeing you again, Joc. You'll have to introduce me to the future Mrs. Tygard."

"Maybe the four of us can go out together some evening."

"We'd like that," Nick said smoothly.

"Later, Danni," Joe said and disappeared into the crowd.

"So Levin skipped town," Nick said.

Despite her bad feeling, she couldn't help but defend her friend. "He went on a romantic getaway with his wife."

"Getaway. Appropriate word."

Uncomfortable with Nick's—and her own—misgivings, Danni clasped his hand and tugged him forward. "Let's find Karen, say our good-byes, then get out of here."

They found the tall blond standing in the center of a small circle of patrolmen. She spotted them immediately and excused herself from the group. Wearing hip-hugger black trousers with black chunky-heeled boots and a snug green knit top, she looked more like a college student than a cop. "I'm glad you two could make it."

Nick smiled. "I doubt you would've even missed us with this mob."

She donned a pout and put an arm around Nick's waist. "I'm hurt you'd think that."

Danni, smelling the liquor on the woman's breath, released Nick's hand and took a step back. How many times had Danni drunk too much here at Hennessy's with her coworkers? Scott had always made sure she made it home safely.

"We just wanted to wish you the best of luck in Denver," Danni said, suddenly wishing to escape the world that had once been hers.

"Thanks, Danni," Karen said warmly. She reached over to clasp Danni's hand. "I wish my dad was half as proud of me as yours was of you."

There was no mistaking the envy in Karen's voice, and Danni's breath stammered in her throat. "I never realized he talked about me so much."

Karen shook her head in tolerant amusement. "You were his favorite topic."

Nick smiled tenderly at Danni. "I keep telling her that, but she won't believe me."

Uncomfortable being the center of attention, Danni changed the topic. "Was Paul Gilsen going to drop by?"

Karen's brow furrowed. "Who?"

"Paul Gilsen. He volunteers at the center in the computer room," Nick explained.

"Is he the nice-looking, dark-haired man who supervises the computer room?" Nick nodded, and Karen continued, "I've seen him around, but didn't know his name. I doubt he'll be here. Why, are you looking for him?"

"We just want to ask him something," Danni replied, stifling her disappointment. "Good luck in Denver, Karen."

"Good luck to you, too, Danni." Karen hugged her, then Nick. "Good-bye."

With the awkward farewell behind them, Danni and Nick made for the exit. However, they were stopped half a dozen times by officers offering belated condolences to Danni for the loss of her father. Once on the sidewalk, Danni breathed deeply of the cool, fresh air.

"I don't want to go through that again," she murmured.

Nick shrugged. "It could've been worse."

"How's that?"

"They could've ignored you completely."

Danni wasn't so certain that would have been worse.

Chapter Nineteen

BECAUSE of their stop at Hennessy's, it was 6:15 when Nick pulled up to Sam's house.

He gazed at the home with its white siding, front porch with a glider swing, well-trimmed lawn, and fenced backyard. A sharp yearning pierced him. More than Paddy's, this house emanated warmth, coziness, and merry Christmases around a tree decorated with ornaments handed down from one generation to the next. All the things he'd never known.

"Are you ready?" Danni asked.

He turned to see her gazing at him, her concern revealed in the corner creases of her eyes. "I was just thinking."

"About?"

"What it would be like to live in a place like this, like a real family."

She appeared startled by his admission. "You mean, complete with a wife, two point four children, and a dog?"

He grinned. "You can keep the point four children, but yeah, something like that."

Danni turned to stare at the house. "I suppose it's like most things—better imagined than actually lived."

"That's a pretty cynical view."

She grinned wryly. "Hey, I grew up in a house a lot like this."

Sam stepped out onto the porch. "Are you two going to come in or stay out there all night?"

"Why do I suddenly feel like I'm fifteen again?" Danni whispered to Nick.

He chuckled, and they stepped out of the truck. He guided Danni, with the backpack over her shoulder, down the walk and up the porch steps.

Nick hung back as Danni and Sam hugged. He hoped, for Danni's sake, the retired cop wasn't involved in anything illegal. Danni stepped away, and Sam held his hand out to Nick, who shook it firmly.

"Good evening, sir," Nick said formally.

Sam's eyes twinkled. "Nice to see you and Danni aren't fighting like cats and dogs anymore."

"We still have our moments," Danni said.

"Life would be pretty boring without them," Nick added.

Sam chuckled and ushered Nick and Danni into the house, which smelled of meat and spices, with the underlying scent of fresh coffee.

"Nancy's in the kitchen," Sam said, steering them in that direction.

The country kitchen was large and airy, with an abundance of cupboards and countertops. An older woman, who had to be Nancy, was stirring something on the stove. She turned, and her thin face lit with a bright smile.

"It's been too long, Danni," she said.

Danni crossed the floor and gave the slender woman a delicate hug. "You weren't supposed to go to any trouble," she scolded Nancy as she released her.

"This? I would've made the same for just Sam and myself." She raised pale blue eyes to Nick. "And you must be Nick."

He smiled. "That's me."

"I met you years ago, when Sam took me over to the youth center. You were with Paddy."

Although there was no sign of censure in her features, Nick detected coolness in her tone and couldn't hide his own defensiveness. "Without Paddy's help, I probably would've ended up another statistic in the prison system."

"I'm sorry," Nancy said sheepishly. "It's just that sometimes I wanted to strangle that man. He left a beautiful, intelligent daughter alone at home while he tried to save the world."

"Only a small part of it," Danni said quietly. "And the more I see of what he did at the center and how much he helped Nick, the more I realize how little I really knew him." She shrugged. "Besides, I didn't need Dad's help to get into trouble. I did that pretty well on my own."

Sam wrapped an arm around her shoulders. "He was a fine man, Danni. I'm glad he and you were starting to reconcile."

Nick suddenly felt like an outsider and realized this must have been how Danni felt all those years while Paddy took care of "his boys" rather than her. It wasn't a pleasant feeling.

"Why don't you get the kids something to drink while I finish up out here?" Nancy suggested.

"The kids are perfectly capable of getting their own drinks," Danni interjected smoothly. "Would you like some help, Nancy?"

"I think everything is done."

Amid teasing and joking, they spooned food into serving bowls and piled sliced beef onto a platter, and carried it all into the dining room. Nick's mouth watered at the banquet of pot roast, potatoes, carrots, and gravy, not to mention a salad and fresh baked bread. It was just the sort of meal the two point four children would expect to eat.

Danni filled water glasses from a pitcher in the refrigerator while Sam poured red wine. Once they were all seated around the table, they bowed their heads as Sam said a prayer. After that, Sam raised his wineglass, prompting Nick, Danni, and Nancy to do the same.

"To Paddy Hawkins," the older man said.

The toast was echoed around the table, then everyone sipped their wine. In the solemn silence, Nick pictured Paddy and mentally raised his glass to him.

Thanks for everything, Paddy. His gaze sidled to Danni. *Especially for your beautiful, passionate daughter.*

Bowls were passed around the table, and plates were filled. The meal was interspersed with compliments to the chef and small talk.

To Nick, it was like being a part of some family TV show. The warmth surrounding Danni and her surrogate parents enveloped him, brought him into a world where he'd previously only been a spectator. He could see why Danni was so adamant about Sam not being involved in anything illegal. It went against baseball, hot dogs, and apple pie to think this nice old couple were accomplices in theft and murder.

Despite Nancy's protests, everyone helped to clear the table.

"Nick and I can take care of these," Sam said, motioning toward the dirty dishes now stacked on the kitchen counter. "Why don't you and Danni go on into the front room and catch up."

Nick caught Danni's concerned gaze, and she made a barely discernible nod toward Nancy. If he hadn't known about her condition, he would still have guessed something was wrong by the yellowish pallor of her skin and the increased trembling of her hands.

"Good idea," Danni said, and Nick could hear her forced cheerfulness. "You have to tell me about your latest trip. Las Vegas, right?"

As Danni and Nancy left the kitchen talking about Wayne Newton and one-armed bandits, Nick found himself alone with Sam.

"She likes to have people over, but it's hard on her," the retired cop said in a low voice.

Nick studied his weary and drawn face. "Hard on you, too."

Sam shrugged as he started the warm water tap. "You rinse, and I'll put them in the dishwasher."

Nick rolled up his shirtsleeves and held the first plate under the running water. He handed it to Sam. "Danni told me about her illness."

"She only knows what I told her."

Nick glanced sharply at the gray-haired man. "What do you mean?"

Sam hunched his shoulders. "Nancy has maybe six months before she won't be able to get around anymore. Then her organs will start failing. She'll be gone in less than a year."

Nick felt Sam's soul-deep anguish. "I'm sorry." He rinsed a handful of silverware. "You should tell Danni."

"I will, but not yet. She just lost her father."

"And she'll be losing the woman who's been like a mother to her in less than a year. She has the right to know." Nick swallowed. "To prepare."

Sam bowed his head, and Nick allowed him his privacy as he continued his task in silence.

"I'm glad Danni's got you now," Sam suddenly said.

Nick jerked his head up. "We're friends. Nothing more."

Sam chuckled, although it held a watery note. "Open your eyes, Rocky."

Nick pressed his lips together. He wasn't ready to pursue that avenue yet. "Danni said you and Nancy have been able to take some trips, do some fishing—things you always wanted to do."

Sam slid the top rack out of the dishwasher and stacked the glasses in it. "A lot of cops end up getting divorced at least once. I was lucky. Nancy sacrificed for me—evenings and holidays alone, putting up with my moods after a rough day at work. Hardly a word of complaint, even when we found out we wouldn't be able to have children. She's been my rock. I owe her everything."

The older man rubbed his face. "If she knew I took out a loan against the house so I can give her those trips and fishing excursions, she would skin me alive." He laughed weakly. "But it's a small price to pay to see her happy."

Thickness filled Nick's throat. Would he ever love someone as much as Sam loved his wife?

Sam closed the dishwasher, and his expression took on its more characteristic gruffness. "That loan is only for you and me to know about. I don't want Nancy finding out from you or Danni."

Nick nodded as he dried his hands on a towel hanging from the refrigerator handle. He'd have to tell Danni where Sam got the money, but he'd make sure she didn't tell Nancy. Although it was a relief to know Sam wasn't using dirty money, the explanation was heartrending.

Sam slapped Nick's shoulder. "What do you say we join the womenfolk?"

Nick grinned at the old-fashioned term and followed Sam to the front room. He spotted Danni and Nancy on the love seat, and when Danni glanced up, he noticed moisture glimmering in her eyes. He took a step toward her, but a brief shake of her head stopped him.

"Nancy was just telling me about the latest fishing trip. Sounds like she's the fisher-person in the family," Danni teased Sam.

Nick, however, saw the stress lining her brow and in her tightly clasped hands. He wondered if Nancy had told her the truth about how long she had to live.

Nick sat back on the sofa across from the love seat and listened to the affectionate repartee between Sam and Danni. He caught Nancy's gaze, and they exchanged amused glances. Clearly, Nancy was accustomed to their banter.

After they'd eaten cheesecake for dessert, Sam asked them about the investigation into Paddy's death. Danni told him about her truck being broken into, about Matt Arbor and Marsel Malone and how they might be related to her dad's "suicide." She glossed over the auto thefts and the details of Nick's book, however, but did include their suspicions about Gilsen.

Sam took a sip of his coffee. "I was afraid of that," he said with a low, rumbly voice. "I tried to help him. Got him into the Marines, but then it was up to him." He looked at Nick solemnly. "You made the right choices, Rocky, but Paul . . . He liked to take the easy route. While he was in the service, he was nearly court-martialed when he was implicated in a supply scam, but there wasn't enough evidence."

Startled, Nick sat up to listen more closely.

"When he got out, he disappeared into southern California," Sam continued. "A few years later, I hear from him. He's doing good, says he's started a security company."

Nick's gaze flew to Danni, whose eyes had widened.

"Home security?" Danni asked Sam.

The ex-cop nodded. "That's right."

"He told me he'd opened his own business in San Diego and done well," Nick said. "He never gave me any details, but I assumed it was a dot com company like he started here."

"So why'd he move back?" Danni asked.

"He said he needed a new challenge, so he sold his company for a nice profit," Sam answered.

"He also said he wanted to help kids like you helped him," Nancy interjected softly.

"Which is why he volunteers at the center," Nick said, although he suspected there was a lot more to it than humanitarianism.

"From a security to an Internet company?" Danni scowled. "Those aren't even close."

Sam's eyes narrowed. "That's why I did a little more digging. It's a dummy company. He's got an office and a phone, but he's never there."

"So, what do you think he's into?"

"Don't play coy with me, Danielle Hawkins. I've known you too long for those kinds of games." The older man sighed and drew a hand across his still-thick hair. "Even though I thought you and Rocky were chasing your tails by looking into Paddy's death, I think you're onto something. If Gilsen thought Paddy was a threat to him, I don't think he'd hesitate to kill him."

Danni broke the ensuing silence. "Why didn't you tell me you were helping Paul? Especially after he tried to rape me."

"That was my fault," Nancy said, her sunken eyes distressed. "I told Sam you'd be hurt if you found out. I knew you'd think he was choosing Paul over you."

Like Paddy chose Rocky over you. The words weren't spoken aloud, but Nick heard them plainly.

Sam reached for his wife's hand, which she clasped between both of hers.

Danni stared at their intertwined hands, and her eyes reflected poignant sadness. Nick ached to hug her and hold her hand, tell her he was there for her, that *he* wouldn't abandon her. But he couldn't make that kind of promise.

He glanced at Nancy and noticed how tired she suddenly appeared. Although it was early—only nine o'clock—he cleared his throat and said, "We should get back to the house. Gus probably needs to be let out."

When Danni glanced at him, he inclined his head toward the older woman. Danni understood immediately and rose.

Nancy roused. "Are you leaving already?"

"I'm afraid so," Danni replied softly. "Nick's dog is staying at Dad's place with us, and we can't leave her alone very long."

Sam helped his wife up, and they escorted Nick and Danni to the door. Danni retrieved her backpack and, after a round of hugs and handshakes, Nick guided her to his SUV. Thcy didn't speak until they were out of the neighborhood.

"She's lost even more weight," Danni said, her voice husky.

Nick remained mute, allowing Danni to talk at her own pace.

"She doesn't have as much time as Sam told me," she continued. "Probably a year, maybe less."

Nick glanced at her as one tear rolled down her cheek to glisten in the muted glow. She didn't seem to notice. He clenched his jaw but only reached for her hand and held it as he rubbed his thumb across her knuckles.

"She said Sam wanted to protect me, like I'm still a little girl." Anger leached into her tone.

"He loves you," Nick said gently. "They both do."

Danni turned her head to gaze out her side window. "I love them, too." She took a deep breath and used her free hand to swipe away the single tear trail, then faced Nick. "Nancy said Sam took out a loan against the house to pay for all their trips."

"She knows?" Nick asked, surprised.

"Nancy always took care of the finances when Sam worked. He took over after she was diagnosed, but she's a smart woman. He couldn't hide it from her."

"When Sam told me about it, he wanted to make sure neither of us told Nancy."

"After she found out what he'd done, she said she was upset. But then she realized why he'd done it, and she didn't have the heart to tell him she knew."

"He did it because he loves her."

Danni nodded.

They lapsed into a lengthy silence.

"Do you think you'll ever love someone that much?" Danni asked softly.

Nick's heart skipped a beat and he concentrated on the feel of Danni's hand in his. "I'd like the chance to find out."

She cast him a quizzical frown, but he ignored it. He couldn't explain, even if he wanted to. Danni was the most exasperating, frustrating, stubborn woman he'd ever met. She was also the most compassionate, exciting, sexy woman he'd ever met. He could grow old with her and never lose his fascination with her—of the facets he'd uncovered and those still unearthed.

Nick turned onto Paddy's street, and Danni tensed. "Look."

He followed her pointing finger to a silver car parked in front of her father's house. As they neared it, the first three letters of the license plate became clear: E C U.

"He's got a lot of balls coming back here," Nick growled.

Danni dug into her backpack and pulled out her cell phone. She punched the On button, but nothing happened. She tried again. Nothing. "Damn it! The battery's dead."

Nick parked along the curb in front of the neighbor's house. "We can use Mrs. Countryman's phone."

Danni nodded as she withdrew her revolver from her backpack. She'd removed her shoulder holster on the way to Sam's, not wanting to wear a weapon to dinner.

Opening her door carefully, she slid out, and Nick joined her, hunched against the side of the SUV. She tilted her head to the side and her brow creased. "It's too quiet."

"It's nearly ten o'clock," Nick said.

Danni grabbed him. "No. Gus should be barking."

Alarm gripped Nick's gut.

Danni's fingers tightened around his arm. "We can't just charge in there. Like you've told me before, we need backup, which means we call nine-one-one."

"But—"

"No. We do it by the book this time."

Mrs. Countryman's front door creaked open, and Nick and Danni spun toward it. The petite woman was wrapped in a long bathrobe with fuzzy slippers on her feet.

"I called the police when he went into Paddy's house," she called out in a low voice.

Nick couldn't help but smile.

"Good work, Mrs. Countryman," Danni said, also keeping her voice down. "How long—" She broke off and ducked behind the Jeep, pulling Nick down with her. "He just came out."

Nick was gratified to see Mrs. Countryman retreat into her house. He peered through the darkness and saw a shadowy figure descend Paddy's porch steps. The man was dressed in black, and he moved with the stealth of a professional soldier . . . or thief.

Nick pressed his back against the Jeep, his arm against Danni's. "Now what?" he whispered.

"I can't let him get away."

Although Nick was torn between taking Gilsen down themselves and waiting for the police, he knew they didn't have much choice this time. Gilsen would get away if they didn't do something.

"You wouldn't happen to have a spare gun, would you?" he asked, his lips close to Danni's ear.

"No. You stay here, out of the line of fire."

Fear flashed through him. "What're you going to do?"

"What I was trained to do." She took a deep breath and suddenly stood, her gun held between her steady hands. "Freeze, Gilsen."

And he did freeze, for a moment. Then he brought his own weapon up and squeezed the trigger. Instead of an explosive bark, there was a muted cough.

A silencer. The bastard was using a silencer.

Danni got off one shot and dropped beside Nick. "He's using a—"

"Silencer. Yeah, I heard."

Loud cursing surprised Nick, and he and Danni peered around the Jeep's front end to see Gilsen kicking a flat tire.

"Good shot," Nick said.

"I didn't do it, but that was going to be my plan."

Suddenly Gilsen swung around toward them and fired two more muffled rounds. Nick and Danni ducked behind the Jeep's protective cover, but Danni popped up to return fire.

"Shit. He's making a run for it," Danni announced, flowing to her feet. "C'mon."

Although worried about Gus, Nick followed Danni. He was glad to find she'd learned her lesson since going after

Gary alone. Nick wasn't certain what he could do without a weapon, but he had no intention of letting Paddy's daughter pursue a murderer without backup.

Without him.

Nick matched his pace to hers and found it was no easy feat, especially with his protesting knees. Tall and athletic, she had kept herself in shape since her days with the police department, while Nick had spent hours sitting in front of a computer since leaving the army.

I definitely need to start working out again.

They ran past the neat rows of houses until Gilsen cut through a yard. A seven-foot wooden fence loomed in front of them. Gilsen jumped up, caught the top, and hauled himself over it. The tear of cloth followed by a muttered curse told him Gilsen had run into something sharp.

Danni slowed down enough to tuck her revolver into the back of her waistband and then launched herself at the wall. She curved her fingers over the top . . . only to cry out and drop to the ground.

"What?" Nick demanded.

"Barbed wire or something like it along the top of the fence." She shook her head, and in the dim light, Nick saw her angry frustration. "Gilsen had gloves on or he wouldn't have made it over."

"Are you all right?"

Danni glanced at her hands and answered wryly, "No gushing blood." She kicked the fence, then turned to Nick. "Let's get back to the house. The police should be arriving."

Nick and Danni used the sidewalk this time as they jogged back to Paddy's.

"Did you get him?" Mrs. Countryman shouted from her own porch as they entered Paddy's yard.

"He got away," Danni replied.

"Drat. I was hoping if I let the air out of one of his tires, he'd be easier to catch."

Nick laughed. "Good thinking, Mrs. Countryman. But

don't you worry. We know who it is, and the police should be able to find him."

"Good. Then you can ask him why he was here the night Patrick died, too."

"Don't worry. They will," Danni said grimly, exchanging a look with Nick. "The police will probably want to talk to you, too."

"Goodness gracious. I'd best make myself presentable." The retired schoolteacher disappeared back into her house.

Nick and Danni walked the remaining distance to the house, and Nick turned the doorknob, not surprised that it was unlocked. He eased the door open as his earlier apprehensions returned and his heart hammered. Gus should've met him at the door. She also should've been barking like crazy at Gilsen. She'd done neither.

"Gus!"

Hushed silence.

Nick fumbled for the light switch, and when his fingers found it, he flicked it on. His gaze immediately fell on Gus . . . and the blood staining the carpet beneath her body.

Chapter Twenty

DANNI stood on her father's porch, watching Nick drive away like the hounds of hell were on his heels. She crossed her arms against the cool, damp drizzle and hoped he'd arrive at the animal hospital in time. Gus was losing blood rapidly and, as with a human, if she lost too much blood, she would die.

Sergeant Rodgers came out to stand beside her. "If Sirocco gets his dog there quick enough, he should make it."

"She," Danni corrected absently.

"You should go inside before you get pneumonia, Hawkins," Sarge said.

She nodded numbly and returned to the house, keeping her gaze averted from the darkening bloodstain where Gus had lain.

Sarge thrust a warm metal cup at her. "Here."

For all his cantankerousness, Sarge wasn't nearly as thick-skinned as he pretended. She sipped the steaming coffee gratefully, and it warmed her from the inside out, although a core of icy dread remained for Nick's dog.

"Think you're up to giving your statement?" Sarge asked.

Danni nodded, then suddenly realized Sarge didn't normally come out on calls. "What're you doing here?"

The veteran cop shrugged. "I heard the call come in from your neighbor and decided to come out with one of the rookies." He pulled out his notebook and a pen. "Go ahead whenever you're ready."

She fixed her professional mask in place. "Sure." Knowing the drill, she told him everything from the moment they pulled onto her dad's street to chasing Gilsen to returning to the house to find Gus bleeding on the floor. "I should've had Gilsen."

"You tried." It was the closest thing to consolation she'd get from the sergeant.

With her statement complete, she gave him her cell phone number in addition to her address and apartment phone number.

"So you figure it's Gilsen behind your dad's death?" Sarge asked.

Danni wondered how trustworthy the crusty sergeant was. Had he come out on the call because he was concerned for her and Nick, or was there another reason? She chose her words carefully. "We think so. We suspect he's working a grand theft auto ring dealing with only high-end vehicles, and Dad found out about it from Matt Arbor, the kid who supposedly committed suicide."

Sarge scowled. "And how did you figure this out?"

"Do you really want chapter and verse now? Or wait until we can give you more than speculation?"

The sergeant didn't look happy, but he didn't press either. "So, you figure Gilsen killed both Paddy and that kid to shut them up."

"More than likely. Only he made them look like suicides, which brings me to the next question. How did he get close enough to both Dad and Matt to kill them without a struggle? Or was it an accomplice who took care of them?"

"Maybe a female accomplice," Sarge murmured. "Paddy was found in his bed."

It was naive for Danni to believe her father had been celibate since her mother left. However, she'd never asked him about his personal life. Truth be told, even as an adult, she didn't like putting her father and sex in the same brain hemisphere.

"The coroner's report didn't say anything about sexual intercourse before his death," Danni said, hoping her face wasn't as red as it felt.

Sarge's eyes narrowed. "How did you see the report?"

Oops.

"That's not important," Danni said quickly. "What *is* important is there was no sign of a struggle, nor of sexual activity, but his body *was* found in bed. And Dad's neighbor saw a light-colored car at his place the night he died. She said it's the same one that's sitting out there with a flat tire. But she saw a person with blond hair, not dark like Gilsen's."

"Maybe Gilsen's accomplice is also his girlfriend."

Danni blinked. She hadn't considered that angle. "I'll ask Nick if Gilsen has a girlfriend."

Sarge glanced at his watch, then at the CSI, who was still working. "There's an APB out on Gilsen, and we'll be getting a search warrant for his place. It's only a matter of time until we get him. But we won't be able to charge him with Paddy's murder, not without evidence."

"But he *can* be charged with attempted murder, B and E, and animal cruelty. That should hold him long enough for us to find something linking him to Dad's death. And Matt Arbor's."

"So you think they're related because of this auto theft ring you won't tell me about?"

Danni ignored his jibe. "Their deaths and Marsel's so-called accident are *all* related."

Sarge whistled low. "Sounds like some goddamned conspiracy."

Her gaze met the sergeant's. "We find Gilsen's partner,

and we've got our conspiracy." She glanced over at the female CSI who was gathering physical evidence and the rookie who was watching with undisguised interest. "How much longer?"

"Ten or fifteen minutes," Sarge replied.

She nodded and handed him back the thermos cup she'd been drinking from. Then she went upstairs to clean the cuts on her hands from the fence, change her shirt, and throw some of Nick's clothes into a bag. She glanced around for her backpack and remembered she'd left it in Nick's Jeep.

She walked into her father's room and blanked her memories to stem her grief. She dug in the back of his closet and found the lockbox containing his backup revolver. Either it didn't interest Gilsen, or he hadn't made it to the second floor to search for Nick's book notes. And Danni had no doubt that was what Gilsen had come to find. She returned the box to its hiding place, then carried Nick's bag downstairs and rejoined Sarge.

"My license is in Nick's Jeep, and my truck's got a broken window," she said. "Any chance you could give me a lift to the Ivywood Animal Hospital?"

"No problem," Sarge said. "It's on my way."

Danni nodded her thanks.

"I'm done here," the CSI announced.

Danni glanced around, her gaze moving quickly across the bloodstain. "I'll lock up."

Once outside, she noticed a tow truck hitching up Gilsen's Audi. She recognized the towing company as one contracted with the police department, which meant the car was being impounded as evidence.

The CSI left in her sedan, but Sarge, the rookie, and Danni waited until the tow truck was ready to go. Danni was anxious to join Nick and chafed at the delay. Even her desire to find her dad's killer became secondary to her need to be with Nick.

Finally, the tow truck left with Gilsen's Audi rolling behind it. Ten minutes later, Sarge stopped in front of the unassuming animal hospital, and Danni got out of the car.

"Thanks for the lift," she said, leaning into Sarge's open window.

Sarge grimaced, his version of a smile. "If you need anything, give me a call. I'll let you know what the lab comes up with."

"Will do." Danni slapped the door lightly and turned away, eager to see Nick and hear how Gus was doing.

"Danni," Sarge called.

She stopped abruptly, startled that he'd used her first name. Shocked that he even knew it. "Yes?"

"Be careful."

Too stunned to speak, she nodded, and Sarge drove away.

Danni hurried into the small hospital. Right inside the entrance was a small waiting room with a sofa and two chairs. Nick perched in a corner of the couch, his elbows propped on his thighs and his face buried in his hands. He looked troubled . . . and alone.

She crossed to him and said softly, "Nick?"

He jerked his head up, and it took a moment for his bleary gaze to focus on her. "What're you doing here?"

Hurt for some unaccountable reason by his question, Danni nearly answered with a sharp retort. But the smear of dried blood on Nick's face and the rust-colored stains on his shirt and jeans extinguished her sarcasm. She sat down beside him. "How's Gus?"

He shook his head and raked a hand through his short, tousled hair. "They just took her into surgery five minutes ago. You didn't have to come down here."

Danni took his hand in hers and met his gaze evenly. "I wanted to. We're in this together, remember?"

"But—"

"No buts." Danni glanced down at their intertwined fingers, at Nick's thumb that caressed the back of her hand. She doubted he was even aware he was doing it. "Besides,

Gus isn't so bad. For a dog." She lifted her gaze, smiling gently.

He stared at her, and Danni's stomach fluttered with nervousness and something else, something far more than attraction or desire.

"Thank you," he said.

"You're welcome." Her voice was husky.

Nick slumped on the sofa, his muscles seeming to melt like hot butter. "Did the police find Gilsen?"

Danni leaned back, her shoulder pressed against Nick's, and their hands still clasped between them. "Not yet, but Sarge thinks it won't be long."

"Paul's smart. It may not be that easy."

She listened to the squeak of rubber soles beyond the waiting room and the occasional bark of one of the hospital's patients. Disinfectant couldn't completely cover the unmistakable animal odor, but it wasn't an offensive smell. Merely different to Danni's unaccustomed nose.

"I found Gus at an animal shelter." Nick's voice startled her. "I'd just moved back here after getting out of the army. The moment I saw that little gold bundle of fur, I knew we were meant to be together." He chuckled. "Sounds like a line from a bad novel, but it's true. She's been with me ever since." He paused, and his gaze became distant. "She's the only friend who's stuck around longer than a year or two."

Moisture burned in Danni's eyes. "She'll be all right, Nick."

He gave her hand a squeeze.

"I brought you some clean clothes." Danni brushed her thumb across the bloodstain on his cheek. "You might want to wash your face, too."

"Thanks." He took the bag from her and walked down to an alcove that had a rest room sign above it.

When he returned with a scrubbed face and wearing clean clothes, he resumed his place by Danni. Seconds ticked into minutes into an hour then another.

Danni shifted her position and eyed the clock on the

wall for the umpteenth time. It was nearly two-thirty in the morning. She tried to stifle a yawn, but it escaped with a jaw-cracking pop.

"You should go home," Nick suggested.

"We stick together."

His lips curled upward. "Stubborn woman."

Warmth flared in Danni's chest at the fond teasing, but before she could speak, a woman dressed in scrubs came out from the back.

"Are you here for Gus?" she asked.

Nick and Danni stood.

"How is she?" Nick asked.

The middle-aged woman smiled. "Better than expected. She came through the surgery with flying colors. The anesthesia will keep her doped up for another two or three hours, but my professional opinion is she was a very lucky lady."

"When can we take her home?" Danni asked.

"We'll see how well she responds, but I'd say in four or five days."

Nick dropped his chin to his chest and released a relieved sigh, then raised his head. "Thank you, Doctor. Can we see her?"

"Just one of you."

"Go ahead, Nick," Danni said. "I'll wait here."

He gave her a hug, and she clung to him for the too-brief moment.

"I'll be back in a minute," he said.

Danni watched him follow the doctor and sank onto the couch. She tipped her head back and said a short prayer of gratitude for Gus's life. Then the long day caught up with her, dragging her toward sleep.

"Wake up, Danni."

She blinked up at Nick, who stood above her. "Wha—How's Gus?"

Nick's smile was a shadow of his usual one. "She looks like hell."

"Do you want to stay and make sure she's okay?"

"No. The doctor says she's doing well, all things considered. If Gus's condition changes, they'll call me." Nick extended his hand to Danni and pulled her to her feet.

He picked up his bag, then wrapped his arm around Danni's waist. She leaned into his welcome strength as they walked out to his Jeep in the night's darkness. Although she was tired, Danni knew Nick was exhausted emotionally and physically. She held out her hand. "I'll drive."

Danni prepared herself for an argument, but Nick dropped the keys into her palm without a word. She hid her surprise and slipped in behind the wheel. As soon as she pulled onto the street, Nick tipped his head back and closed his eyes. Smiling fondly, she remained quiet as she drove.

"We're here," she said to Nick.

He jerked awake and looked around. "Where's here?"

"Since Gilsen knows where we've been staying, I figured it wouldn't matter if we came here instead." She didn't mention the real reason—Gus's blood staining the living room carpet at Paddy's.

"Your place?"

She was impressed he recognized it, since he'd only been here once during the day. "That's right."

He shrugged. "Okay."

Danni heaved a mental sigh of relief. She grabbed her backpack, and Nick took his bag.

Without the dirty clothes lying around, her place didn't look too bad. The air, however, was stale inside, and Danni cracked open some windows.

Nick lowered himself to the sofa. "Do you have a spare pillow and blanket?"

"Yes, but they're on my bed." She held out her hand. "C'mon, let's go."

After a moment's hesitation, he took her hand and allowed her to lead him into her bedroom.

Once there, Nick stripped down to his underwear, then crawled into Danni's bed. Without a word, she changed into an oversized T-shirt and slid in beside him. She lay down on her side, and Nick spooned behind her, putting his arm around her.

"Good night, Danni," he whispered and kissed her cheek.

She clasped his hand that rested between her breasts. "Good night."

Despite everything that had happened that night, she felt safe and protected, and sleep claimed her within minutes.

"DANNI," Nick said, giving her a gentle nudge.

She opened her eyes blearily and tried to remember where she was. The disorientation evaporated as she recognized her familiar apartment bedroom and her increasingly frequent bed partner. She focused on Nick's face close to hers. "Wha—"

"Where's your cell phone?"

A ring penetrated her sleep-fogged brain. Groping blindly for the phone on the nightstand where it'd been recharging, she nabbed it and brought it to her ear. " 'Ello."

"Hawkins?"

Danni shook her head to clear the lingering cobwebs. "Sarge?"

"Yeah. Thought you might be interested in what I found out about Gilsen."

She scooted up and leaned against the headboard. "Go ahead."

The cobwebs disappeared completely as Sergeant Rodgers gave her a rundown of what he'd learned. Despite the power of Nick's gaze on her, she kept her attention on the phone conversation.

"Thanks, Sarge. I owe you a big one," she said, once he'd finished.

"Yeah. I should've been home hours ago."

Although his tone was blustery, Danni knew he wasn't angry. "I'll get you tickets for the next baseball game."

"Make it wrestling, and it's a deal."

"You got it."

She punched off her phone and turned to look at Nick, who was reclining on his pillow gazing up at her with incredibly blue eyes. Only a sheet draped him, outlining every angle and curve of his six foot-plus frame. Danni's libido kicked into overdrive, reminding her that his hard, hot body had pressed against her all night.

"Well?" Nick asked.

His impatient query put her mind back on track, although her body refused to fall into line. She ignored its morning horniness . . . for now.

"That was Sergeant Rodgers. He did a background check on Gilsen. Came up with what Sam told us about him having his own security business. Only Sarge has a friend in San Diego who gave him the real scoop. Seems Gilsen was arrested for suspicion of B and E after two of his clients were robbed while on vacation. Only they jumped the gun on the charges, and Gilsen had a good lawyer. It didn't even go to trial. Right after that, Gilsen sold the business and moved here." Danni frowned, recalling the missing link Sarge had mentioned.

"What?"

"The cops in San Diego suspected Gilsen had a partner, but they came up empty. It could be a girlfriend." At Nick's puzzled expression, Danni explained the theory that Mrs. Countryman might have seen a woman get into Gilsen's car the night Paddy was killed.

"Paul never mentioned a girlfriend," Nick said thoughtfully. "But then, if she was also his accomplice, he'd want to keep her identity secret."

"He's also moved up from B and E to grand theft auto."

"And murder." Nick's expression was grim. "Did the police search Paul's place?"

Danni nodded. "But by the time Detective Rearden got a search warrant, Gilsen had been there and gone. He didn't leave behind any incriminating evidence. Same with his office, which, by the way, had only a desk and a phone in it."

"He's too smart to leave anything behind," Nick said with disgust.

Although she hated to admit it, Nick was right. Gilsen was a bastard, but he was an intelligent bastard.

She glanced at the digital clock radio: 10:45. Later than she'd expected. It'd been over seven hours since they'd left Gus recovering at the hospital.

"I'm going to call the hospital and see how Gus is doing," Nick said, as if reading her mind. "Do you have a phone book?"

"In the kitchen, in the drawer beneath the phone."

Nick got out of bed and picked up his clothes lying on the floor. Danni only had time to appreciate the quick flash of his backside profiled by black boxer briefs as he left. She sighed in regret.

While Nick was calling the hospital, Danni appropriated the bathroom. Twenty minutes later, she escaped the steam cloud wearing only a towel that covered her from breasts to thigh. She called down the hallway, "How's Gus?"

Nick appeared in the narrow entrance of the hall, the sunlight in the living room backlighting his athletic body. "She's come out of the anesthesia, and Dr. Cookson said they're watching her closely. But she thinks Gus is doing as well as can be expected."

Danni breathed a sigh of relief. "After we have something to eat, we'll go see her."

"All right, but we have one other item to take care of before we eat." Nick's voice had taken on a husky note.

He stalked up the hall toward her, his movements reminding Danni of a big cat on the prowl. With her as the prey.

Barefoot and bare-chested, with thc button of his jeans undone, he halted in front of her. She shivered under the intensity of his gaze but met it without flinching.

Nick didn't speak but only stared down at her, his pupils

nearly obscuring his blue irises. Slowly, deliberately, he slipped a finger beneath Danni's towel, between her breasts. He gave a little tug. The towel unfurled and dropped to the floor.

Danni made no move to cover herself. Nick's gaze scorched her skin and sent ripples of desire through her belly and moisture between her thighs.

"Like what you see?" she asked, her voice rough with desire.

He took her hand and pressed her palm against the front of his jeans. His hard length pulsed beneath her. "What do you think?"

Danni massaged his erection through denim and stepped closer, her bare toes brushing Nick's. "I think you should get naked."

Nick's eyes flared with lust, and he wrapped his arms around her waist and kissed her.

With their mouths fused and Danni's fingers in his belt loops, they shuffled into the bedroom. The back of her knees hit the bed, and she dropped down, pulling Nick on top of her.

"Anxious, are we?" Nick's tone was teasing, but his breathlessness told Danni he was just as hot on the trigger.

She growled. "Shut up and get rid of the jeans."

Nick laughed but didn't waste a second fulfilling her request.

IT was after noon when Danni and Nick walked across the street to a corner diner she frequented. The food wasn't anything special, but she wasn't picky, and the price was right. Besides, the servings were large, and after the late morning lovemaking, she was famished.

By the pile of food Nick ordered, he, too, needed to replenish his energy.

They ate in silence, but Danni caught him looking at her, and she tipped her head in question. He merely grinned boyishly and shrugged, which created an odd lightness in her chest.

Nick paid the bill and Danni left the tip, then they walked hand in hand back to her apartment. Danni could almost forget that they were in the middle of a dangerous investigation, that someone had tried to kill them more than once.

Entering her apartment, she heard her cell phone ringing in the bedroom where she'd left it to continue recharging. She ran down the hall to answer it. "Hawkins."

"May I speak with Nick Sirocco?"

With a sense of foreboding, Danni carried the phone into the living room and handed it to Nick. "It's for you."

He frowned as he took it. "Hello."

She watched his expression turn grave as he listened to the person at the other end.

"I'm on my way," he said and clicked off the phone. "It's Gus. Something's wrong. They want to open her up again."

Danni's heart jumped into her throat as she followed Nick out to his Jeep.

Chapter Twenty-one

Nick sat in the same corner of the sofa he'd claimed twelve hours ago and watched Danni, fretting and anxious, pace in front of the waiting area.

When they'd arrived, a different veterinarian had told them Gus's condition had taken a bad turn. He wasn't certain what was causing the problem but suspected the dog was bleeding internally. Nick had given his approval for the doctor to open Gus up again.

"Coffee?" Danni asked.

"No thanks." His stomach was already upset.

Danni crossed her arms and gazed at him miserably. "I'm sorry. I should've known something like this could happen."

"So, you're a clairvoyant now?"

"You know what I mean."

Nick pushed himself upright and went to stand in front of her. He placed his hands on her shoulders, noting the tension that hadn't been there earlier when they'd made love. "Hindsight isn't going to help, Danni. Put your energy into finding Gilsen."

"His accomplice could be hiding him." Danni's cell

phone interrupted her. "Hawkins." She scowled and covered her other ear with her hand. "I can barely hear you. What number are you at, Sarge?"

She hung up, glaring at her phone. She lifted her irritated gaze to Nick. "I need a new cell. I'm going to call Sarge back on a real phone. I'll be back in a few minutes."

She crossed to the receptionist's desk and returned five minutes later, her expression grim.

Nick met her in the middle of the corridor. "What's wrong?"

Her eyes held banked anger, and her jaw clenched. "Gilsen bought three airline tickets for three different flights departing within thirty minutes of each other. Those departure times were two hours ago."

"Why did it take them so long to track him down?"

"Rearden was checking his credit card activity, and Gilsen used cash."

"Dammit! So did they have police waiting for him at the three arrival points?"

"Too late for the flights to Salt Lake City and Minneapolis, but Atlanta did send someone out. Gilsen didn't show," Danni said grimly.

"So either he's in Salt Lake City or Minneapolis."

"Or neither. He could've used cash and a fake ID for his real destination."

"Was anyone traveling with him?"

"Sales were for single tickets only."

Fatigue and disappointment flowed through Nick. To be so close and have Gilsen slip through their fingers . . . "What now?"

Danni walked over to the waiting area and dropped into a chair. "I don't know."

Nick sat across from her on the couch, his knees touching hers. He rested his hand on her fist. "Whatever you want, I'm here to help."

She opened her fist and turned her hand over, intertwining her fingers with his. Nick stared down at their interlaced hands, noting how deceptively delicate hers appeared.

"I could go to the hospital and talk to Marsel, see if there's anything else he remembers," she said quietly. "Maybe he can point me in the direction of Gary Otis. I have this feeling he's right in the middle of everything."

"All right. Let's go."

He started to rise, but Danni's firm grip stayed him.

She shook her head. "No. You stay here. If it looks like Gus won't make it, you'll want to be here with her."

Nick's throat tightened, but he wasn't certain if it was caused by the possibility of Gus's death or Danni's understanding. She hadn't liked Gus in the beginning, but it was clear her attitude had changed. And not only regarding Gus, either. However, he didn't like Danni going off alone, even if Gilsen had fled the city.

"What about being in this together?" he asked.

She smiled, but it seemed strained. "We can't stay connected at the hip forever. You have your life, and I have mine. Besides, Gilsen is gone."

A week ago Nick would've been overjoyed to have his life back—his mundane, routine, everyday life. But after being with Danni, that vanilla life wasn't what he wanted anymore. "What about *our* life?"

Danni averted her gaze. "We spent a lot of time together, Nick. What happened between us was inevitable, but once we're not living in each other's shadow, things will return to normal."

He didn't believe it—didn't want to believe it. "Do you *want* to go back to the way our lives were before?"

Danni suddenly tugged away from him and stood. She wrapped her arms around herself. "It doesn't matter what I want. That's just the way it is."

Nick narrowed his eyes, studying her. Danielle Hawkins was scared. Normally courageous to the point of foolhardy, she was terrified of him and what they could have together. He'd have to show her that he wouldn't abandon her, like her mother did. Or make her feel second best, like Paddy did.

"I'll go talk to Marsel," Danni said, the words tumbling out. "Will you call me as soon as you know anything about Gus?"

Nick rose and walked over to her tense figure. "I promise."

Danni took a deep breath and held up his car's keys. "You take these. I'll call a taxi."

"No. You take the Jeep. You can pick me up later."

Danni curled her fingers around the key ring. "Thanks."

"You're welcome." Nick kissed her, his lips lingering on hers. "Be careful."

"You, too." Her hand rested on his forearm, and she stared at him, as if memorizing his face. Then she whirled around and fled.

Nick suspected Danni wanted to be alone right now, and she'd be safe enough with Gilsen out of the picture.

So why, if it was safe, did he have this gnawing feeling in his gut urging him to run after her?

DANNI looked left before making a right turn and hit the brakes when a car went through a red arrow. She opened her mouth to make a comment to Nick's empty seat about imbecilic drivers, but snapped it shut. Six days with the man and she would've thought they'd been together for six years.

Annoyed with herself, Danni focused on the early afternoon rush hour. A few minutes later she turned off the backed-up main thoroughfare onto a side street. Having been a patrol cop, she knew the city—especially this part—like her own backyard. The route took her within five blocks of the youth center, and she considered stopping, but remembered it was closed this weekend so the broken windows could be replaced.

She caught sight of a familiar figure pushing a cart.

After parking, she trotted down the sidewalk to catch up to the homeless man. "Southpaw," she called out.

He glanced over his shoulder and grinned. "Sorry, Danni, but I ain't got any more tickets. Done gave them all away for tomorrow's game."

Danni smiled back at him, joining him in his fantasy world. "That's okay. I have to work, but I'll be rooting for you. I figure you won't have any problem putting away the visiting team. You played them before?"

Southpaw's pleased expression faded slightly. "Yeah. I know the pitcher. Hometown boy. Went to be a hero but come back. Plays dirty. Wild pitches. Don't care who he hurts."

Again, Danni realized Southpaw was trying to tell her something in his odd baseball vernacular. She played along. "I heard the same thing. Doesn't care about his own teammates. In it for himself."

Southpaw nodded vehemently. "That's right. Took one of his own outta the game the other day. Saw him with my own eyes during practice."

Danni frowned. "Was that yesterday morning?"

"Yep. Had to bring out the trainers. Carried him off."

She glanced around and realized Marsel had been hit by the Taurus less than two blocks away. Had Southpaw witnessed Gilsen running down Marsel? "I heard about that but didn't know it was one of his teammates."

"Wasn't so sure myself. Tall, gangly kid—taller'n most players."

Southpaw's description could definitely be Marsel. "Have you seen the pitcher lately?"

Southpaw leaned into his cart and picked out an aluminum can. He kept his gaze on it as he spoke. "Seen him and his catcher. They was tradin' signs."

Danni willed her expression to remain calm. "When was this?"

"Coupla hours ago. Figured they was gettin' ready for the big game tomorrow." Southpaw's brow creased. "Didn't look right, though."

"How's that?"

"Catcher didn't know the signals. Nearly missed the ball when the pitcher fired one home."

Frustration gnawed at Danni's patience as she tried to decipher his cryptic words. "Can you tell me anything more about the catcher?"

Southpaw shrugged and raised his head. His eyes seemed to focus clearly. "Seen her around. With your daddy. But she don't know baseball like he did. Not like you neither."

She?

"So you've seen her before?"

"Yep. Never trusted her. Got gold hair. Never trust a woman with gold hair." Southpaw's eyes glazed again, and he tossed his aluminum can back in his cart. "Got to get me a good night's sleep afore the game tomorrow. I be showin' my best stuff."

He pushed his cart down the sidewalk, mumbling to himself, and Danni knew she wouldn't get any more information from him. She found a few dollars in her jacket pocket amid old notes and straightened paper clips and caught up to the old man.

"Thanks, Southpaw," she said, pressing the bills into his rough hand.

He looked at them, then gave her a wide, gap-toothed grin.

As Danni hurried back to the Jeep, she tried to make sense of Southpaw's ramblings. If the pitcher was Gilsen, that meant he hadn't left town after all, and Nick was still a target. But he was safe enough at the animal hospital. Even if Gilsen knew he was there, he wouldn't try anything in a public place during the day.

So, if Gilsen was the pitcher, who was the gold-haired catcher? Gilsen's elusive accomplice? Or were both the pitcher and the catcher merely characters in Southpaw's make-believe world?

No, Southpaw had told her as clear as he was capable that Gilsen had run down Marsel.

She climbed into the Jeep and stared after the old man's fading figure. He said he'd seen the gold-haired woman with Paddy.

Suddenly, it all came together, and Danni sagged under the revelation.

Karen Crandle had been Paddy's partner, and her hair could be called gold. *She* was the blond Mrs. Countryman saw at Paddy's the night he was killed. *She* used DMV records to tell Gilsen who had cars worth stealing once he had the names of people going out of town. *She* ensured that she and Paddy weren't patrolling the area when Gilsen heisted a car.

Danni started Nick's Jeep with a roar and made a tire-squealing one eighty. Driving ten miles above the speed limit to Karen's apartment, Danni could only imagine how her father must've felt when he realized his own partner was going to kill him.

She felt lightheaded and sick with betrayal and fury. Her dad had trusted Karen, and the two-faced bitch had murdered him.

Fifteen minutes later, Danni parked in front of the Blue Meadow Apartments. She checked her weapon to make sure it was loaded.

Her gaze fell on her cell phone. She had to call the police. Even a wet-behind-the-ears rookie knew how important backup was going into a potentially dangerous situation. And she owed it to Nick to call him and share her information. Despite her initial mistrust of him and the years-old pain he'd unearthed, he'd become a valuable partner. Someone she could trust . . . and care for.

She reached for the phone and pressed the On button. Nothing happened. She punched it again. It was dead. Disgusted, she tossed it back on the passenger seat.

Danni glanced up and down the street for a pay phone, but couldn't spot one. If she wanted to call 911 and Nick before confronting Karen, she'd have to find a convenience store or gas station.

Before Danni could decide what to do, she spotted

Karen through the building's glass entrance door. The cop was wearing a coat, as if preparing to go somewhere. If Danni wanted to talk to her, this might be her only chance.

Determined, but with a twinge of apprehension, she crossed the street and entered the sunlit foyer. It was empty. She pushed the button for Karen's apartment and shuffled her feet impatiently. No answer. Had Karen already left? Danni tried again.

"Who's there?" Karen asked through the intercom.

Danni's pulse kicked up. "Danni Hawkins. Do you mind if I come in?"

She crossed her fingers during the ensuing pause, then the door buzzed, and she quickly entered the building. Standing by Karen's apartment door, Danni heard the soft bluesy strains of a saxophone. Not exactly what she expected from a fleeing suspect.

The door swung open. "I wasn't expecting you." A smile tempered Karen's words.

Looking past the casually dressed woman who had shed her coat, Danni saw boxes littering the floor. Obviously she'd been packing. Doubts about Southpaw and the assumptions she'd drawn from his statements crept across Danni's mind. "I was in the neighborhood and thought I'd drop by to see if you needed any help."

Karen propped a hand on her hip. "That's sweet of you, Danni, but I've got things under control."

Danni smiled. "You're more organized than I am." Knowing she had little ground to stand on, she risked a bluff. "Last night you told me you didn't know Paul Gilsen. I just talked to someone who said he saw you two together earlier today."

Karen blinked. "It wasn't me. I've been packing all day."

She'd been wearing a jacket less than five minutes earlier, which meant she was lying. Karen had played Danni, Nick, Paddy, and everyone else for fools, but no more. She wasn't going to get away with murdering Danni's father. Red-hot anger clouded Danni's judgment and made her reckless. "Did you kill my father?" She tensed, waiting for Karen's outraged denial.

Instead, the woman smiled coldly. "Yes."

Shock froze Danni for a split second, long enough to feel a dull jab in her side.

"Nice of you to stop by," came an all-too-familiar, oily voice.

A shove of the gun barrel forced Danni into the apartment, and Karen locked the door behind them. Her hands raised, Danni turned around slowly and glared at Gilsen. "So those plane tickets were only a smoke screen."

Gilsen, looking disgustingly suave in pleated trousers and an expensive polo shirt, shrugged. "I have some unfinished business."

Danni trembled inwardly but remained poised. "Did you forget to kill someone?"

"As a matter of fact . . ." Gilsen swung a strap off his shoulder and revealed her backpack. He must've gone out to the Jeep while Danni had come to Karen's apartment. "Now that I have what I've been looking for, I can dispose of you and Sirocco."

Danni's blood ran cold. If he learned those papers had nothing to do with him or his theft ring, she couldn't predict how he'd react. Better to let him think he'd won.

"Nice little operation you had going," Danni said conversationally, hoping to get him to talk. Buying time, *any* time. "Find out when someone's on vacation, then bring in your boys to steal the car while you take out the security system."

Gilsen's dark eyes narrowed. "So, Nick must've told you the story."

Danni almost laughed at his choice of words, but Gilsen was deadly serious. "The only thing we couldn't figure out was the identity of your accomplice." She deliberately looked at Karen. "Looks like I found her."

"Cut the chatter," Karen said, annoyed. "Lose the gun."

Danni gritted her teeth and, using two fingers, lifted her

revolver out of the shoulder holster. She held it out to her captors, and Karen took it, then the cop frisked her.

"Facedown on the floor." This time it was Gilsen's command.

Every cell in Danni's body screamed to disobey, but having a nine millimeter aimed in her direction convinced her otherwise. She did as he ordered.

"Hands behind your back."

She did so reluctantly and felt a knee drop onto the small of her back, then Karen snapped handcuffs around her wrists. The blond removed her knee and stood.

Gilsen grabbed Danni's arm and yanked her to her feet, nearly dislocating her shoulder in the process.

Impotent anger made Danni's gut churn. She'd walked right into this like some baby-faced rookie just out of the Academy. Without backup. She studied Karen, seeing her for the murderer she was. "You killed Dad, and Matt Arbor, too."

"Hey, Paul did Matt," Karen said petulantly, as if Gilsen had stolen the boy's homework rather than murdered him.

"Why kill my father?" Danni asked, her heart pounding.

"He was onto us. Oh, he tried to hide it from me—his own partner—but I saw his notes. He and Sirocco thought they were being so secretive." Karen's lips curled into an ugly sneer. "That night I went over to Paddy's, tried to seduce him. Probably would've succeeded if I hadn't had to kill him."

Danni choked back sour bile rising in her throat. "You're a cold-blooded bitch."

Paul chuckled, but Karen's eyes narrowed.

"Better a bitch than a corpse," Karen said.

Danni took an instinctive step backward and stumbled on a box, falling over and landing on her butt.

Karen laughed, a cruel rendering of true laughter. "Don't worry." She moved closer to Gilsen, who wrapped an arm around her waist, and she stared down at Danni. "Once we get your partner, there's going to be a tragic accident at the youth center."

Danni's mouth was so dry she couldn't swallow. She'd uncovered the truth, but what good was it when she'd take it to her grave?

"MR. Sirocco?"

Nick, his palms slicked with sweat, rose as the veterinarian approached him. "How's Gus?"

"Much better," the doctor said with a tired but kindly smile. "The bullet nicked an artery. It was so small it probably didn't start bleeding until she moved around this morning."

Nick rubbed his brow. "Will there be any more surprises?" He didn't mean for it to come out as an accusation, but he was tired and worried, about both Gus and Danni.

Fortunately, the doctor was accustomed to harried pet owners. "After I fixed up the bleeder, I did a thorough search for any more. I can say with ninety-nine point nine percent surety that there won't be any more unpleasant surprises."

Nick's shoulders slumped in relief. "Thanks, Doctor."

"My pleasure, Mr. Sirocco. Gus will be out of it for a few more hours."

"Could I see her?"

"Follow me."

Nick trailed after him to the same small room where he'd been taken after the initial surgery. He shook hands with the vet, who then left him alone with his pet.

Gus's entire middle was swathed in white, and her side moved up and down in shallow, even breaths. An IV had been inserted into her left front leg and was wrapped in blue gauzy tape. Nick gently laid a hand on her head, feeling the familiar soft hair beneath his palm. Tremors skated along her skin, but Nick had felt that last time, too. The vet had said it was normal for an animal under anesthesia.

"Hey, girl, this time everything's going to be okay,"

Nick said quietly, stroking her head. "Before you know it, you'll be home."

Nick paused, wondering which home they'd be returning to—his, Paddy's, or Danni's? With Gilsen out of the city, he suspected he'd be going back to his lonely apartment. Funny how he'd thought of his apartment as his refuge before meeting Danni.

He took a deep breath, and exhaustion tugged at him. It'd been a hell of a long week. He glanced at his wristwatch and realized Danni had been gone—and out of touch—for nearly two hours. A shiver crawled down his spine. He tried to ignore it. She was only visiting Marsel.

With one final pat for Gus, Nick left the room and stopped by the front desk to use their phone. He called Danni's cell and was connected to her voice mail. That was strange. He hung up, wondering if her phone had quit working completely. Borrowing a phone book, Nick called Memorial Hospital and asked to speak to Marsel.

"Hello," came a woman's tentative voice.

"Olivia, this is Nick Sirocco. Danni Hawkins and I stopped by yesterday. How's Marsel doing?"

"He woke up for a few minutes about an hour ago," Olivia replied, her relief obvious in her voice. "The doctor says he'll sleep for a while now, but it's a natural sleep."

Nick smiled. "That's good news, Olivia. Did Danni happen to stop by there this afternoon?"

"I've been here since noon, and she ain't come by."

"Thanks. Next time Marsel wakes up, tell him we're thinking of him. Bye." Nick hung up the phone and stared at it. Danni told him she was going to see Marsel, but she never arrived. Had she lied to him? Or had something happened to her?

He called the police department and asked for Sergeant Rodgers but was told he wouldn't be in until Monday night, and they wouldn't give out his home phone number. Alex Levin was in Seattle, so contacting him wasn't an option.

Fumbling in his pockets, Nick found a spare key to

Paddy's house. It was after four when a taxicab dropped him off there, and he paused on the sidewalk, gazing at Danni's truck. Maybe she'd left a set of keys for it in the house.

He entered the foyer, and his gaze was drawn to the bloodstain on the carpet. Hot embers of anger flared within him, but close on its heels came icy fear. He imagined Danni's blood spilled in some alley, her life seeping away.

Swallowing hard against his rising dread, he escaped into the kitchen. There was a message on the phone's answering machine, and he punched the button eagerly. But it wasn't Danni.

"Danni, it's Alex. I talked to Joe and he said you and Sirocco were looking for me. What's up? Give me a call at 206-555-8301."

Nick replayed the message and jotted down Levin's phone number on a piece of paper. Since Levin was in Seattle, Nick doubted he'd be of much help finding Danni, but it wouldn't hurt to ask the cop about Gary Otis. It was a long shot, but Nick had nothing to lose.

He dialed the number on Paddy's rotary phone.

"Bay Point Bed and Breakfast," a woman's perky voice said.

"May I speak to Alex Levin?"

"May I tell him who's calling?" the hostess asked him.

"Nick Sirocco."

"Hold on. I believe I just saw him come downstairs."

There was the thud of the receiver being laid on a hard surface and distant voices. Then the phone was picked up.

"This is Alex Levin."

"Levin, it's Nick Sirocco. Do you remember the other night at the center when you told Danni and me that you hadn't seen Gary Otis?"

"I remember."

"One of the kids said he saw Gary Otis go into the computer room while you were there."

"He must've seen somebody who looked like Gary, because I didn't see him." Defensiveness crept into Levin's tone.

"He was fairly certain it was Gary."

"Then he needs glasses." Nick could hear his irritation clearly. "Look, Karen Crandle was supervising the lab when I showed up, and she talked me into staying until Gilsen came in. Said she had a basketball game to referee. Maybe she saw Gary."

Nick squeezed the bridge of his nose between his thumb and forefinger, trying to figure out if Levin was lying. "All right. Thanks."

"What's going on, Sirocco? Why didn't Danni call back?"

Nick paused, debating whether he should tell him or not, then decided it didn't matter. "She's missing."

"What?"

"You heard me," Nick said gruffly. "I think Paul Gilsen got her."

"Gilsen? Why?"

Levin sounded genuinely confused. Nick explained what had happened the night before with Gilsen breaking into Paddy's home. "We think he's involved in an auto theft ring. We also think he's got an accomplice on the police force. Is it you?" Nick knew he was taking a big risk, but he was desperate.

"Hell, no." Heavy silence filled the line, then he said with less assurance, "It might be Karen Crandle."

"Why do you think it's her?"

"She's Gilsen's girlfriend. One evening about two months ago, my wife and I saw her with Gilsen in a restaurant. They were sitting at a corner table, and you could tell they weren't strangers, if you get my drift," Levin said, his tone dry. "Crandle walked right by me, like she didn't know me. I asked her about it next time I saw her, and she said I was mistaken. But I know it was her."

Nick weighed his words. Was Levin lying to protect himself and incriminate Karen? Or was he telling the truth?

Danni had trusted him, and Nick trusted Danni.

"Do you know where she lives?"

"Yeah, Blue Meadow Apartments at Summit and Reynard."

"Thanks, Levin."

"Call me as soon as you know something," Levin said.

"I will," Nick promised. He hung up and took a shaky breath.

Sick with worry, Nick retrieved Paddy's backup gun from the closet. He hadn't used a gun since he got out of the military, but he wouldn't hesitate to use this one if it meant saving Danni's life.

Chapter Twenty-two

Nick parked Danni's truck on the street in front of the Blue Meadow Apartments, then scanned the area for his Jeep but didn't spot it.

He walked across the street to the building entrance and found Karen's name listed among the occupants. Figuring it might be better to surprise her, he waited impatiently until he spotted a tenant coming toward the outer door. Nick squatted down, pretending to tie his shoe.

The renter unlocked the security door, and Nick slipped in behind him. He hurried down the hallway on the ground floor, conscious of Paddy's gun stuck in the back of his waistband. He found Karen's apartment at the end of the hall and pressed his ear against the door but didn't hear anything. Frowning, he knocked loudly.

"Hold on," came Karen's annoyed voice. "Why didn't you use—" She opened the door and halted in midquestion. "Nick. What're you doing here?"

Nick leaned against the doorjamb in a deceptively casual pose. "Where's Danni Hawkins?"

"How should I know? I haven't seen her since yesterday."

"She told me she was coming by your place this afternoon," he bluffed.

Karen crossed her arms and looked back at him with just the right mix of curiosity and concern. "I've been here all day packing, and she hasn't shown up."

"You mind if I come in and take a look around?"

She frowned but swung the door wide open. "Knock yourself out. But you won't find anything. Danni hasn't been here."

Nick felt a frisson of unease but didn't hesitate to plunge into the apartment. It didn't take long for him to search the two-bedroom apartment, since most everything was packed in boxes.

Nick returned to the living room to see Karen sitting on a box. "Sorry, Karen. I'm just worried about Danni."

She rose and offered, "I can call the department and see if she's been reported in an accident."

Nick tried to see past her apparent sincerity, but there was nothing but concern. "Thanks, but it's only been a few hours. Maybe she just lost track of time."

"I'm sure that's it. Go back to Paddy's and wait there for her. I bet she'll show up."

"Yeah, you're probably right. Thanks."

Disappointed, Nick glanced around the living room one more time, but there was only the usual packing odds and ends on the carpet: packing peanuts, tape, and silver wire. He raised his gaze to Karen and extended his hand. "Good luck in Denver."

She shook it firmly and smiled. "Thanks, Nick."

Once Nick was in Danni's truck, he slumped in the seat. A week ago Danni would've run off without telling him where she was going or how long she'd be gone. Now, he'd bet his life that she would've called him . . . if she could. Which meant she was in serious trouble. For a moment, he tried not to think, not to imagine a hundred different scenarios for Danni's fate, each worse than the previous.

Where was she?

Obviously, she wasn't in Karen's apartment. However, something niggled at the back of his mind. Closing his eyes, he tried to recall each room in detail. He remembered the silver wires on the carpet and frowned, thinking they looked familiar. His eyes flashed open.

Straightened paper clips.

How often had he watched Danni unbend paper clip after paper clip in her office? A nervous quirk that had bugged him at first, but now evidence that Karen had lied.

Son of a bitch. Crandle was involved up to her crooked little eyeballs.

So where was Danni now?

Nick slipped out of the truck and made his way around the apartment building. If his Jeep wasn't in front, maybe it was in back.

An asphalt parking lot lay behind the building, obviously for the tenants' cars. Nick crouched behind a shrub near the corner of the building. Seven vehicles were parked in the lot, and a rental truck sat close to the back entrance of the building. Probably Karen Crandle's.

But no sign of his Jeep.

He spotted Crandle's Camaro parked in the lot, and an idea formed. If she knew where Danni was, sooner or later she might go there. All Nick had to do was follow her.

The smart thing now was to contact the police and have them take Karen in for questioning. But Crandle was one of them—brothers in blue—and he wasn't. All he had was Levin's word linking her to Gilsen, and slim circumstantial evidence tying her to Danni's disappearance. Karen would deny everything, and Nick would lose his chance to find Danni. No, he'd have to do this himself.

He quickly ran back to Danni's truck, drove it around the block, and parked across the street, where he had a clear view of Crandle's Camaro. Now all he could do was watch and wait. And hope.

• • •

DANNI struggled against the ropes that bound her to the chair in front of the farthest computer station from the door, but it was a hopeless cause. Even if she succeeded in freeing herself, pistol-toting Gary Otis and his spiky-haired girlfriend Angela would ensure she didn't get far.

Gilsen had brought her to the computer lab via a back door hours ago . . . or so it seemed. It was hard to say, since she was in a room with no windows and unable to ask the time due to the duct tape over her mouth.

She berated herself for not taking the time to find a pay phone to call Nick before confronting Karen. Danni had been given another chance with a partner, and she'd blown it. Again.

Worse, she should've told Nick how she felt about him, but she'd been a coward.

Afraid to trust him.

Afraid to trust herself.

Afraid to love.

Sitting in the chair at the computer station across from Danni, Gary Otis yawned widely. "God, this is boring. When did the boss say he'd be back?"

"Whenever he wants," Angela replied. "He *is* the boss."

Although the girl was only two desks away from her, Danni couldn't see her because of the privacy partitions between each station.

Gary shot Angela an annoyed look. "When did you start kissin' up to the boss?"

Angela peered around the divider at her boyfriend. "I'm not kissing up. But he is paying me to do what Matt did." As she spoke, Danni could see a flash of silver in her pierced tongue.

Gary scowled. "It's no big deal. Just type in some stuff, and there it is."

Angela rolled her eyes, making her look like a landed fish with three silver hoops in her left eyebrow and another through her left nostril. "You are so fuckin' clueless, Gary. Hacking into a security company's system isn't like getting into a porn chat room."

So that was how they knew when people would be on vacation. And there'd be no common denominator with the security company, because they could hack into various companies.

"But *you* don't know how to hot-wire a car," Gary shot back peevishly.

"I'm so impressed." Angela's tone implied the opposite.

"What do you know," the boy muttered. He stood and crossed to Danni, the gun held loosely in his right hand. "Wonder what she knows anyhow."

Before Danni realized what he was going to do, he'd ripped the tape off her mouth. The abrupt sting made her gasp and her eyes water, but her throat was too dry to do anything more.

"So, you're Paddy Hawkins's daughter," Gary began. "You're a helluva lot better lookin' than I figured you'd be."

"Gary—" Angela began.

"I'm bored," he interrupted. "Might be fun to have a captive audience." He threw back his head and laughed, as if it were the funniest thing he'd ever said.

Danni glared at him.

Gary pulled his chair closer to her, turned it around and straddled it. "You wanna know about your old man? Or maybe about Matt? Or how about my old friend Marsel?"

Danni refused to be baited.

Gary shrugged and skimmed his fingers over the pistol's barrel, like he was caressing a lover. "None of the others know anything about them, but I do. I'm the boss's right-hand man."

"I thought Karen Crandle was," Danni said.

Gary scowled. "Sometimes she thinks she's in charge. Tellin' the boss to do this or not to do that. If she was my girlfriend, I'd lose her."

"I don't think Mr. Gilsen wants you tellin' her this stuff," Angela said.

Gary laughed. "Who's she gonna tell? She's gonna be dead by tomorrow morning."

Not if I can help it, Danni thought with a surge of determination.

"Crandle killed your old man," Gary continued. "She dressed up real hot and went over there. The old guy really thought she wanted him to fuck her."

Danni was going to throw up if she heard any more about Crandle and her father. "Who killed Matt?"

"That was the boss. I went over to see Matt, played his pal, slipped him some stuff, and when he was out of it, I let the boss in. Matt didn't hardly do anything when the boss slashed his wrists." Gary paused and took a breath, the first sign of remorse in his young face. "I used to like him, but then he turned rat. Stupid bastard. Didn't know a good thing when he had it."

"Wasn't Marsel your friend, too?"

"We hung out until he got religion. He knew what was going on but didn't know who the boss was. Tried to find out a couple of days ago. That's when he had to be reminded what happens to rats."

Danni shivered inwardly. Gary Otis may not have been so cold-blooded a year ago, but he'd obviously learned from Gilsen. The kid was on a one-way road to prison, or worse.

"So why was Gilsen trying to kill Nick Sirocco and me?" she asked. Maybe if she kept him talking, he'd give her an opening to try to escape.

"Because you had something I wanted," Gilsen replied as he entered the room. He strode to Gary and glared down at him. "Why the hell isn't she gagged?"

Gary flushed. "We were just talking."

Gilsen dismissed him with a shake of his head and faced Danni. "Where is he?"

She suspected "he" was Nick, and intense relief washed through her. If Gilsen was asking her, he obviously hadn't found him. And Danni had no intention of helping him. "Who?"

Anger glittered in his eyes. "Nick Sirocco. I spent over two hours watching Paddy's place. He never showed."

Danni shrugged as well as she could in her bonds. "I'm not his mother."

"You two have been like Siamese twins for the past week."

"Since everyone figured you had left the city, we didn't think there was a reason to stick together any longer."

"I guess I'll just have to be satisfied with Nick's notes." Gilsen smiled without warmth. "But you, I'm afraid, I'll have to kill."

NICK shifted his butt as he remembered his first stakeout five days ago on the passenger side of this same unyielding bench seat. That time he and Danni had been watching a sleazy two-timer hook up with his overendowed girlfriend. This time the stakes were a hell of a lot higher than gathering evidence against a wandering husband.

Nick's stomach growled, and he wished he'd at least thought to grab a bottle of water when he left Paddy's. The streetlamps and security lights in the parking lot had come on an hour ago. If Crandle didn't come out soon, he would have to resort to plan B, whatever the hell that was.

The building's back door opened, creating a shaft of light with a body silhouetted in the opening. The person halted on the stoop and glanced around. Karen Crandle. Finally.

She hurried over to her Camaro and got inside. Moments later, Crandle turned onto the street, heading away from Nick's position. He started Danni's truck and followed.

Although he'd never tailed a person, he'd watched enough cop shows to know he couldn't stay on her bumper. But no matter what, he couldn't lose her. She was the key to finding Danni.

Nick concentrated on keeping her sports car in sight as she jockeyed back and forth through the traffic. She was in a hurry, that much was obvious.

The neighborhood became more familiar, and he realized she was heading to the youth center. Confident of her destination, he hung back and drove past the center when Crandle turned toward the rear of the building. Nick parked by the curb, and as soon as he switched off the engine, he sprinted around to the back of the center.

He halted and peeked around the corner. Crandle stood by a back door as she spoke into a cell phone. Then she closed the phone and waited. Nick assumed she'd called someone in the center to let her in. Pressed against the old brick, he glanced around, and his heart missed a beat when he spotted his Jeep.

If he hadn't been certain before that Crandle was involved with Gilsen, he was now. The foreboding he'd felt earlier mushroomed. He'd bet his next book that Gilsen hadn't left town and was inside the center waiting for his girlfriend.

Nick again debated calling the police but realized he didn't have time. Someone, probably Gilsen, would let Crandle in at any moment.

He reached back and withdrew Paddy's revolver from where it was tucked into his waistband. He adjusted the revolver's grip in his right hand and waited.

The door opened.

"It's about time," Karen grumbled. She entered, and the door began to close behind her.

Nick raced over and grabbed the handle carefully, allowing the door to continue swinging shut, but stopped its movement before it automatically locked. He stood there, his breathing harsh in his ears as he strained to hear sounds from within the center. There were only fading voices. Fortunately, neither Crandle nor whoever let her in bothered to make certain the door closed behind them.

He remained outside for a count of sixty, then entered soundlessly and found himself in the dark hallway that ran between the administrative area and the gym. Using his Ranger skills, he moved down the hall stealthily until he reached the door that led into the main corridor. He cracked it open and peeked through to see if anyone was around. Nothing moved, nor did he hear any voices.

Keeping his body flush with the wall, he sidled into the wide hallway and crept down to the computer lab. If Gilsen were still in town, there was a good chance he'd be in there.

He wasn't surprised to see the lab door shut. Pressing his ear against it, he listened and was rewarded with Crandle's voice. He shoved the door open and surged into the room. Three people stood between the two rows of computer stations, and their startled gazes fell on him.

"Hold it," he ordered.

Gary Otis's eyes slid to where a pistol lay, six feet away.

"Don't try it," Nick warned the teenager, but then addressed the trio. "Raise your hands where I can see them."

Gary glared at him but didn't make a move toward the weapon. Angela shifted closer to her boyfriend, fear in her expression. Only Karen Crandle appeared unruffled.

"So you figured it out?" she asked.

Nick ignored her question. "Where's Danni Hawkins?"

He heard a muffled voice and shifted to the left. Danni was tied to a chair at the end of the row, hidden by the stations' dividers. Her eyes were wide, and she was trying to speak, but tape covered her mouth.

Nick's knees wobbled with relief. The sight of her wild chestnut curls and huge dark blue eyes gave him a moment of lightheadedness. A part of him had been terrified that Danni was already dead.

Although he wanted nothing more than to untie Danni and hold her, he had more pressing problems to deal with.

"Karen and Gary, on the floor, facedown and hands behind your backs."

Rebellion filled their faces, but they did as he ordered. A loaded weapon was a powerful motivator.

"Angela, untie Danni," Nick said, his voice a shade gentler with the girl.

Her face pale, Angela stooped down to untie Danni's ankles from the chair. As the teen moved to release her hands, Danni's eyes widened. She yelled something in a muffled voice, but Nick couldn't understand.

Until he heard Gilsen's voice. "I've been looking all over for you, Nick. Nice of you to come to me."

Nick glanced over his shoulder to see Gilsen holding a gun and framed in the doorway. His heart sank. "You won't get out of the city. Your picture's plastered everywhere—airport, bus station, rental car agencies."

"But I don't need any of them. I've got Karen and a moving truck."

As a teenager, Gilsen had had everything: girlfriends, brains, and athletic prowess. Even a successful career, except Nick hadn't known at the time that Paul's success was illegally gained. It seemed Paul had always bested Nick, no matter what measuring stick was used.

But this time Gilsen couldn't win. If he did, both Nick and Danni were dead. And Nick had no intention of seeing the woman he loved killed.

DÉJÀ vu flooded Danni. Two years ago, it had been Scott who'd died because of her inadequacy. Now it would be Nick. And people would go on believing Patrick Hawkins had taken the easy way out, instead of being murdered by a dirty cop.

Karen and Gary climbed to their feet and brushed off the front of their clothing. The teenager took Nick's revolver, which Danni recognized as her father's.

"Now what?" Nick asked Gilsen conversationally.

"As soon as the stage is set, you and Danni will come to an unfortunate end." The thief and murderer sounded almost apologetic.

"Why?"

He shrugged. "It's not good business practice to leave loose ends. I'll still have to change my name, but you two are the only ones who know where we're going."

"To use kids—" Nick motioned to Gary and Angela. "Like them, again?"

Gilsen glanced at the teenagers. "I paid you well, didn't I?"

"Yes, sir, you did," Gary answered.

"Did I use you?"

"No, sir."

Gilsen, with a condescending smile, turned back to Nick. "See, I don't use kids. I *employ* them."

A muscle flexed in Nick's jaw, and Danni knew how difficult it was for him to curb his anger. Yet without Paddy Hawkins's guidance, Nick might very well have turned out like Gilsen.

"How are you going to get rid of us?" Nick asked calmly.

Startled, Danni looked at Nick, who met her gaze. Despite the flippancy of his tone, his eyes were intense, as if trying to tell her something. She watched as his gaze deliberately slid to Gilsen and the weapon in his hand, then back to her. Nick was going to try to take Gilsen.

Her partner would need a diversion.

She struggled to free her hands but was bound too tightly to the chair. However, her feet were free, and Gary Otis had shifted so he was directly in front of her. . . .

She caught Nick's eye and nodded minutely. For a moment, she thought he didn't understand. Then she felt it—like the final knot unraveling. He placed his faith in her and she placed hers in his. Without reservations.

Danni listened to Gilsen describe to Nick, in detail, how he was going to make their deaths look like a murder and suicide. But her attention remained focused on Gary, and when the teenager looked away from her, Danni surged upward. Head lowered, she rammed into Gary, who stumbled back against a chair and flailed for balance. But Danni's momentum tipped the scales, and Gary fell under her weight. The boy's head hit the floor with a sickening thud, and Gary lay unmoving. Danni, still lashed to the wooden chair, registered a wrenching ache in her shoulders as she lay on top of the teenager.

Angela screamed and stood frozen as she stared down at her unconscious boyfriend.

Danni rolled off Gary and renewed her struggle to free her arms. There was slack in the rope that hadn't been there before, and she took advantage of it, tugging free of the chair with only a mild hiss of pain. But she still wore the handcuffs behind her, and she quickly rolled onto her back and drew her knees to her chest. Straining against the metal, Danni drew her cuffed hands down the back of her thighs and behind her knees, past her calves, and finally over her feet. Although the handcuffs still held her, at least she had her hands in front of her now.

She ripped the tape from her mouth and barely noticed the sting, then did a quick visual reconnaissance. Nick had taken advantage of her diversion and grappled with Gilsen, who still had his pistol, but the barrel was pointed upward. However, Nick's red face showed the strain he exerted to keep the weapon away from him.

Danni swung around and came face-to-face with Karen Crandle, who had snatched up a pistol and aimed it at Danni. Her finger was poised on the trigger.

"Shoot him," Gilsen suddenly yelled.

Karen swung the weapon toward Nick.

Danni's heart missed a beat. She dived for her father's revolver where it lay on the floor and rolled to a kneeling position with the weapon held between her hands.

"Drop it," Danni barked.

Please drop it. Two years ago she'd frozen, and her partner had been killed. This time it was Nick's life in the balance.

She saw the flex in Karen's right hand as if in slow motion, and this time she didn't hesitate. The old revolver kicked in her hands as the gunshot registered. Karen crumpled to the floor, the pistol falling from her hand as she went down with a bullet in her shoulder.

She kicked Karen's weapon under a computer station. Then she swung her attention to Nick and Gilsen in time to see Nick throw a right hook that sent Gilsen tumbling backward. Gilsen's head cracked against the corner of a desk on the way down. He lay motionless.

Nick stumbled over to Danni. "Are you all right?"

She trembled as she looked from Gary and Angela, who'd fallen to her knees beside her boyfriend, to Karen and Gilsen. The only one who moved was Angela, but it was with grief, not menace.

Danni finally settled her gaze on Nick. His concern for her reflected in his face and eyes and the warm, strong hands that clasped her arms. A bruise was already forming on his cheekbone, and blood trickled from a split lip, but he was alive. And so vibrant and handsome that he stole her breath. And her heart.

She leaned forward to rest her head against his chest, and his heartbeat calmed her. "Definitely all right."

Nick enveloped her within his arms and kissed the top of her head. "Keep an eye on them, and I'll call nine-one-one."

She nodded and stepped back, using every ounce of energy left in her adrenaline-drained body to stay upright. Listening to Nick's authoritative tone on the phone, she couldn't help but smile. Her father had helped mold the man Nick had become—the man she loved.

Her throat felt tight as she smiled.

Thank you, Dad.

Epilogue

As Nick parked the Jeep behind a familiar sedan, Danni wasn't surprised to see Sam and Nancy Richmond standing at her father's graveside. Their heads were bowed, and they held hands.

"Looks like they had the same idea as us," Nick said.

Danni nodded absently, concerned by Nancy's fragile appearance. "Nancy couldn't come to the funeral, but Sam told me she wanted to pay her respects."

She opened her door and stepped into the sunny warmth of the early afternoon. She waited for Nick to come around, and when he took her hand, she clung to his welcome strength. They walked across the luxuriant green grass with the reverence a cemetery invoked.

They stopped at the foot of the grave, and Sam glanced up, startled, then gave them a brief nod. But Danni could see he was focused on his pale wife who dabbed at her eyes with a lace-trimmed handkerchief.

Danni lowered her head and listened to nearby birdsong and the far-off drone of traffic. One week ago she'd stood in this exact place surrounded by grieving people, but she had felt isolated and alone as she'd stared dry-eyed at her father's casket. Today, with the three people she cared for most, she felt their sorrow keenly but also felt their love and acceptance.

Nancy sniffed and wiped her nose. "I wanted to say good-bye," she said softly.

Danni raised her head and smiled tremulously at the woman who'd baked her cookies and helped her shop for school clothes. "I know Dad appreciates it."

Nancy reached out and clasped Danni's hand. Her fingers were cool and waxen, but there was still strength in her grip. "He loved you so very much, Danni. He just didn't know how to show it."

A lump filled Danni's throat, and she could barely speak around it. "I know."

Sam wrapped an arm around Nancy's thin shoulders. "I owe you both an apology," he said to Nick and Danni.

"Why's that?" Nick asked.

"I didn't believe you," the older man admitted with a shake of his head. "I was Paddy's partner for over twenty years. I should've known he'd never take the easy way out."

"Don't feel bad, Sam. Nick had to struggle to convince me." She glanced up and met Nick's warm gaze. "He was the only one who had faith in Dad."

"You had faith, too," Nick said. "It just took you a little longer to find it."

No one had ever placed as much confidence and trust in her as Nick did, and it both humbled and empowered her.

"What's going to happen to those people who killed him?" Nancy asked.

"Paul Gilsen and Karen Crandle are going away for life with the testimonies of Gary Otis, Angela, and the other kids who did Gilsen's dirty work," Danni replied.

"Good," Sam said forcefully, then melancholy crept across his seamed face. "I had such high hopes for Paul."

"You did everything you could, Sam," Nancy said. "He was just determined to follow the wrong path." She began to cough.

Sam held her until the fit passed, but Nancy's face had grown even paler. "Time to go home and take a nap," he said softly to his wife.

Nancy raised her gaze and there was a hint of sassiness in her eyes. "Care to join me, big guy?"

Danni smiled, amazed at Nancy's spirit. She glanced at Sam's tender expression, and the depth of his love stopped her breath. For a moment, she ached to know that kind of love.

Sam kissed his wife's wrinkled cheek. "I never could refuse you." He lifted his gaze to Nick and Danni. "We'll have you two over for dinner again real soon."

"We'd like that," Danni said. She hugged Sam and then Nancy, taking care not to embrace the frail woman too tightly.

Nick shook Sam's hand and gave Nancy a peck on the cheek.

Danni watched Sam lead Nancy back to their car, an arm around her as if she were made of spun glass. Their shared love was almost tangible.

Nick sighed, and Danni glanced at him.

"Why do shitty things happen to nice people?" he asked.

"Why was Dad murdered? Why did you have such rotten parents?" Danni shrugged. "At least with Sam and Nancy, they had a good life together. Maybe in the long run, that's all that counts."

Nick studied her. "Maybe."

Danni turned back to her father's grave. "Do you think he's at peace now?" she asked.

"Are *you* at peace?"

She met Nick's compassionate gaze and answered as honestly as she could. "I was so angry with him for not being the father I wanted him to be and for dying before he could become that man." She licked her dry lips and listened to a distant siren. "But . . . But he *was* a good father. A-and a good man. Y-you opened my eyes. . . ."

Her voice broke, and the tears she hadn't shed a week

ago would no longer be denied. She turned her face into Nick's jacket and allowed herself to grieve for her father and for herself.

Danni had no idea how long she cried, but she was aware of Nick's arm around her, his quiet, soothing words, and his own mirroring sorrow for Paddy. With a shaking hand, she wiped away the moisture on her cheeks and straightened but remained close to Nick's side.

"Feel better?" Nick asked softly.

She nodded as the heat of the sun dried the remaining tear tracks.

Nick wrapped his arm around her waist, and she allowed him to guide her back to his Jeep. Once seated inside, Danni said, "You should write the book."

"It's not fiction anymore."

"Then write it as true crime. I've heard they're popular."

Nick gazed out the window toward Paddy's grave. "I think he'd like that."

"Dad would *love* that. He liked having his name in the paper."

Nick chuckled. "Remember that scrapbook he kept?"

Danni laughed. "Oh, yeah. In fact, it's at his house if you want to come by and borrow it for research."

"That's a good idea. But I'm going to need your help with the book, too. I mean, I'm not a cop, and I don't know all the jargon. I bet you've got some stories about Paddy, too."

A merry-go-round of memories swirled through Danni, of a younger Paddy Hawkins and a little girl with curly hair, dark blue eyes, and a stubborn chin. She lifted her gaze to Nick and smiled. "I might have a few."

"I'd like to hear them." Sincerity warmed his voice.

Danni nodded, then changed the subject to a less emotionally charged one. "When can you take Gus home?"

"Tomorrow. She's doing really well. I only wish I had a ground-floor apartment."

"Why don't you stay at Dad's place? The carpet was

cleaned yesterday, and there's a backyard for Gus. What more could you ask for?"

"You."

Danni blinked, uncertain if she'd heard him correctly. "What?"

"I love you," he said without hesitation.

The depth of love in his eyes stopped her breath, and in that instant, she recognized what he was offering . . . what she'd ached to possess all her life. Nick was offering her what Sam and Nancy shared. Her eyes filled with moisture, but she managed a cocky grin. "Funny you should say that. I kinda fell in love with you, too."

"Did you now?"

Nick's slow, sexy smile sent Danni's libido into overdrive.

"In fact, I thought we might even make pretty good partners. How does Hawkins and Sirocco, Private Investigators, sound?" Danni asked.

"I kinda like it."

"I thought you might," Danni said smugly.

"We should probably seal the partnership with a kiss."

"Better than a handshake."

"Infinitely."

They leaned toward one another and were barely able to touch lips between the bucket seats. Laughing, they returned to their respective seats before they fell out of them.

"We'll just have to firm up the deal this evening," Danni said, waggling her eyebrows.

Before Nick could respond, Danni's new cell phone interrupted them. She dug it out of her coat pocket. "Hawkins."

"It's Cathy. You've got a prospective client."

As she listened to her administrative assistant, Danni's smile grew. She closed her phone and looked at Nick.

"Hawkins and Sirocco have their first case. Remember the man who wanted to hire me last week?"

"The one with the two grand bonus?"

Danni nodded. "He wouldn't take no for an answer.

He's upped the bonus to two and a half grand plus the normal fees and expenses if we retrieve the diamond ring he gave his mistress. Cathy set an appointment with him for two o'clock today."

Nick glanced at his watch. "That gives us just enough time to get over there. Who is it?"

"You know him. He was very impressed with another job we did."

"We?" Nick's eyes widened. "Not Willy the Jungle King and his redheaded temptress?"

Danni smirked. "Welcome to my world."

Turn the page for a special preview of
Maureen McKade's next novel

CONVICTIONS

Coming soon from Berkley Sensation!

OLIVIA tried to concentrate on her book, a recent Oprah pick, but she'd reread the same page three times and still had no idea what was going on. She grimaced, dog-eared the page to mark her place, and tossed the book on the window seat beside her.

Pressing aside the gauzy curtain, she gazed out at the activity in the ranch yard. Men were milling about, getting their day's orders from Buck, the foreman. Despite her aversion to the convicts, she couldn't help but search for them among the legitimately hired men. They were fairly easy to spot with their black caps—most everyone else wore a wide-brimmed hat.

Buck directed the Hispanic and the youngest prisoner toward the farthest barn. By their expressions, they weren't pleased with their assignment. Olivia figured they'd been given the task of shoveling manure. She wrinkled her nose, not envying them but not sympathizing either. The shifty convict, who reminded Olivia of a fat-cheeked gopher, and the prisoner who looked like a wrestler were sent with a group of men into the back of a big truck. It appeared they'd drawn fence-mending duty.

Although Olivia knew her father handpicked the prisoners who came to work on the ranch, icy fingers of dread crawled down her back. Nobody could predict how those men would act once they were outside the prison walls. One of them could slip away from his work detail and find his way to the house. . . .

Taking a deep breath, Olivia pictured the gun cabinet in her father's study. She knew exactly where he kept the key to it and which drawer the revolver was in. One day not long after she'd returned home, when her father was out talking to the foreman, she'd unlocked the cabinet and lifted out the gun. Her father had taught her how to shoot when she was a teenager, and with the weapon in her hands she'd felt safe for the first time since the attack. Another day when he was outside, she'd timed how long it took her to get from the front room to the study to retrieve the gun. She'd wrapped that knowledge around her like a security blanket. No one would catch her unaware or unarmed again.

Feeling more in control, Olivia shifted her attention to the remaining convict, the one who'd spotted her peeking out the window five days ago, when they'd first arrived. He stood silently with his hands clasped behind his back, as he listened to Buck give him his day's task. She had a clear view of the man's expression, which was bland almost to the point of insolence. Out of the five prisoners, this was the one who made her hackles rise. Even from behind her glass wall, she could feel his cold resentment. She'd seen that kind of emotion before, from conscienceless murderers and heartless rapists.

The convict nodded to Buck, then pivoted slowly to face the window. His gaze locked onto Olivia's as if he knew she was there. She ordered her fingers to release the curtain, to let it shield her from his hypnotic glare, but they wouldn't obey her. Instead, she remained trapped by the prisoner's dark eyes, as helpless as she'd been when—

A cry escaped her throat and she blundered to her feet, dropping the curtain into place. She stumbled away from the window seat, but she nearly crumpled to her knees at the pain of her bad leg. Scrabbling for balance, she thrust out a hand and caught herself on the back of the sofa.

She registered the sound of the front door opening and heavy footsteps coming toward her. No time to get the gun. She'd failed to protect herself. Again.

Throwing an arm across her face, she cried, "No! Leave me alone."

"Olivia, it's just me, your father," came a calming voice. "It's all right, honey. There's nobody here but you and me. I promise."

Olivia's breath rasped raggedly. She focused on her father's soothing timbre, on the familiarity of the tone, and her terror faded. Lowering her arm, she opened her eyes, half expecting to see her attacker again, but instead saw her father standing a wary distance away. She slumped against the sofa. "I—I'm sorry."

He closed the gap between them and carefully wrapped his arms around her. "It's all right, Livvie. You're safe here."

Her father's use of her childhood name should've calmed her, but instead her anger rose sharp and ugly. She pulled out of his embrace and reached for her cane, another reminder of the horrible night that had robbed her of something infinitely more valuable than money and physical health.

"I hate this," she hissed as she limp-paced behind the couch.

Her father dropped his gaze to the floor. "The doctor said it would take time to heal." He lifted his head and apology shone in his eyes. "Both physically and psychologically."

"How long? It's been over two months." She stopped, closed her eyes and tipped her head back, fighting tears. "Over two months I've been afraid of my own shadow. I just want to be like I was."

She heard her father's heavy sigh. "You were stalked and assaulted, Liv. A person doesn't recover from that overnight. Or even a few weeks or months. The son-of-a-bitch stole your feelings of security and safety."

Olivia had heard it all before—from her fellow assistant district attorneys and her shrink. Same old overplayed tune.

She opened her eyes and faced her father. "I know that and accept it, so why can't I move past it?"

"You can't run before you can walk."

She managed a tight smile and raised her cane. "How appropriate, Dad."

Impatience twitched his lips. "Locking yourself away in this house isn't helping you heal."

"If you hadn't brought those convicts here, I'd still be taking my morning walks around the yard," she said, knowing she was being irrational and petty, but not caring.

He shook his head, not falling for her offensive ploy. "They're an excuse. Any time you want to go outside, I'll walk with you." He paused and eyed her shrewdly. "Or don't you trust me?"

She should've known he'd use any weapon in his arsenal, including guilt, to get his way. "You know I trust you."

He arched his brow. "Then let's go see Misty's new foals."

"Foals?"

"She had twins—a filly and a colt—last night."

For a moment, Olivia forgot her fears. "Are they all right?"

"Right as rain. And cuter 'n two bugs in a rug." He canted his head, mutely asking her to accompany him outside to see the newborns.

Olivia's mouth lost all moisture. Walk outside? Leave her sanctuary?

"You haven't left the house for five days," her father said, as if reading her thoughts. "Not even to go to your physical therapy sessions."

"Pat volunteered to come here." Her defensiveness was obvious even to her ears.

"So you can take two steps backward in your recovery?"

The disappointment in her father's eyes hurt.

"You say you want to be like your old self? You can't do that while hiding in here."

She hated it when he used her own words against her. But then, that's what a lawyer was trained to do. She should know.

She glanced down the foyer, at the solid oak door. All she had to do was swing the door open and step outside into the sunlight. Outside where the convicts were.

She turned to look down the hall, at the door to her father's study where the gun was kept. Maybe she could take it with her. Nobody would know if she tucked it into her jacket pocket.

I would know.

Wrestling with her fear, Olivia closed her eyes. She used to be called the "risk taker" in the Chicago district attorney's office. It was time to start living up to that name again.

Her heart hammered in her chest but she nodded firmly. "All right. You'll stay with me?"

He smiled warmly. "I promise."

Olivia braced herself and started to the door. Her father followed and when she stopped, he gave her shoulder a gentle squeeze.

"Gotta walk before you can run," he said softly.

Olivia shook her head, amused in spite of her belly-cramping dread. With a shaking hand she reached out and turned the doorknob. Redolent fresh air washed across her face as the door swung open.

Steeling herself, she hobbled out to stand in the center of the wide porch. The scent of sage drifted past her and Olivia took a deep breath of the pungency. Her father's familiar aftershave mixed with the sage and her pulse slowed its frantic beat.

"Whenever you're ready," he said.

Olivia gripped her cane tightly and kept her gaze

averted from the activity around the corral. Continuing down the steps, she used the porch post to help keep the weight off her bad leg. To get to Misty and her foals, Olivia would have to walk past the men saddling and loading horses into a trailer. Could she do it?

She had to—to prove she could.

Her father walked close beside her but didn't physically aid her. She was grateful for that. It was difficult enough to accept her emotional dependence on him. He kept himself between her and the hired men, but many of them touched their hat brims and greeted her with sincere respect and pleasure. Most had worked on the ranch for years, since before she moved away, and Olivia relaxed amid the familiar faces.

She glanced over at the corral and met the remaining prisoner's cold eyes. Her footsteps faltered.

"Is something wrong?" her father asked.

"Who is he?" she demanded.

He followed her line of sight. "One of the prisoners on the work-release program."

"I know that. What's his name?"

"Hank Elliott. Do you recognize him?"

Olivia tried to swallow but her mouth was too dry. "No."

"I'll introduce you," he offered, obviously not understanding her curiosity. But before she could argue, he called out, "Elliott. Come here."

The rangy man swaggered over to them and stopped a few feet away, one hip cocked. "Yes, sir?"

"This is my daughter, Olivia. Olivia, this is Hank Elliott."

"Ma'am," Elliott drawled.

Olivia couldn't have spoken if her life depended on it. All she could do was nod.

"We were just going to peek in on Misty's foals. Care to join us?" her father asked him.

Olivia shot him a disbelieving look but he didn't seem to notice.

Elliott didn't reply, but fell into step on the other side of Olivia. Her heart hammered in her breast as the man's intensity battered her already-strained defenses. She could easily visualize him in the defendant's chair in a courtroom, his expression contemptuous as he dared the jury to convict him. And if Olivia had been the prosecutor, she would've fought to have him put away for a very long time.

His long legs moved with smooth stealthy motions as his thighs surged against denim. He swung his arms easily, and Olivia couldn't help but notice the flexing of his forearms beneath the rolled-up sleeves of his chambray shirt. Pure masculinity radiated from him like blinding rays of sunlight, and both were equally scorching.

Attracted to him despite everything, Olivia reminded herself that Ted Bundy had been good-looking, too. So was the man who'd attacked her.

To deflect her downward spiraling thoughts, she glanced away and found her attention captured by the worn brown boots encasing Elliott's feet. Something told her he was no stranger to ranch work.

At the entrance to the barn, Olivia went in first with her father behind her. Elliott brought up the rear but Olivia was hyperaware of his presence. Her father's hand on her back guided her past a half dozen stalls before they arrived at Misty's.

Olivia leaned against the gate and peered through the slats to see the newborn foals. Their spindly legs appeared too thin to hold them upright, but the young horses were surprisingly steady. The colt was sucking on one of his mother's teats while the filly butted her brother.

Olivia laughed softly at their antics. "They're beautiful."

"Without Hank, they wouldn't have survived," her father said.

Olivia straightened in surprise to glance at him.

Her father answered her unspoken question. "The first one had to be turned before either of them could come out.

The vet wasn't going to get here in time but Hank was able to do it and save both of them."

Olivia turned her attention to the flat, hazel eyes that gazed at her. Her mouth grew dry but she forced herself to ask, "How did you know what to do?"

Elliott shrugged, insolence written in the careless gesture. "I grew up on a ranch."

"He wants to be a veterinarian," her father added.

A flash of annoyance streaked across Elliott's face, but he only shrugged again. "*Wanted* to be a veterinarian."

Olivia, feeling a bit more confident, asked, "So what happened that kept you from going to vet school?"

His hard lips curled upward but there was no warmth in the expression. "Prison happened."

She shivered and shifted closer to her father's solidness, but a tiny kernel of her former self asserted itself. "That happens when you break the law."

His jaw muscle knotted. "Yes, ma'am."

Although the words were correct, his disdainful tone caused her to flinch.

"You should get going. The men probably have the horses loaded up," her father said to Elliott.

"Yes, sir." He spun around and stalked out of the barn.

Olivia scowled at the convict's back. "How can you trust him?"

"Don't judge him until you get all the facts, Liv," her father said with a glimmer of his stern judge persona. "As a lawyer, you should know that."

"Obviously he's already been judged and found guilty or he wouldn't have gone to prison. What did he do?"

"Accessory to felonious assault. He pleaded not guilty."

Olivia snorted. "They all plead their innocence. It doesn't mean a damn thing."

"Right. Every person in prison deserves to be there." His tone was rife with sarcasm.

"You said it. I didn't."

Her father shook his head. "The system isn't perfect,

Liv. You know that. Sometimes the innocent are convicted."

"And too often the guilty aren't."

"You have your mother's stubbornness."

"And that's a bad thing?"

"Only when you let it blind you."

Olivia gripped the wood beneath her hand. "Stubbornness didn't blind me to the bastard who did this." She glanced down at her leg. "He'd already stalked and assaulted at least two other women. I tried to get him in prison where he belonged."

"You did your best."

"And look where it got me. I'm thirty-one years old and living with my father because I'm too scared to live on my own." She choked on the last word, hating herself for what she'd become.

Her father put his arm around her shoulders but she shrugged it off and moved away from the stall. Knowing he was only trying to help made her feel guilty, but she was too full of self-disgust and anger.

Outside the barn, she stood for a moment, taking long breaths to loosen the constricting band around her chest. A clang caught her attention and she looked over to see Elliott closing the back end of the horse trailer.

As if knowing she was there, he turned and swept his hungry gaze up and down her body. Elliott wore his virility like a suit of armor and wielded his sultry gaze like a sword. However, even knowing this knight possessed no chivalry, Olivia couldn't deny the arrow of heat streaking through her.

Although Olivia's attacker hadn't raped her, lying in her hospital bed afterward, she'd believed she'd never experience a woman's desire for a man again. But this convicted felon stirred something deep and primal within her. Something she thought was as lost as her self-confidence.

"Do you want to continue walking?" her father asked from close beside her.

Olivia jerked, startled. But before she could answer,

Elliott spun away and joined three other men in the quad cab of the pickup. She watched the truck and horse trailer bump down the driveway.

Breathing a sigh of relief that Elliott was gone and the yard was now deserted, she replied, "Yes. It's nice to be outside."

Although he didn't say anything, Olivia knew her father was pleased that she didn't scurry back into her hidey-hole. She reached out and linked her arm with his. He patted her hand and they continued walking.

"Where are they going?" she asked, motioning toward the fading pickup and trailer.

"Antler Creek. Some cattle are getting out in that area. They're going to gather up the strays then find the break in the fence."

"I'm surprised you let Elliott go with them. Aren't you afraid he'll keep riding?"

"No. He won't chance ruining the possibility of getting out a few months early. Besides, he's already proven himself. Right after he got here."

"When he saved the farrier?"

"You saw that?"

"I was looking out the window," she admitted.

"Then you know he put himself in danger to help a stranger. In my book, that's not the act of your typical convict."

"Maybe he only did it to gain your trust." Olivia wasn't about to let Hank Elliott off the hook that easily.

Her father shrugged. "It's possible, but it seemed more instinctive than calculated."

Olivia pressed her lips together, not accepting the prisoner's supposedly selfless motives as quickly as her father.

She had yet to meet a convict who didn't have an agenda, an angle. She'd discover Elliott's, one way or another.

National bestselling author

LYNN ERICKSON

WITHOUT A TRACE

With a serial rapist and killer on the loose in Western ski towns, burned-out police sketch artist Jane Russo joins FBI agent Ray Vanover on the case. With his help, she must confront a demon from her own past to catch a madman.

0-425-19325-X

Lynn Erickson is the author who...

"Keeps fans on edge." —BookBrowser

"Creates...masterful suspense."
—*Midwest Book Review*